POPULAR**MMOS**

PAT + JEN, the stars of PopularMMOS, are two of the most popular YouTubers in the world. With over 16.9 million subscribers and 14 billion combined views, their *Minecraft*-inspired channel is one of the most-watched channels on YouTube. To learn more, visit Pat and Jen on YouTube @PopularMMOS and @GamingwithJen.

For my Bumpa—D.J.

A special thanks to Joe Caramagna for all his creative help!

HarperAlley is an imprint of HarperCollins Publishers.

 For information address HarperCollins Children's Books, a division of HarperCollins Publishers, 195 Broadway, New York, NY 10007.
www.harpercollinschildrens.com

ISBN 978-0-06-308041-6 (trade) — ISBN 978-0-06-327357-3 (special edition) — ISBN 978-0-06-327914-8 (special edition)

The artist used an iPad Pro and the app Procreate to create the digital illustrations for this book.
Typography by Erica De Chavez 22 23 24 25 26 PC/WOR 10 9 8 7 6 5 4 3 2 1 ❖ First Edition

POPULARMMOs

PRESENTS

THE END OF ALL THE THINGS

By PAT+JEN from POPULARMMOs
Illustrated by DANI JONES

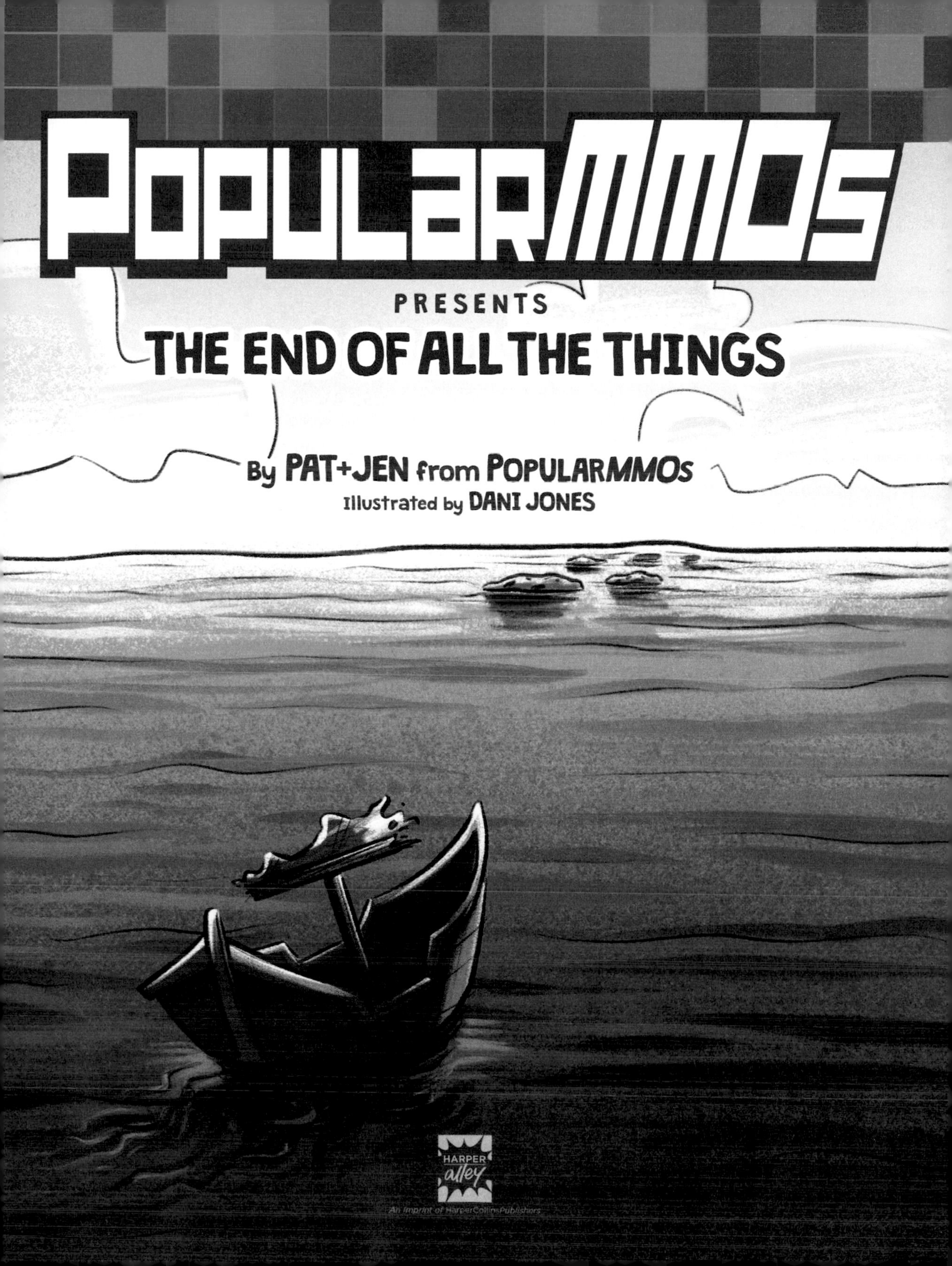

HARPER alley
An Imprint of HarperCollinsPublishers

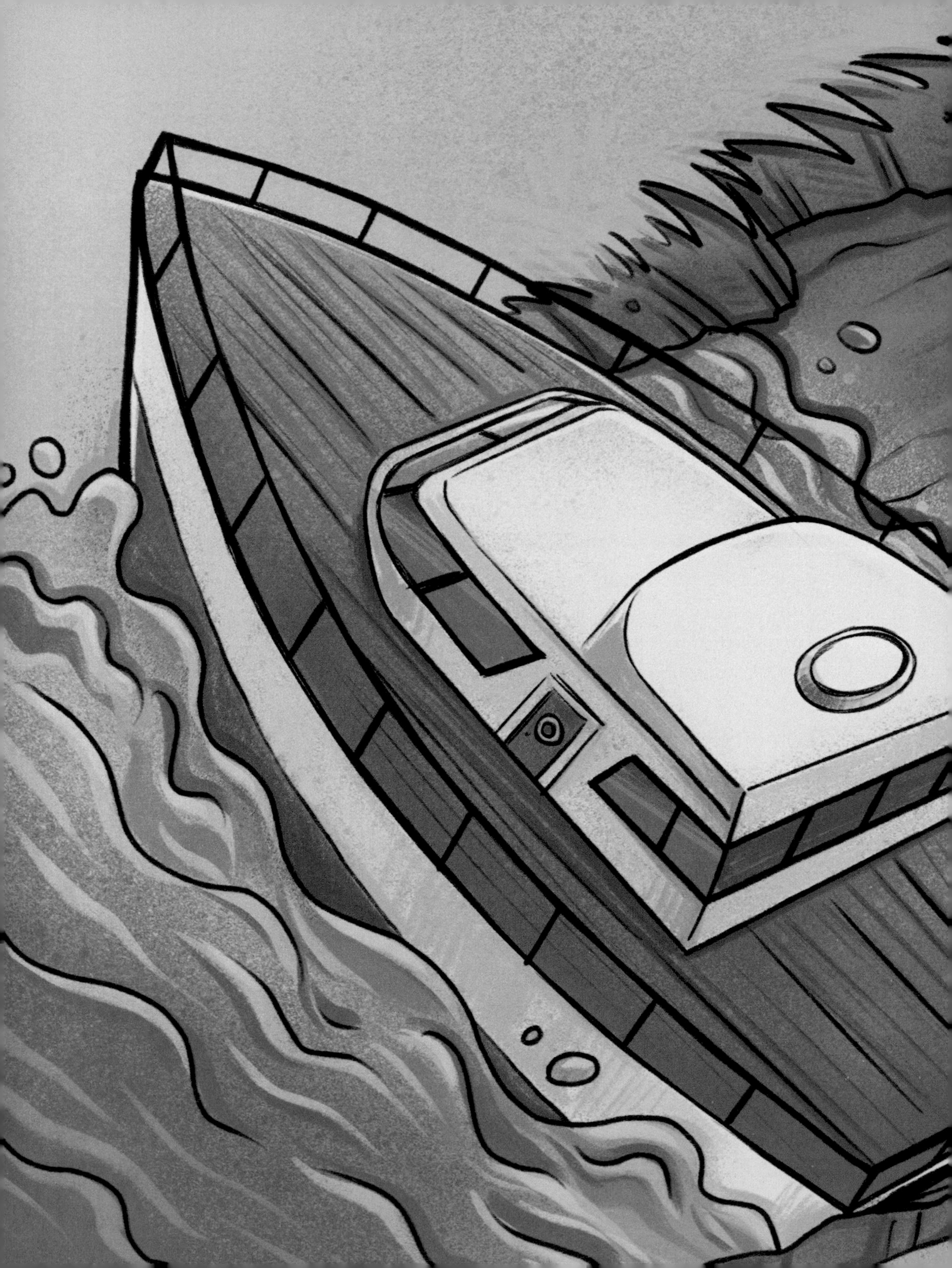

Hey, what's going on, guys!

It's Pat and Jen again, and we're so thrilled that you're reading the fifth and final book in this crazy series! So much has happened since *A Hole New World* launched us on this unbelievable adventure. Jen's discovered that Evil Jen is her sister, that Herobrine is her father, and that Bob(!) is her brother. Pat's become friends (sort of) with Carter. Captain Cookie may even be on the right path to discovering the Cookie Islands. There's only one very important piece of the puzzle left for Jen to unearth if she's going to reunite her family. . . . We're not going to spoil it, but let's just say that if she succeeds it may really be the end of all the things.

Anyway, we hoped you've enjoyed reading and playing and creating along with us. Having good friends like you along for the ride has meant SO much to both of us. It's no fun going on an adventure alone, right? And at the end of the day, these stories are about the power of friendship, the importance of family, and doing the right thing—especially when doing the right thing isn't easy to do. So even though this adventure is over, that doesn't mean the fun is done. Keep on reading. Keep on dreaming. Make up your own stories. That's what we did. Just watch out for all the holes!

Have fun! Read on! And thanks for being a fan.

Pat + Jen

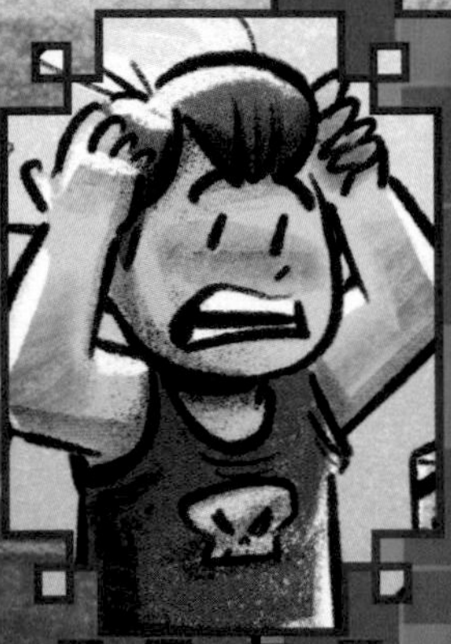

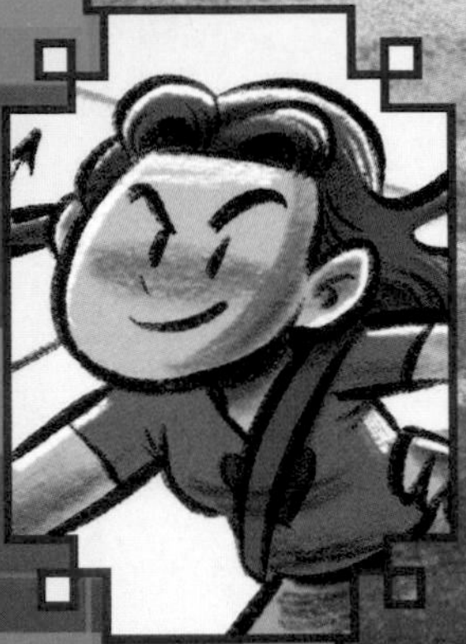

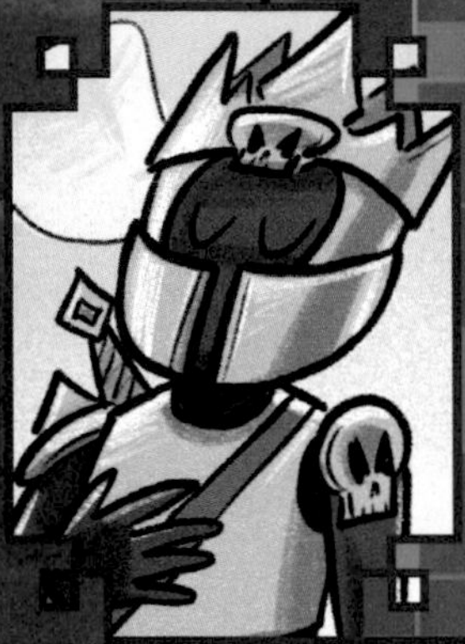

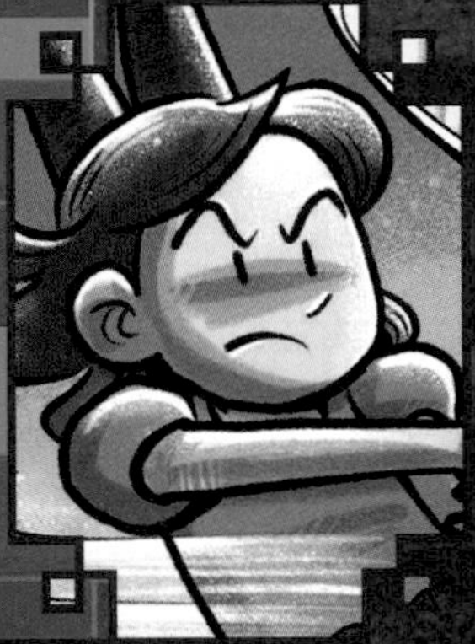

PAT & JEN

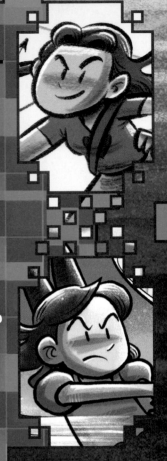

Pat is an awesome dude who's always looking for an epic adventure with his partner, Super Gamer Jen. Pat loves to have fun with his friends and take control of every situation with his cool weapons and can-do attitude. Jen is the sweetest person in the world and loves to laugh, but don't let her cheeriness fool you—she's also fierce. In fact, she could be an even greater adventurer than Pat . . . if she weren't so clumsy. Even when they go on their own separate adventures they—along with their savage cat, Cloud—have a bond that can never be broken.

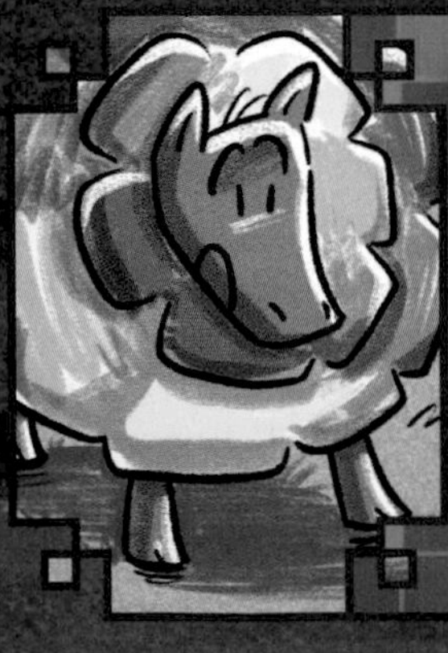

MR. RAINBOW

Mr. Rainbow is a magical sheep whose wool can appear to be any color of the rainbow. He is always ready, willing, and able to help his friends Jen and Pat whenever they need it!

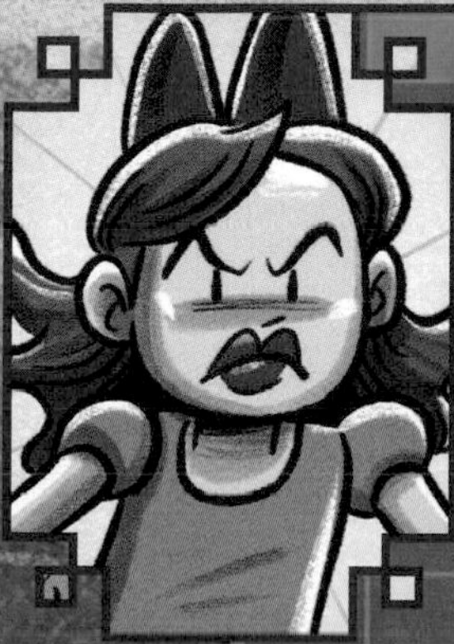
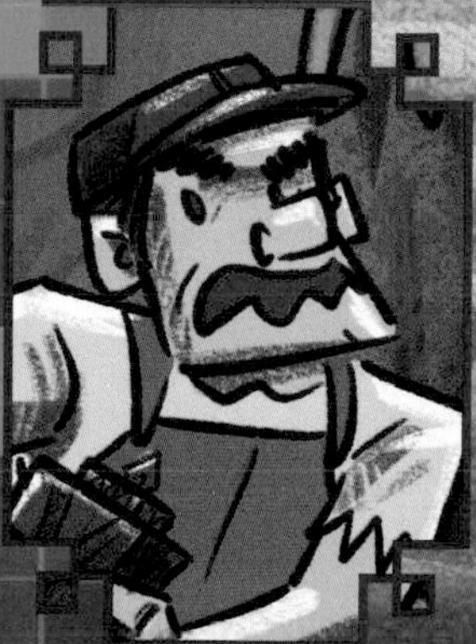

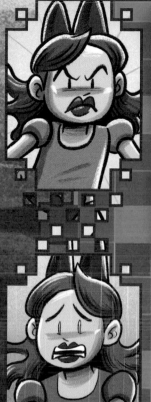

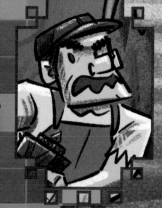

EVIL JEN (EJ) & BOB

EJ & Bob are Jen's long-lost sister and brother. They both were once evil and worked for the nefarious Herobrine but have since decided to join Jen on an adventure to be the first people to ever find the Cookie Islands!

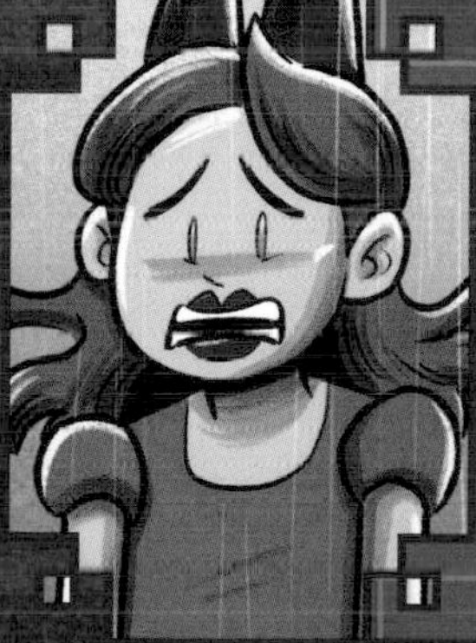
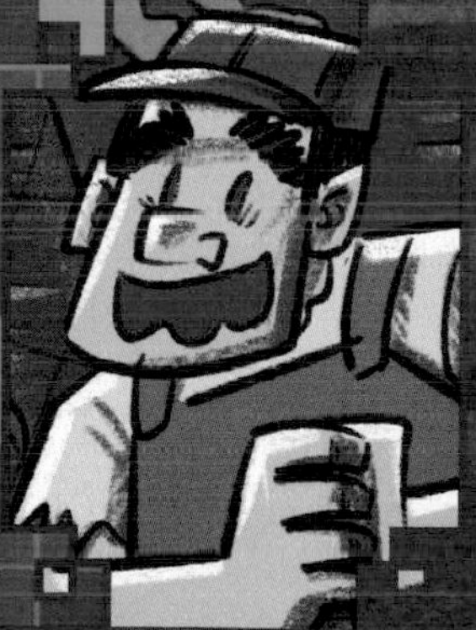

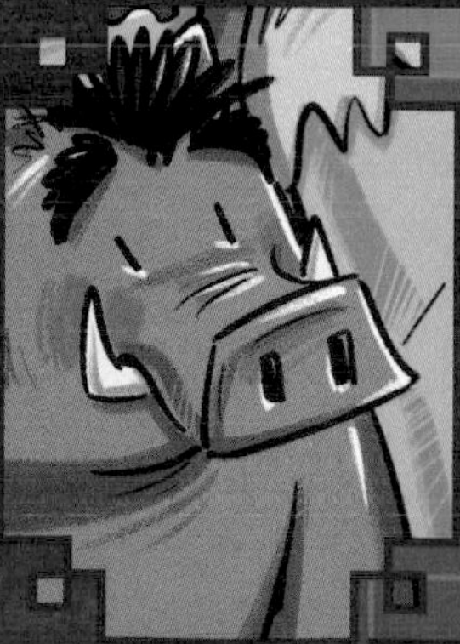

REUBEN THE PIG

Reuben is Bob's comfort pig. How could you not feel loved and comforted by this cute li'l fella? OINK!

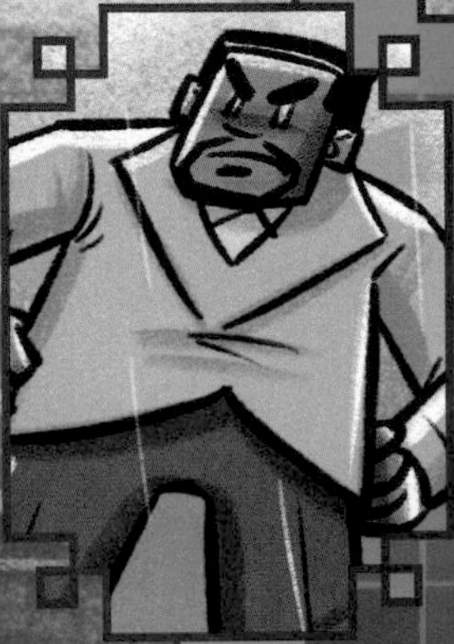

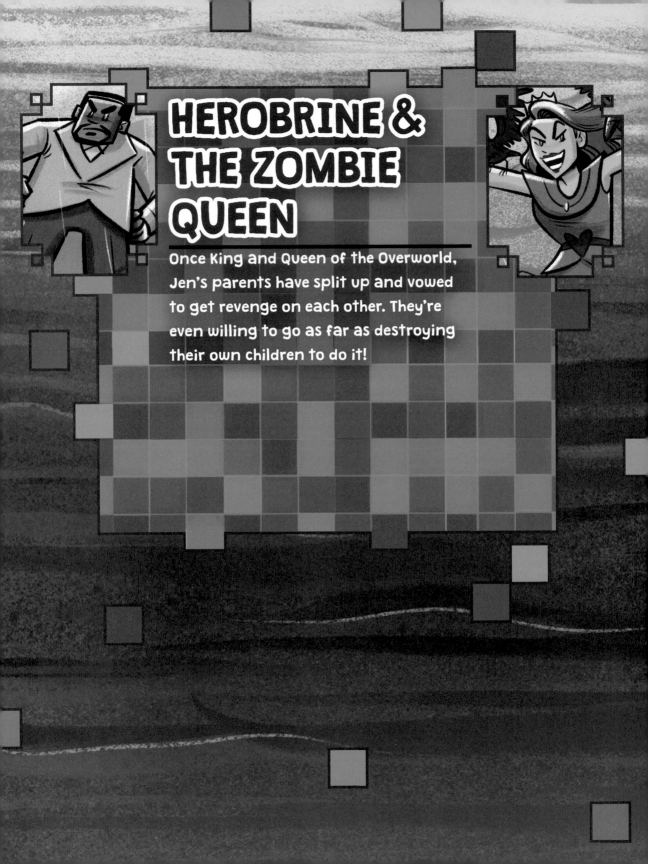

HEROBRINE & THE ZOMBIE QUEEN

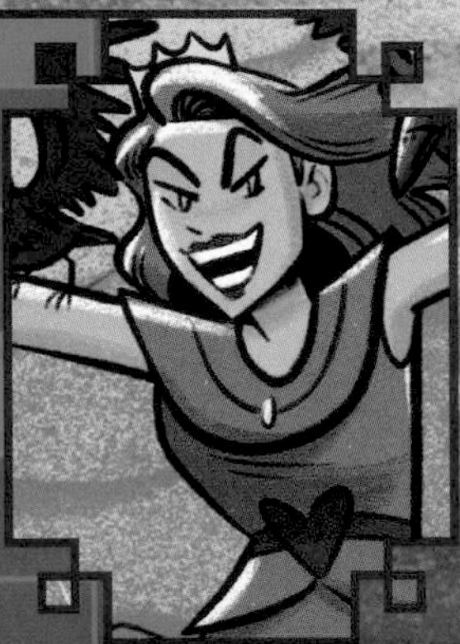

Once King and Queen of the Overworld, Jen's parents have split up and vowed to get revenge on each other. They're even willing to go as far as destroying their own children to do it!

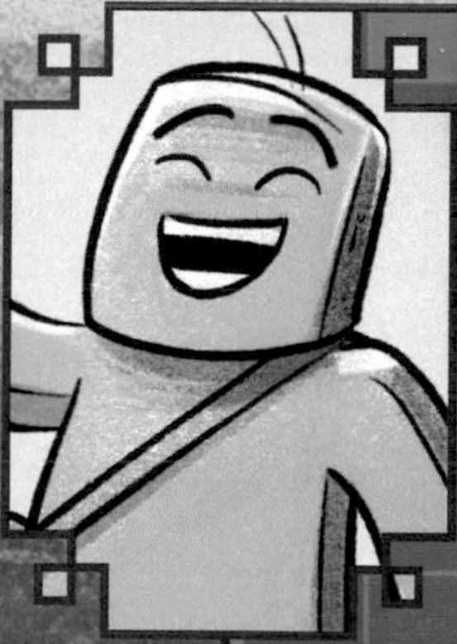

BOMBY, CARTER, & CAPTAIN COOKIE

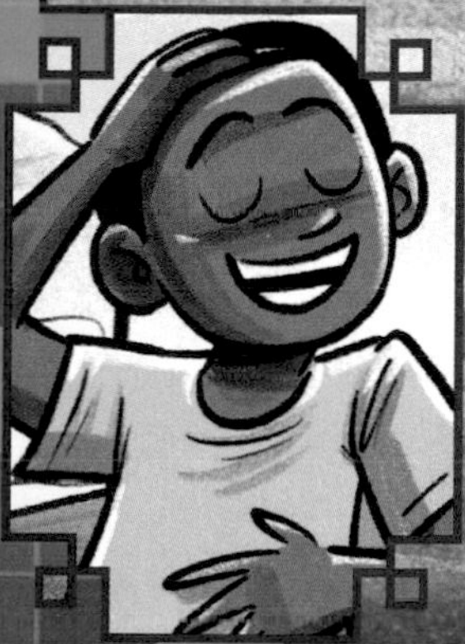

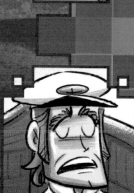

Ever since Jen left, Bomby, Carter, and Captain Cookie have been Pat's family. They're always up for an adventure, especially since it gives Carter a chance to prove his love for Jen and to wield his pickle sword!

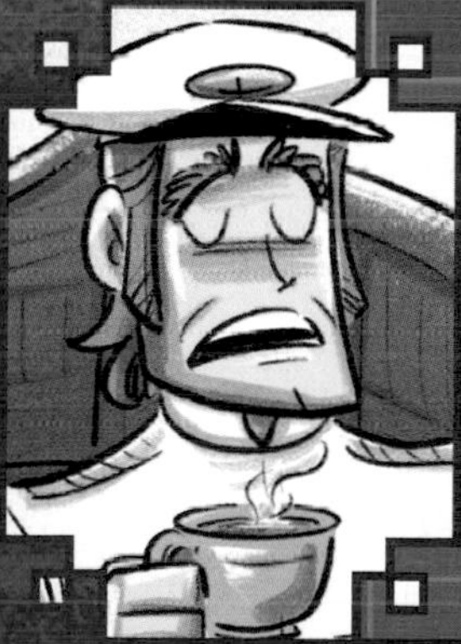

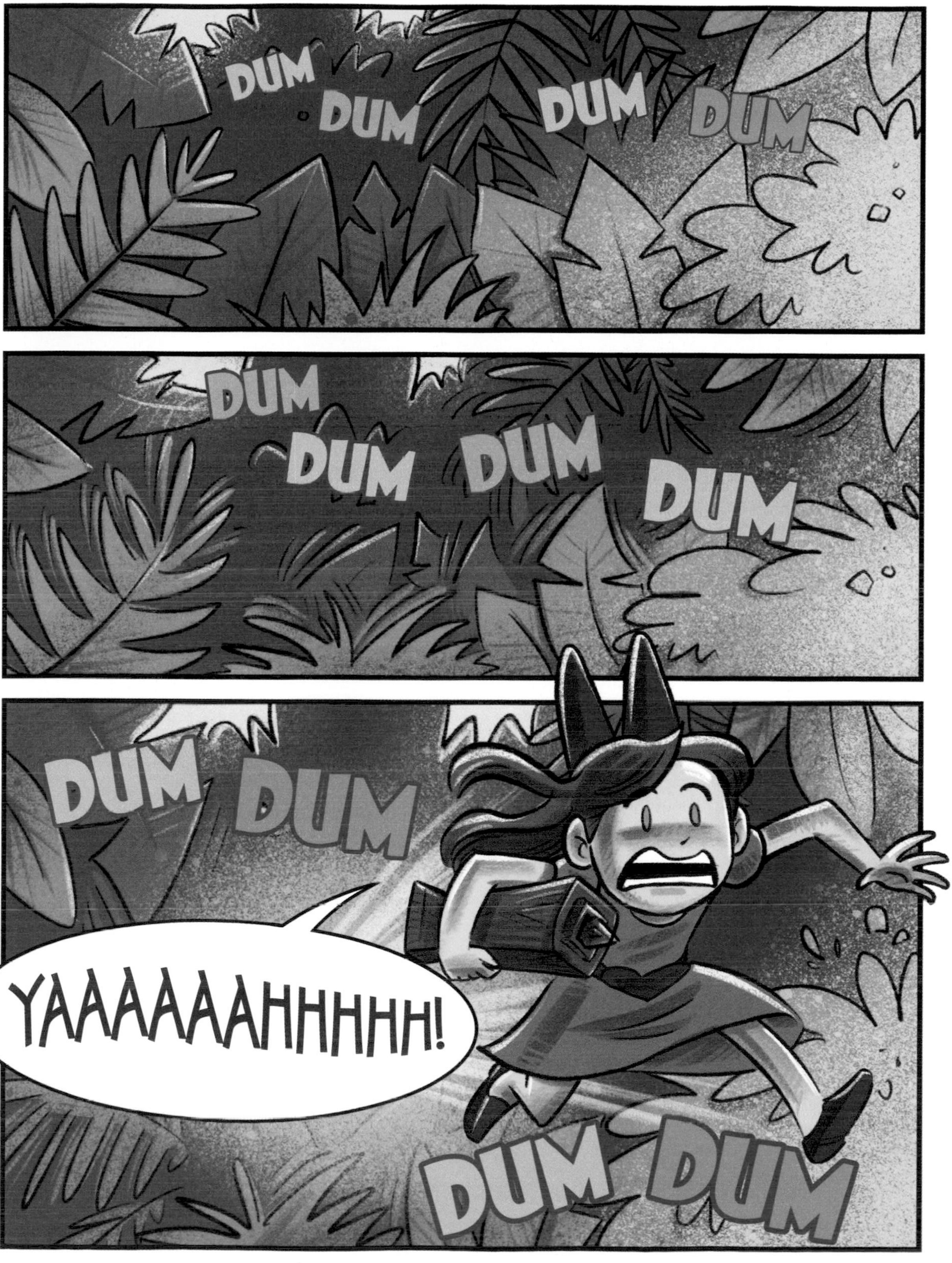
DUM
DUM
DUM
DUM
DUM
DUM
DUM
DUM
DUM
DUM
YAAAAAAHHHHH!
DUM
DUM

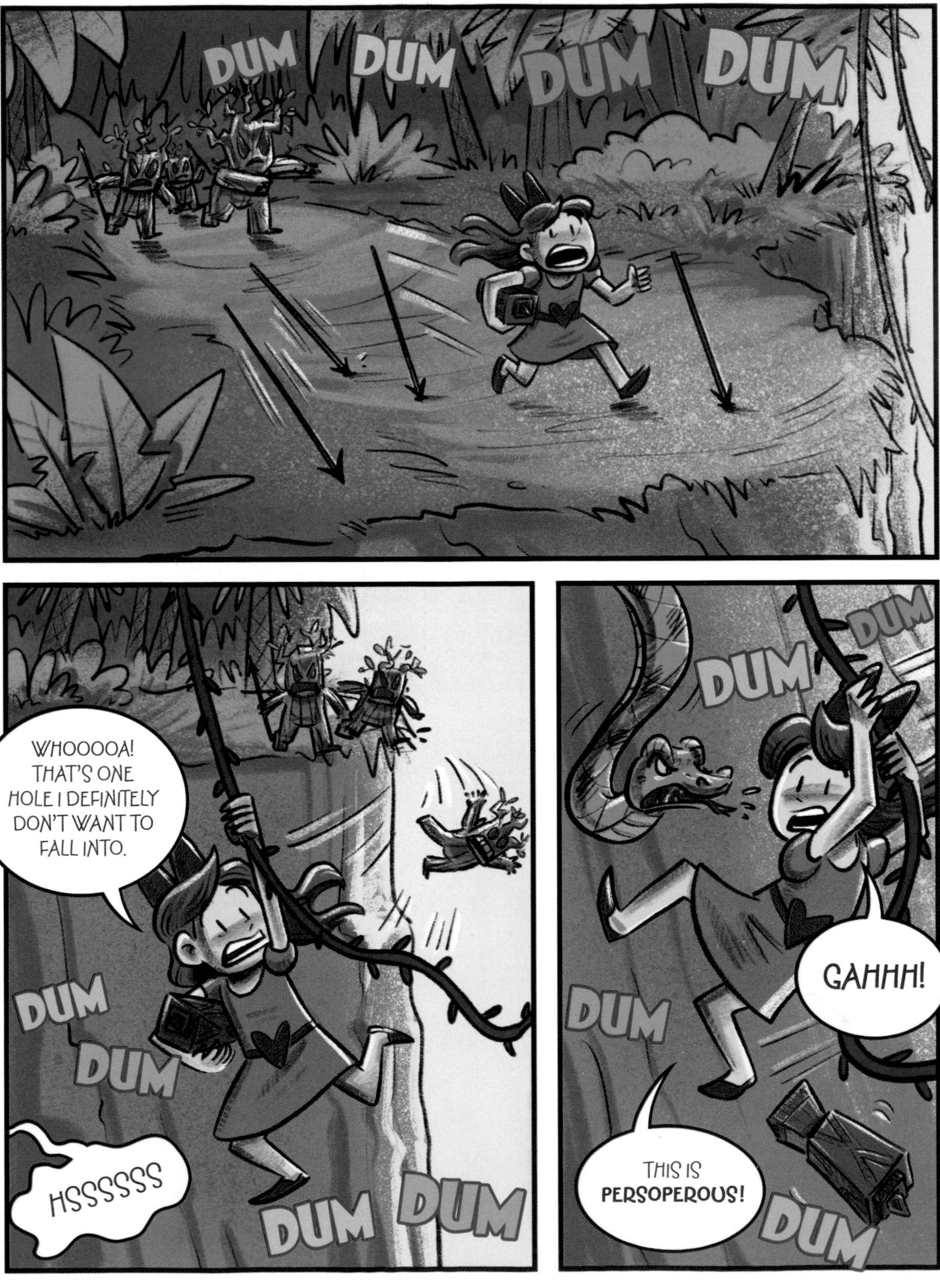
DUM DUM DUM DUM
WHOOOOA! THAT'S ONE HOLE I DEFINITELY DON'T WANT TO FALL INTO.
DUM
DUM
HSSSSSS
DUM DUM
DUM
DUM
GAHHH!
DUM
THIS IS **PERSOPEROUS!**
DUM

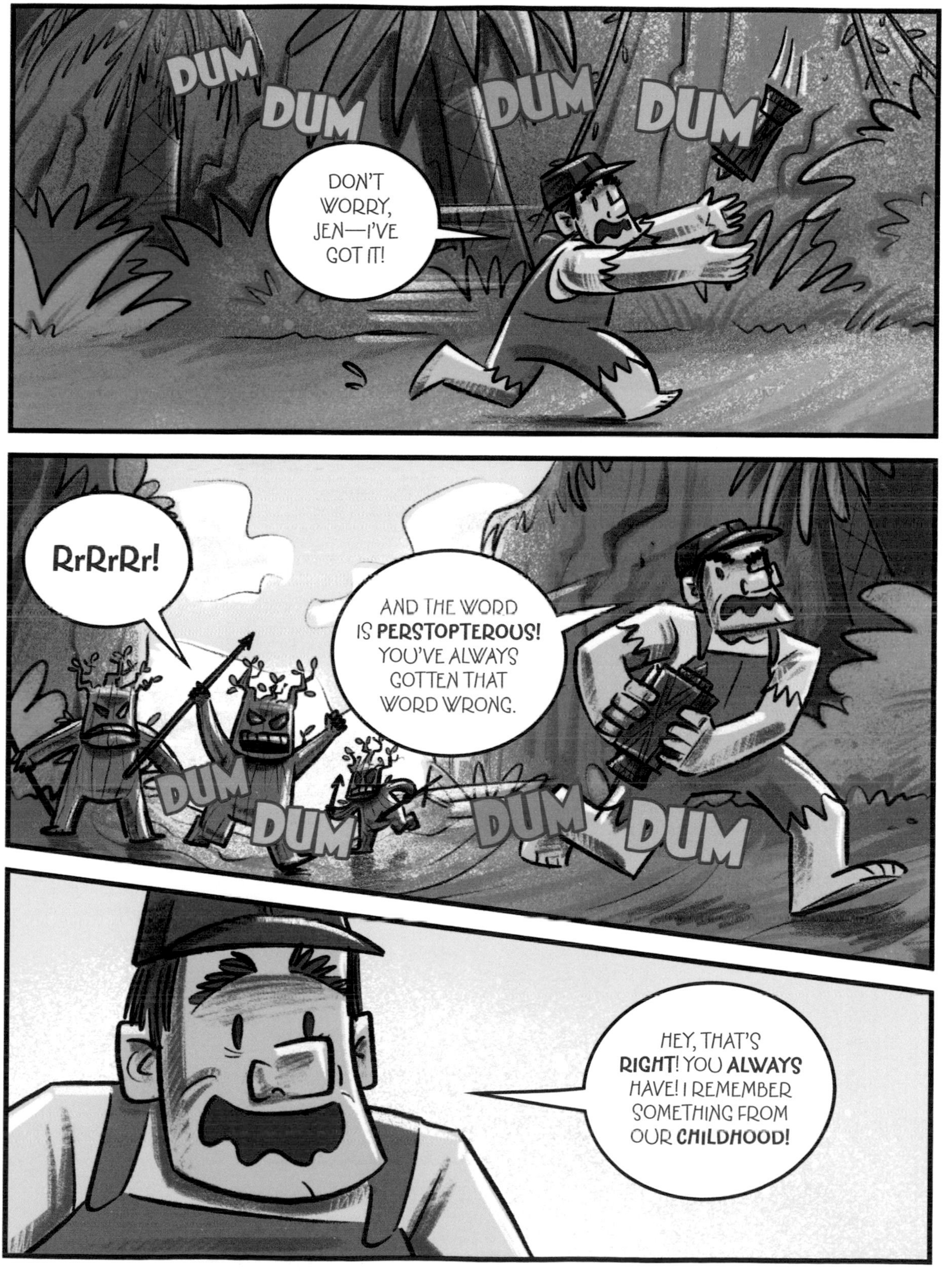
DUM
DUM
DUM
DUM
DON'T WORRY, JEN—I'VE GOT IT!
RrRrRr!
AND THE WORD IS **PERSTOPTEROUS!** YOU'VE ALWAYS GOTTEN THAT WORD WRONG.
DUM
DUM
DUM
DUM
HEY, THAT'S **RIGHT**! YOU **ALWAYS** HAVE! I REMEMBER SOMETHING FROM OUR **CHILDHOOD!**

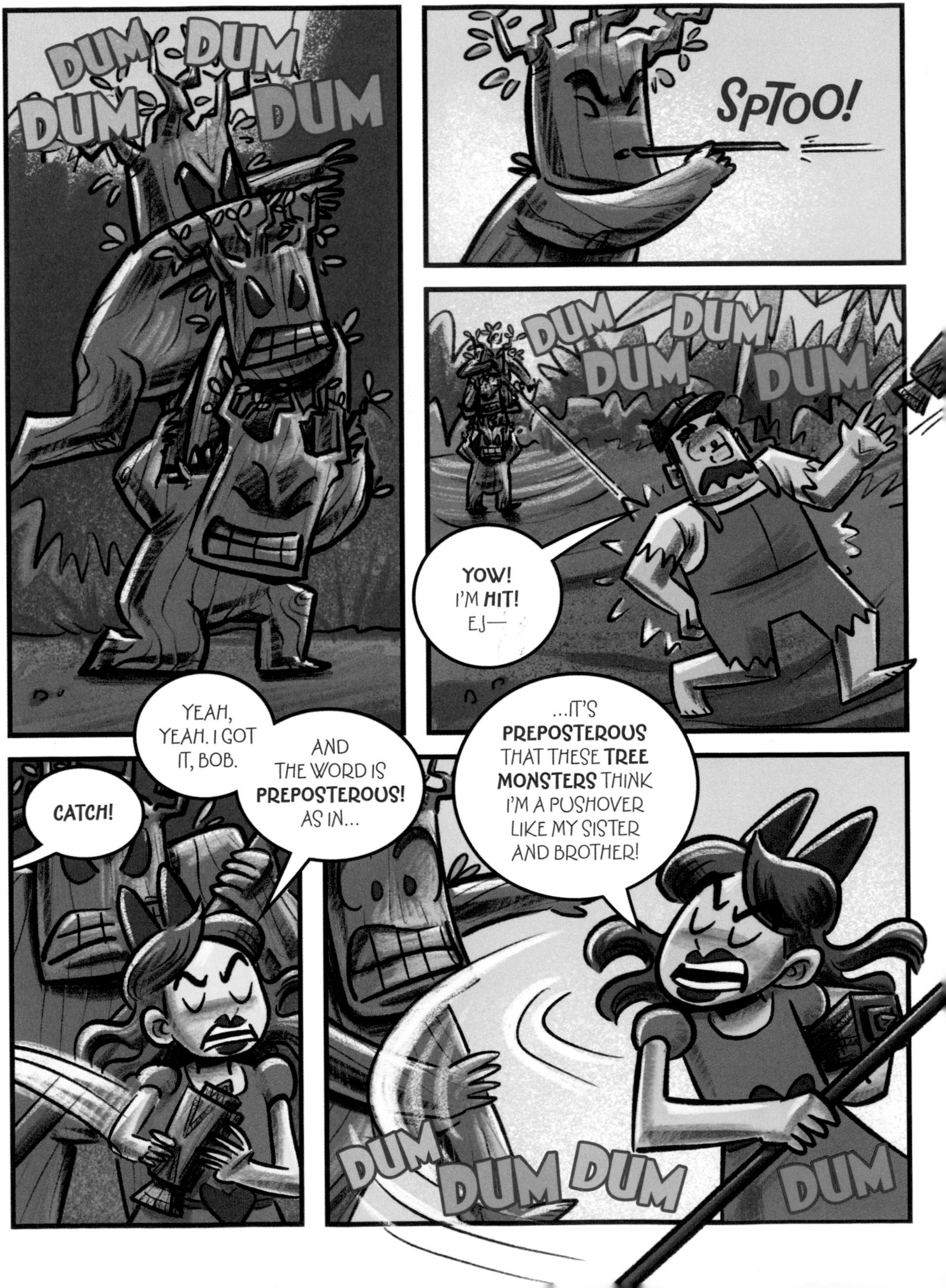
DUM DUM
DUM DUM
SPTOO!
DUM DUM
DUM DUM
YOW! I'M HIT! EJ—
CATCH!
YEAH, YEAH. I GOT IT, BOB.
AND THE WORD IS PREPOSTEROUS! AS IN...
...IT'S PREPOSTEROUS THAT THESE TREE MONSTERS THINK I'M A PUSHOVER LIKE MY SISTER AND BROTHER!
DUM DUM DUM DUM

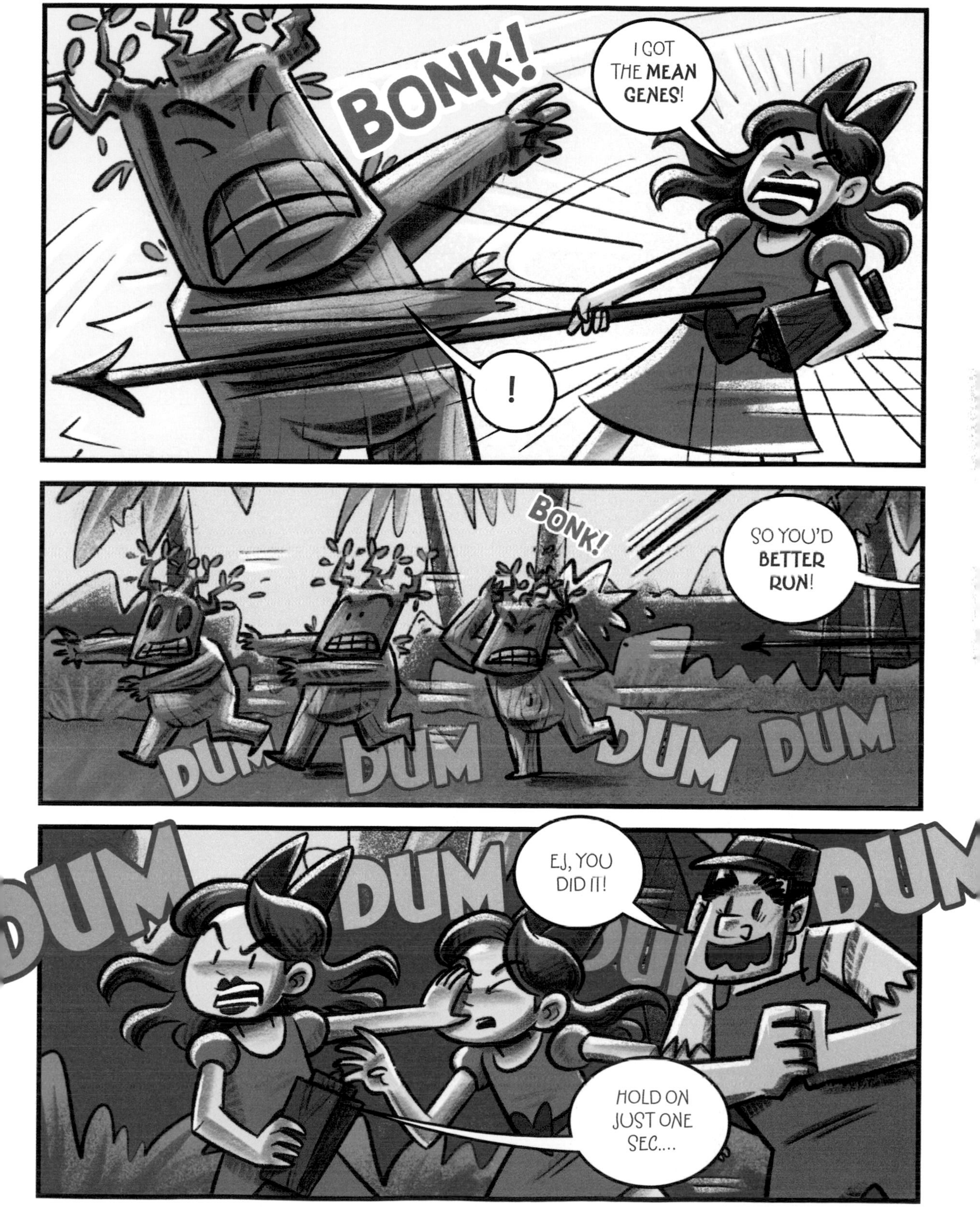
BONK!
I GOT THE MEAN GENES!
!
BONK!
SO YOU'D BETTER RUN!
DUM DUM DUM DUM
DUM DUM DUM
EJ, YOU DID IT!
HOLD ON JUST ONE SEC....

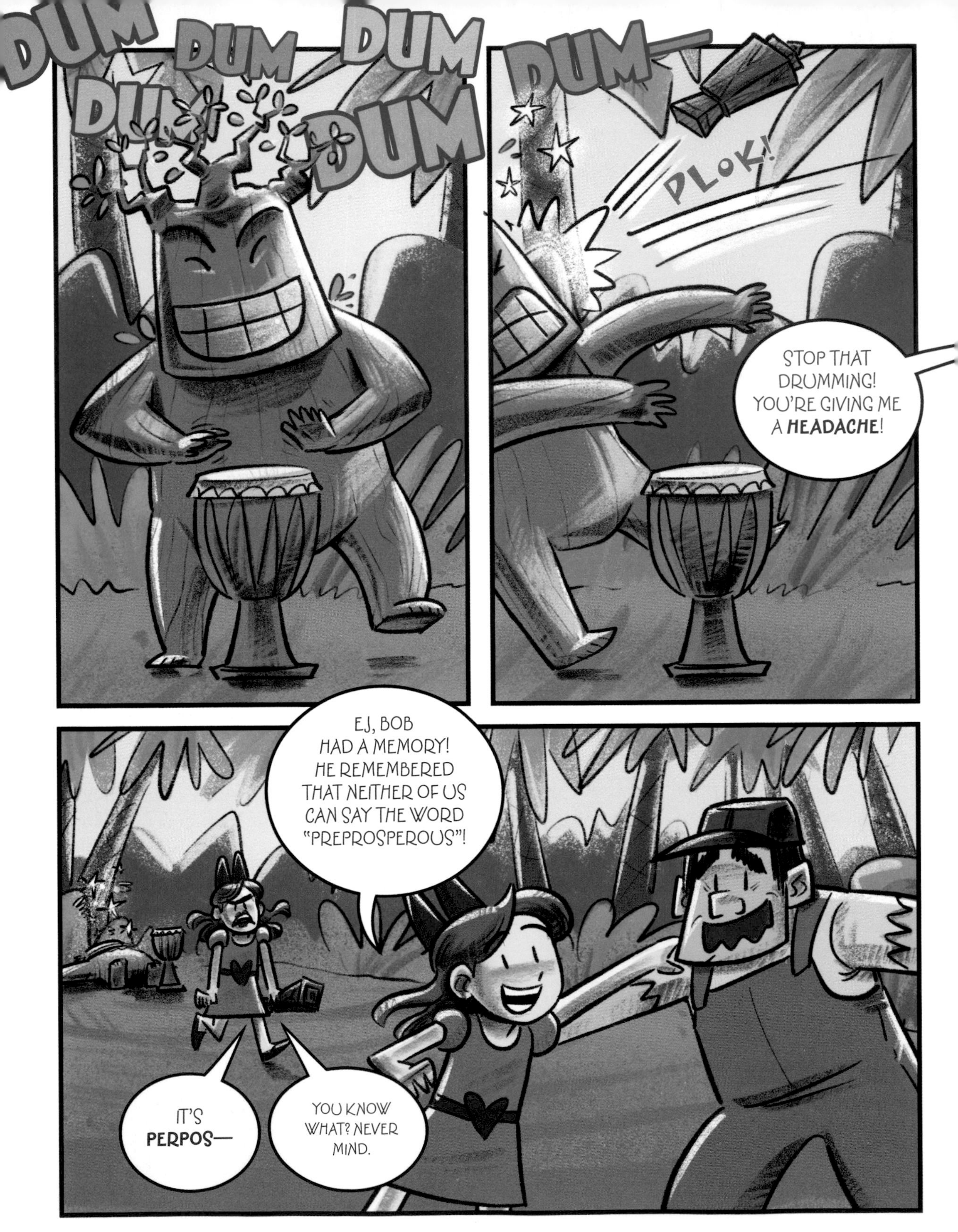
DUM DUM DUM DUM DUM DUM DUM—
PLOK!
STOP THAT DRUMMING! YOU'RE GIVING ME A **HEADACHE**!
EJ, BOB HAD A MEMORY! HE REMEMBERED THAT NEITHER OF US CAN SAY THE WORD "PREPROSPEROUS"!
IT'S **PERPOS—**
YOU KNOW WHAT? NEVER MIND.

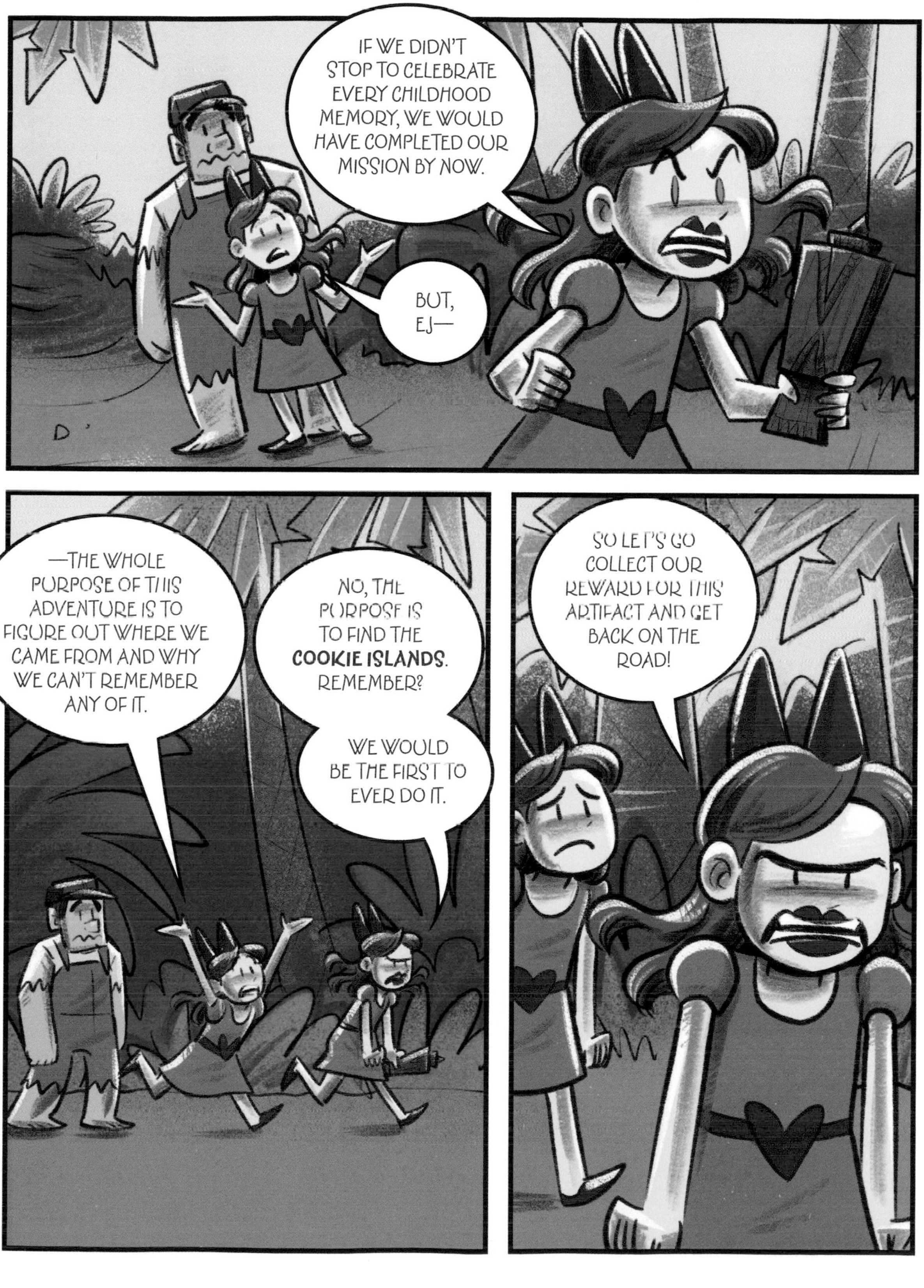
IF WE DIDN'T STOP TO CELEBRATE EVERY CHILDHOOD MEMORY, WE WOULD HAVE COMPLETED OUR MISSION BY NOW.
BUT, EJ—
—THE WHOLE PURPOSE OF THIS ADVENTURE IS TO FIGURE OUT WHERE WE CAME FROM AND WHY WE CAN'T REMEMBER ANY OF IT.
NO, THE PURPOSE IS TO FIND THE **COOKIE ISLANDS**. REMEMBER?
WE WOULD BE THE FIRST TO EVER DO IT.
SO LET'S GO COLLECT OUR REWARD FOR THIS ARTIFACT AND GET BACK ON THE ROAD!

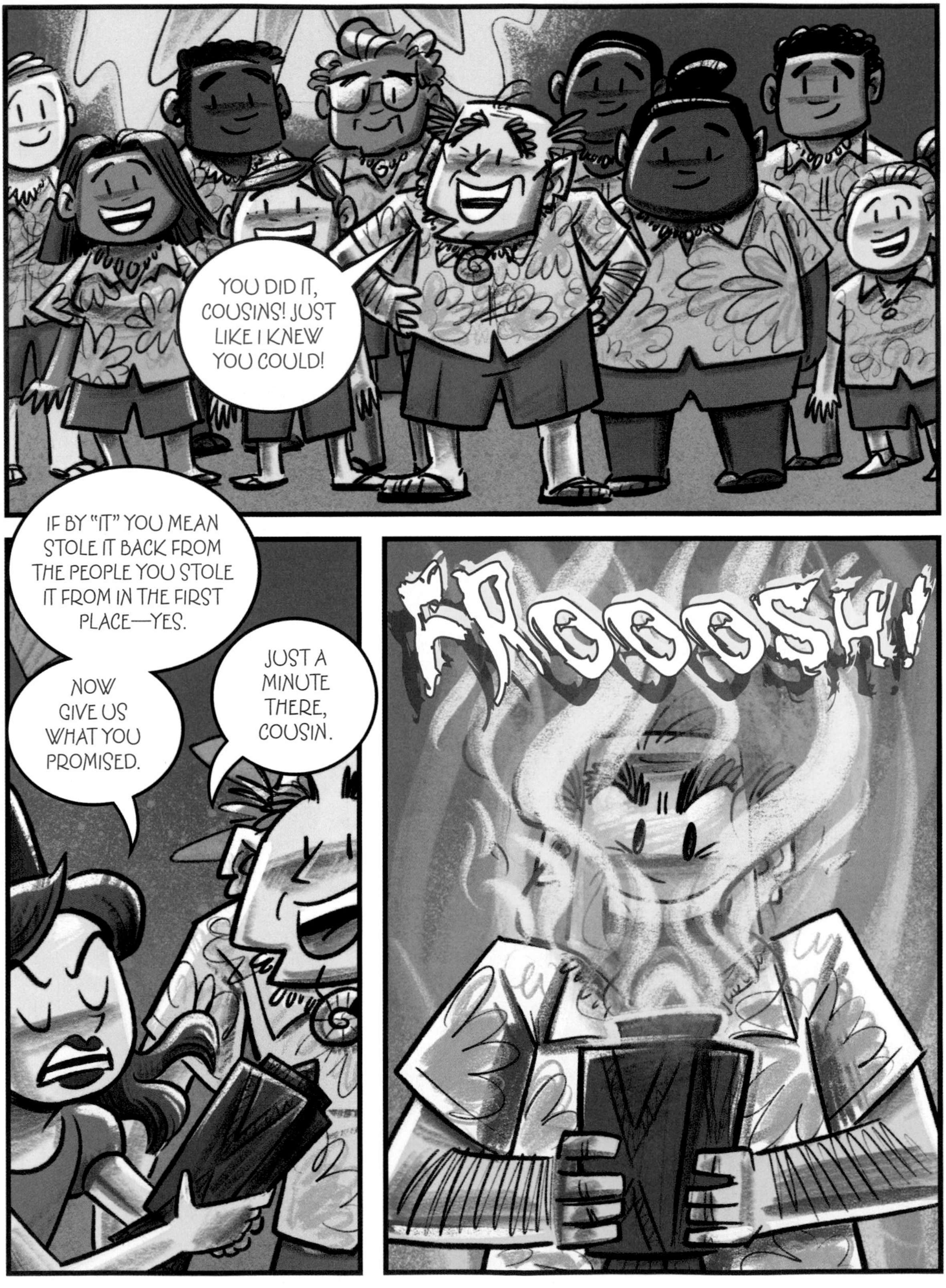
YOU DID IT, COUSINS! JUST LIKE I KNEW YOU COULD!
IF BY "IT" YOU MEAN STOLE IT BACK FROM THE PEOPLE YOU STOLE IT FROM IN THE FIRST PLACE—YES.
NOW GIVE US WHAT YOU PROMISED.
JUST A MINUTE THERE, COUSIN.
FROOOOSH!

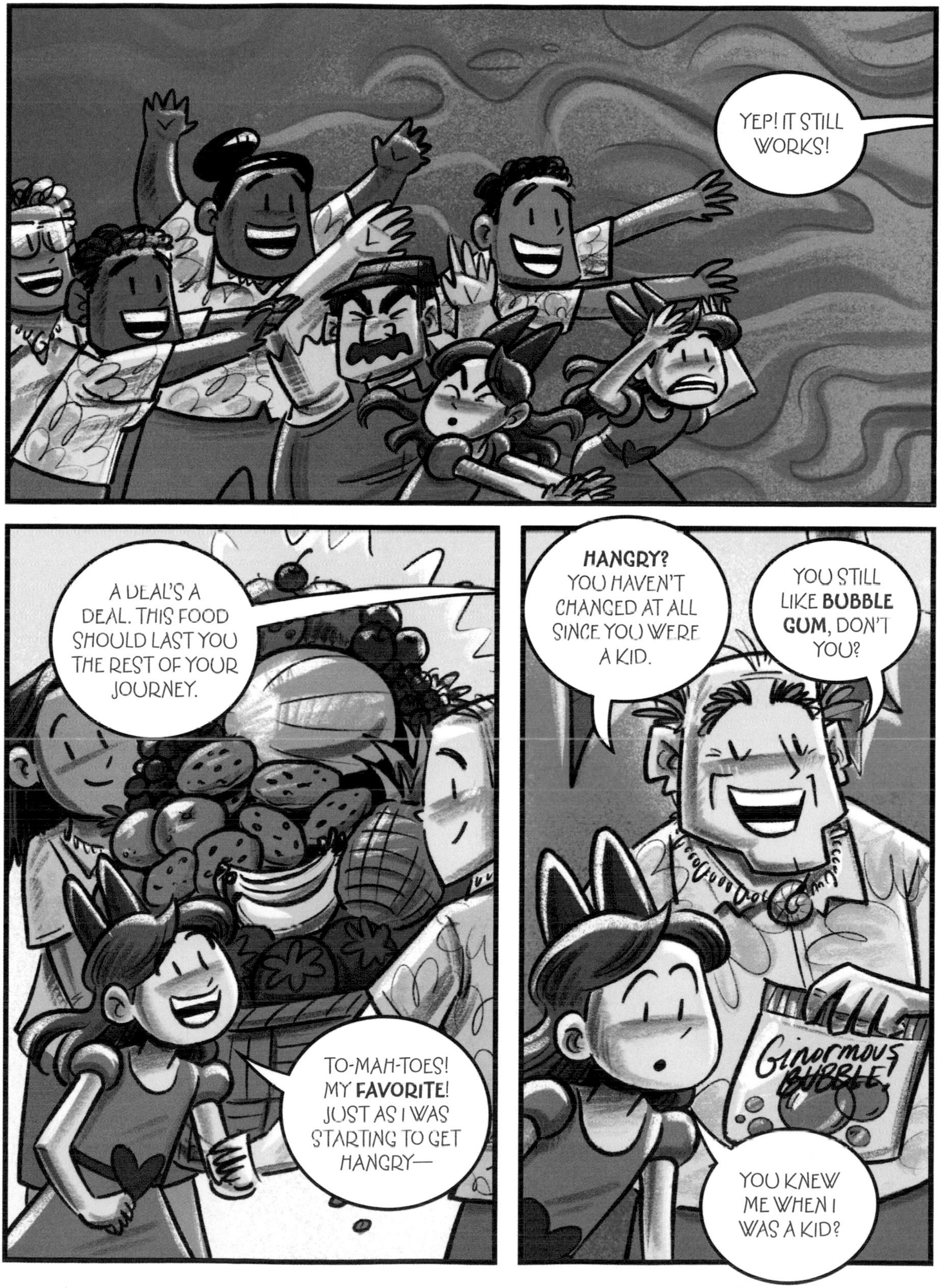
YEP! IT STILL WORKS!
A DEAL'S A DEAL. THIS FOOD SHOULD LAST YOU THE REST OF YOUR JOURNEY.
TO-MAH-TOES! MY **FAVORITE**! JUST AS I WAS STARTING TO GET HANGRY—
HANGRY? YOU HAVEN'T CHANGED AT ALL SINCE YOU WERE A KID.
YOU STILL LIKE **BUBBLE GUM**, DON'T YOU?
Ginormous BUBBLE!
YOU KNEW ME WHEN I WAS A KID?

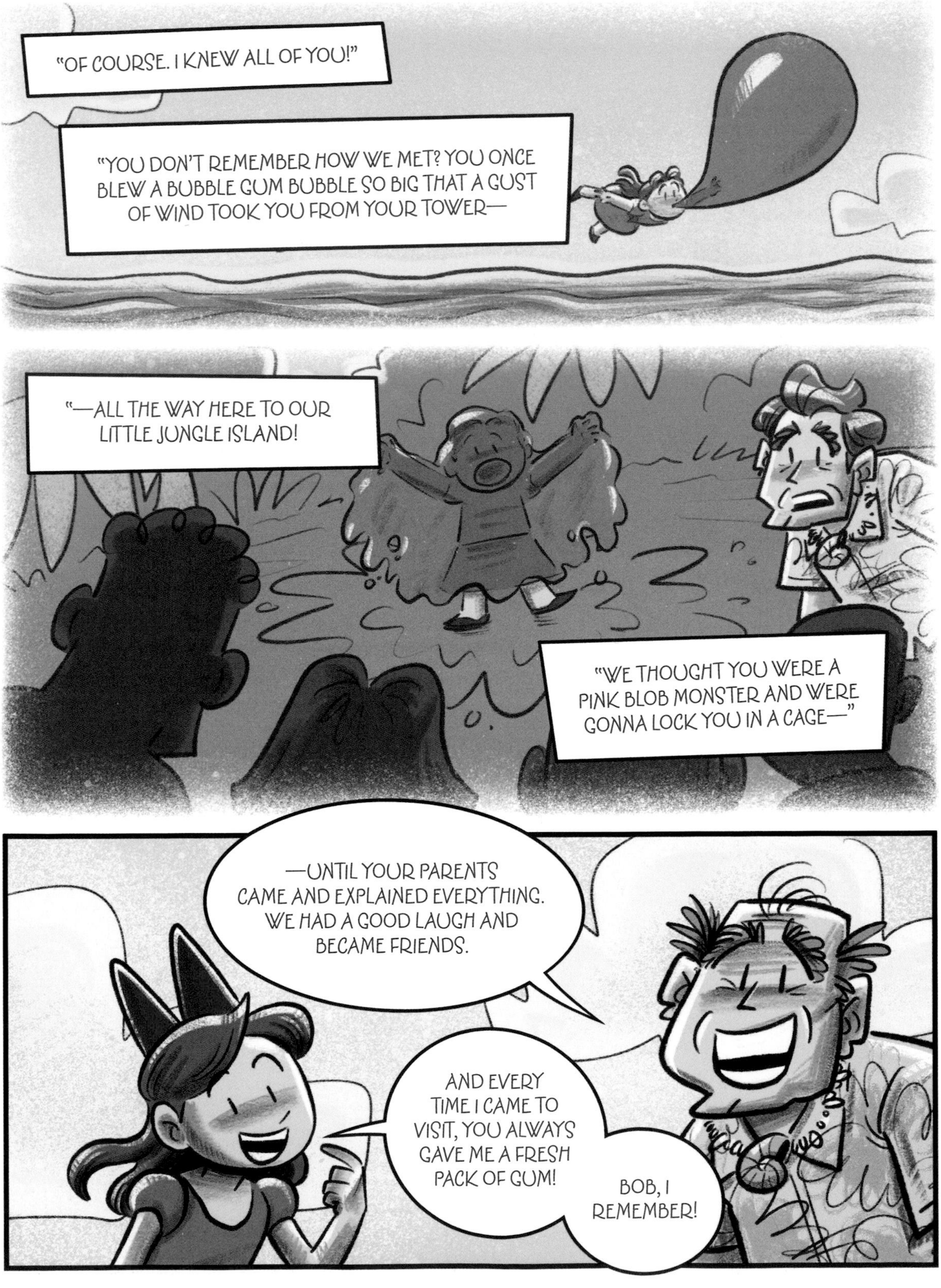
"OF COURSE. I KNEW ALL OF YOU!"
"YOU DON'T REMEMBER HOW WE MET? YOU ONCE BLEW A BUBBLE GUM BUBBLE SO BIG THAT A GUST OF WIND TOOK YOU FROM YOUR TOWER—
"—ALL THE WAY HERE TO OUR LITTLE JUNGLE ISLAND!
"WE THOUGHT YOU WERE A PINK BLOB MONSTER AND WERE GONNA LOCK YOU IN A CAGE—"
—UNTIL YOUR PARENTS CAME AND EXPLAINED EVERYTHING. WE HAD A GOOD LAUGH AND BECAME FRIENDS.
AND EVERY TIME I CAME TO VISIT, YOU ALWAYS GAVE ME A FRESH PACK OF GUM!
BOB, I REMEMBER!

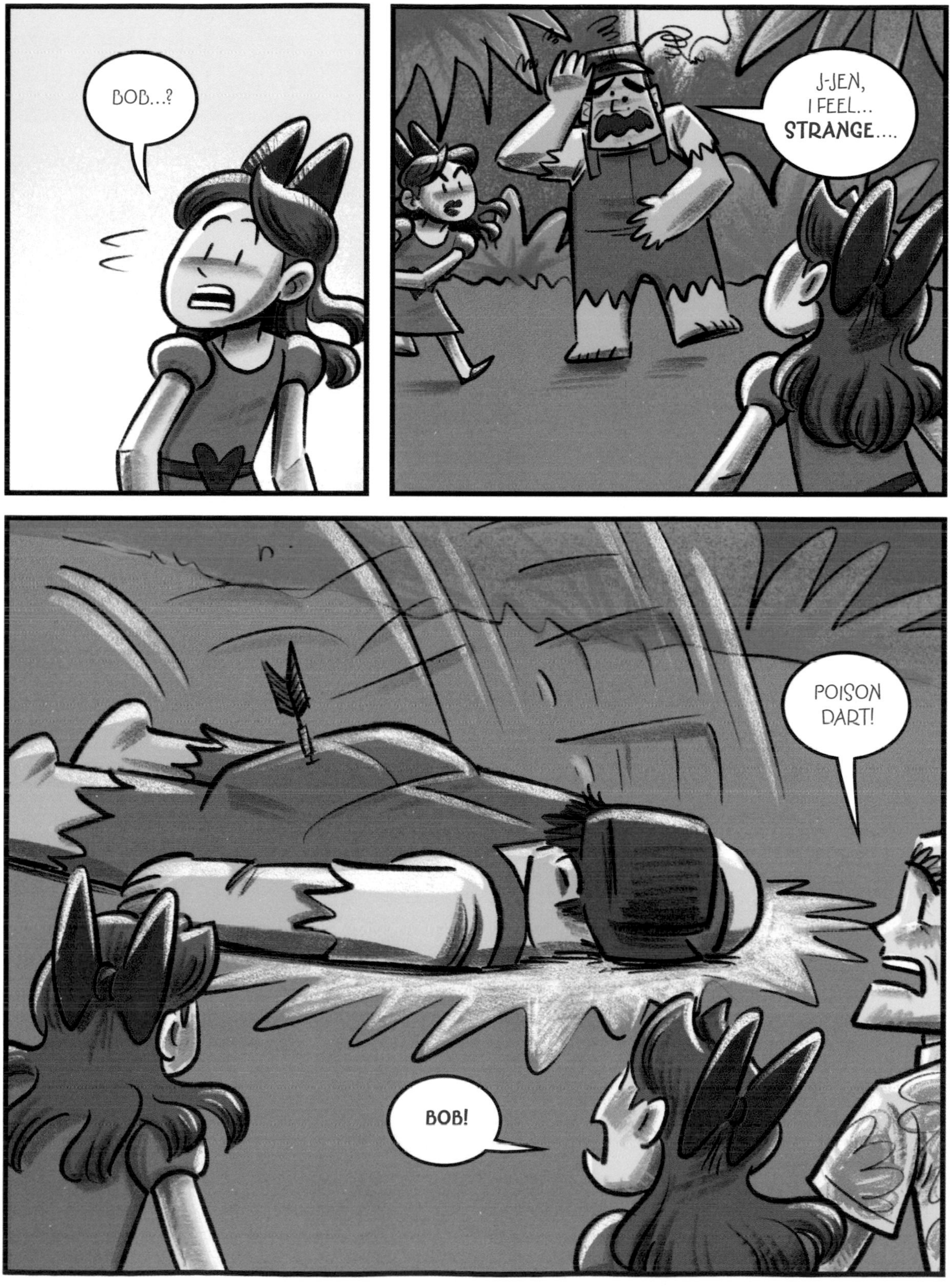
BOB...?
J-JEN, I FEEL... STRANGE....
POISON DART!
BOB!

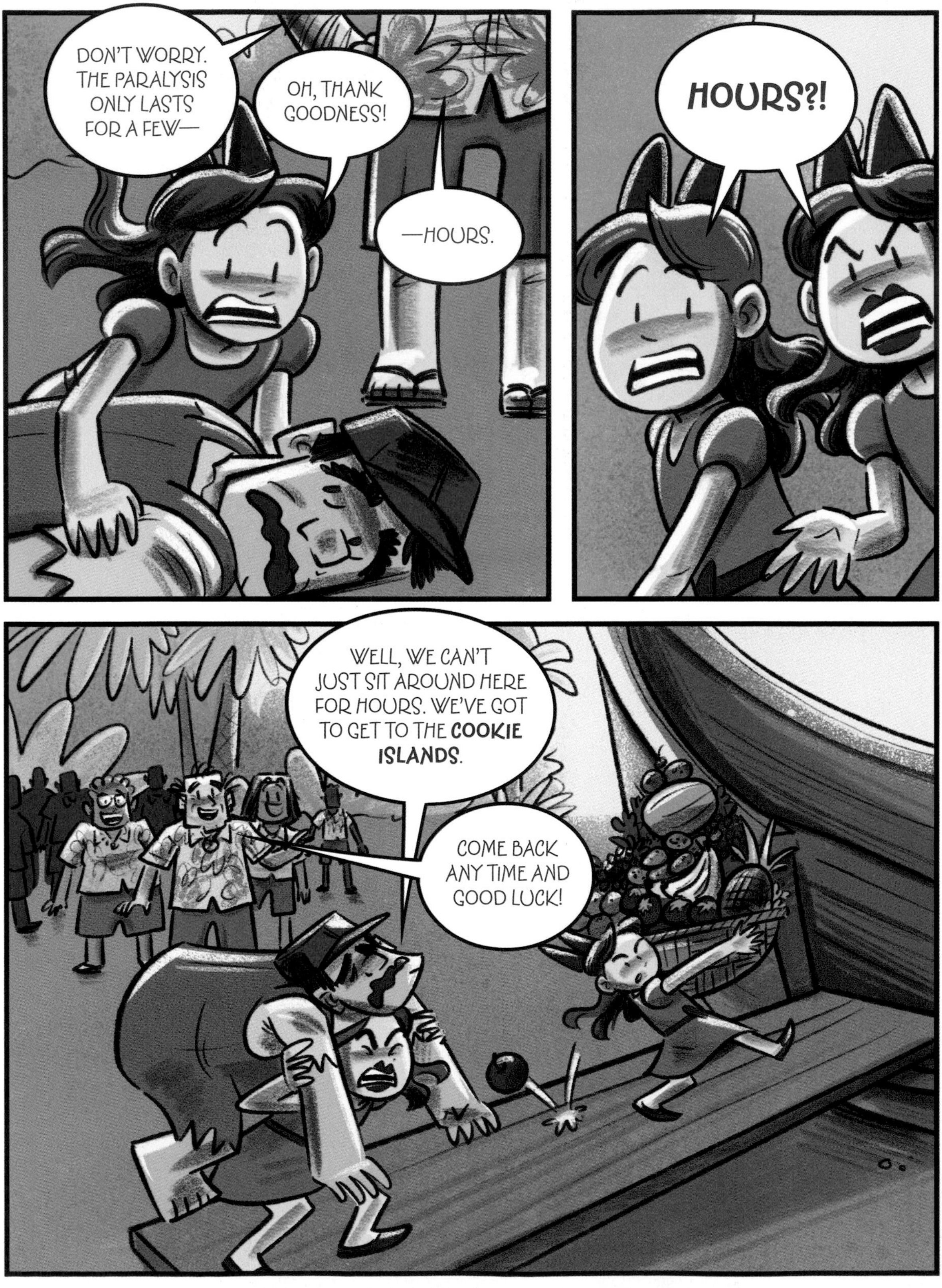
DON'T WORRY. THE PARALYSIS ONLY LASTS FOR A FEW—
OH, THANK GOODNESS!
—HOURS.
HOURS?!
WELL, WE CAN'T JUST SIT AROUND HERE FOR HOURS. WE'VE GOT TO GET TO THE COOKIE ISLANDS.
COME BACK ANY TIME AND GOOD LUCK!

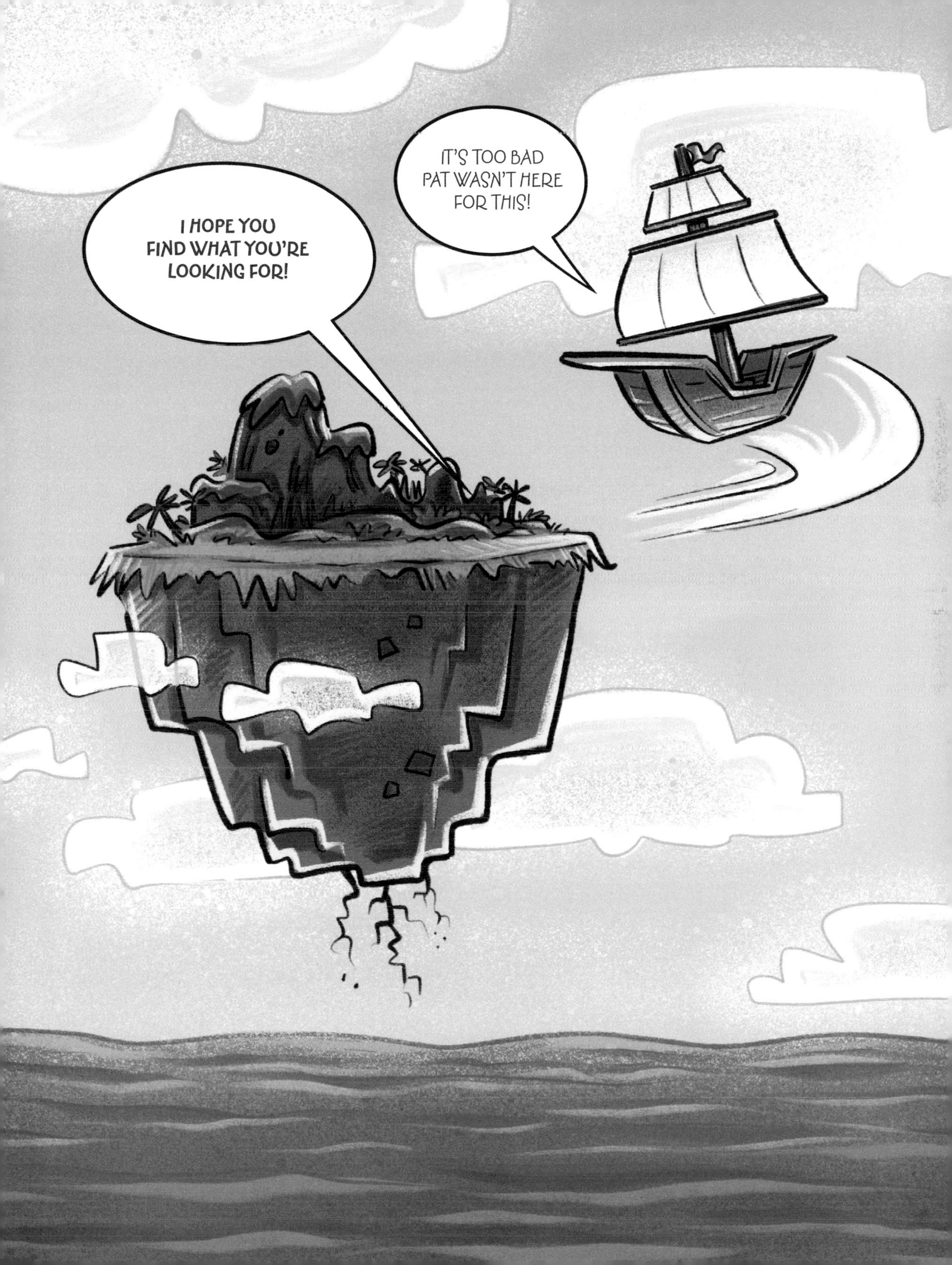
IT'S TOO BAD PAT WASN'T HERE FOR THIS!
I HOPE YOU FIND WHAT YOU'RE LOOKING FOR!

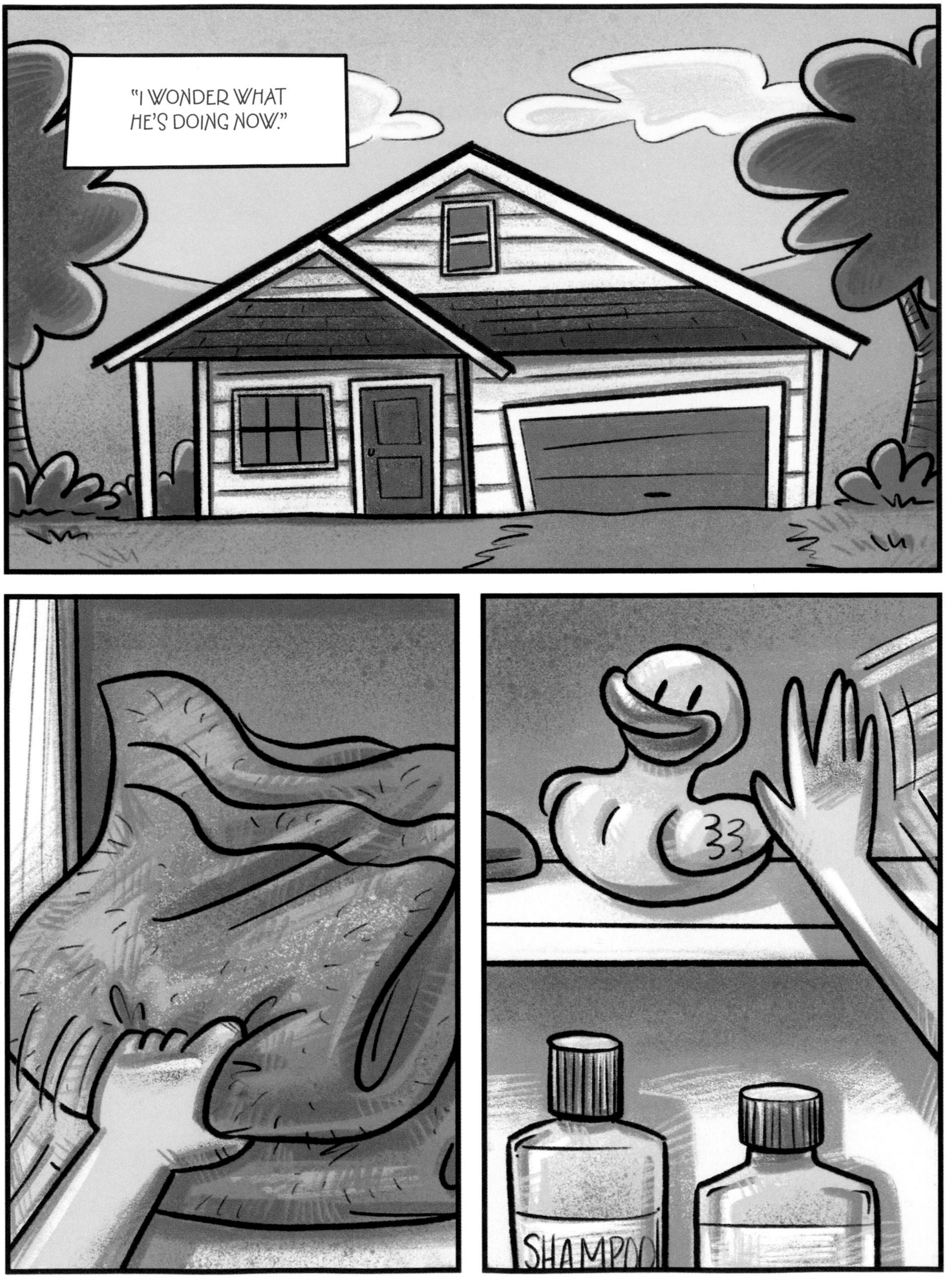
"I WONDER WHAT HE'S DOING NOW."
SHAMPOO

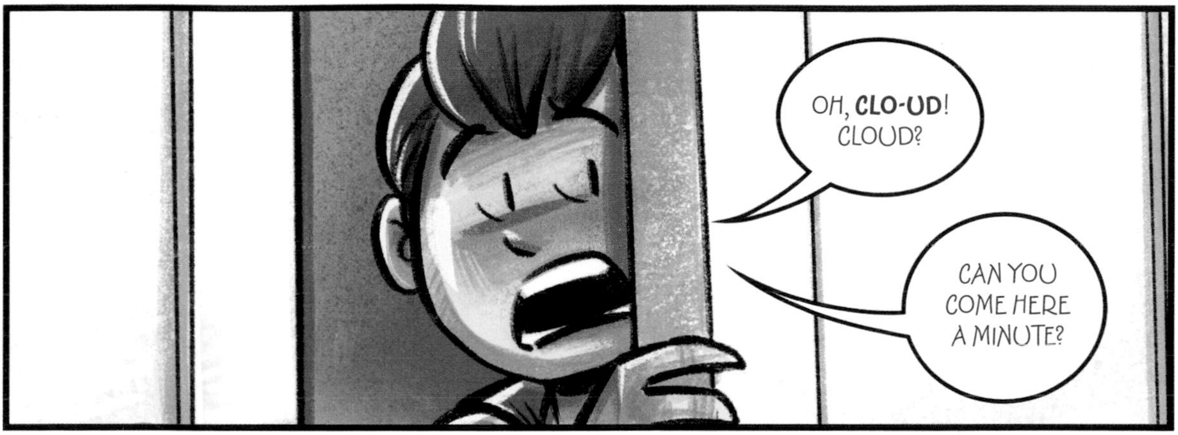
OH, **CLO-UD**! CLOUD?
CAN YOU COME HERE A MINUTE?

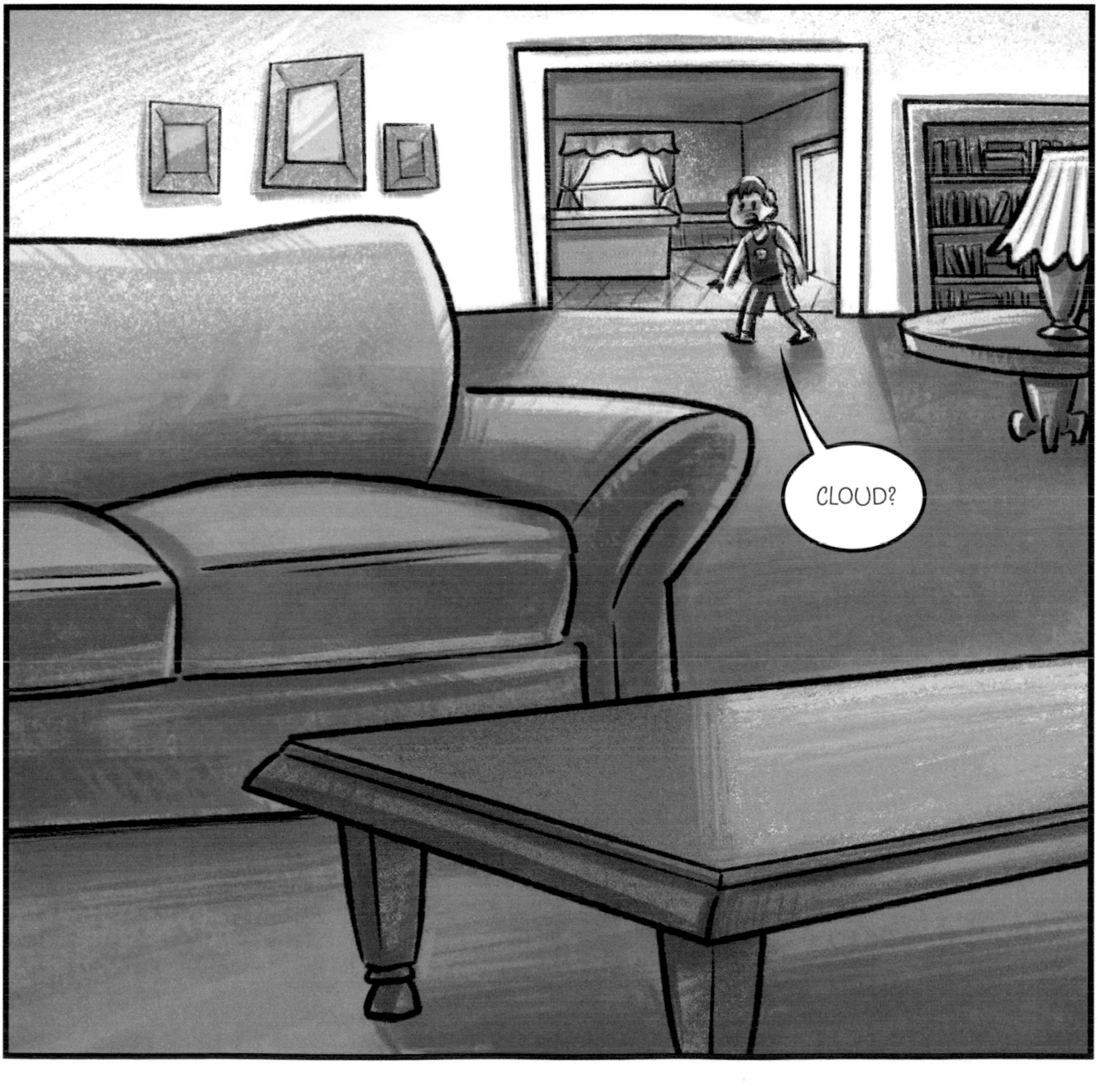
CLOUD?

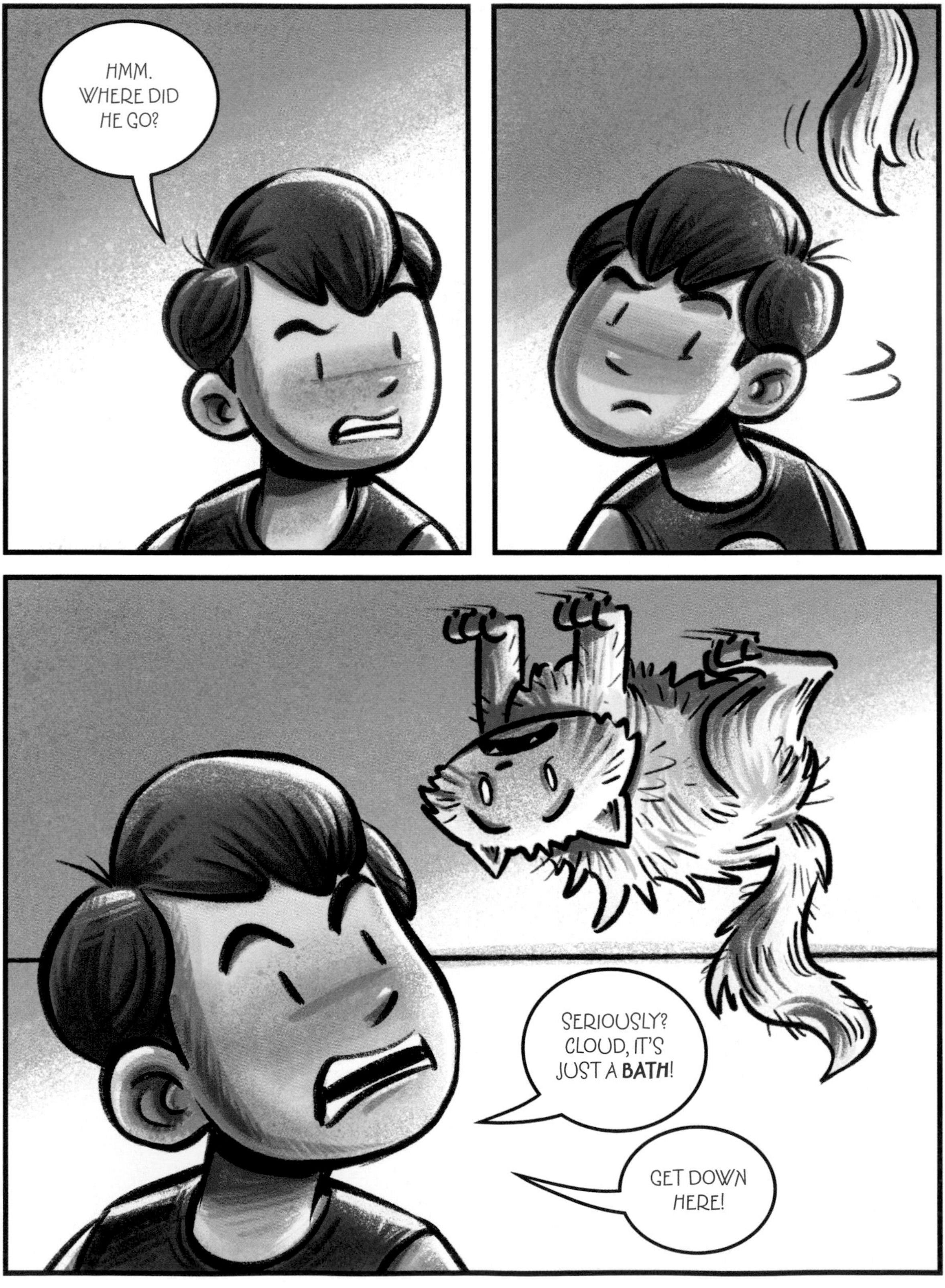
HMM. WHERE DID HE GO?
SERIOUSLY? CLOUD, IT'S JUST A **BATH**!
GET DOWN HERE!

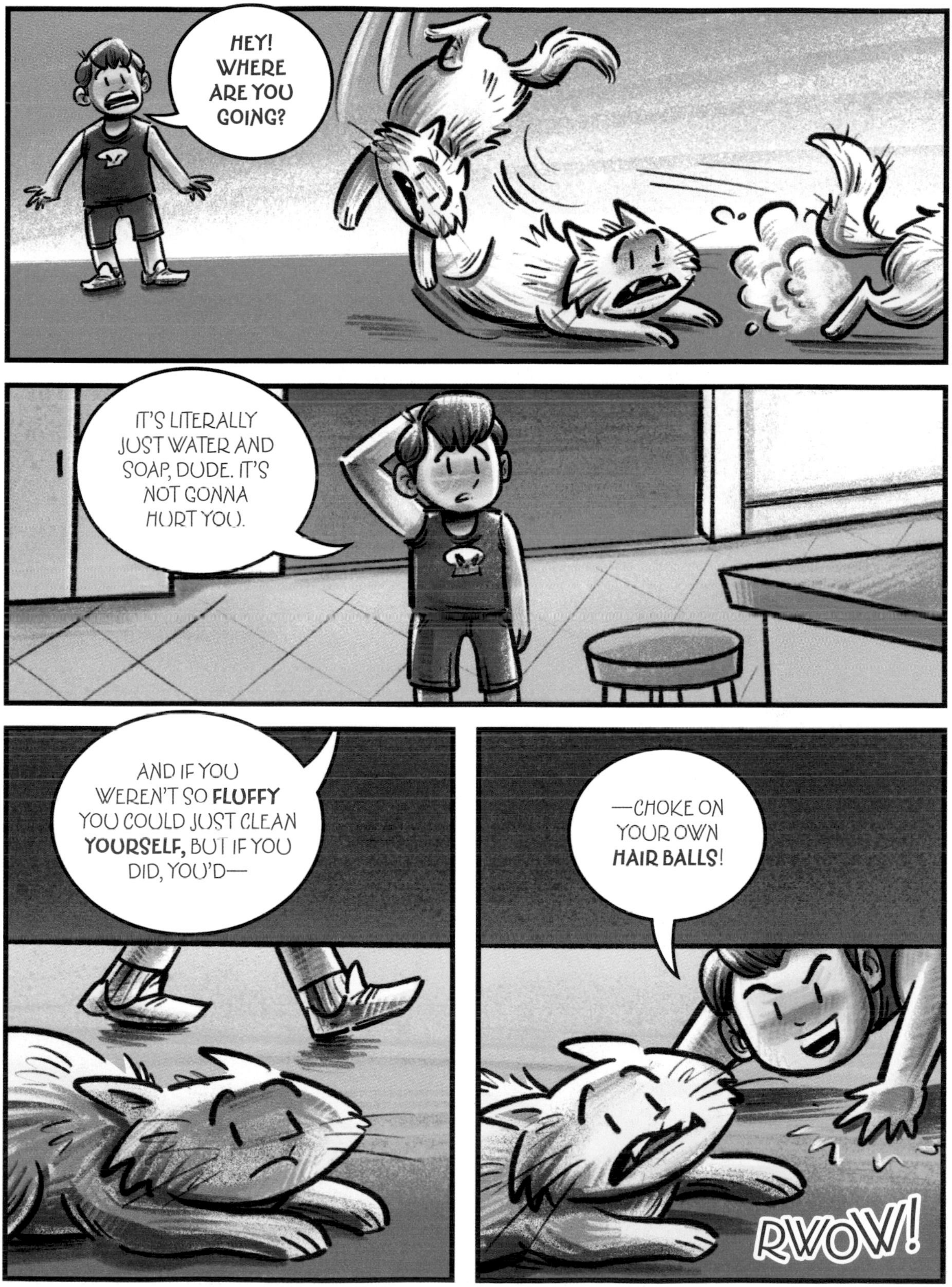
HEY! WHERE ARE YOU GOING?
IT'S LITERALLY JUST WATER AND SOAP, DUDE. IT'S NOT GONNA HURT YOU.
AND IF YOU WEREN'T SO FLUFFY YOU COULD JUST CLEAN YOURSELF, BUT IF YOU DID, YOU'D—
—CHOKE ON YOUR OWN HAIR BALLS!
RWOW!

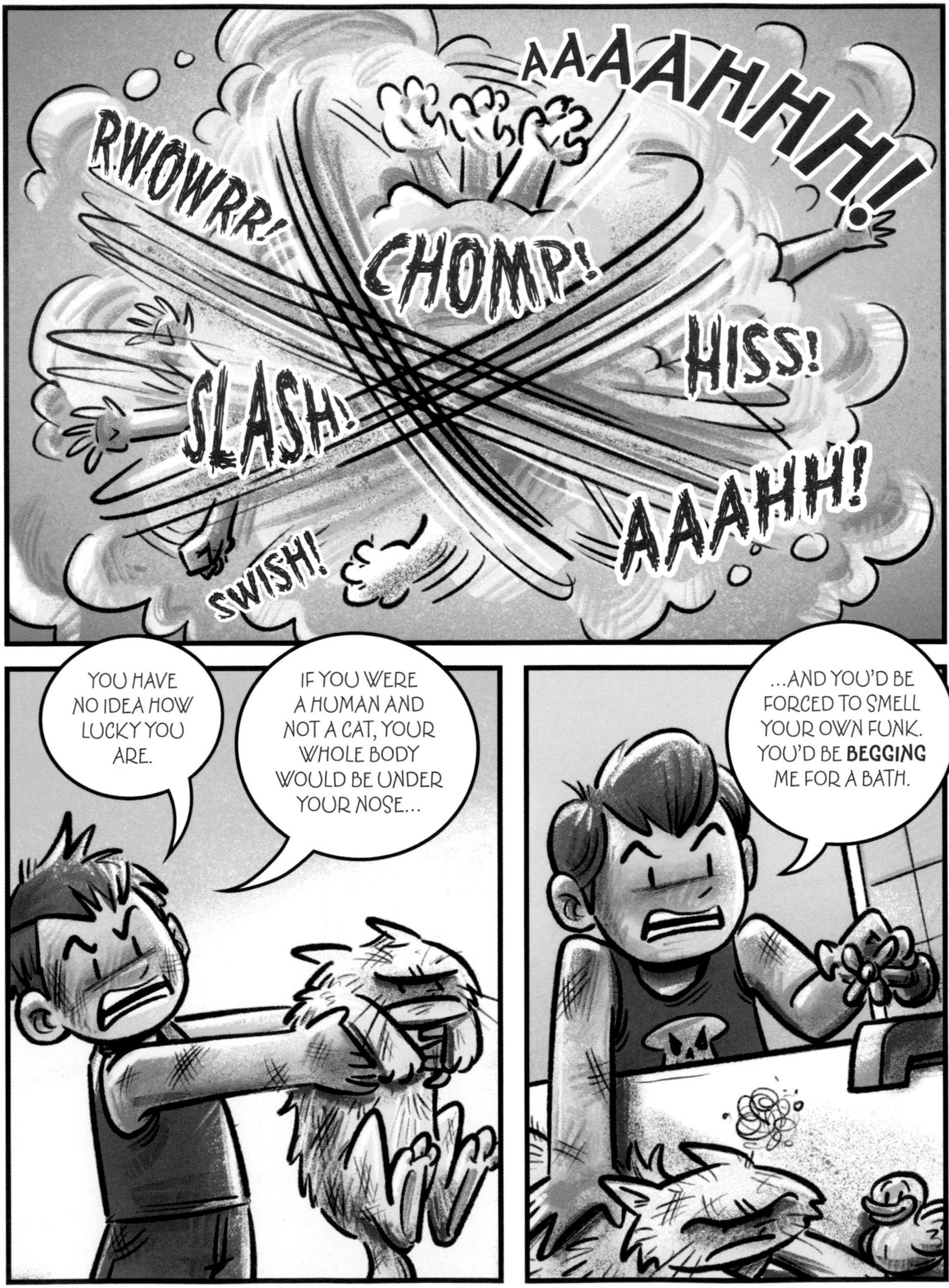
AAAAHHHH!
RWOWRRR!
CHOMP!
HISS!
SLASH!
AAAHH!
SWISH!
YOU HAVE NO IDEA HOW LUCKY YOU ARE.
IF YOU WERE A HUMAN AND NOT A CAT, YOUR WHOLE BODY WOULD BE UNDER YOUR NOSE...
...AND YOU'D BE FORCED TO SMELL YOUR OWN FUNK. YOU'D BE **BEGGING** ME FOR A BATH.

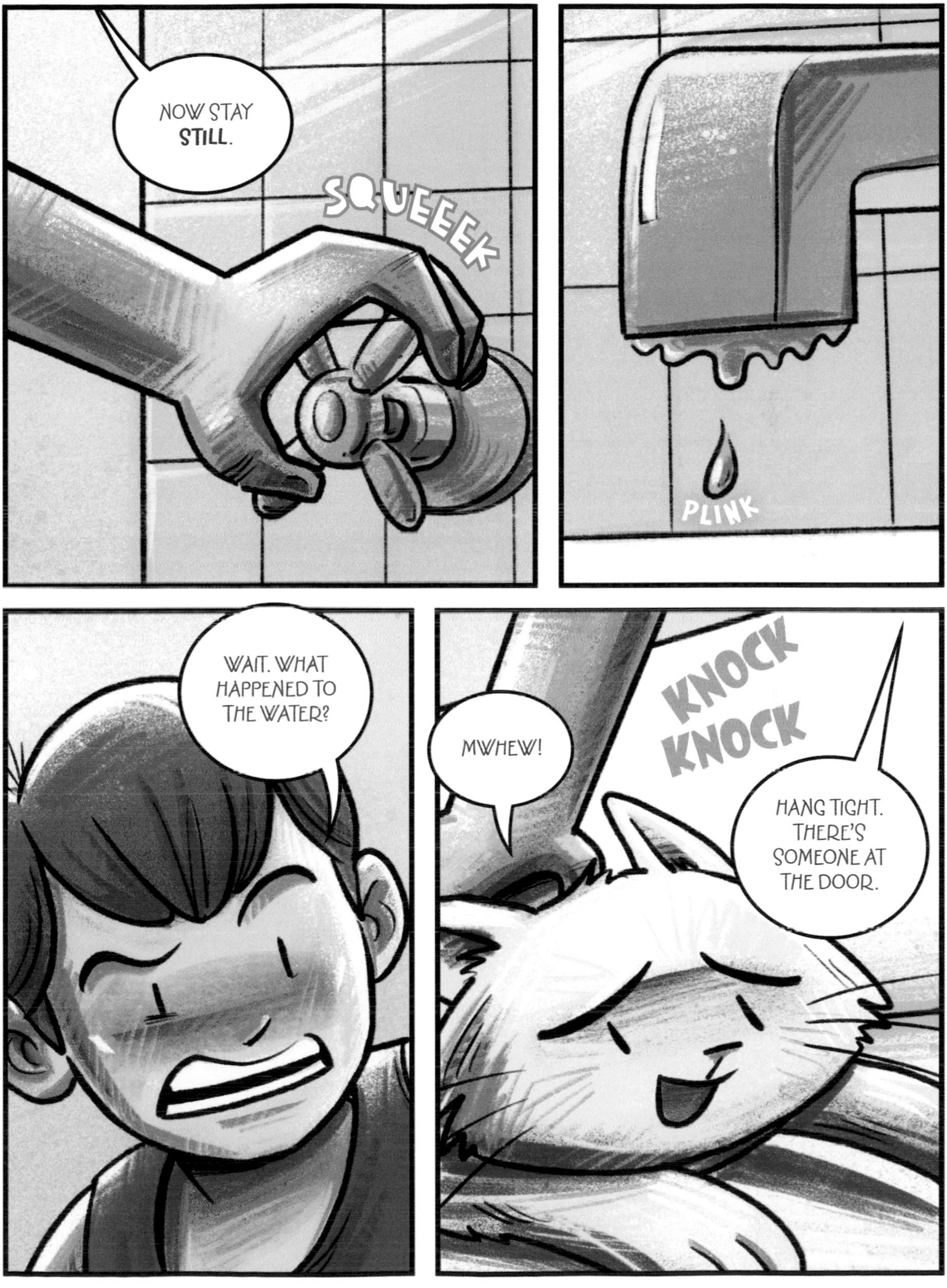
NOW STAY STILL.
SQUEEEEK
PLINK
WAIT. WHAT HAPPENED TO THE WATER?
MWHEW!
KNOCK KNOCK
HANG TIGHT. THERE'S SOMEONE AT THE DOOR.

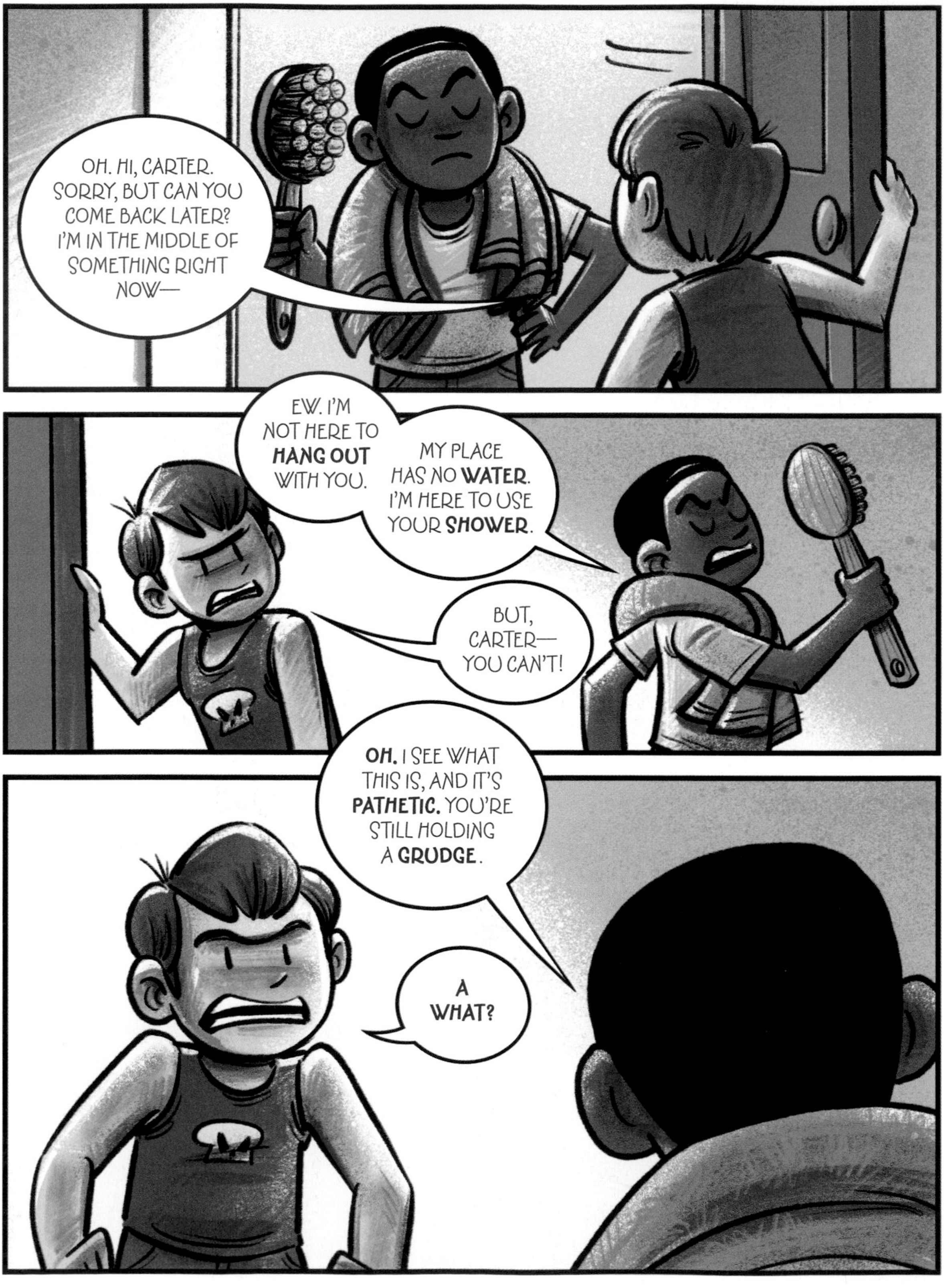
OH. HI, CARTER. SORRY, BUT CAN YOU COME BACK LATER? I'M IN THE MIDDLE OF SOMETHING RIGHT NOW—
EW. I'M NOT HERE TO HANG OUT WITH YOU.
MY PLACE HAS NO WATER. I'M HERE TO USE YOUR SHOWER.
BUT, CARTER— YOU CAN'T!
OH. I SEE WHAT THIS IS, AND IT'S PATHETIC. YOU'RE STILL HOLDING A GRUDGE.
A WHAT?

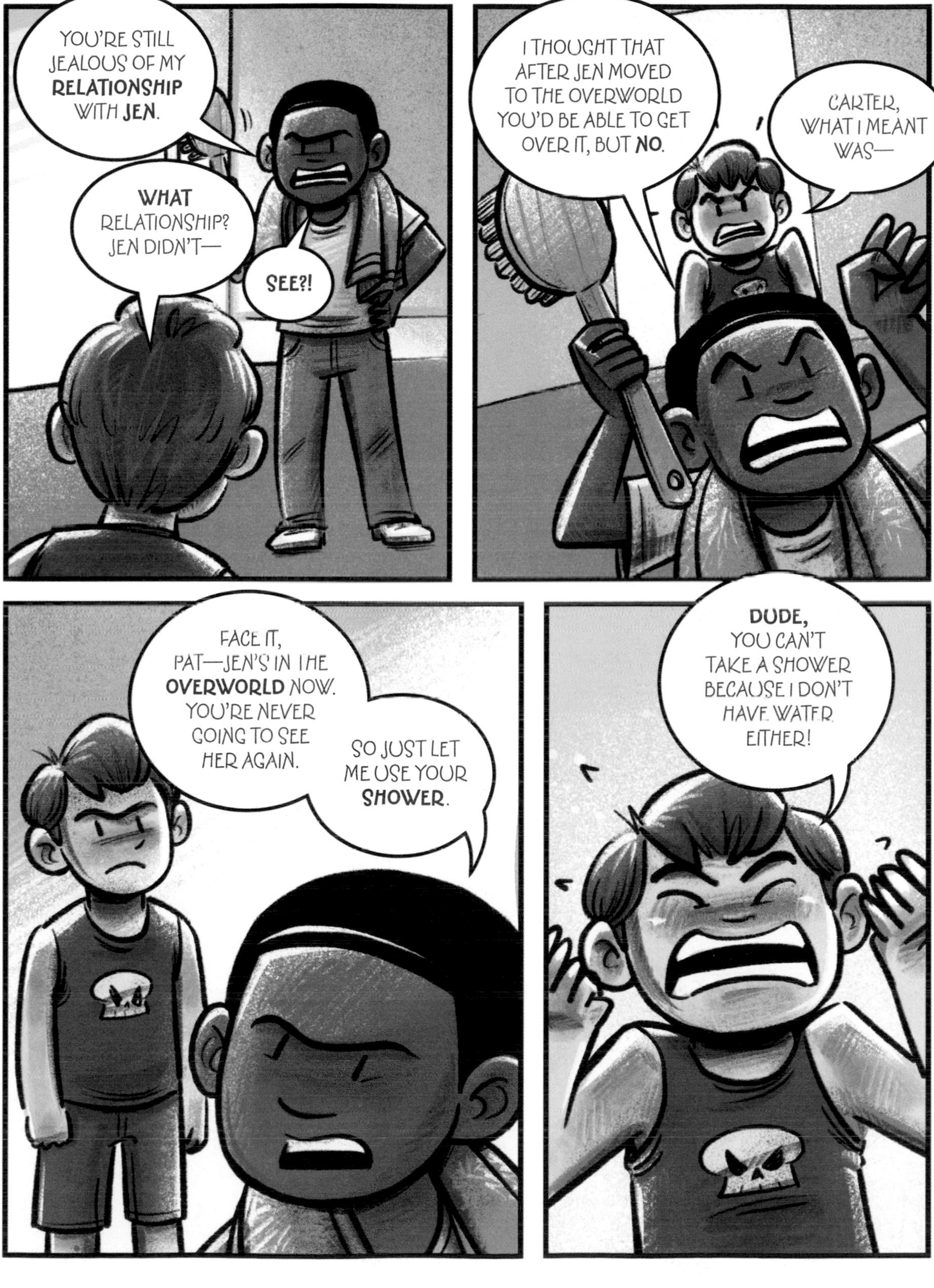
YOU'RE STILL JEALOUS OF MY **RELATIONSHIP** WITH **JEN**.
WHAT RELATIONSHIP? JEN DIDN'T—
SEE?!
I THOUGHT THAT AFTER JEN MOVED TO THE OVERWORLD YOU'D BE ABLE TO GET OVER IT, BUT **NO**.
CARTER, WHAT I MEANT WAS—
FACE IT, PAT—JEN'S IN THE **OVERWORLD** NOW. YOU'RE NEVER GOING TO SEE HER AGAIN.
SO JUST LET ME USE YOUR **SHOWER**.
DUDE, YOU CAN'T TAKE A SHOWER BECAUSE I DON'T HAVE WATER EITHER!

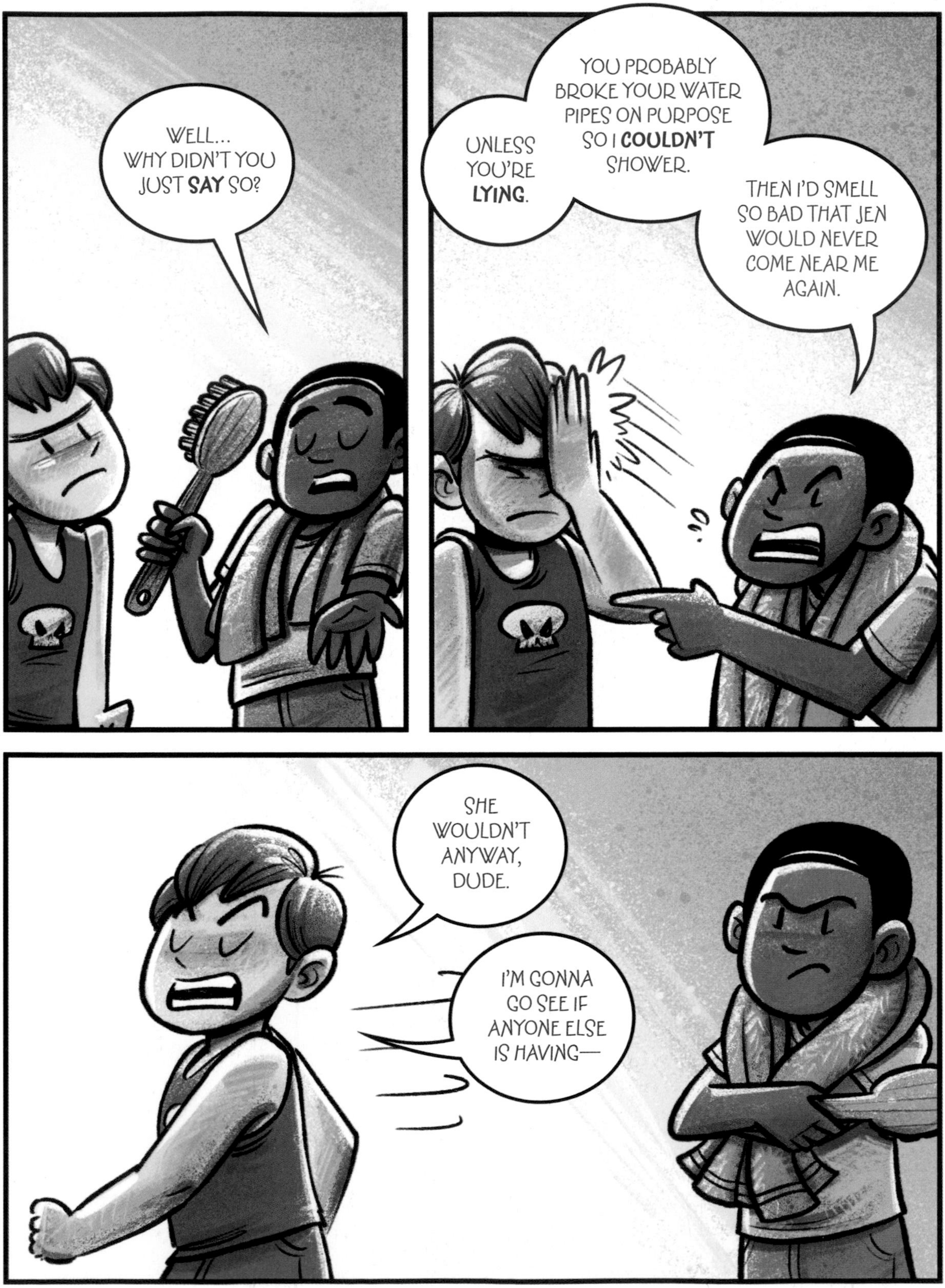

WELL... WHY DIDN'T YOU JUST **SAY** SO?
UNLESS YOU'RE **LYING**.
YOU PROBABLY BROKE YOUR WATER PIPES ON PURPOSE SO I **COULDN'T** SHOWER.
THEN I'D SMELL SO BAD THAT JEN WOULD NEVER COME NEAR ME AGAIN.
SHE WOULDN'T ANYWAY, DUDE.
I'M GONNA GO SEE IF ANYONE ELSE IS HAVING—

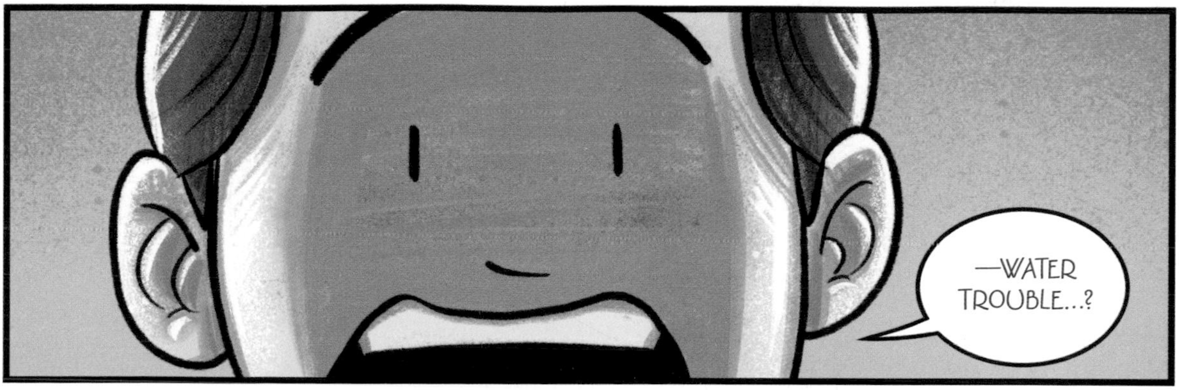
—WATER TROUBLE...?

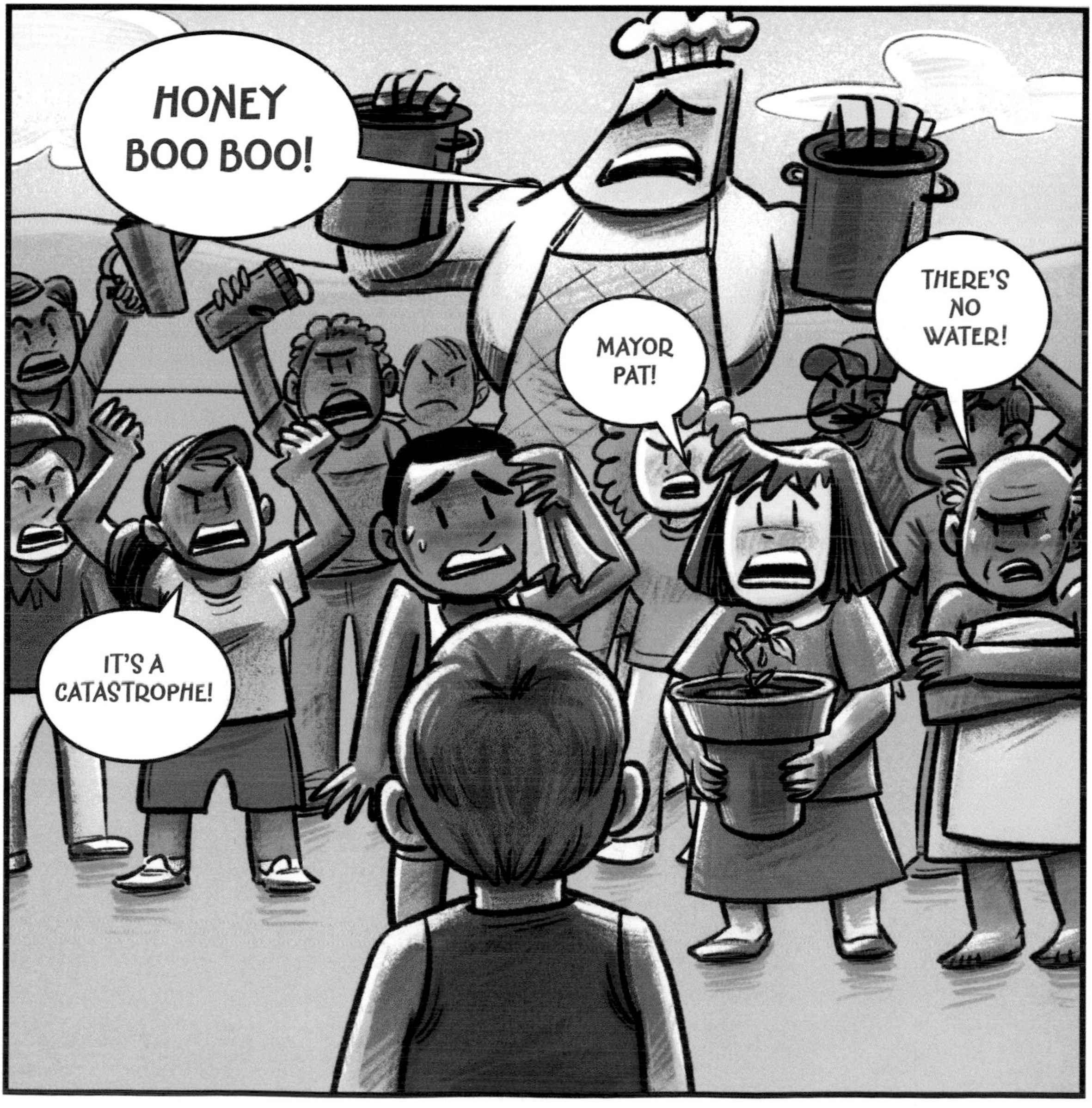
HONEY BOO BOO!
THERE'S NO WATER!
MAYOR PAT!
IT'S A CATASTROPHE!

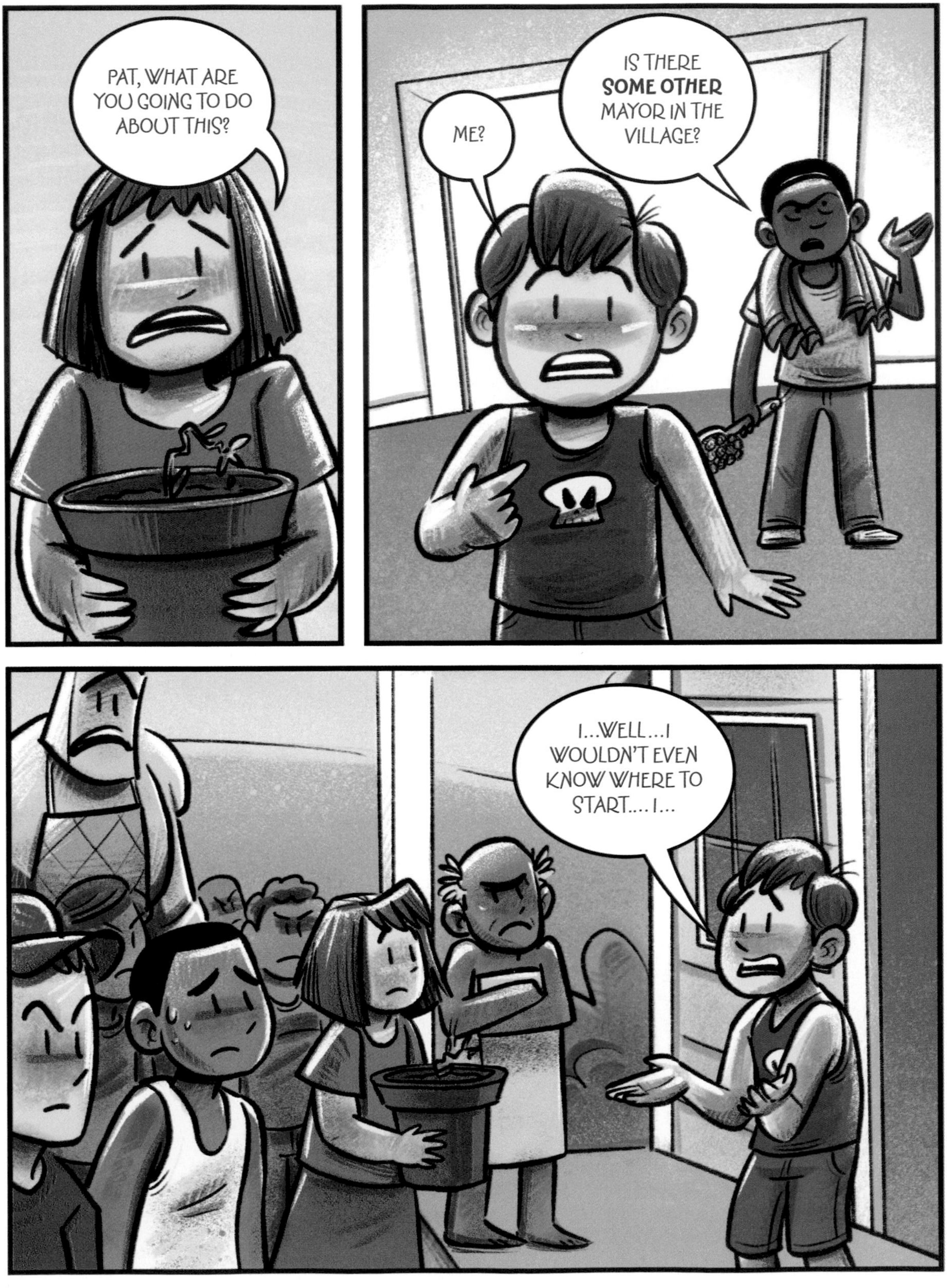
PAT, WHAT ARE YOU GOING TO DO ABOUT THIS?
ME?
IS THERE **SOME OTHER** MAYOR IN THE VILLAGE?
I...WELL...I WOULDN'T EVEN KNOW WHERE TO START.... I...

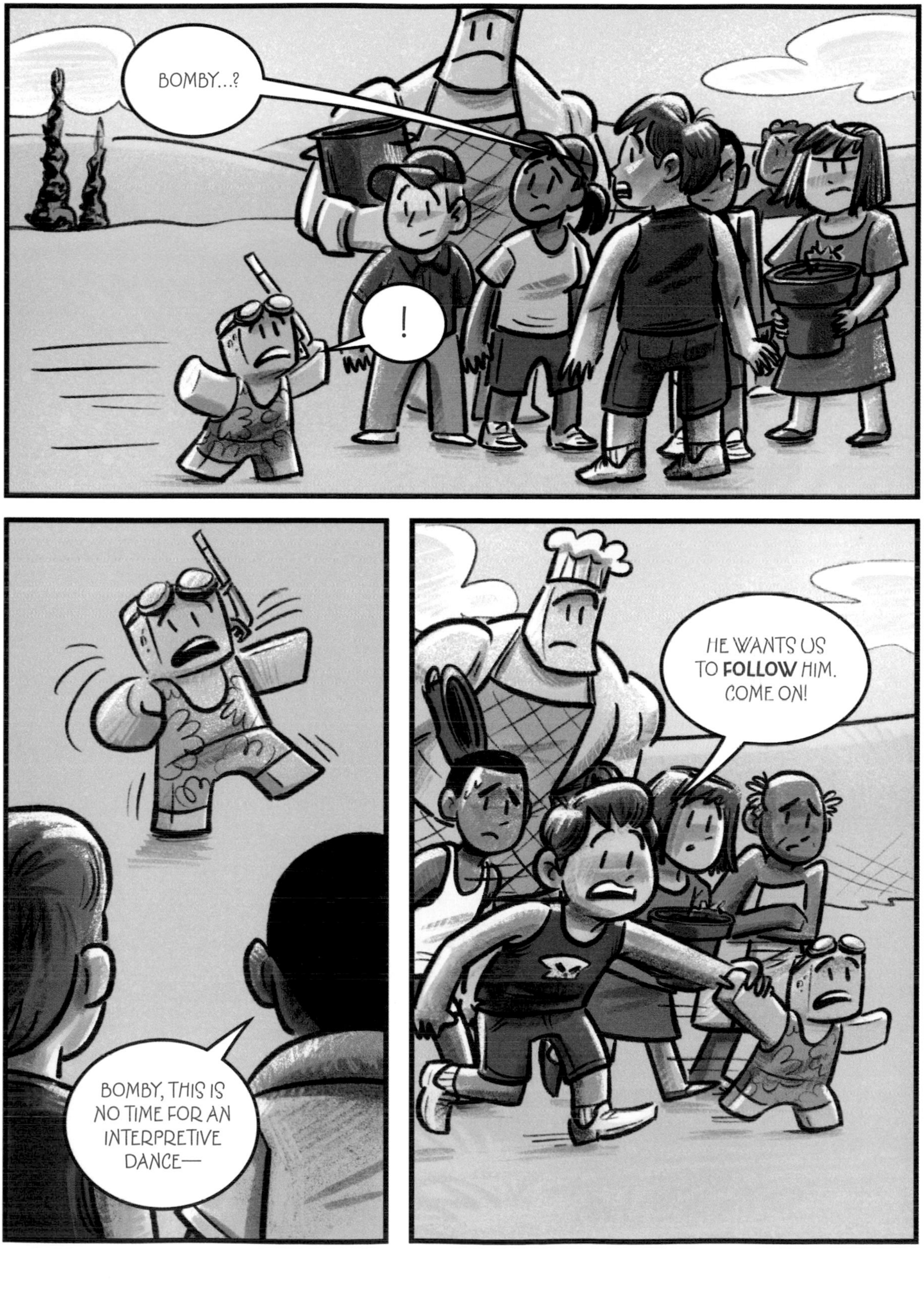
BOMBY...?
!
BOMBY, THIS IS NO TIME FOR AN INTERPRETIVE DANCE—
HE WANTS US TO **FOLLOW** HIM. COME ON!

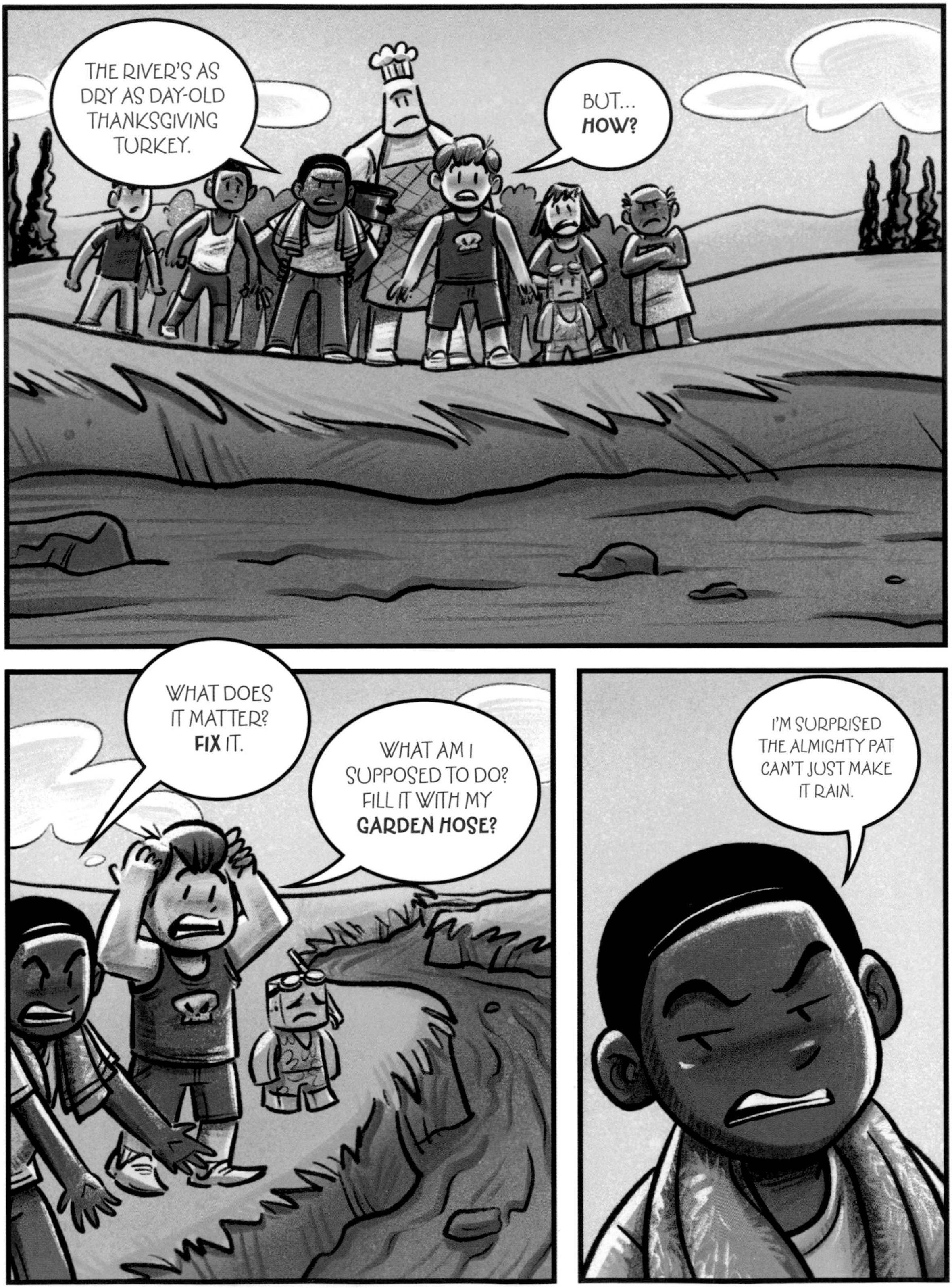
THE RIVER'S AS DRY AS DAY-OLD THANKSGIVING TURKEY.
BUT... **HOW?**
WHAT DOES IT MATTER? **FIX** IT.
WHAT AM I SUPPOSED TO DO? FILL IT WITH MY **GARDEN HOSE?**
I'M SURPRISED THE ALMIGHTY PAT CAN'T JUST MAKE IT RAIN.

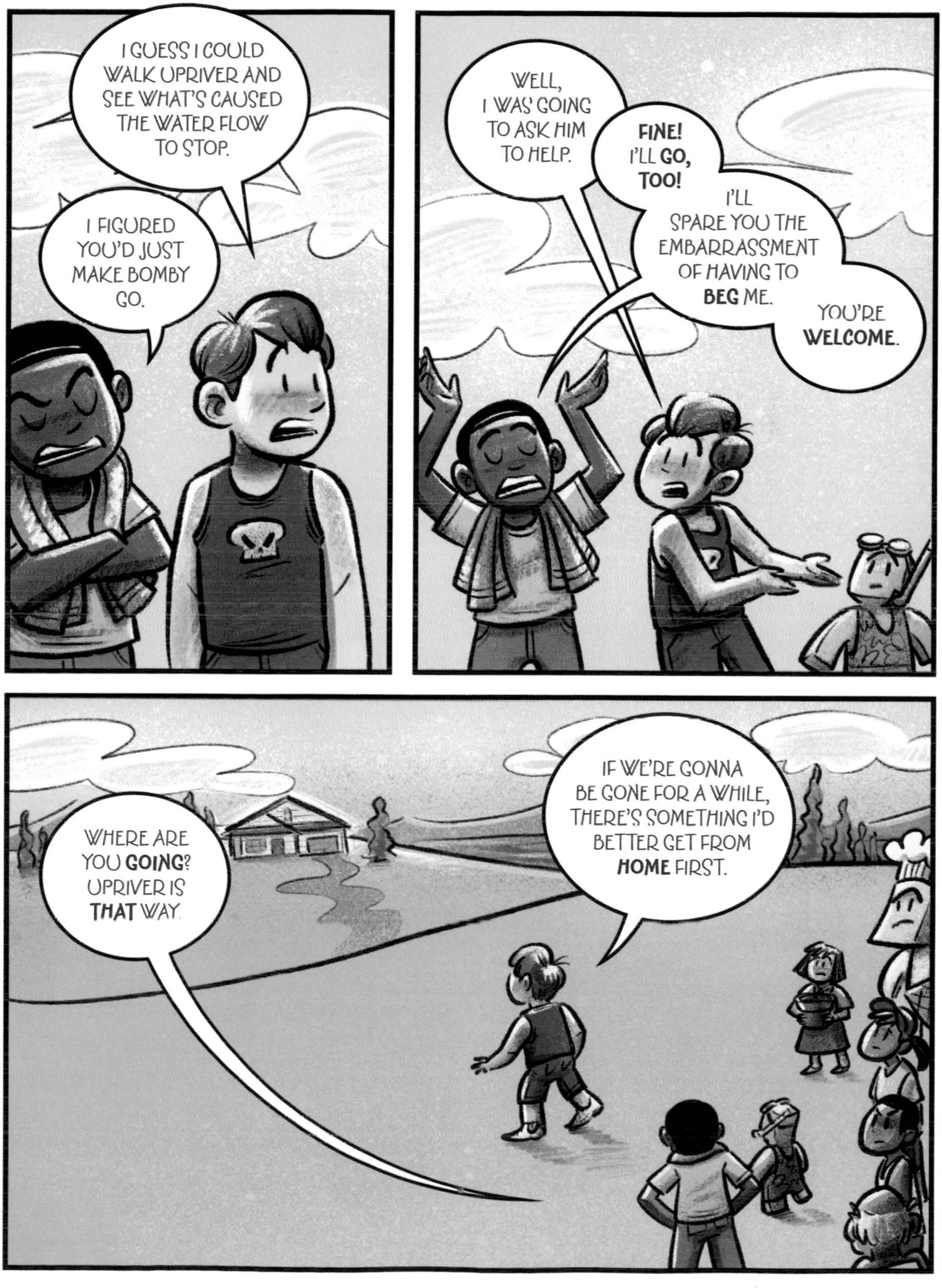
I GUESS I COULD WALK UPRIVER AND SEE WHAT'S CAUSED THE WATER FLOW TO STOP.
I FIGURED YOU'D JUST MAKE BOMBY GO.
WELL, I WAS GOING TO ASK HIM TO HELP.
FINE! I'LL **GO, TOO!**
I'LL SPARE YOU THE EMBARRASSMENT OF HAVING TO **BEG** ME.
YOU'RE **WELCOME**.
IF WE'RE GONNA BE GONE FOR A WHILE, THERE'S SOMETHING I'D BETTER GET FROM **HOME** FIRST.
WHERE ARE YOU **GOING**? UPRIVER IS **THAT** WAY.

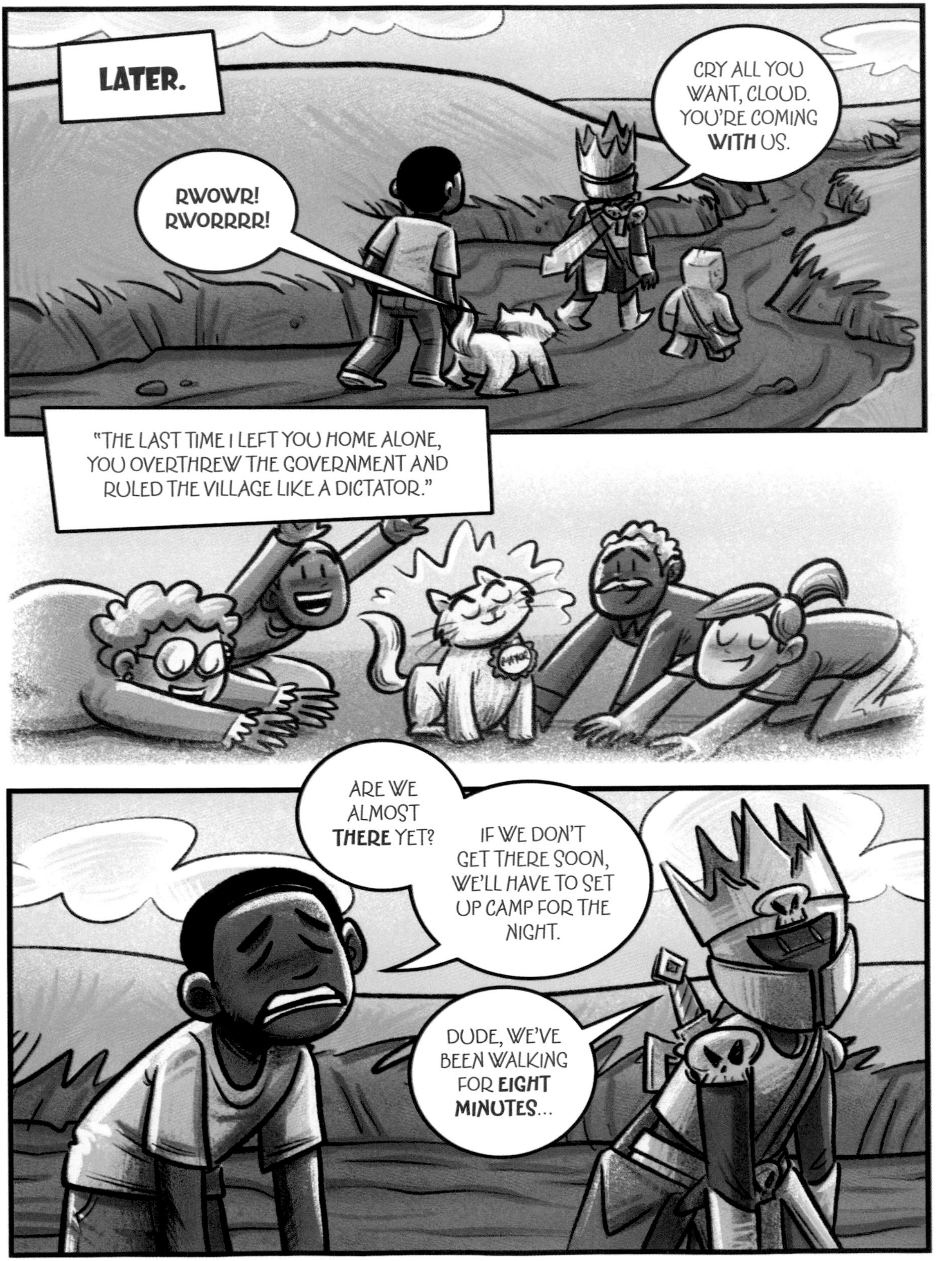
LATER.
CRY ALL YOU WANT, CLOUD. YOU'RE COMING **WITH** US.
RWOWR! RWORRRR!
"THE LAST TIME I LEFT YOU HOME ALONE, YOU OVERTHREW THE GOVERNMENT AND RULED THE VILLAGE LIKE A DICTATOR."
ARE WE ALMOST **THERE** YET?
IF WE DON'T GET THERE SOON, WE'LL HAVE TO SET UP CAMP FOR THE NIGHT.
DUDE, WE'VE BEEN WALKING FOR **EIGHT MINUTES**...

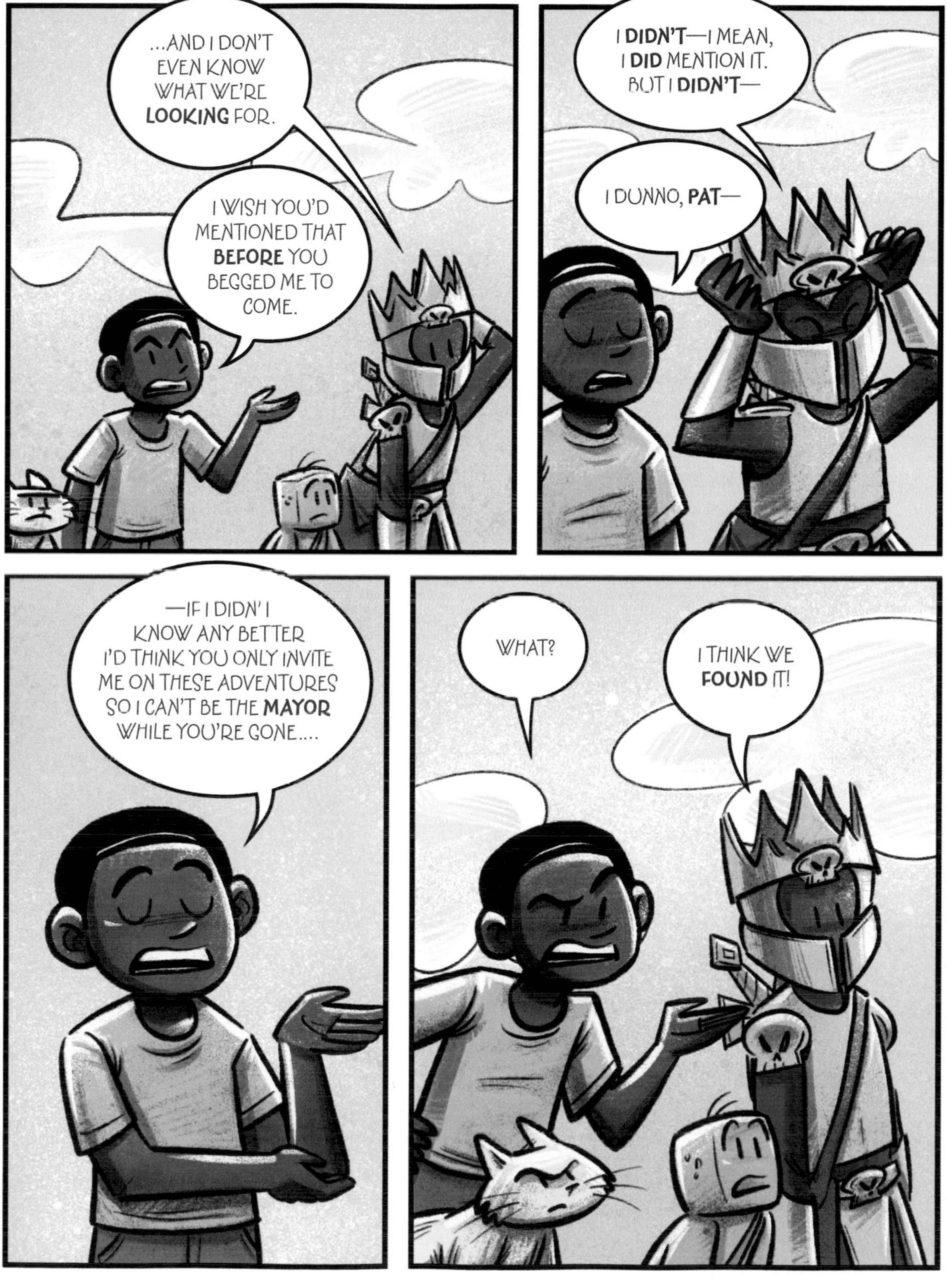
...AND I DON'T EVEN KNOW WHAT WE'RE **LOOKING** FOR.
I WISH YOU'D MENTIONED THAT **BEFORE** YOU BEGGED ME TO COME.
I **DIDN'T**—I MEAN, I **DID** MENTION IT. BUT I **DIDN'T**—
I DUNNO, **PAT**—
—IF I DIDN'T KNOW ANY BETTER I'D THINK YOU ONLY INVITE ME ON THESE ADVENTURES SO I CAN'T BE THE **MAYOR** WHILE YOU'RE GONE....
WHAT?
I THINK WE **FOUND** IT!

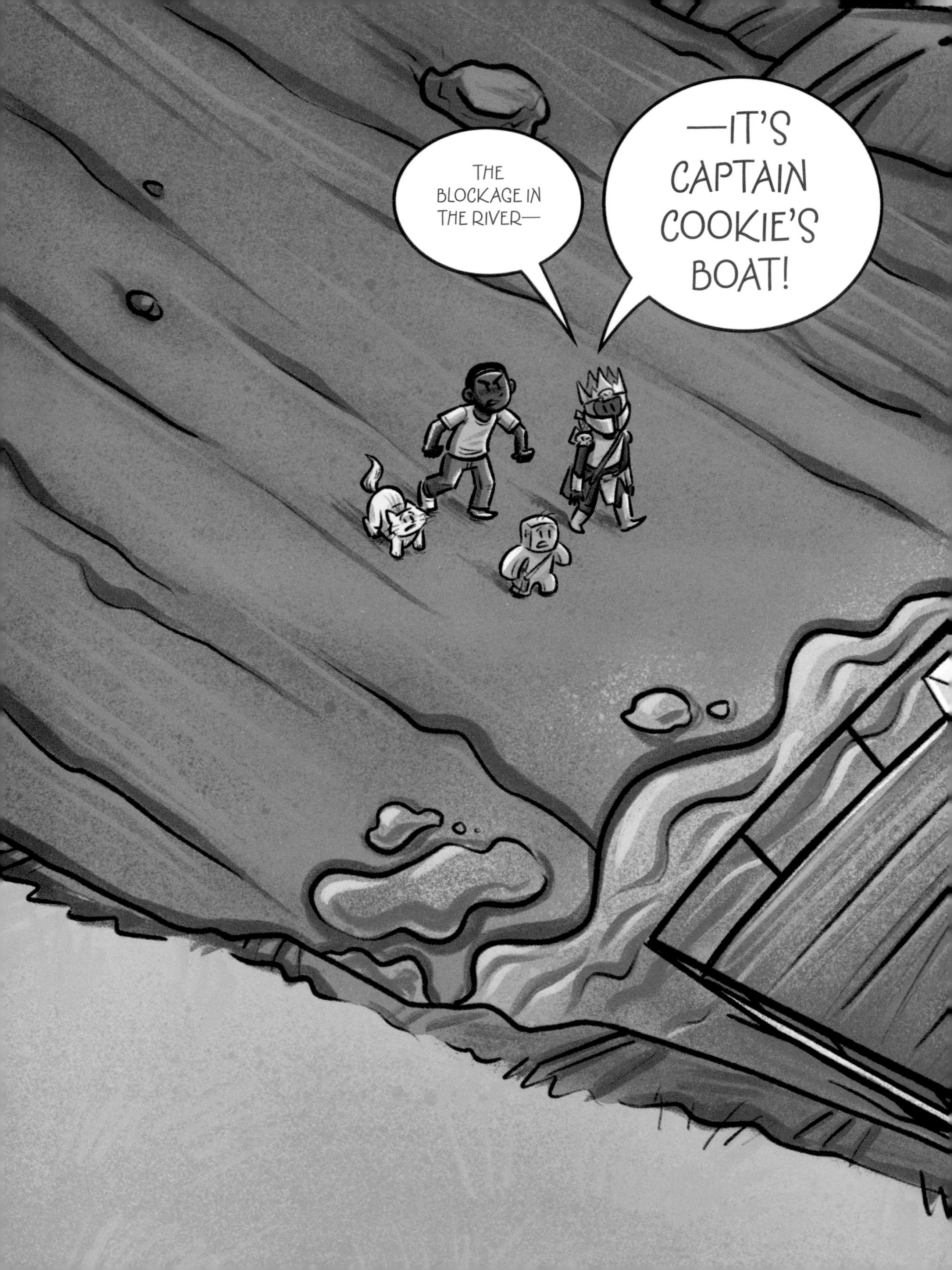
THE BLOCKAGE IN THE RIVER—
—IT'S CAPTAIN COOKIE'S BOAT!

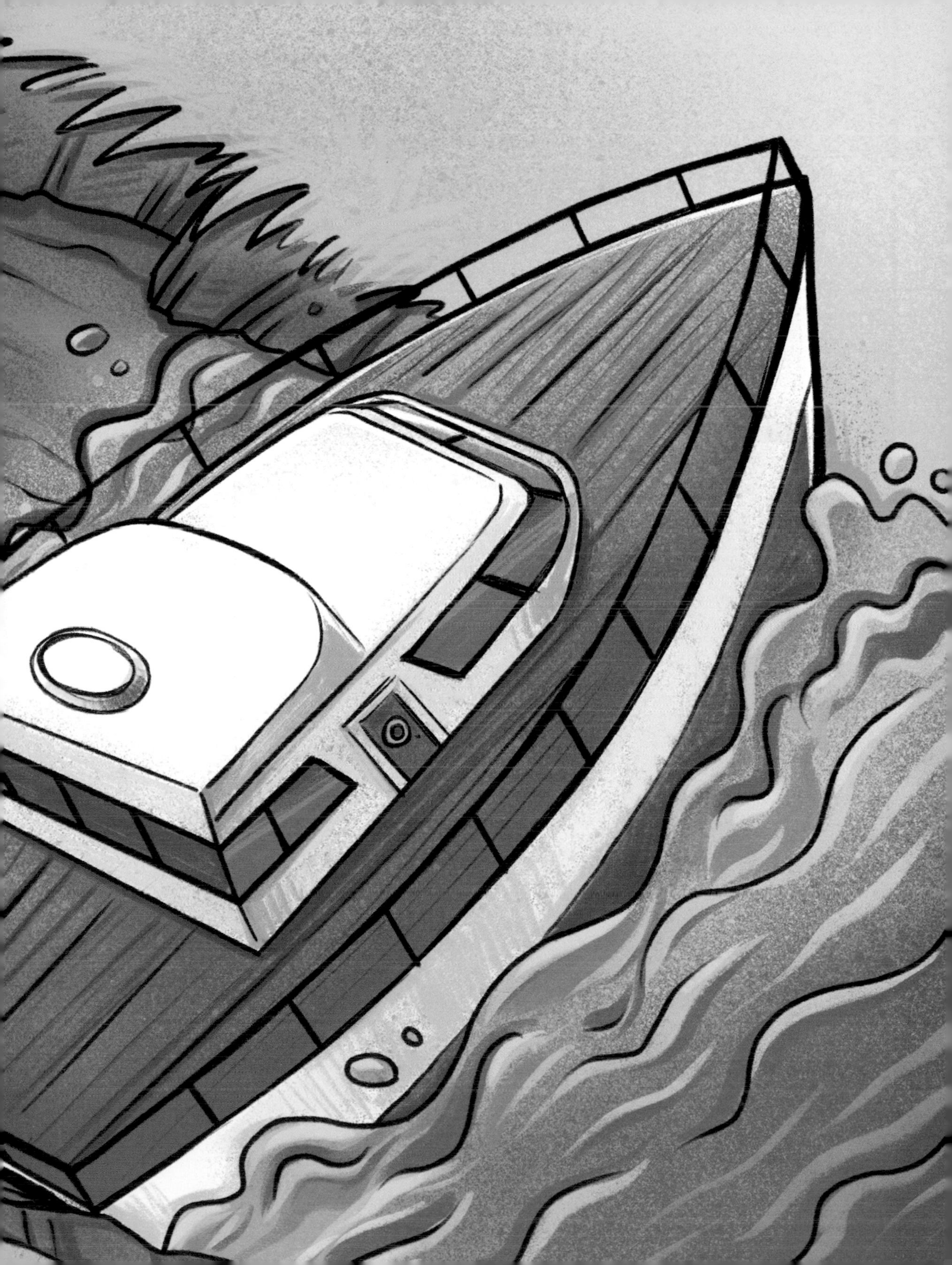

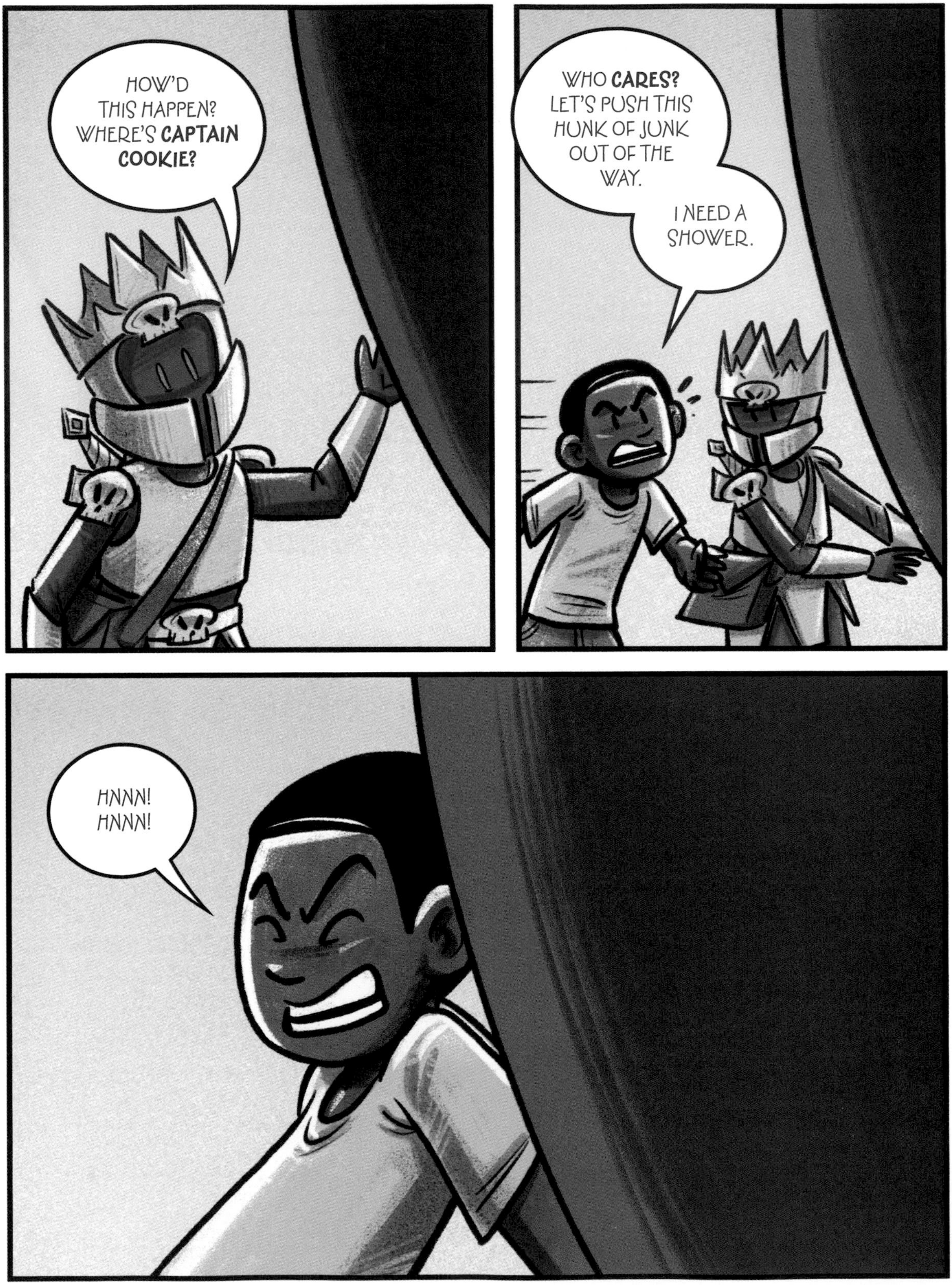
HOW'D THIS HAPPEN? WHERE'S **CAPTAIN COOKIE?**
WHO **CARES?** LET'S PUSH THIS HUNK OF JUNK OUT OF THE WAY.
I NEED A SHOWER.
HNNN! HNNN!

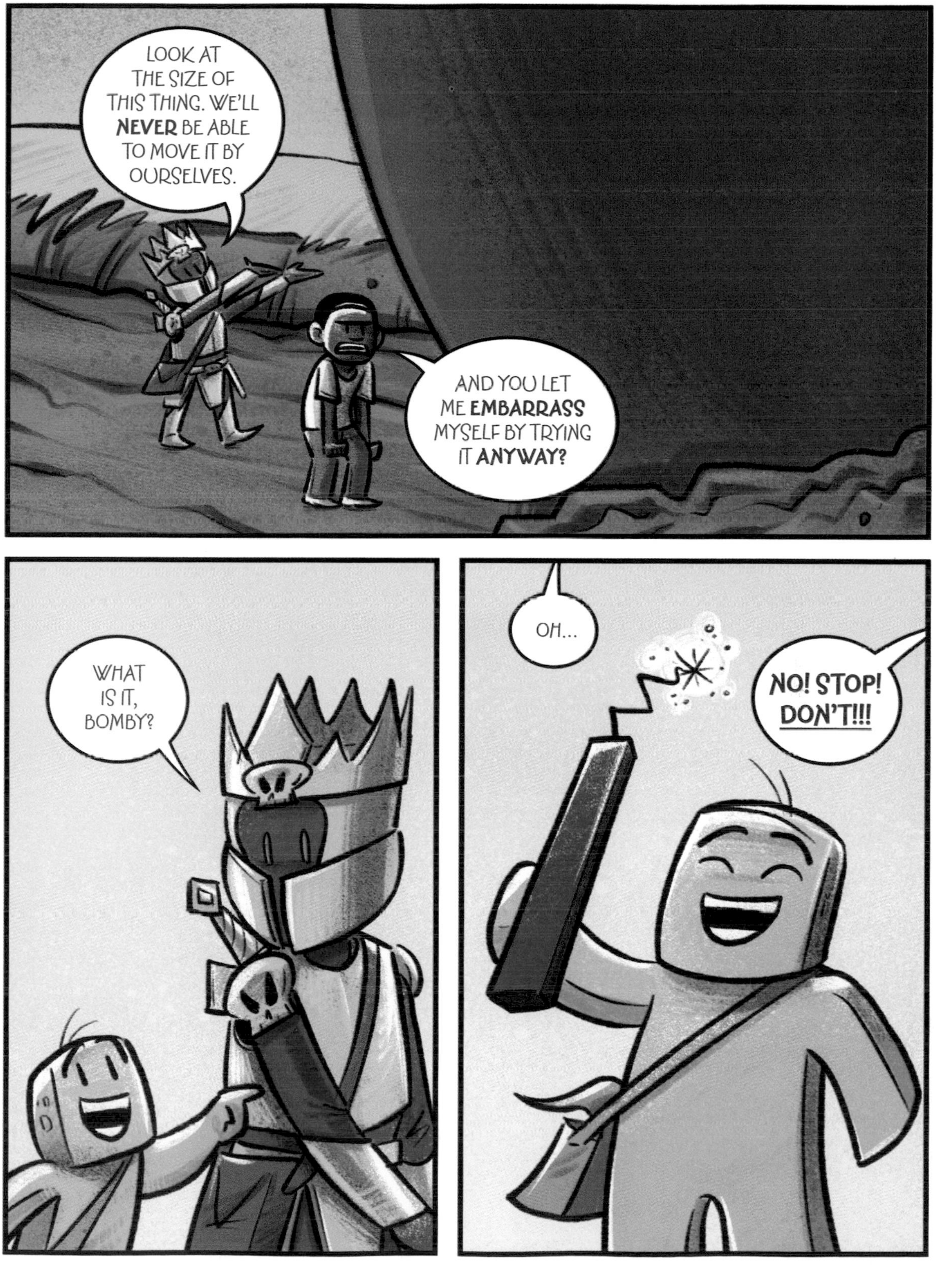
LOOK AT THE SIZE OF THIS THING. WE'LL **NEVER** BE ABLE TO MOVE IT BY OURSELVES.
AND YOU LET ME **EMBARRASS** MYSELF BY TRYING IT **ANYWAY?**
WHAT IS IT, BOMBY?
OH...
NO! STOP! DON'T!!!

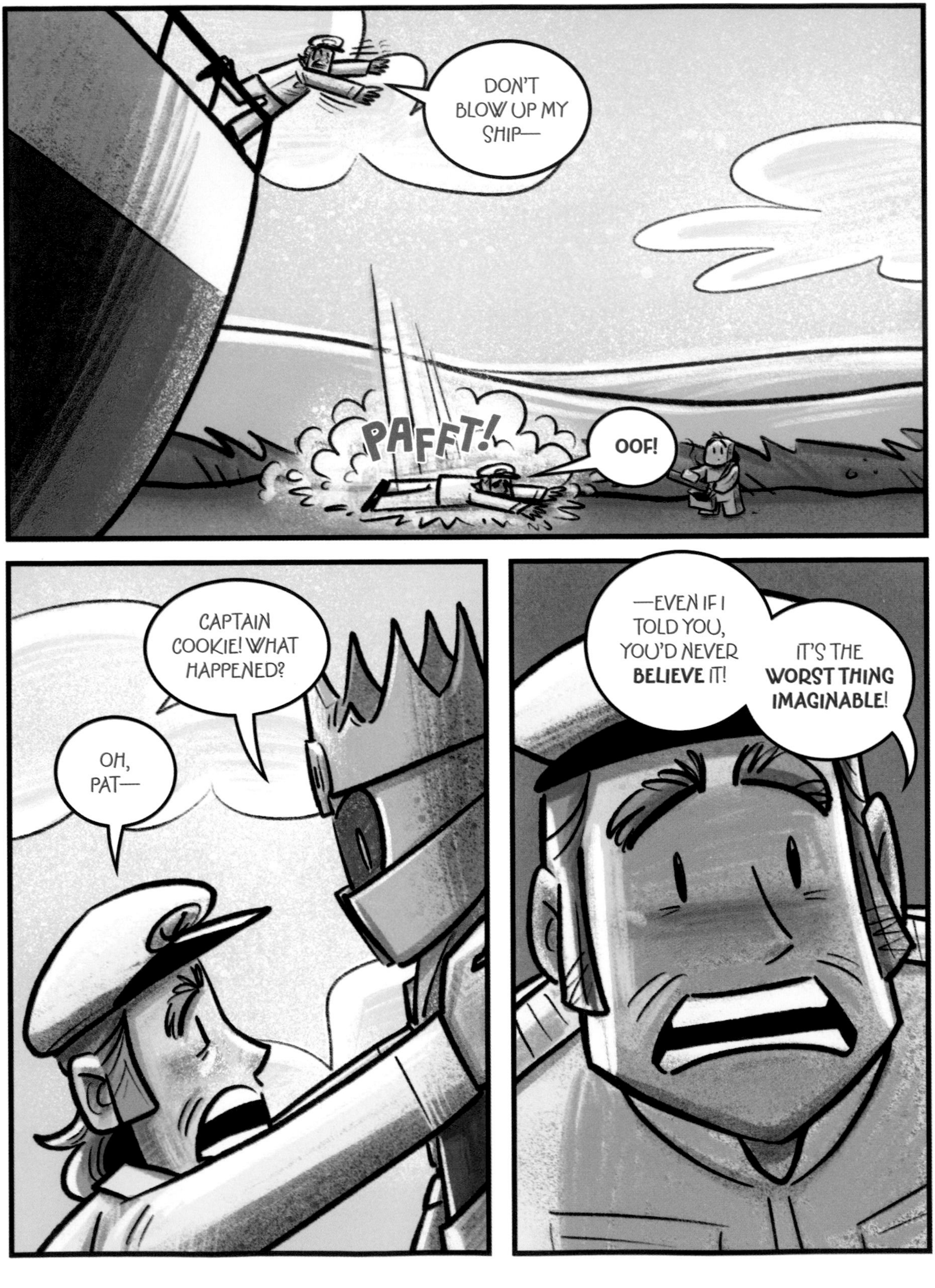
DON'T BLOW UP MY SHIP—
PAFFT!
OOF!
CAPTAIN COOKIE! WHAT HAPPENED?
OH, PAT—
—EVEN IF I TOLD YOU, YOU'D NEVER **BELIEVE** IT!
IT'S THE **WORST THING IMAGINABLE**!

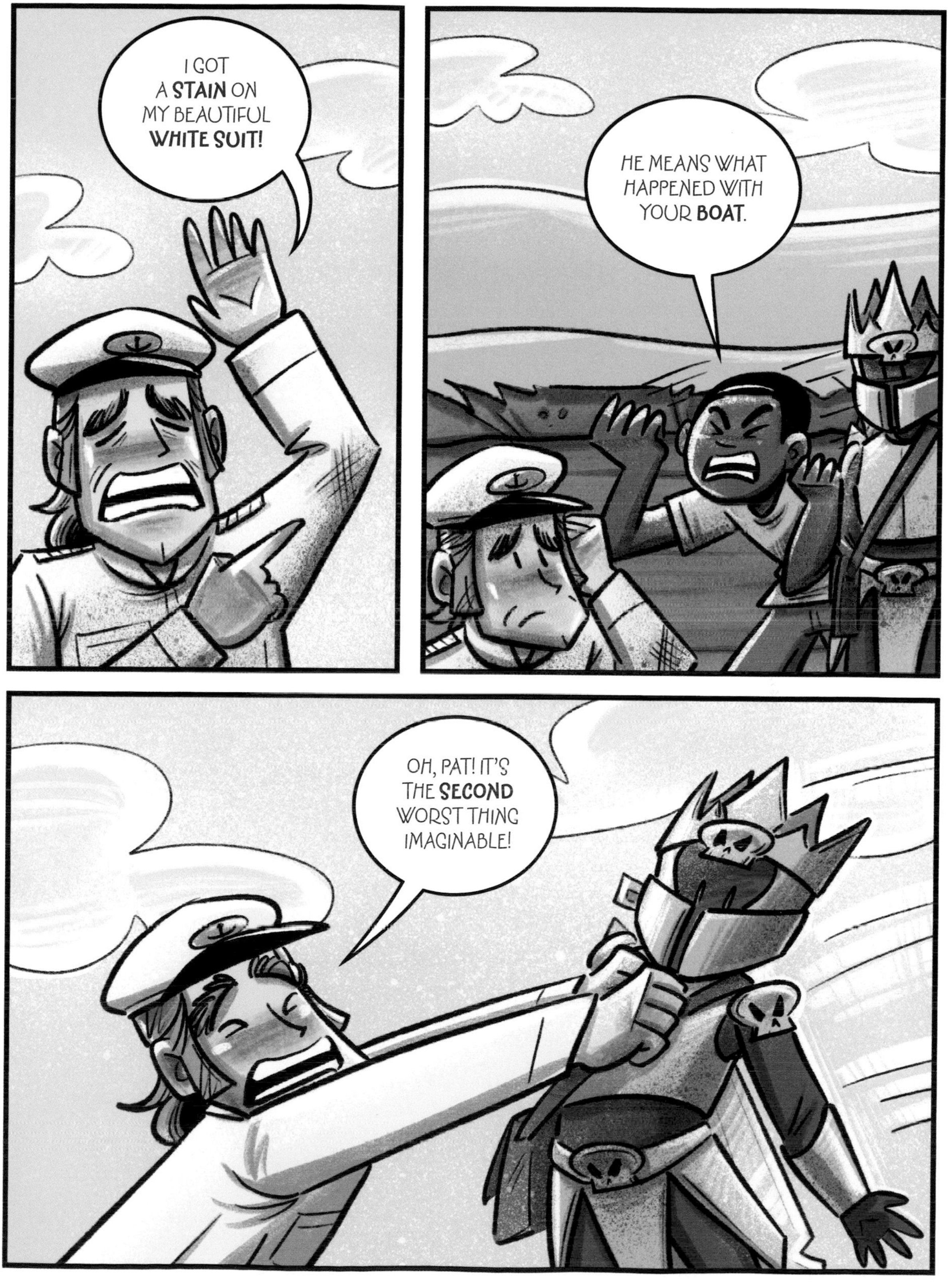
I GOT A **STAIN** ON MY BEAUTIFUL **WHITE SUIT!**
HE MEANS WHAT HAPPENED WITH YOUR **BOAT**.
OH, PAT! IT'S THE **SECOND** WORST THING IMAGINABLE!

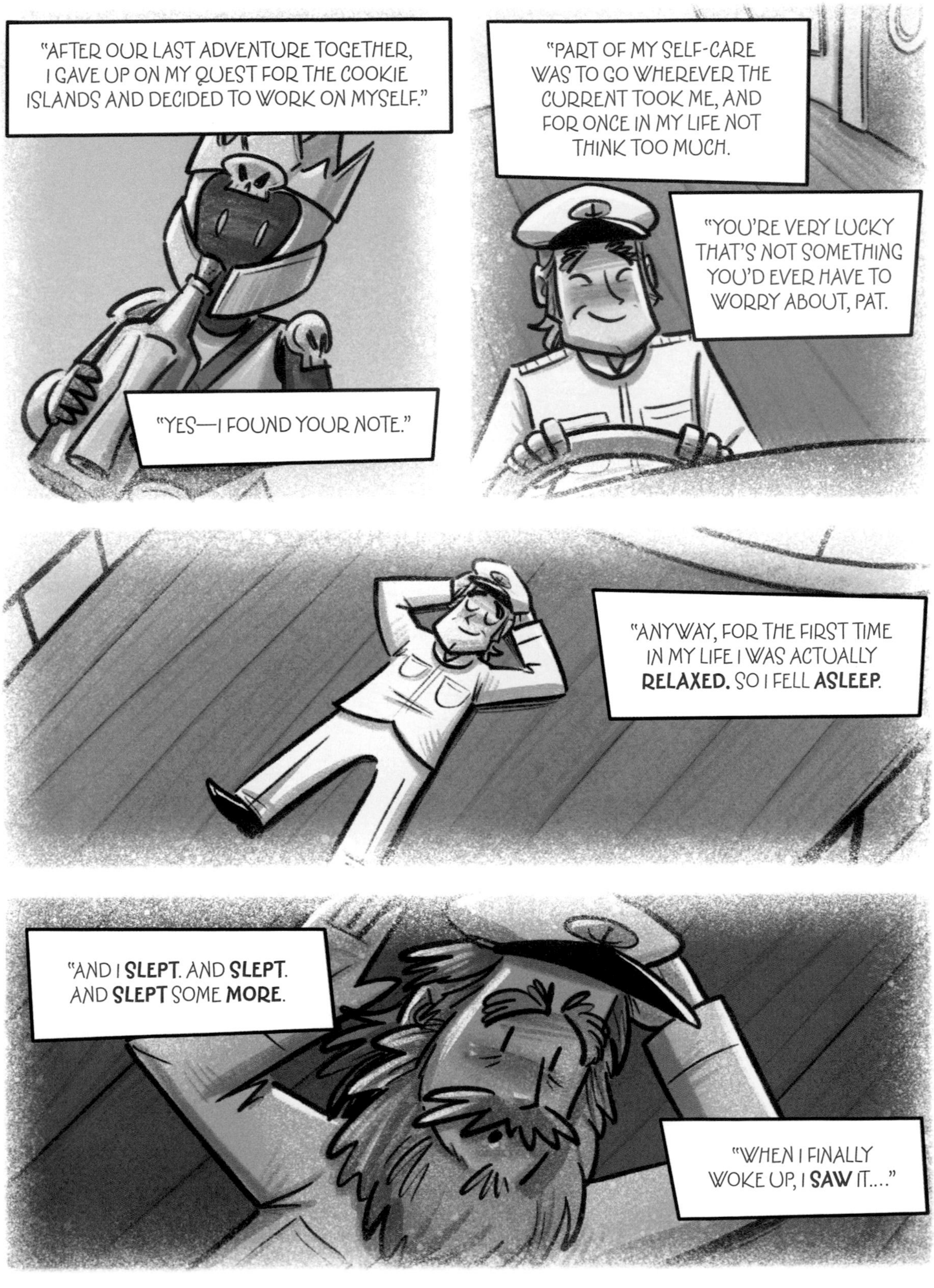
"AFTER OUR LAST ADVENTURE TOGETHER, I GAVE UP ON MY QUEST FOR THE COOKIE ISLANDS AND DECIDED TO WORK ON MYSELF."
"YES—I FOUND YOUR NOTE."
"PART OF MY SELF-CARE WAS TO GO WHEREVER THE CURRENT TOOK ME, AND FOR ONCE IN MY LIFE NOT THINK TOO MUCH.
"YOU'RE VERY LUCKY THAT'S NOT SOMETHING YOU'D EVER HAVE TO WORRY ABOUT, PAT.
"ANYWAY, FOR THE FIRST TIME IN MY LIFE I WAS ACTUALLY **RELAXED.** SO I FELL **ASLEEP**.
"AND I **SLEPT**. AND **SLEPT**. AND **SLEPT** SOME **MORE**.
"WHEN I FINALLY WOKE UP, I **SAW** IT...."

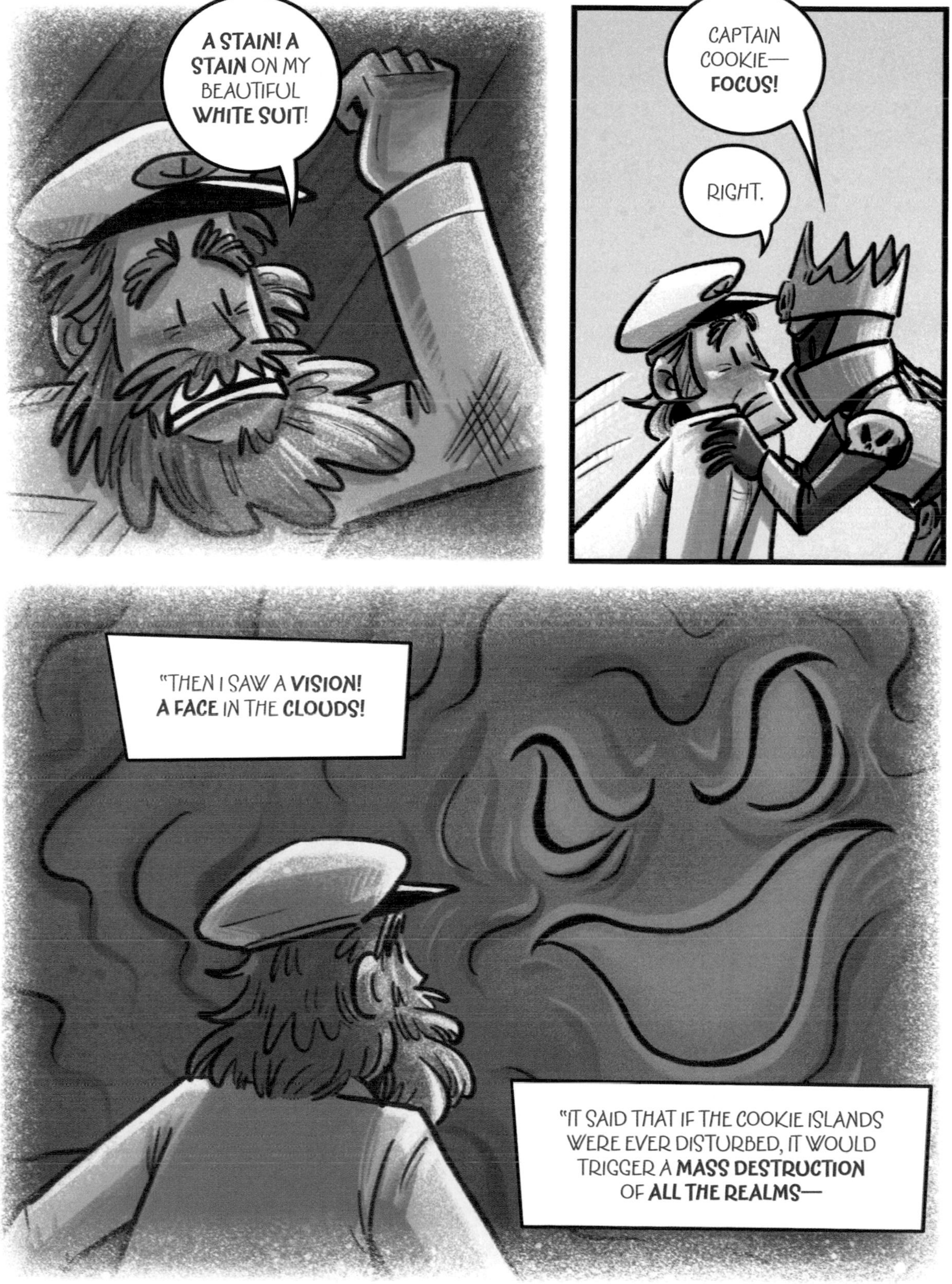
A STAIN! A STAIN ON MY BEAUTIFUL WHITE SUIT!
CAPTAIN COOKIE—FOCUS!
RIGHT.
"THEN I SAW A VISION! A FACE IN THE CLOUDS!
"IT SAID THAT IF THE COOKIE ISLANDS WERE EVER DISTURBED, IT WOULD TRIGGER A MASS DESTRUCTION OF ALL THE REALMS—

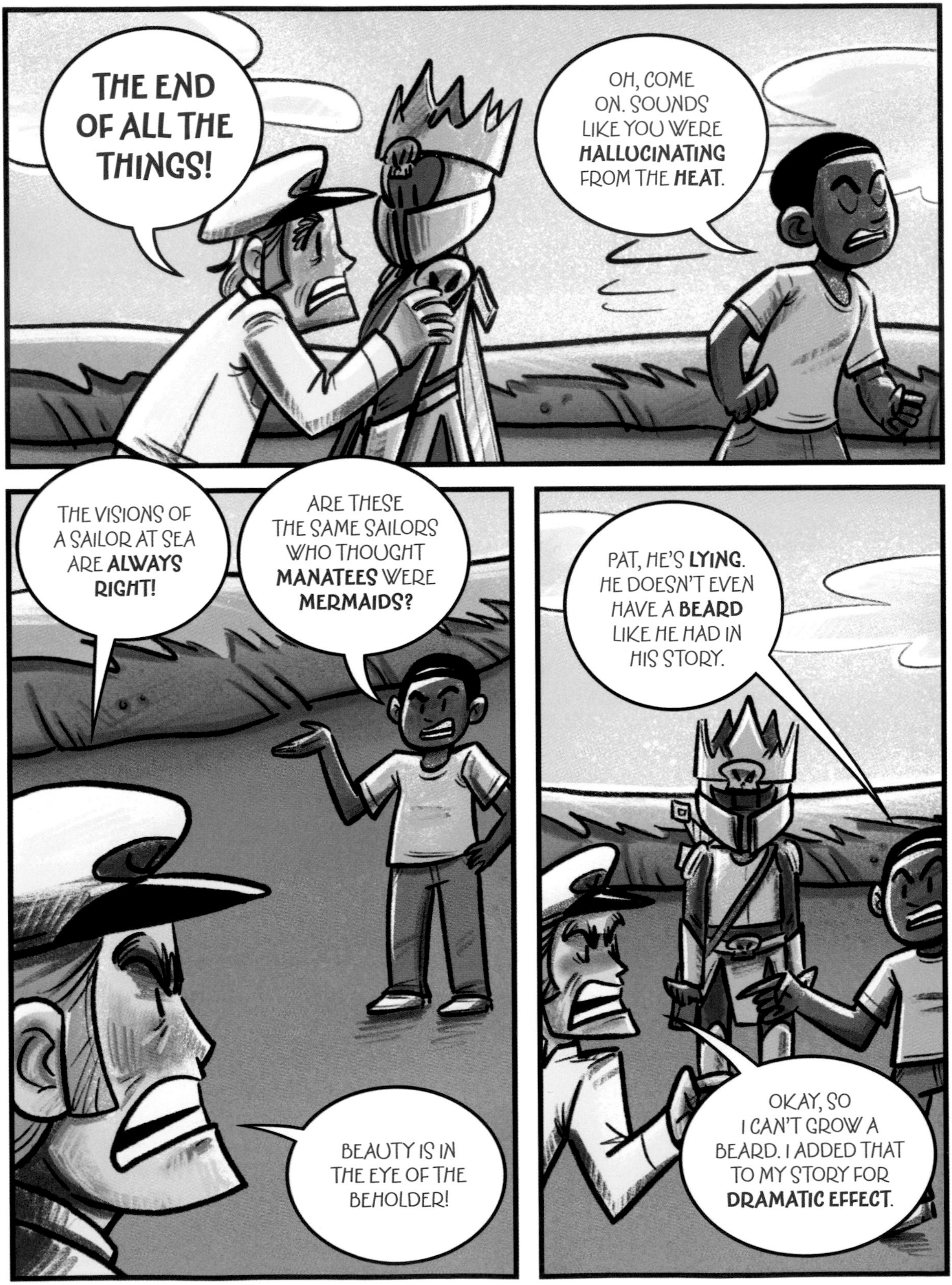
THE END OF ALL THE THINGS!
OH, COME ON. SOUNDS LIKE YOU WERE **HALLUCINATING** FROM THE **HEAT**.
THE VISIONS OF A SAILOR AT SEA ARE **ALWAYS RIGHT!**
ARE THESE THE SAME SAILORS WHO THOUGHT **MANATEES** WERE **MERMAIDS?**
BEAUTY IS IN THE EYE OF THE BEHOLDER!
PAT, HE'S **LYING**. HE DOESN'T EVEN HAVE A **BEARD** LIKE HE HAD IN HIS STORY.
OKAY, SO I CAN'T GROW A BEARD. I ADDED THAT TO MY STORY FOR **DRAMATIC EFFECT**.

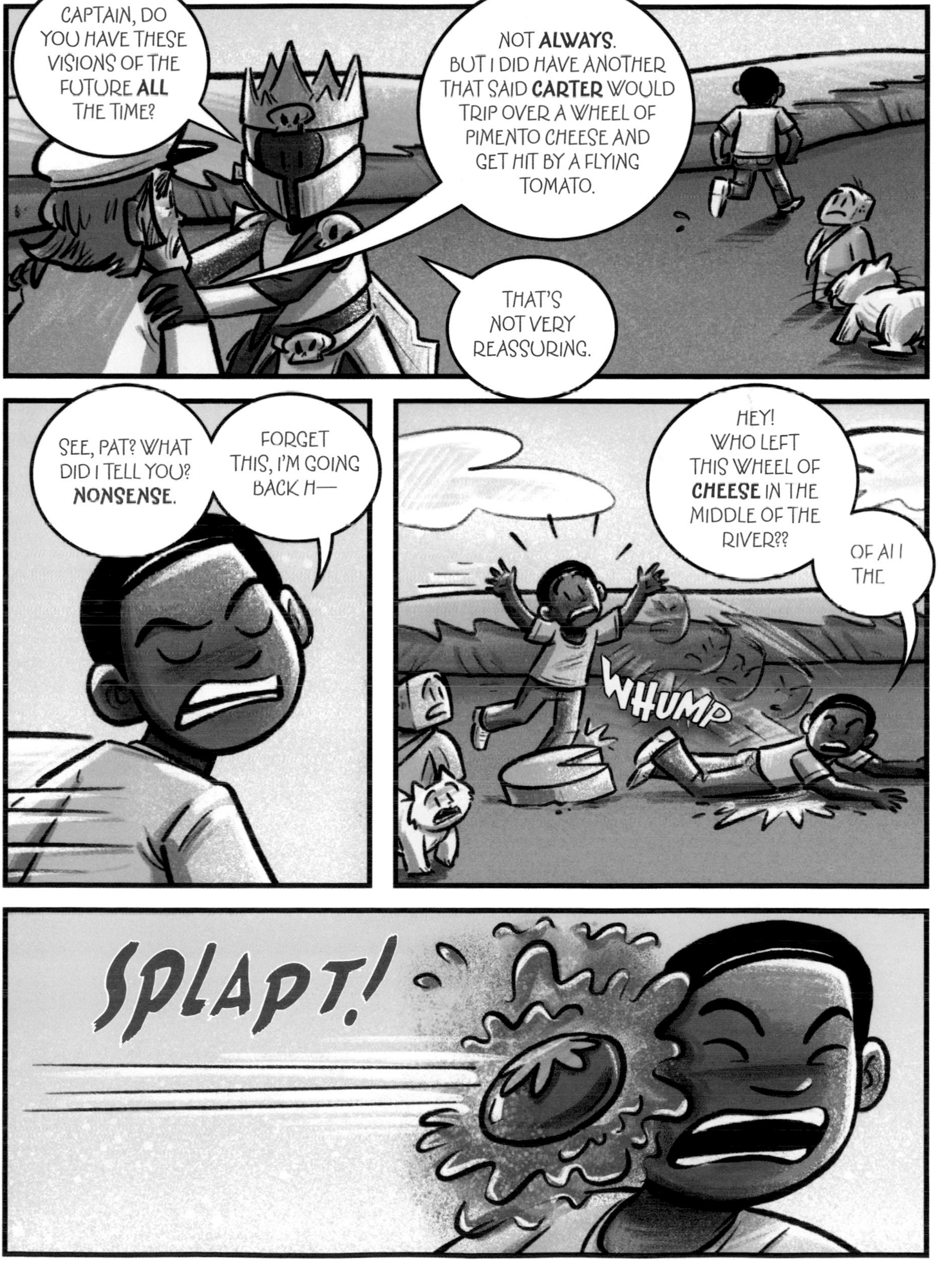
CAPTAIN, DO YOU HAVE THESE VISIONS OF THE FUTURE ALL THE TIME?
NOT ALWAYS. BUT I DID HAVE ANOTHER THAT SAID CARTER WOULD TRIP OVER A WHEEL OF PIMENTO CHEESE AND GET HIT BY A FLYING TOMATO.
THAT'S NOT VERY REASSURING.
SEE, PAT? WHAT DID I TELL YOU? NONSENSE.
FORGET THIS, I'M GOING BACK H—
HEY! WHO LEFT THIS WHEEL OF CHEESE IN THE MIDDLE OF THE RIVER??
OF ALL THE
WHUMP
SPLAPT!

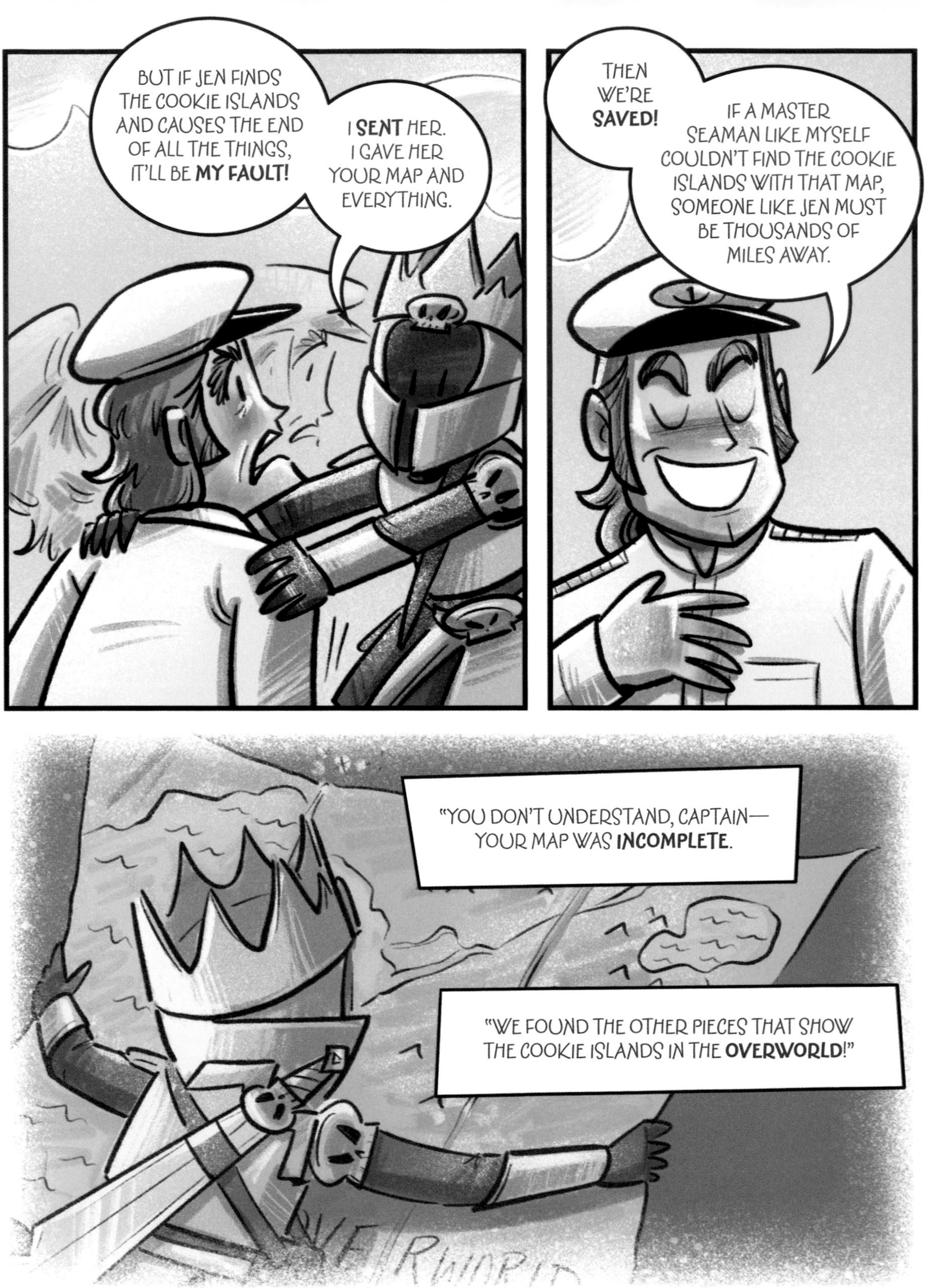
BUT IF JEN FINDS THE COOKIE ISLANDS AND CAUSES THE END OF ALL THE THINGS, IT'LL BE **MY FAULT!**
I **SENT** HER. I GAVE HER YOUR MAP AND EVERYTHING.
THEN WE'RE **SAVED!**
IF A MASTER SEAMAN LIKE MYSELF COULDN'T FIND THE COOKIE ISLANDS WITH THAT MAP, SOMEONE LIKE JEN MUST BE THOUSANDS OF MILES AWAY.
"YOU DON'T UNDERSTAND, CAPTAIN— YOUR MAP WAS **INCOMPLETE**.
"WE FOUND THE OTHER PIECES THAT SHOW THE COOKIE ISLANDS IN THE **OVERWORLD**!"

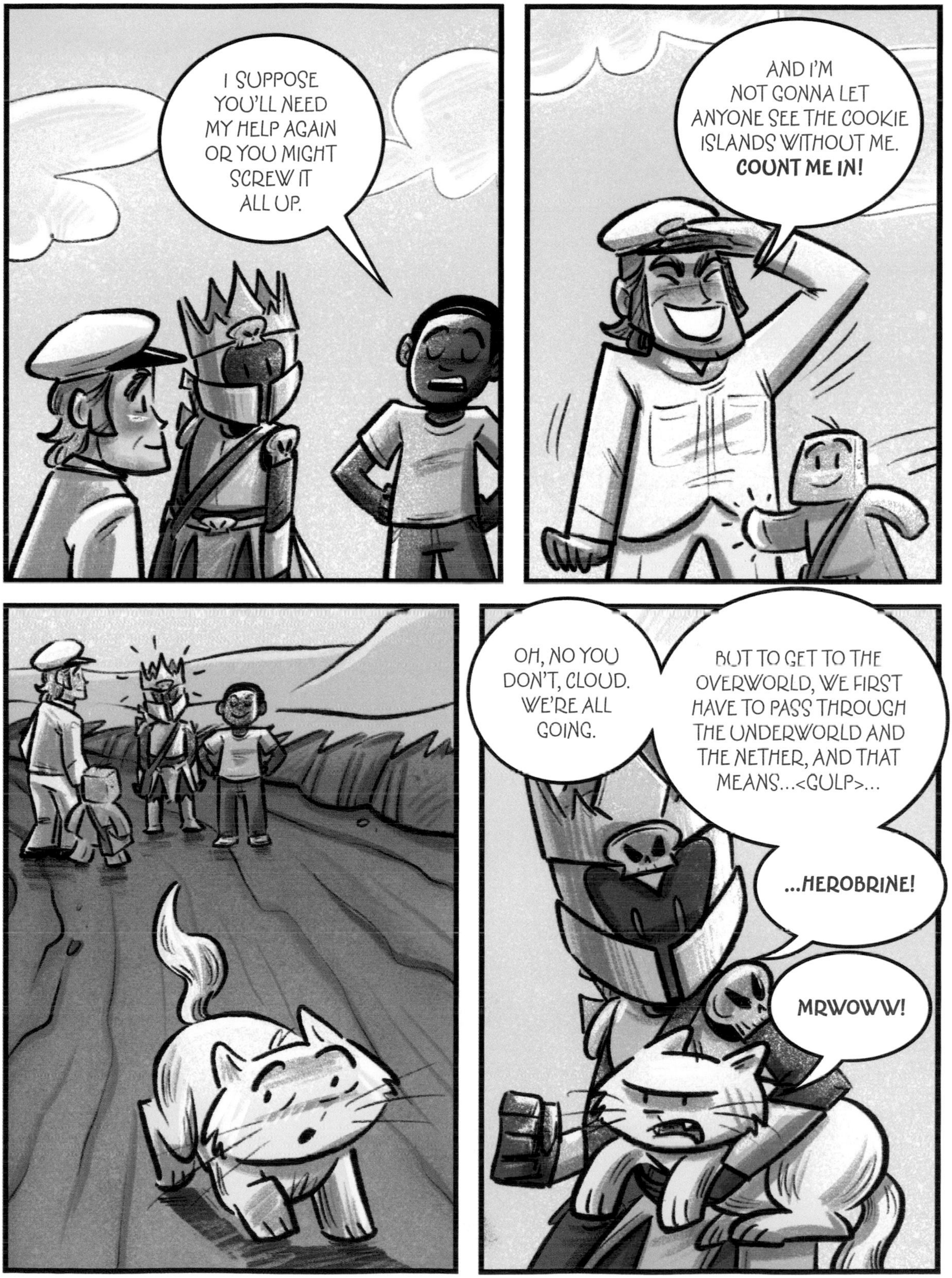
I SUPPOSE YOU'LL NEED MY HELP AGAIN OR YOU MIGHT SCREW IT ALL UP.
AND I'M NOT GONNA LET ANYONE SEE THE COOKIE ISLANDS WITHOUT ME. **COUNT ME IN!**
OH, NO YOU DON'T, CLOUD. WE'RE ALL GOING.
BUT TO GET TO THE OVERWORLD, WE FIRST HAVE TO PASS THROUGH THE UNDERWORLD AND THE NETHER, AND THAT MEANS...<GULP>...
...HEROBRINE!
MRWOWW!

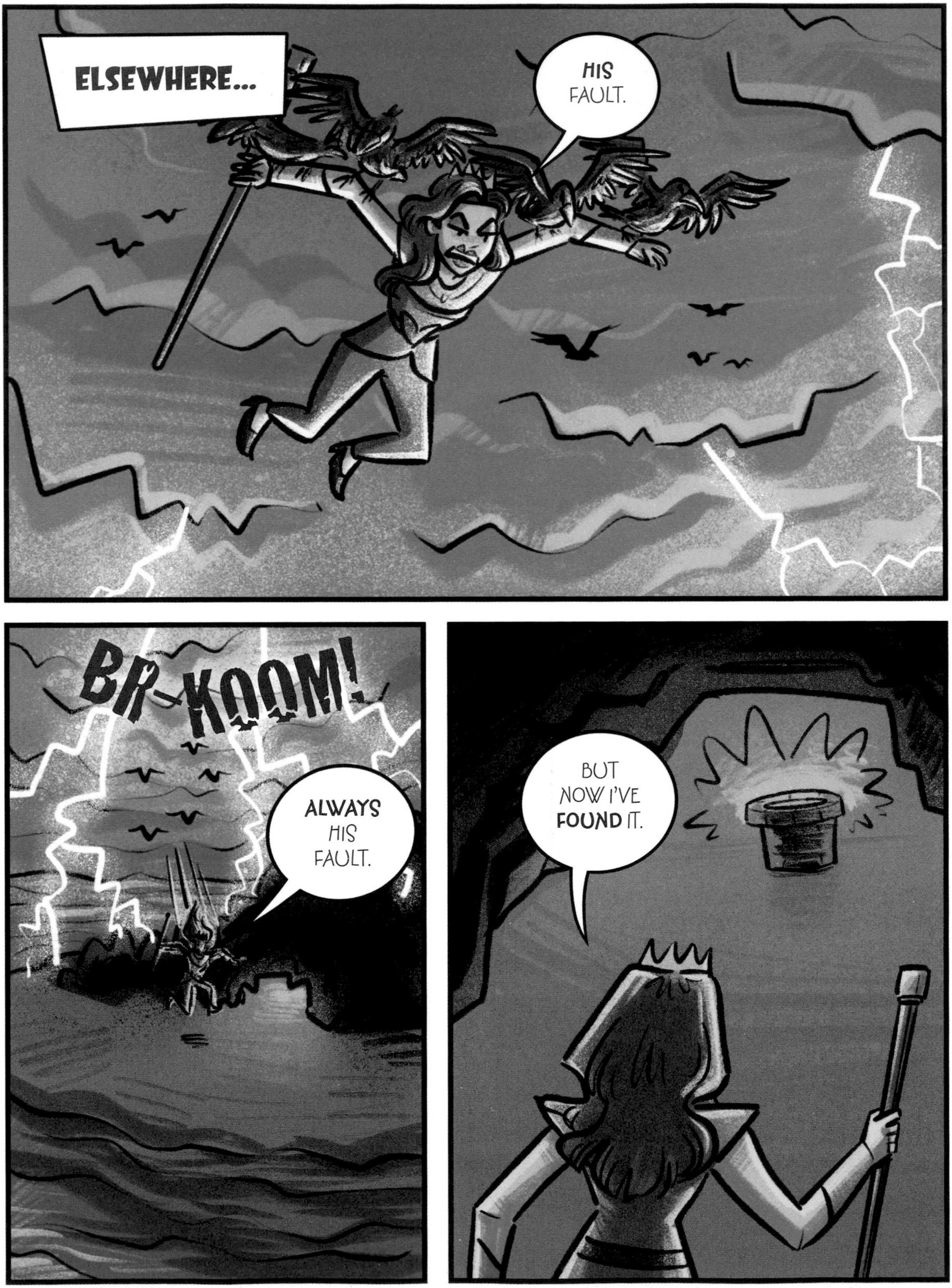
ELSEWHERE...
HIS FAULT.
BR-KOOM!
ALWAYS HIS FAULT.
BUT NOW I'VE FOUND IT.

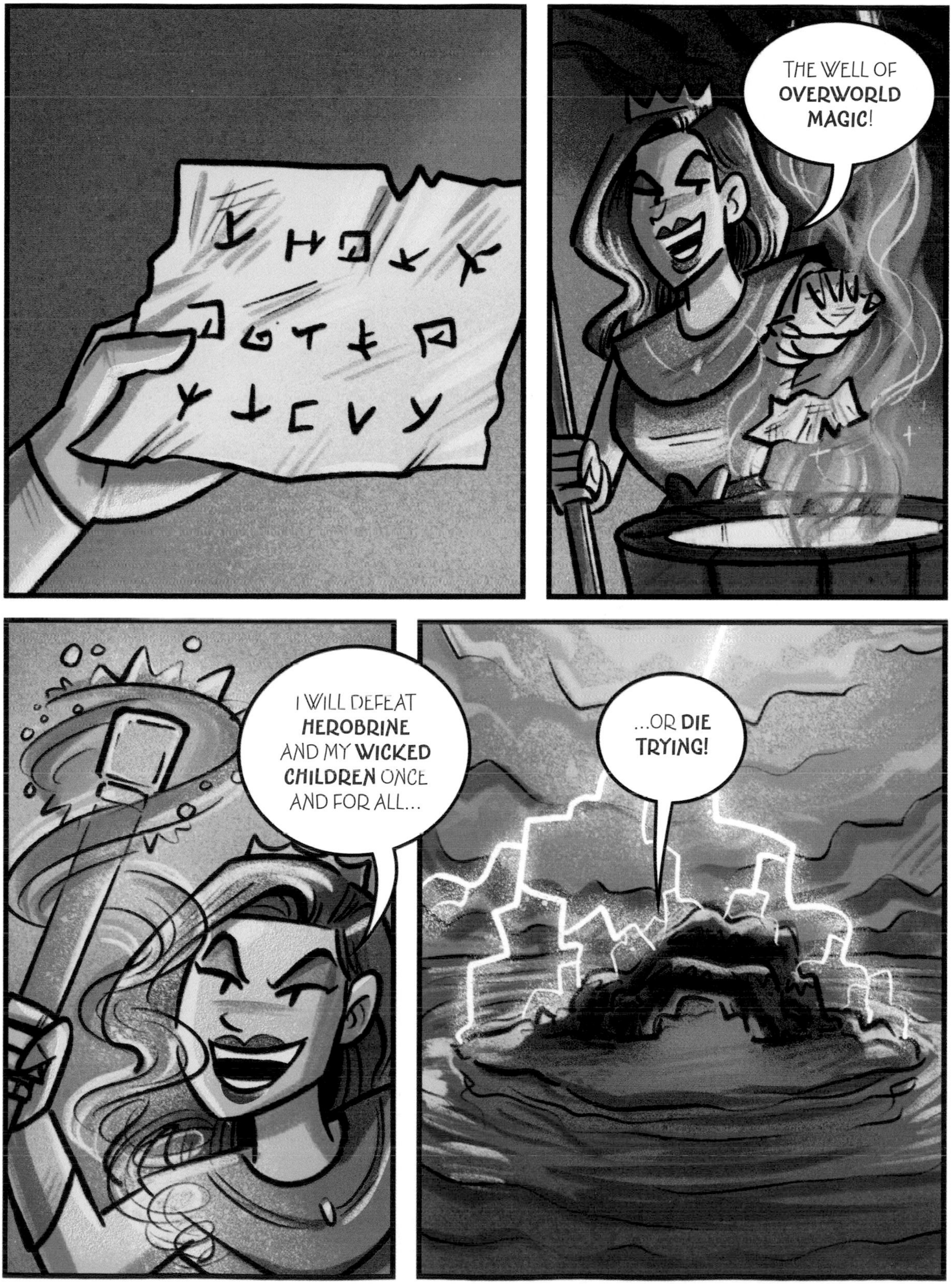
THE WELL OF OVERWORLD MAGIC!
I WILL DEFEAT HEROBRINE AND MY WICKED CHILDREN ONCE AND FOR ALL...
...OR DIE TRYING!

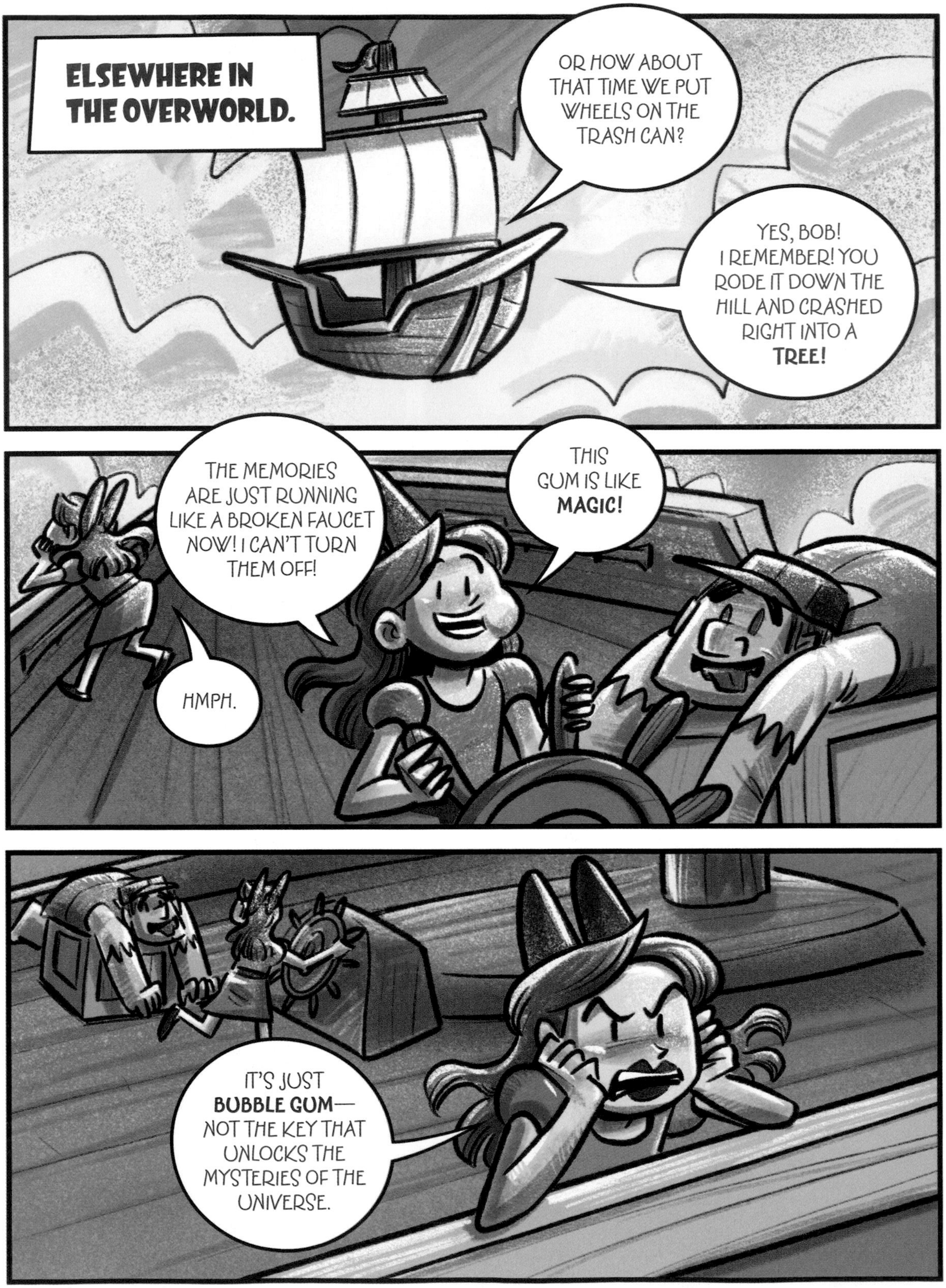
ELSEWHERE IN THE OVERWORLD.
OR HOW ABOUT THAT TIME WE PUT WHEELS ON THE TRASH CAN?
YES, BOB! I REMEMBER! YOU RODE IT DOWN THE HILL AND CRASHED RIGHT INTO A **TREE!**
THE MEMORIES ARE JUST RUNNING LIKE A BROKEN FAUCET NOW! I CAN'T TURN THEM OFF!
THIS GUM IS LIKE **MAGIC!**
HMPH.
IT'S JUST **BUBBLE GUM**— NOT THE KEY THAT UNLOCKS THE MYSTERIES OF THE UNIVERSE.

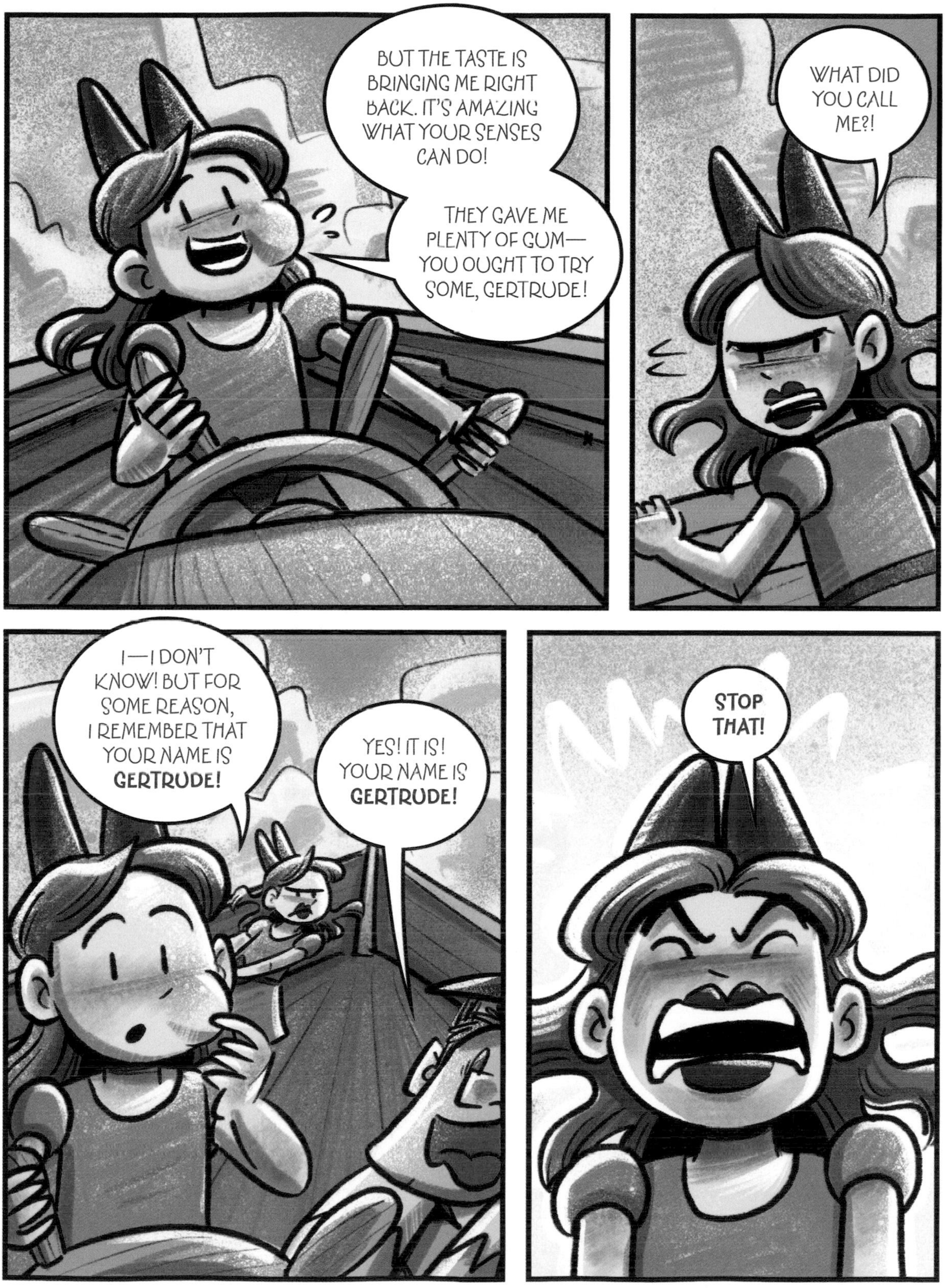
BUT THE TASTE IS BRINGING ME RIGHT BACK. IT'S AMAZING WHAT YOUR SENSES CAN DO!
THEY GAVE ME PLENTY OF GUM— YOU OUGHT TO TRY SOME, GERTRUDE!
WHAT DID YOU CALL ME?!
I—I DON'T KNOW! BUT FOR SOME REASON, I REMEMBER THAT YOUR NAME IS **GERTRUDE!**
YES! IT IS! YOUR NAME IS **GERTRUDE!**
STOP THAT!

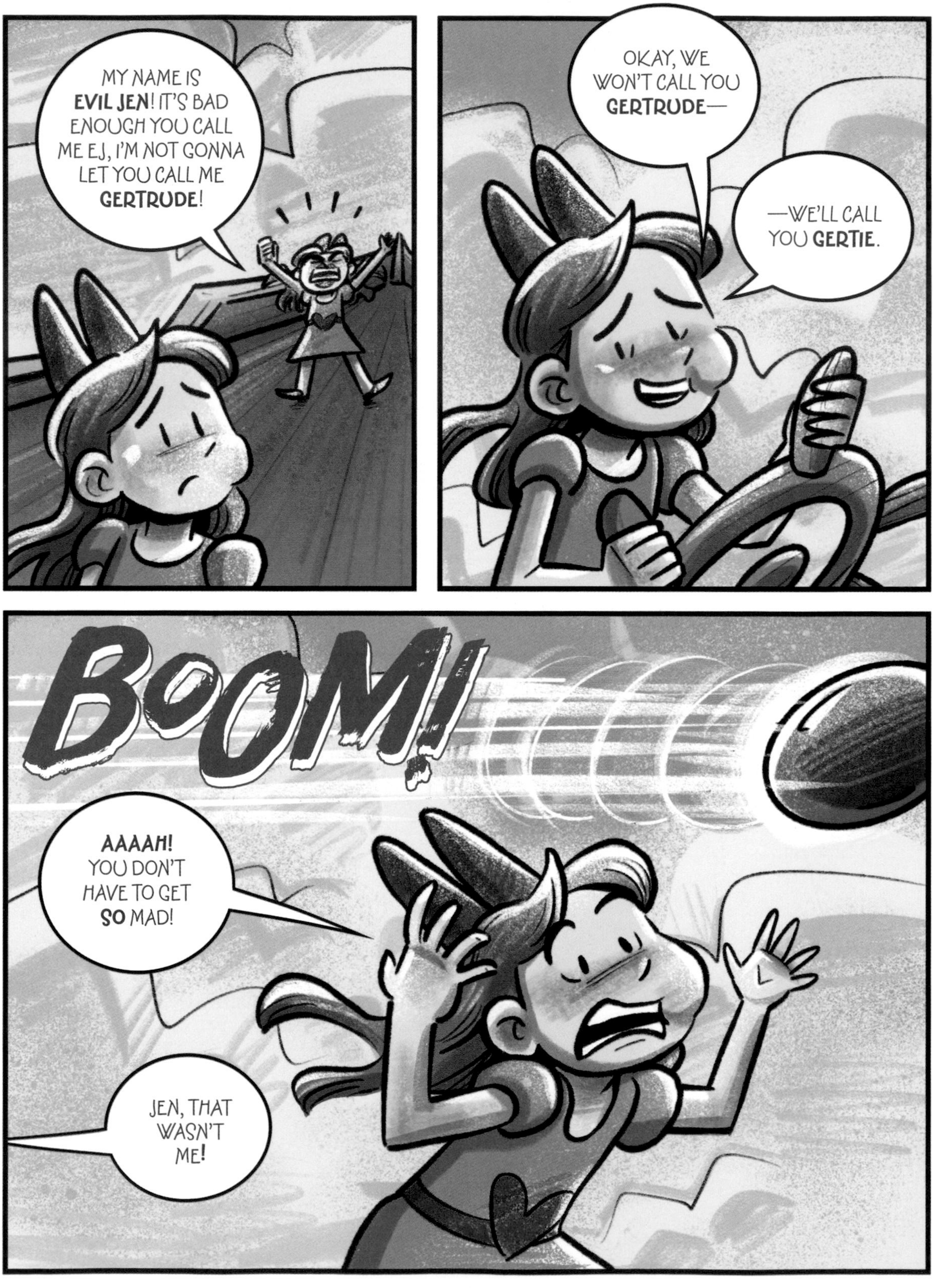
MY NAME IS **EVIL JEN**! IT'S BAD ENOUGH YOU CALL ME EJ, I'M NOT GONNA LET YOU CALL ME **GERTRUDE**!
OKAY, WE WON'T CALL YOU **GERTRUDE**—
—WE'LL CALL YOU **GERTIE**.
BOOM!
AAAAH! YOU DON'T HAVE TO GET **SO** MAD!
JEN, THAT WASN'T ME!

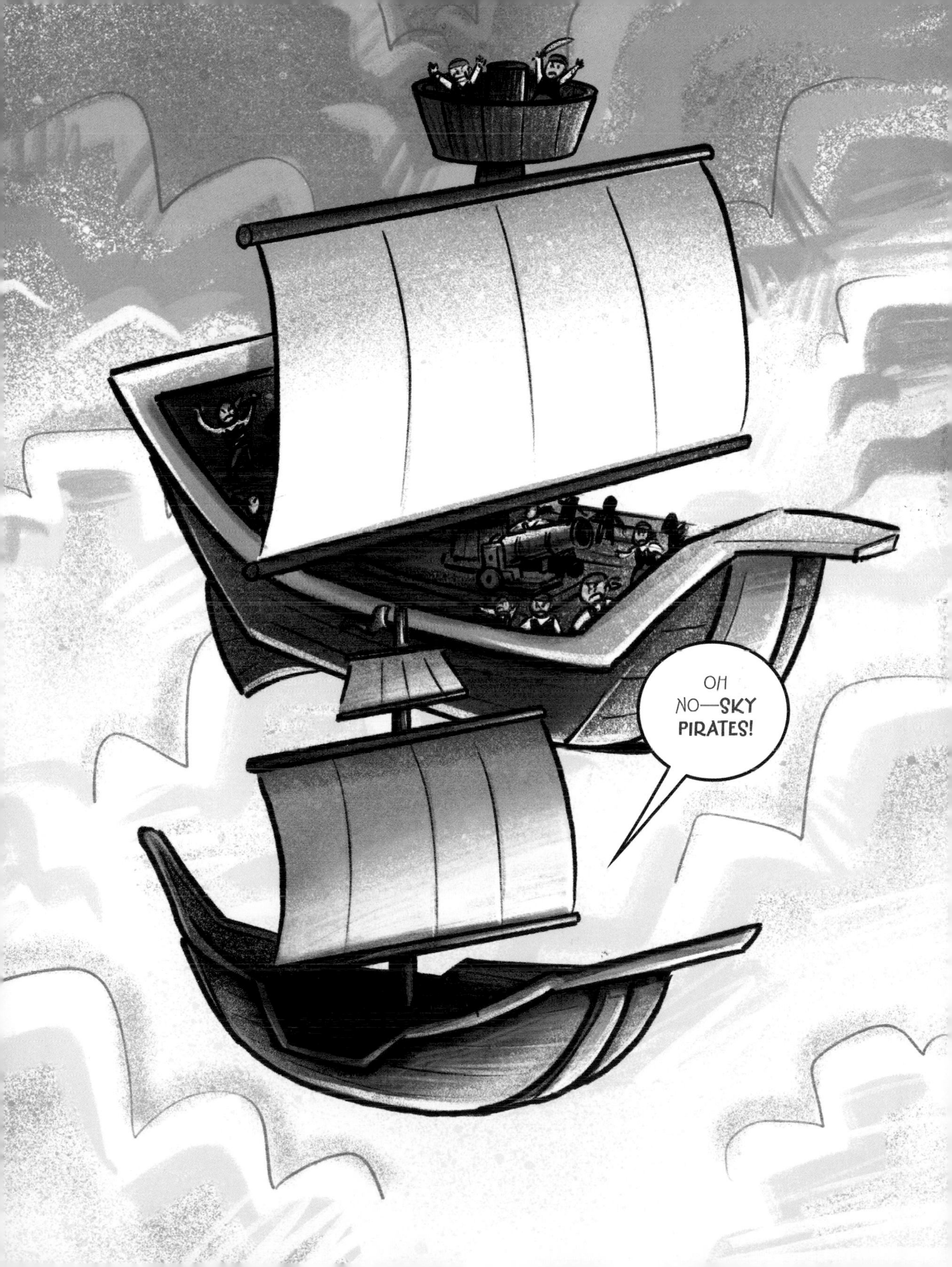
OH NO—**SKY PIRATES!**

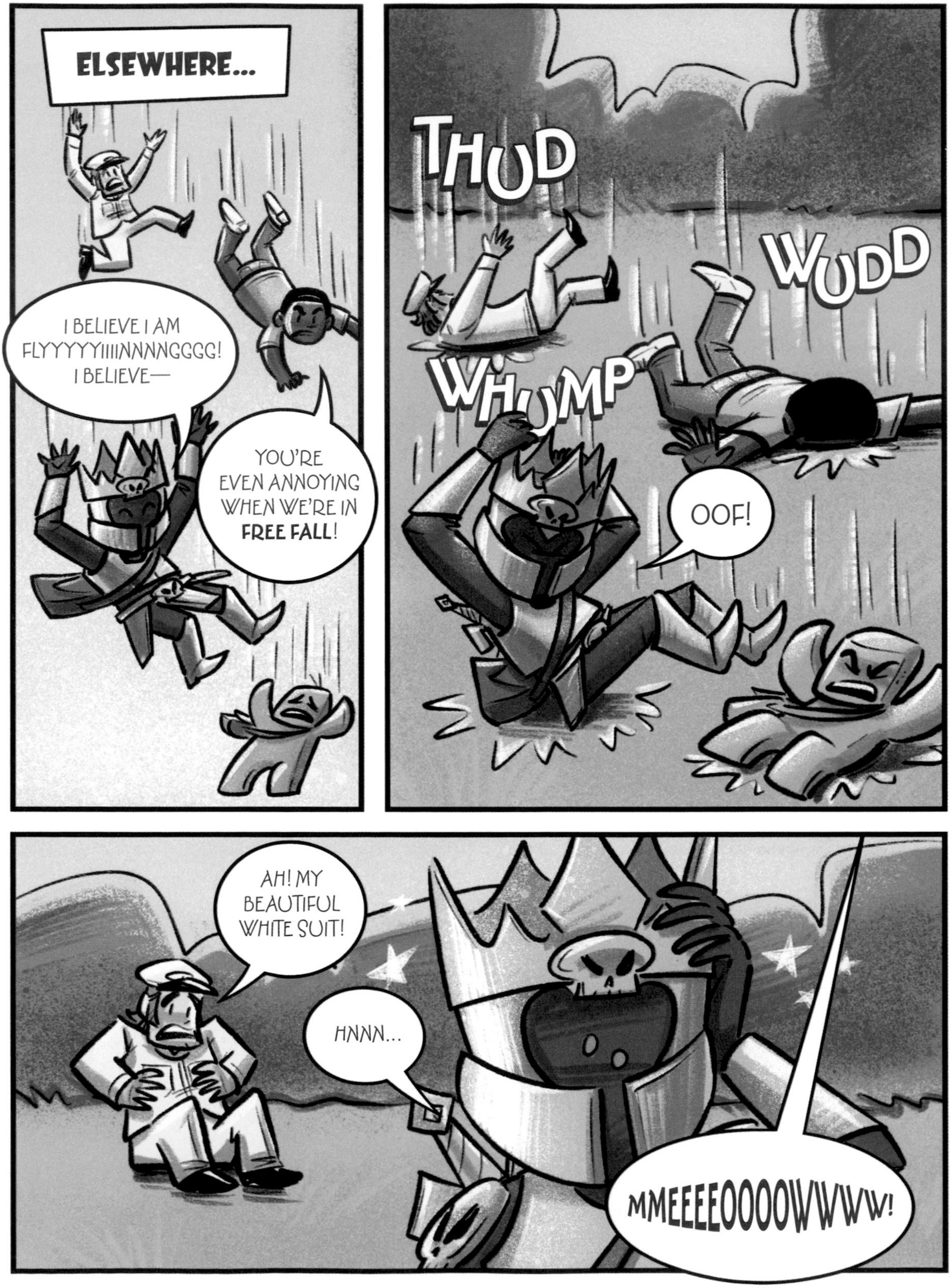
ELSEWHERE...
I BELIEVE I AM FLYYYYYIIIINNNNGGGG! I BELIEVE—
YOU'RE EVEN ANNOYING WHEN WE'RE IN FREE FALL!
THUD
WUDD
WHUMP
OOF!
AH! MY BEAUTIFUL WHITE SUIT!
HNNN...
MMEEEEOOOOWWWW!

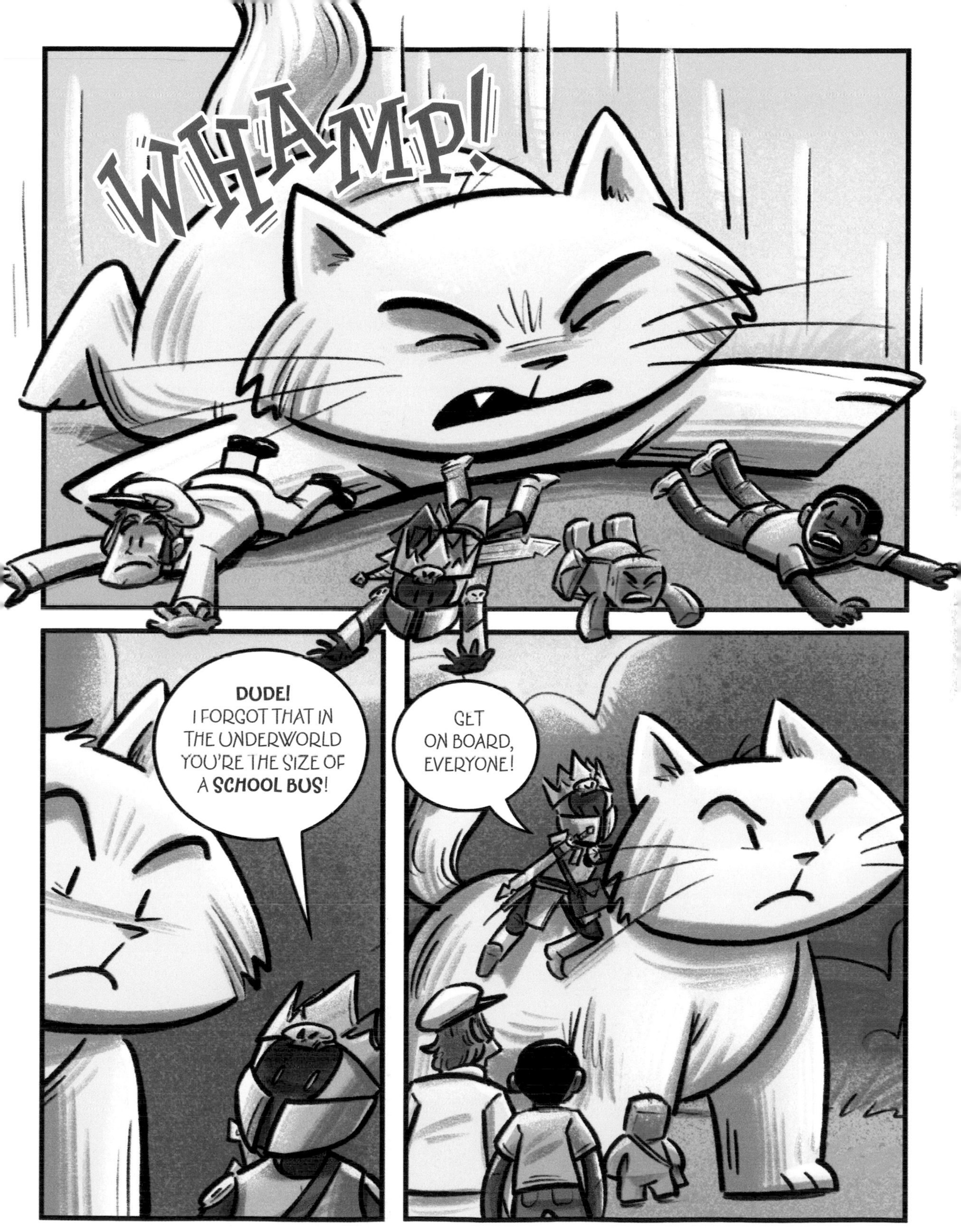
WHAMP!
DUDE! I FORGOT THAT IN THE UNDERWORLD YOU'RE THE SIZE OF A SCHOOL BUS!
GET ON BOARD, EVERYONE!

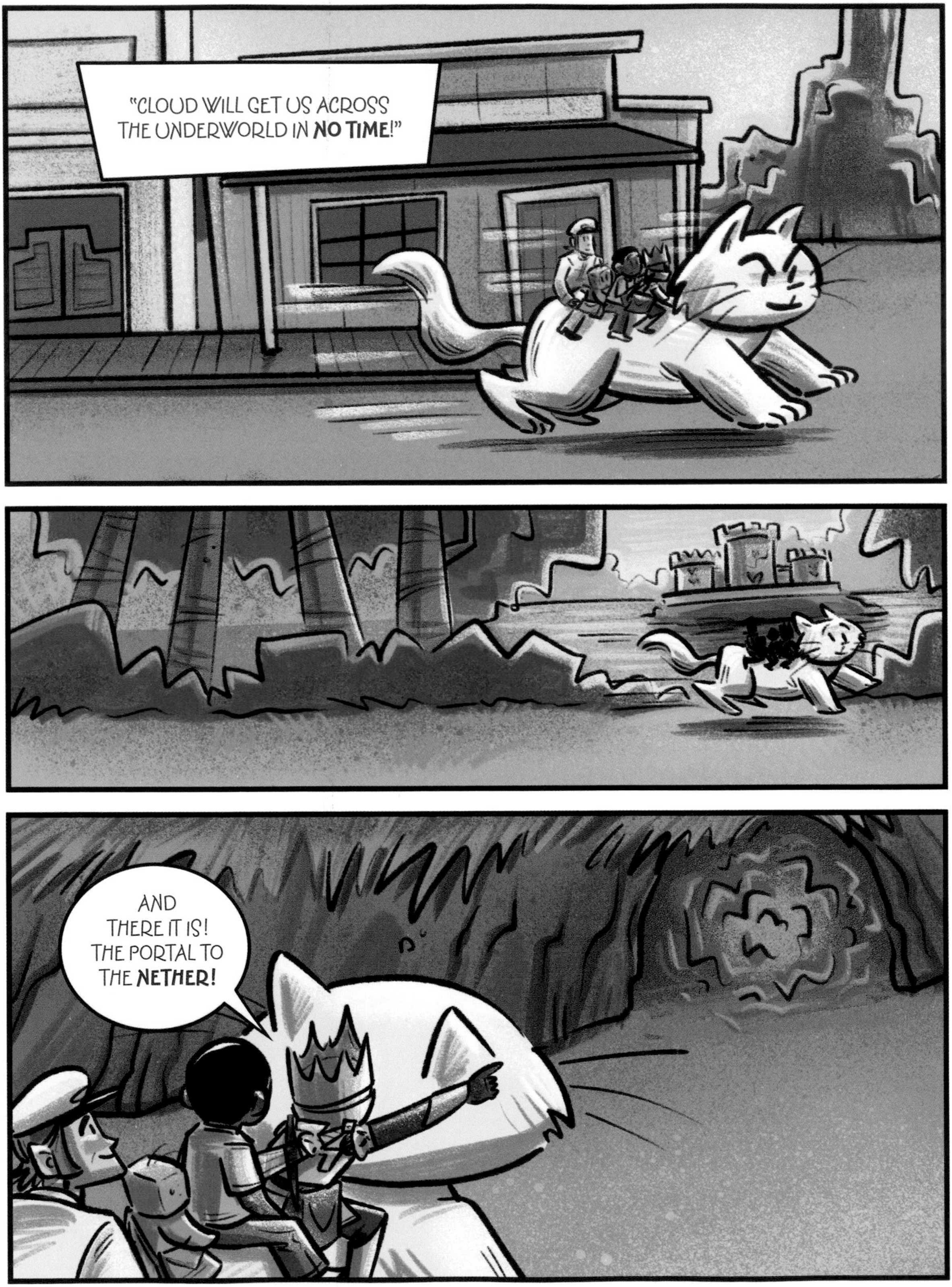
"CLOUD WILL GET US ACROSS THE UNDERWORLD IN NO TIME!"
AND THERE IT IS! THE PORTAL TO THE NETHER!

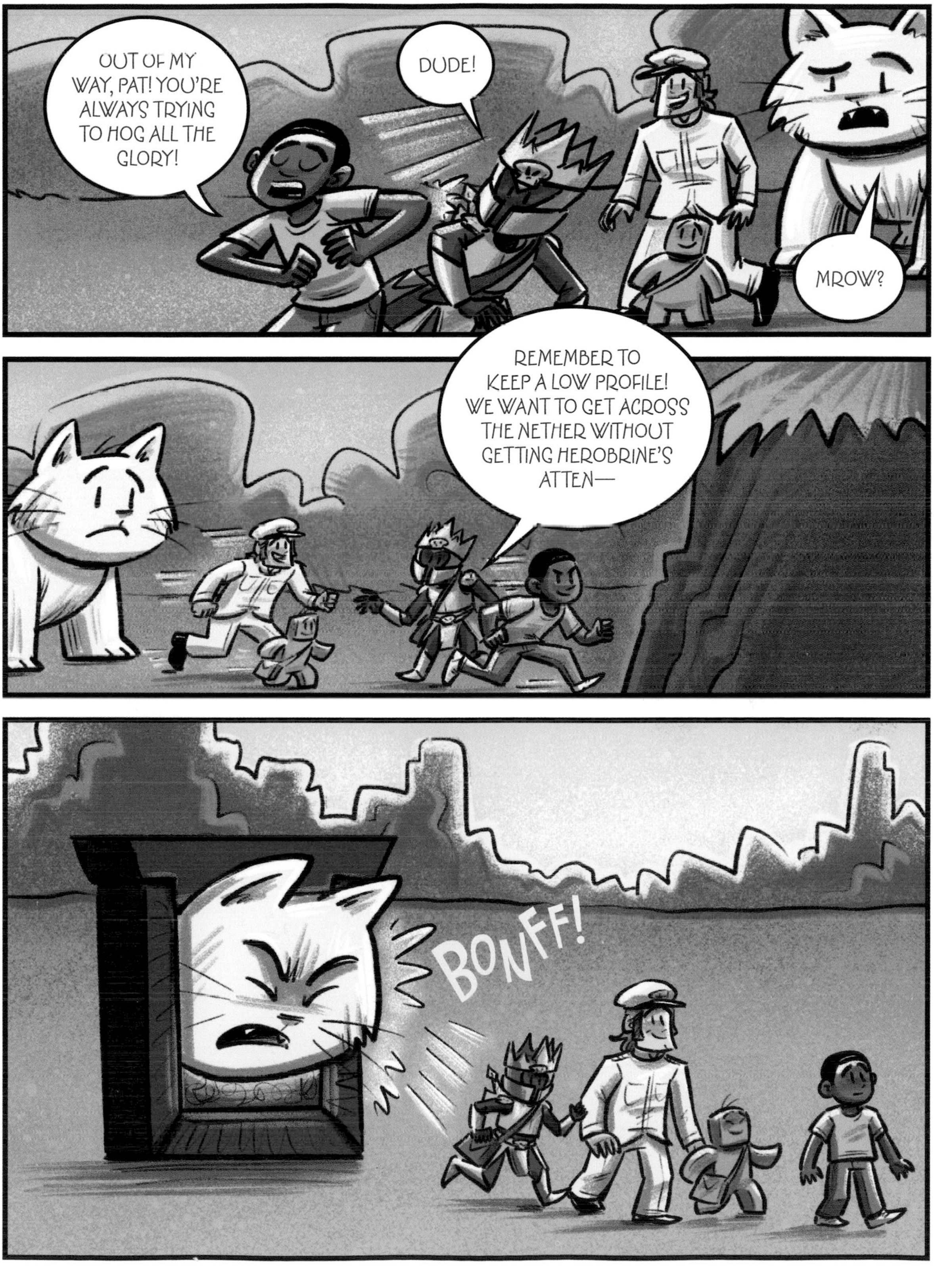

OUT OF MY WAY, PAT! YOU'RE ALWAYS TRYING TO HOG ALL THE GLORY!
DUDE!
MROW?
REMEMBER TO KEEP A LOW PROFILE! WE WANT TO GET ACROSS THE NETHER WITHOUT GETTING HEROBRINE'S ATTEN—
BONFF!

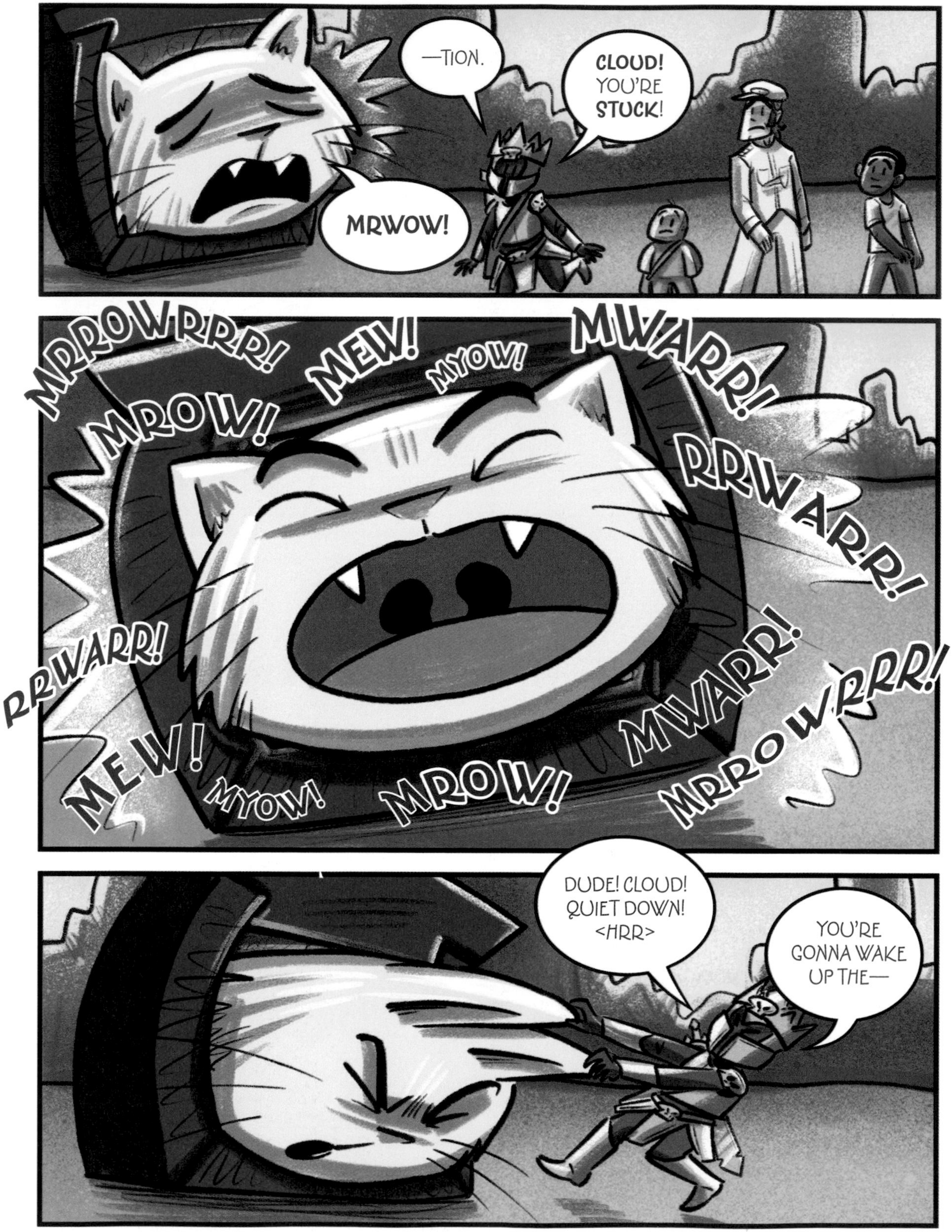
—TION.
CLOUD! YOU'RE STUCK!
MRWOW!
MRROWRRR!
MEW!
MYOW!
MWARR!
MROW!
RRWARR!
RRWARR!
MWARR!
MRROWRRR!
MEW!
MYOW!
MROW!
DUDE! CLOUD! QUIET DOWN! <HRR>
YOU'RE GONNA WAKE UP THE—

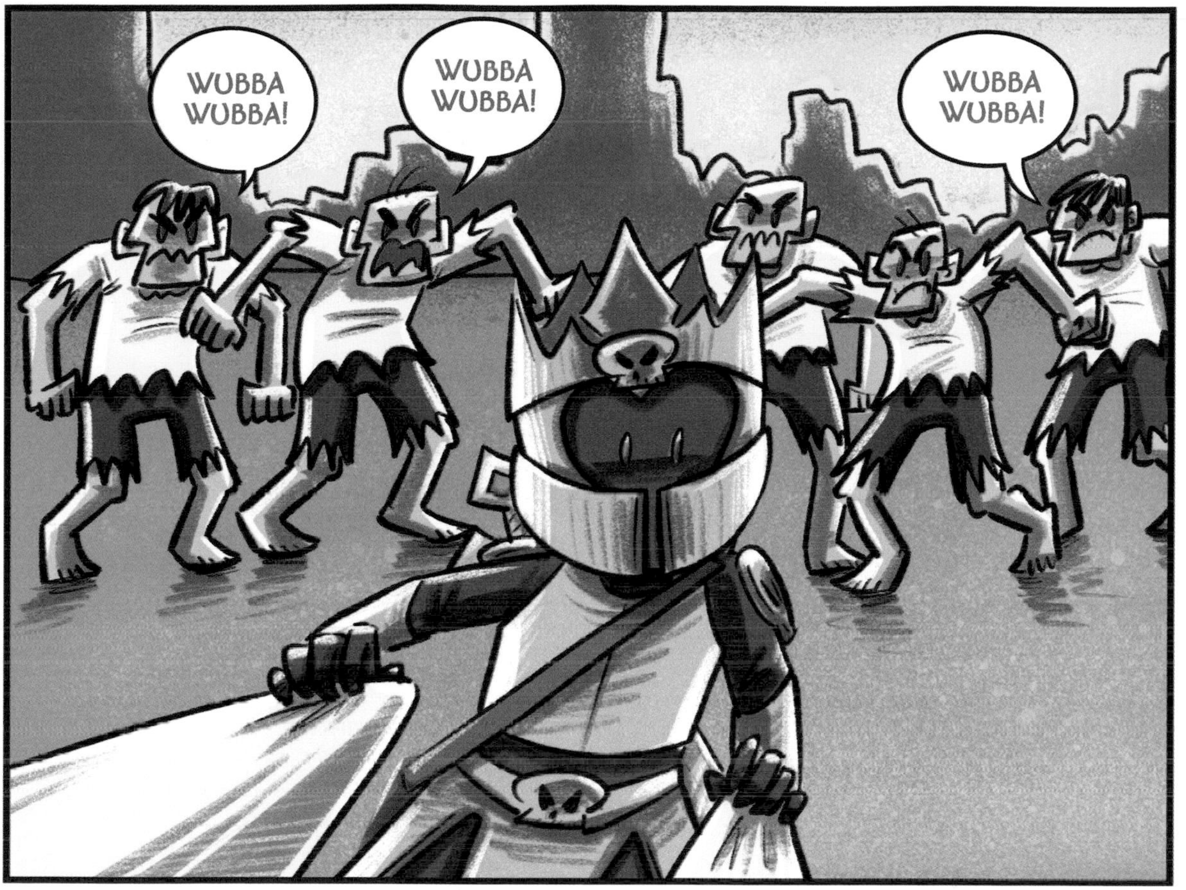
WUBBA WUBBA!
WUBBA WUBBA!
WUBBA WUBBA!

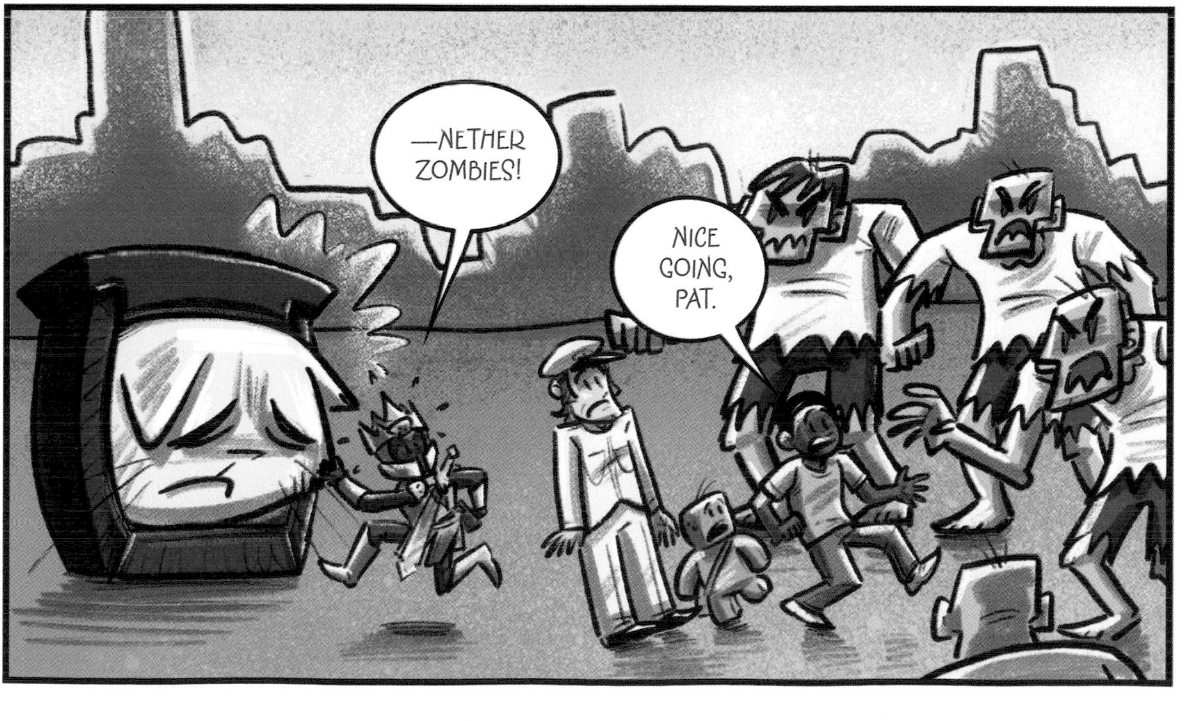
—NETHER ZOMBIES!
NICE GOING, PAT.

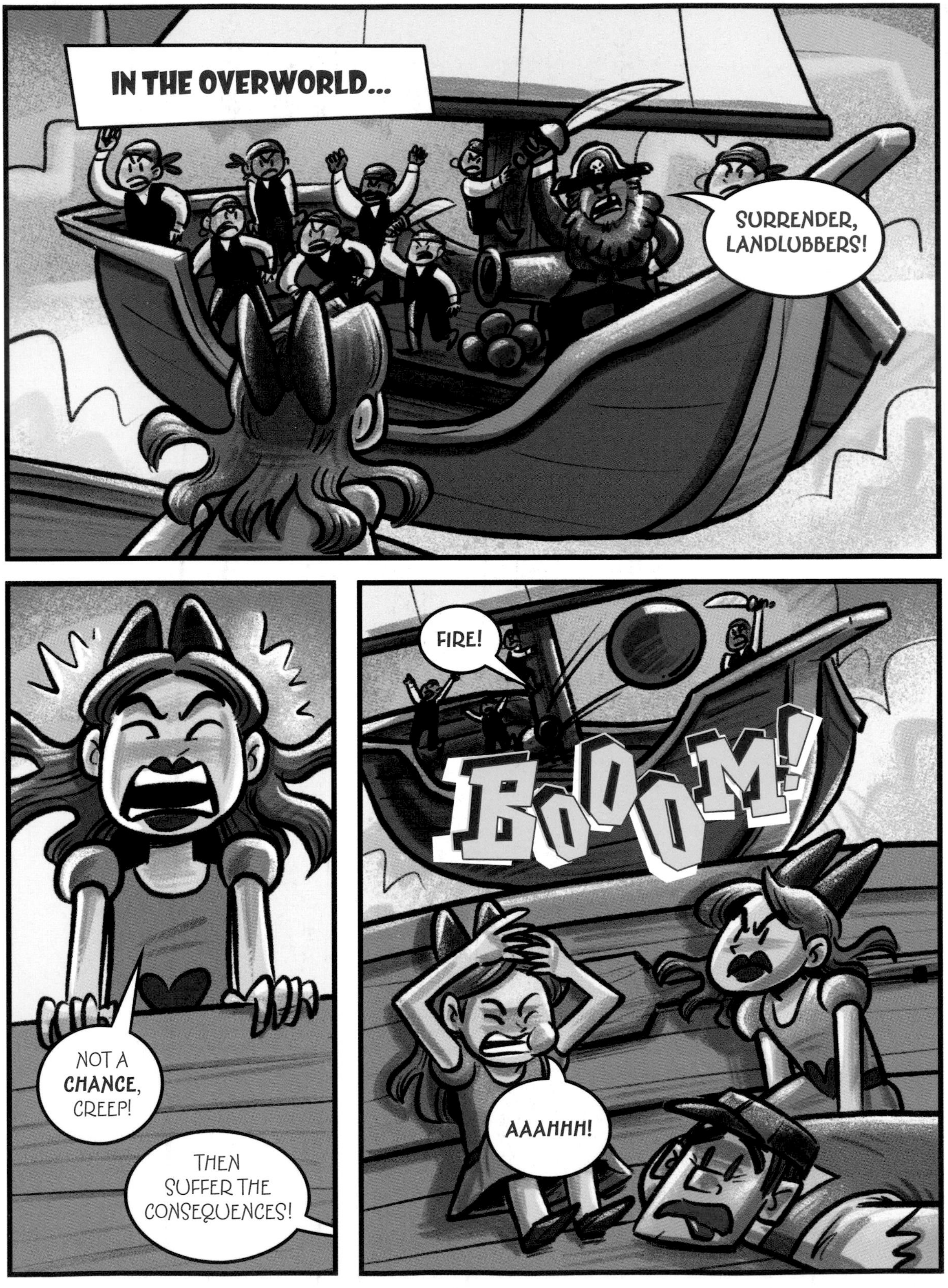
IN THE OVERWORLD...
SURRENDER, LANDLUBBERS!
NOT A **CHANCE**, CREEP!
THEN SUFFER THE CONSEQUENCES!
FIRE!
BOOOM!
AAAHHH!

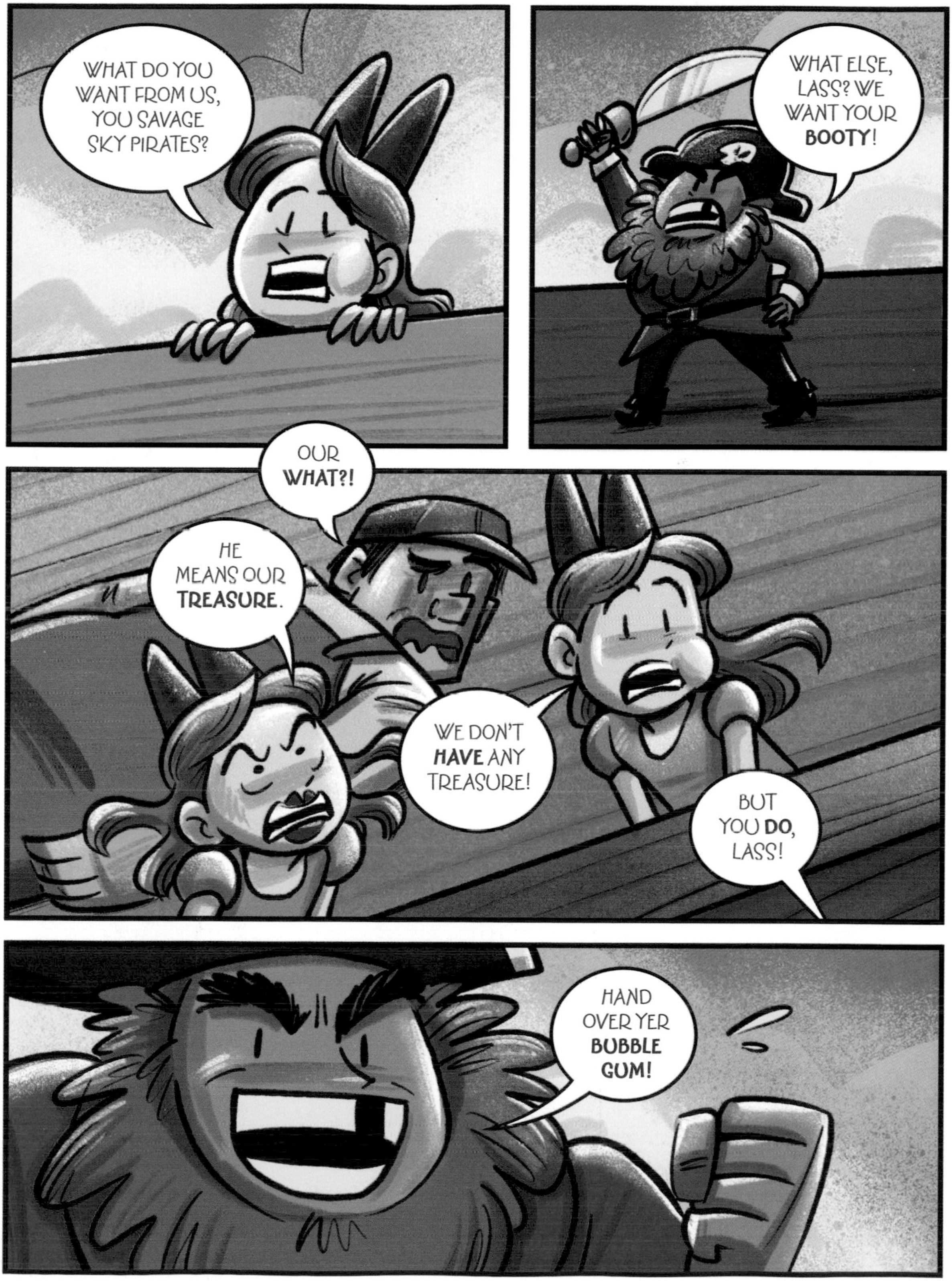
WHAT DO YOU WANT FROM US, YOU SAVAGE SKY PIRATES?
WHAT ELSE, LASS? WE WANT YOUR **BOOTY**!
OUR **WHAT?!**
HE MEANS OUR **TREASURE**.
WE DON'T **HAVE** ANY TREASURE!
BUT YOU **DO**, LASS!
HAND OVER YER **BUBBLE GUM!**

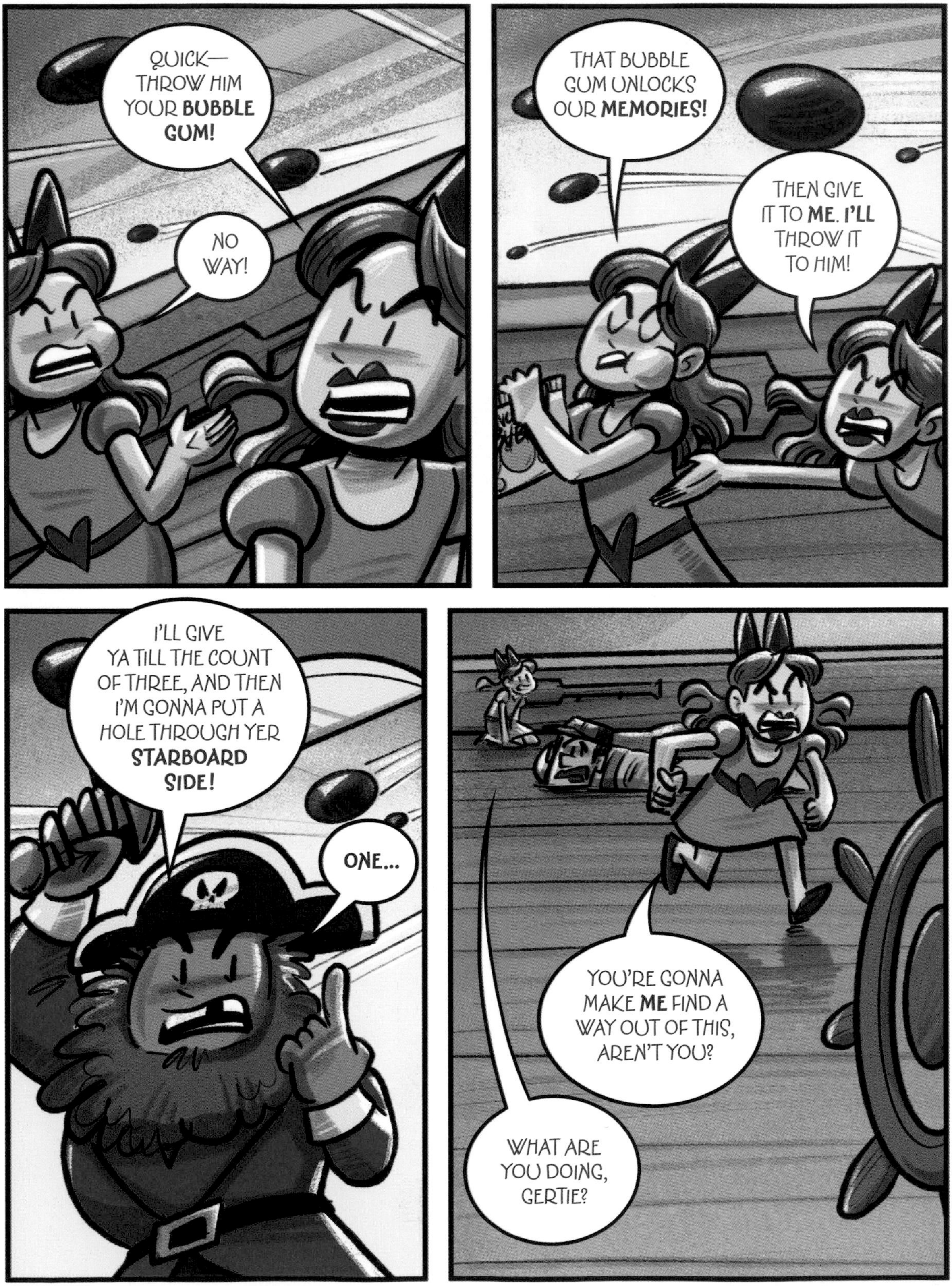

QUICK—THROW HIM YOUR **BUBBLE GUM!**
NO WAY!
THAT BUBBLE GUM UNLOCKS OUR **MEMORIES!**
THEN GIVE IT TO **ME. I'LL** THROW IT TO HIM!
I'LL GIVE YA TILL THE COUNT OF THREE, AND THEN I'M GONNA PUT A HOLE THROUGH YER **STARBOARD SIDE!**
ONE...
WHAT ARE YOU DOING, GERTIE?
YOU'RE GONNA MAKE **ME** FIND A WAY OUT OF THIS, AREN'T YOU?

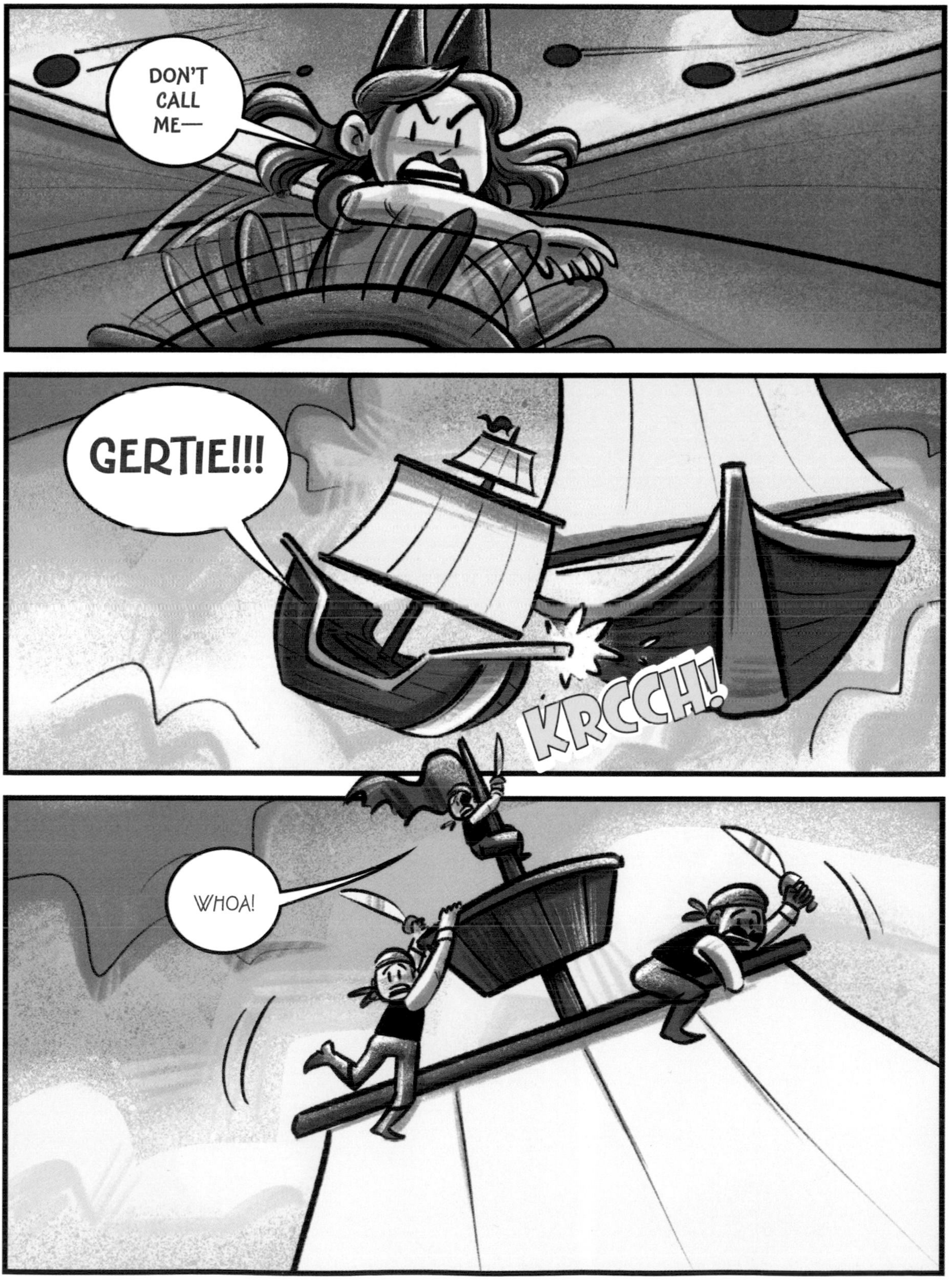
DON'T CALL ME—
GERTIE!!!
KRCCH!
WHOA!

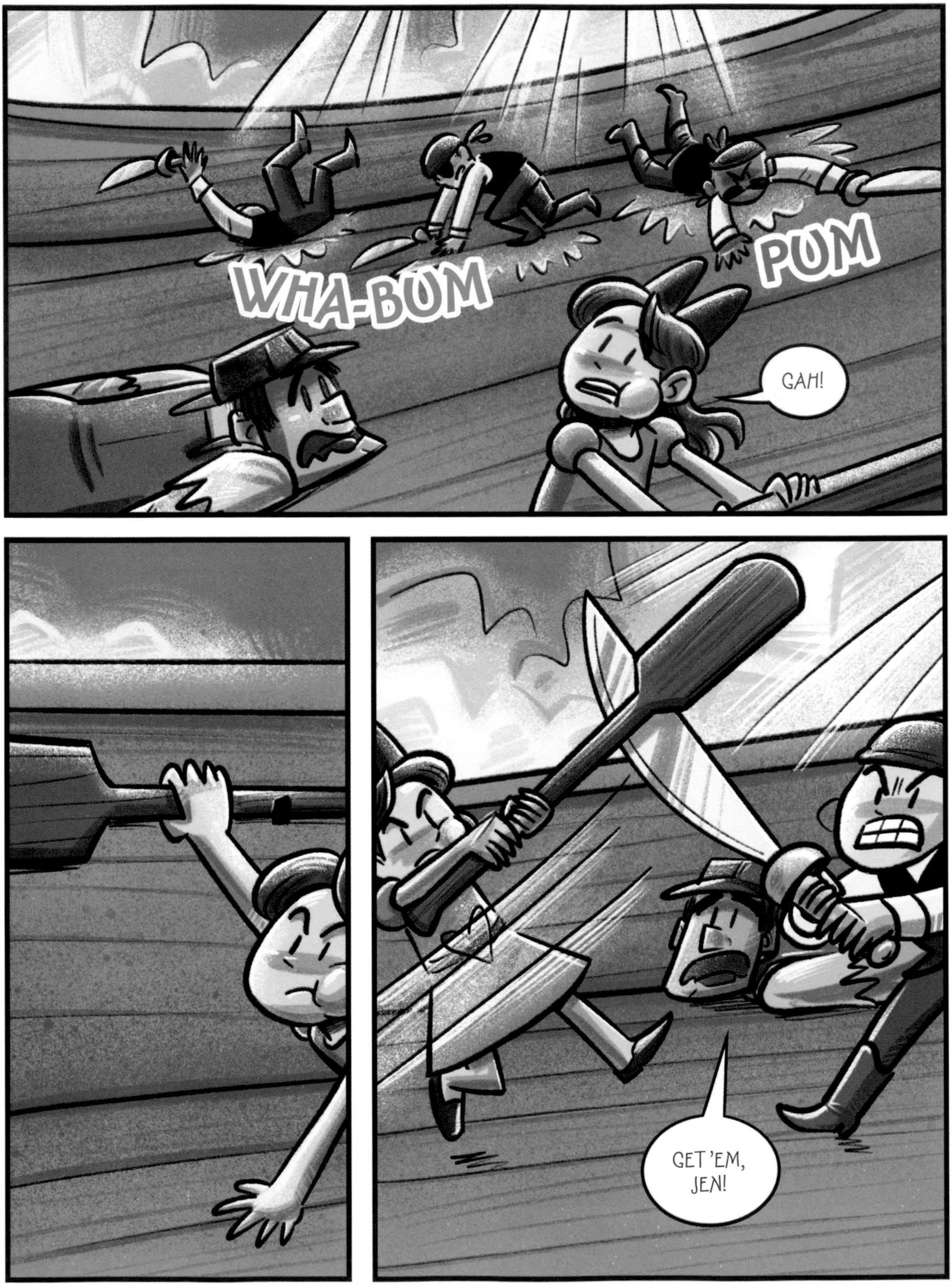
WHA-BUM
PUM
GAH!
GET 'EM, JEN!

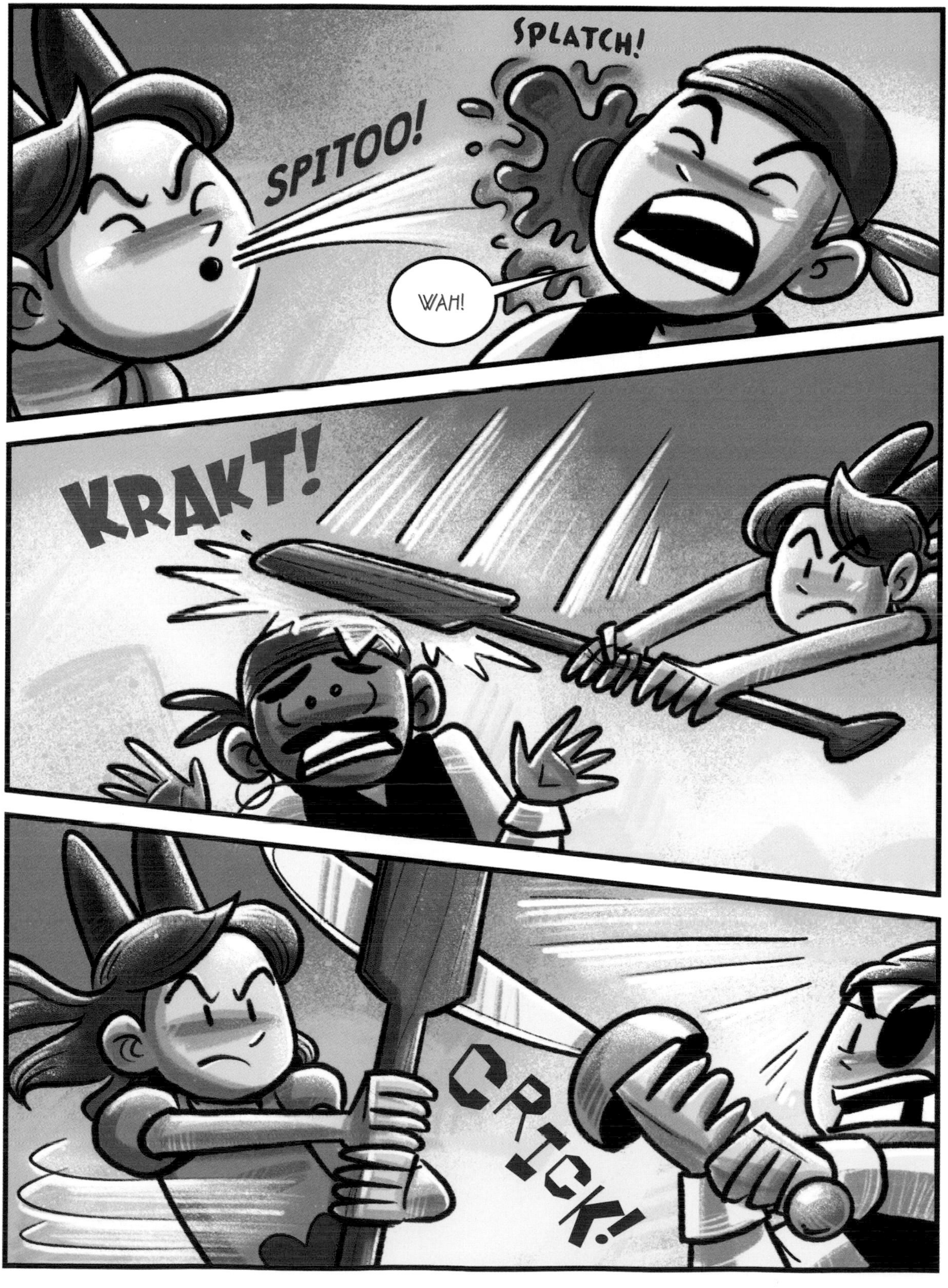
SPITOO!
SPLATCH!
WAH!
KRAKT!
CRICK!

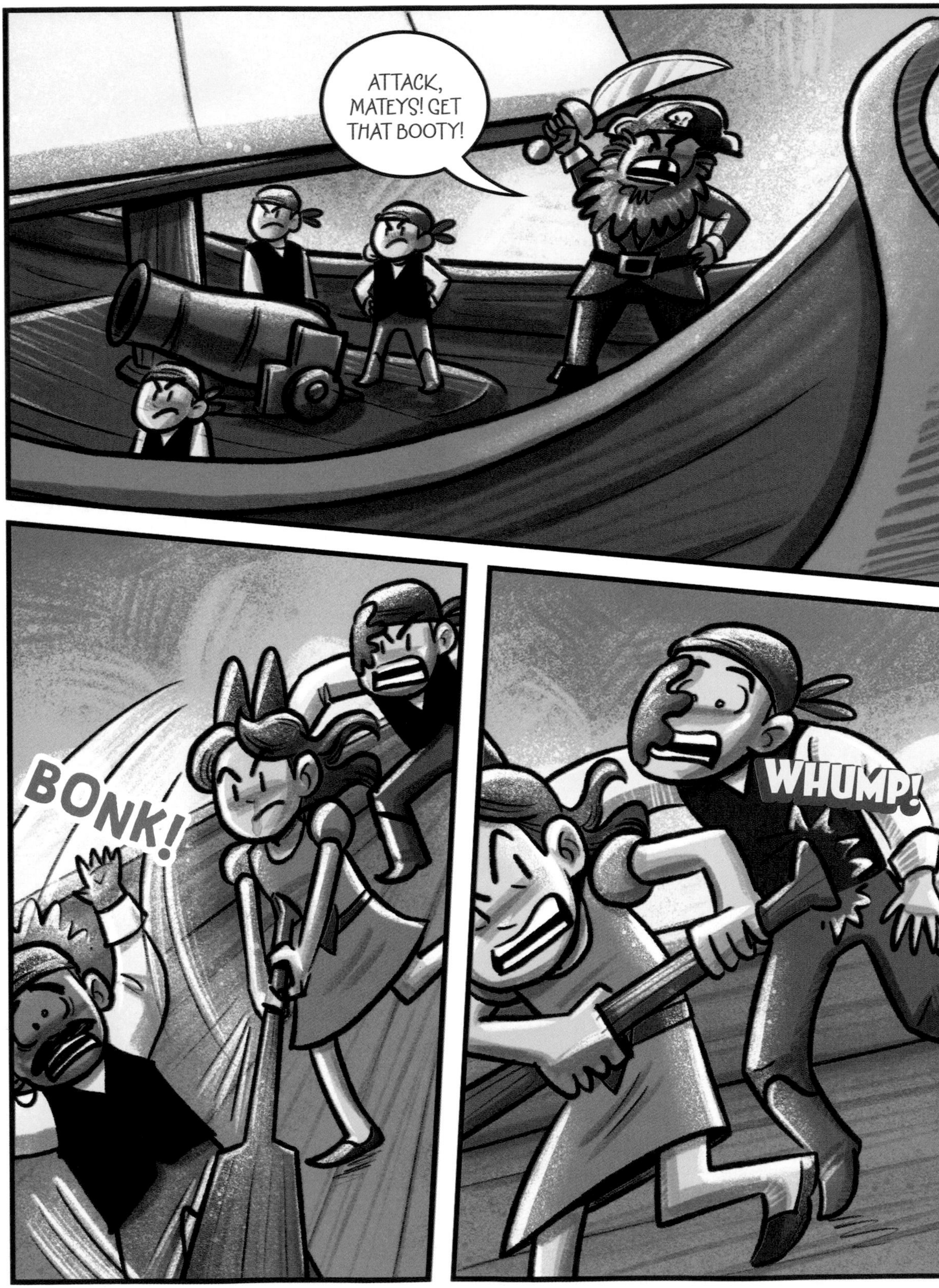
ATTACK, MATEYS! GET THAT BOOTY!
BONK!
WHUMP!

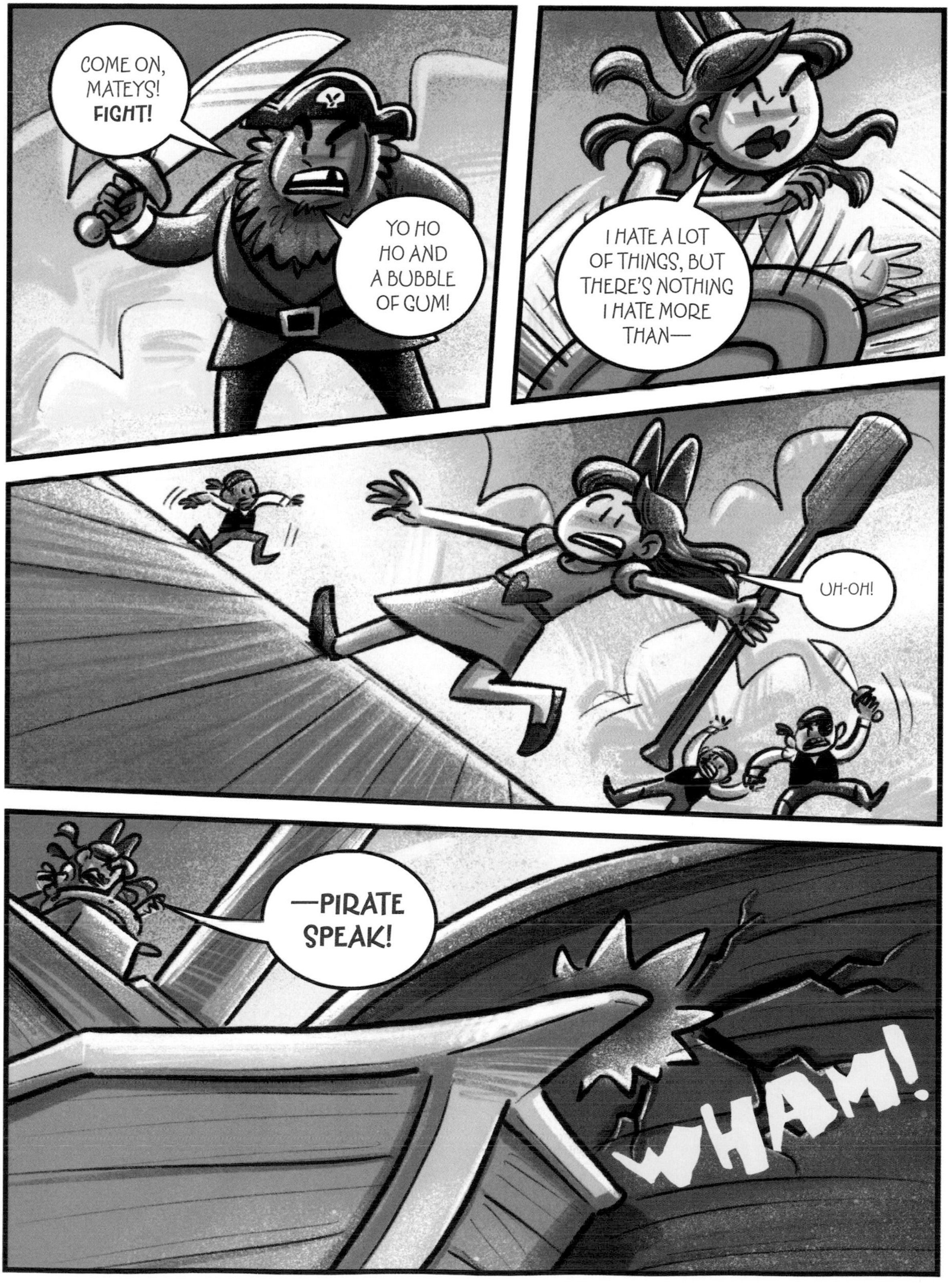
COME ON, MATEYS! **FIGHT!**
YO HO HO AND A BUBBLE OF GUM!
I HATE A LOT OF THINGS, BUT THERE'S NOTHING I HATE MORE THAN—
UH-OH!
—PIRATE SPEAK!
WHAM!

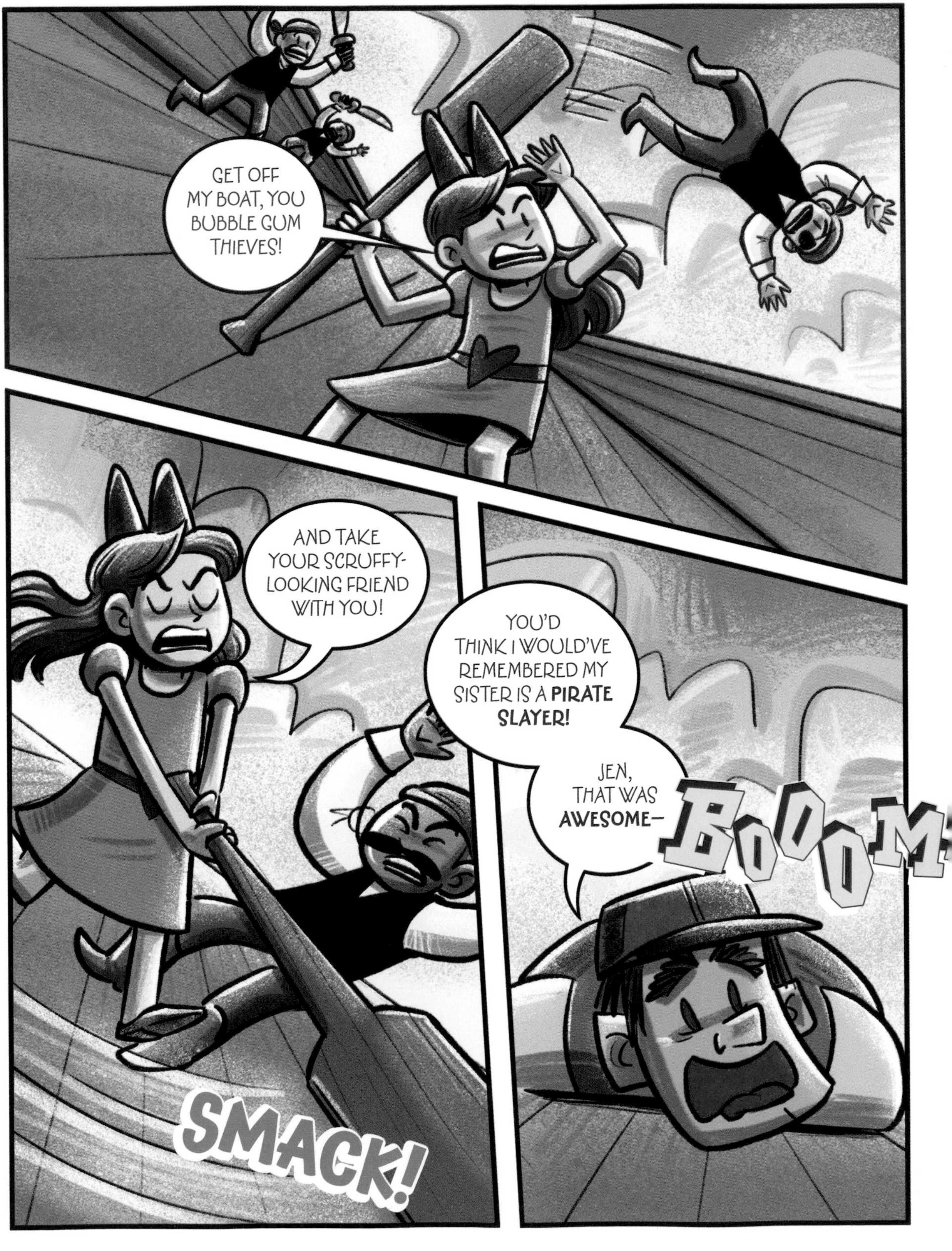
GET OFF MY BOAT, YOU BUBBLE GUM THIEVES!
AND TAKE YOUR SCRUFFY-LOOKING FRIEND WITH YOU!
SMACK!
YOU'D THINK I WOULD'VE REMEMBERED MY SISTER IS A **PIRATE SLAYER!**
JEN, THAT WAS **AWESOME—**
BOOOM!

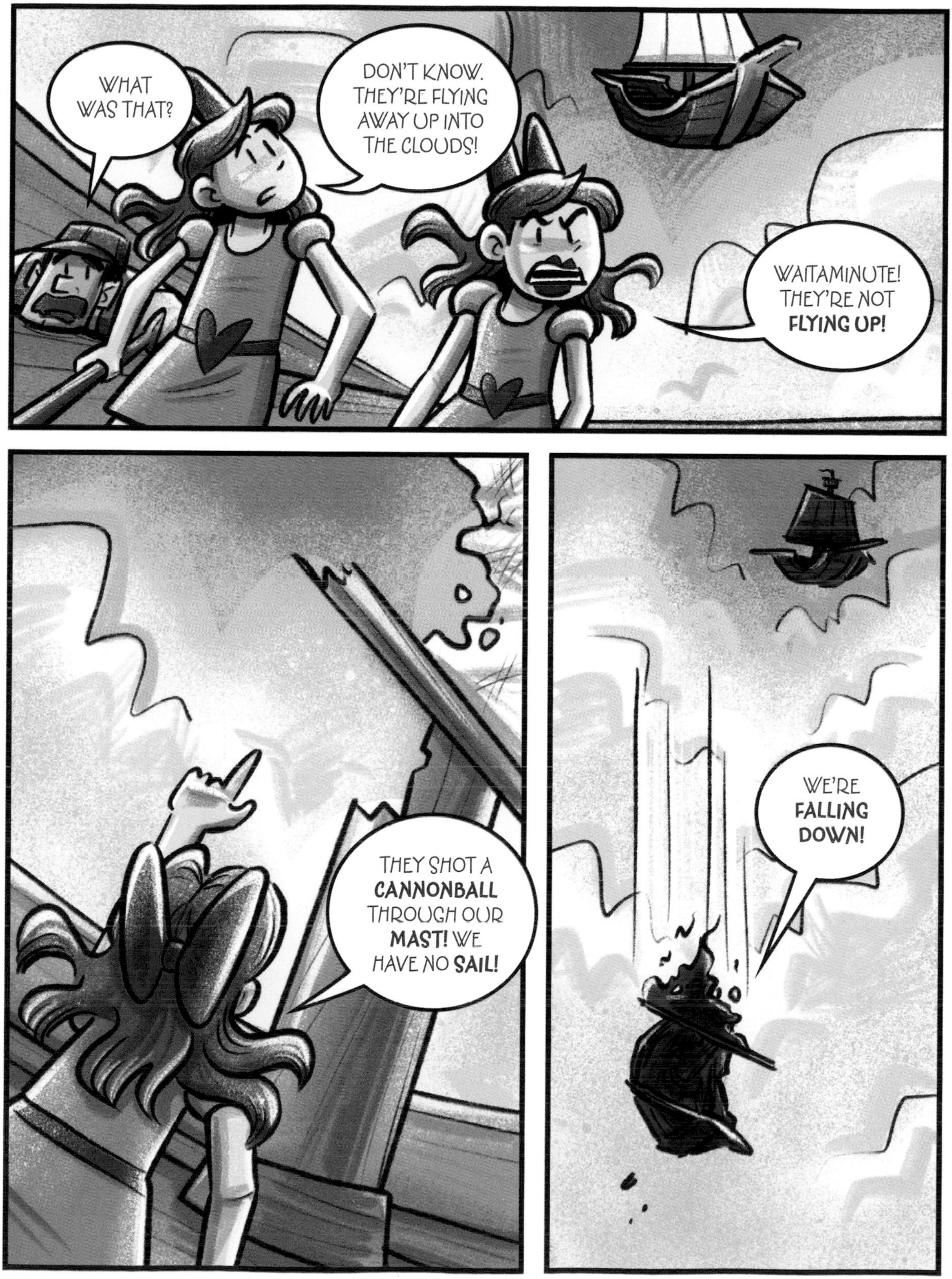
WHAT WAS THAT?
DON'T KNOW. THEY'RE FLYING AWAY UP INTO THE CLOUDS!
WAITAMINUTE! THEY'RE NOT **FLYING UP!**
THEY SHOT A **CANNONBALL** THROUGH OUR **MAST!** WE HAVE NO **SAIL!**
WE'RE **FALLING DOWN!**

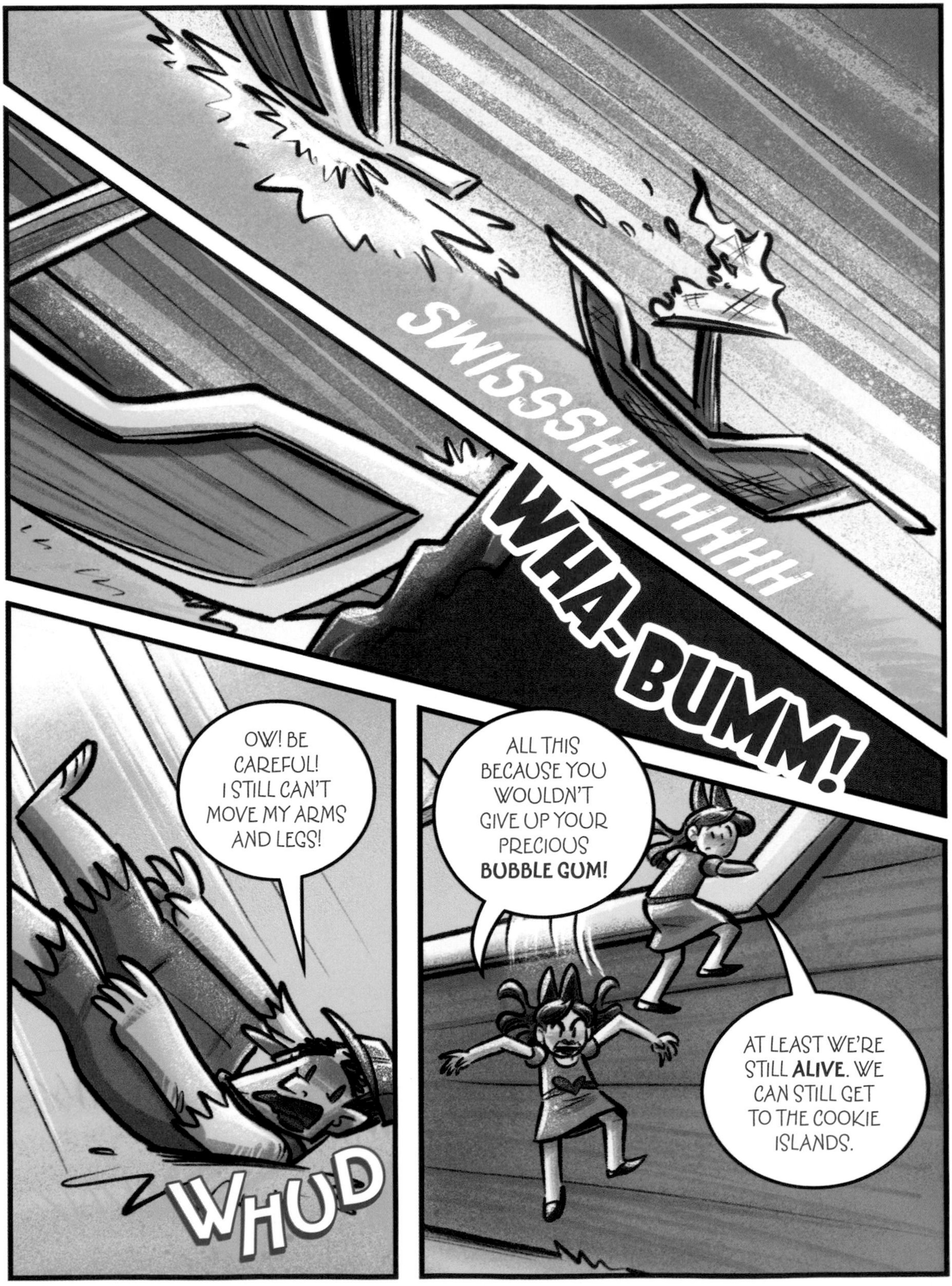
SWISSSHHHHHHH
WHA-BUMM!
OW! BE CAREFUL! I STILL CAN'T MOVE MY ARMS AND LEGS!
WHUD
ALL THIS BECAUSE YOU WOULDN'T GIVE UP YOUR PRECIOUS **BUBBLE GUM!**
AT LEAST WE'RE STILL **ALIVE**. WE CAN STILL GET TO THE COOKIE ISLANDS.

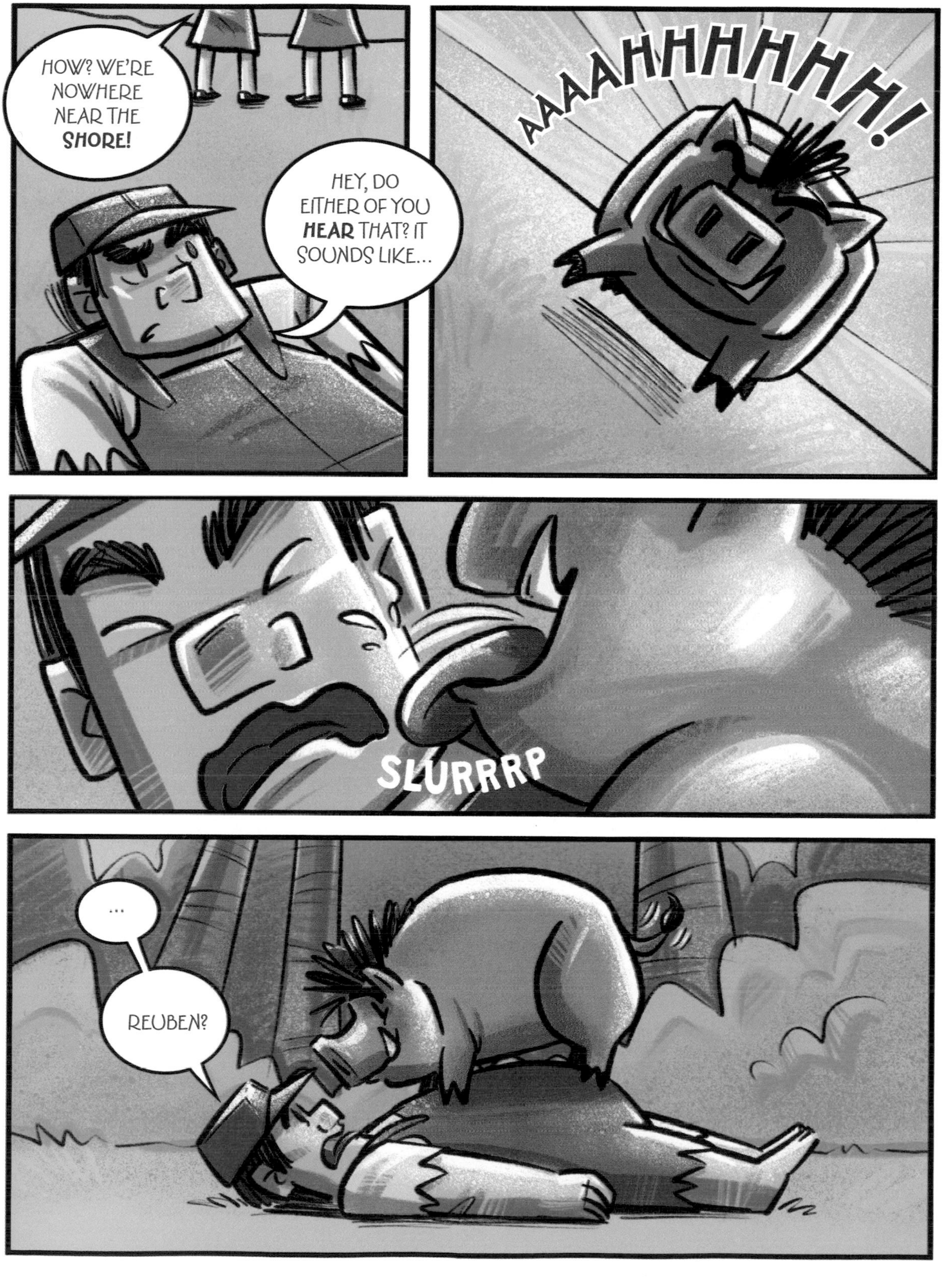
HOW? WE'RE NOWHERE NEAR THE **SHORE!**
HEY, DO EITHER OF YOU **HEAR** THAT? IT SOUNDS LIKE...
AAAAHHHHHHH!
SLURRRP
...
REUBEN?

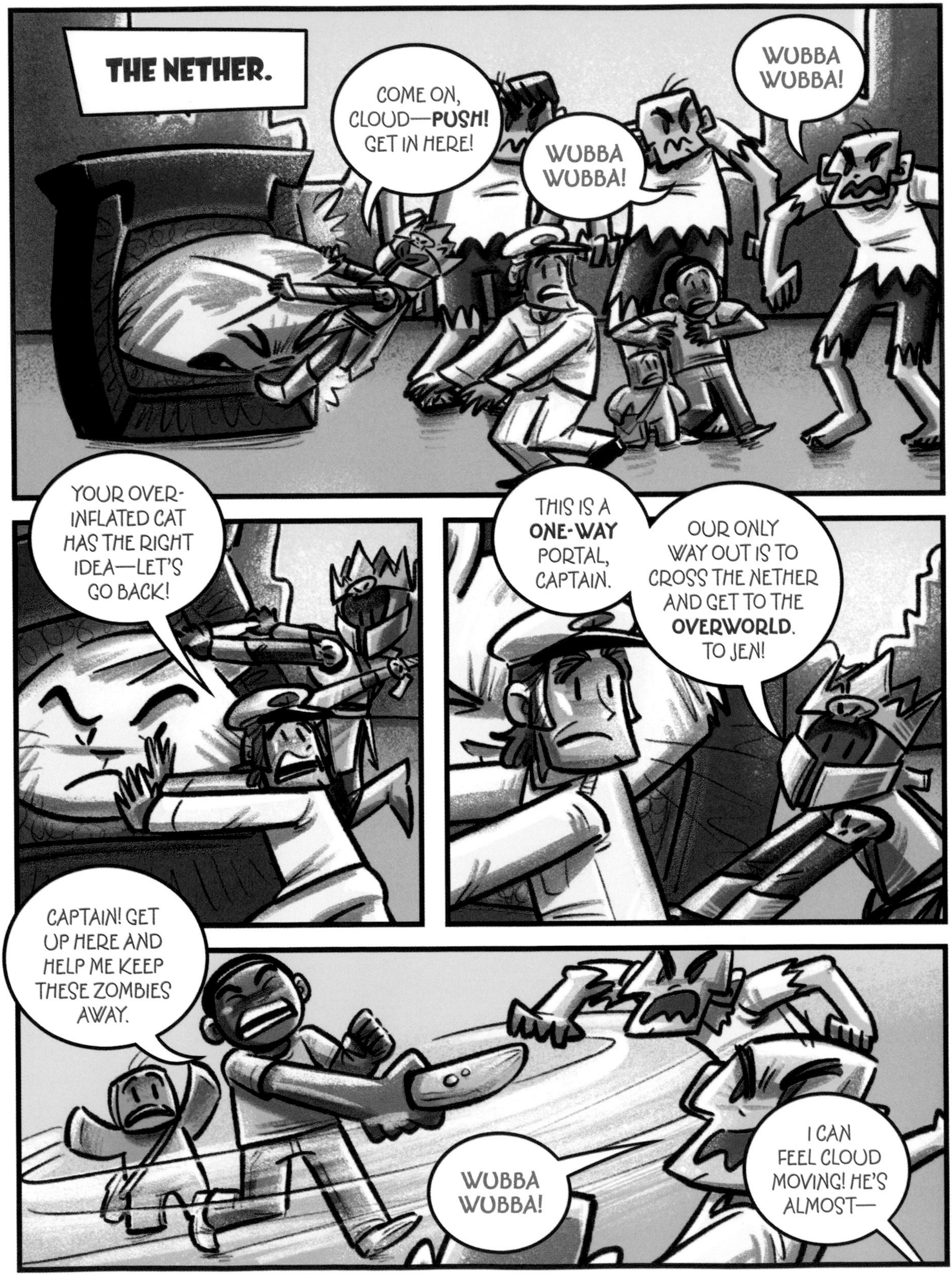
THE NETHER.
COME ON, CLOUD—PUSH! GET IN HERE!
WUBBA WUBBA!
WUBBA WUBBA!
YOUR OVER-INFLATED CAT HAS THE RIGHT IDEA—LET'S GO BACK!
THIS IS A ONE-WAY PORTAL, CAPTAIN.
OUR ONLY WAY OUT IS TO CROSS THE NETHER AND GET TO THE OVERWORLD. TO JEN!
CAPTAIN! GET UP HERE AND HELP ME KEEP THESE ZOMBIES AWAY.
WUBBA WUBBA!
I CAN FEEL CLOUD MOVING! HE'S ALMOST—

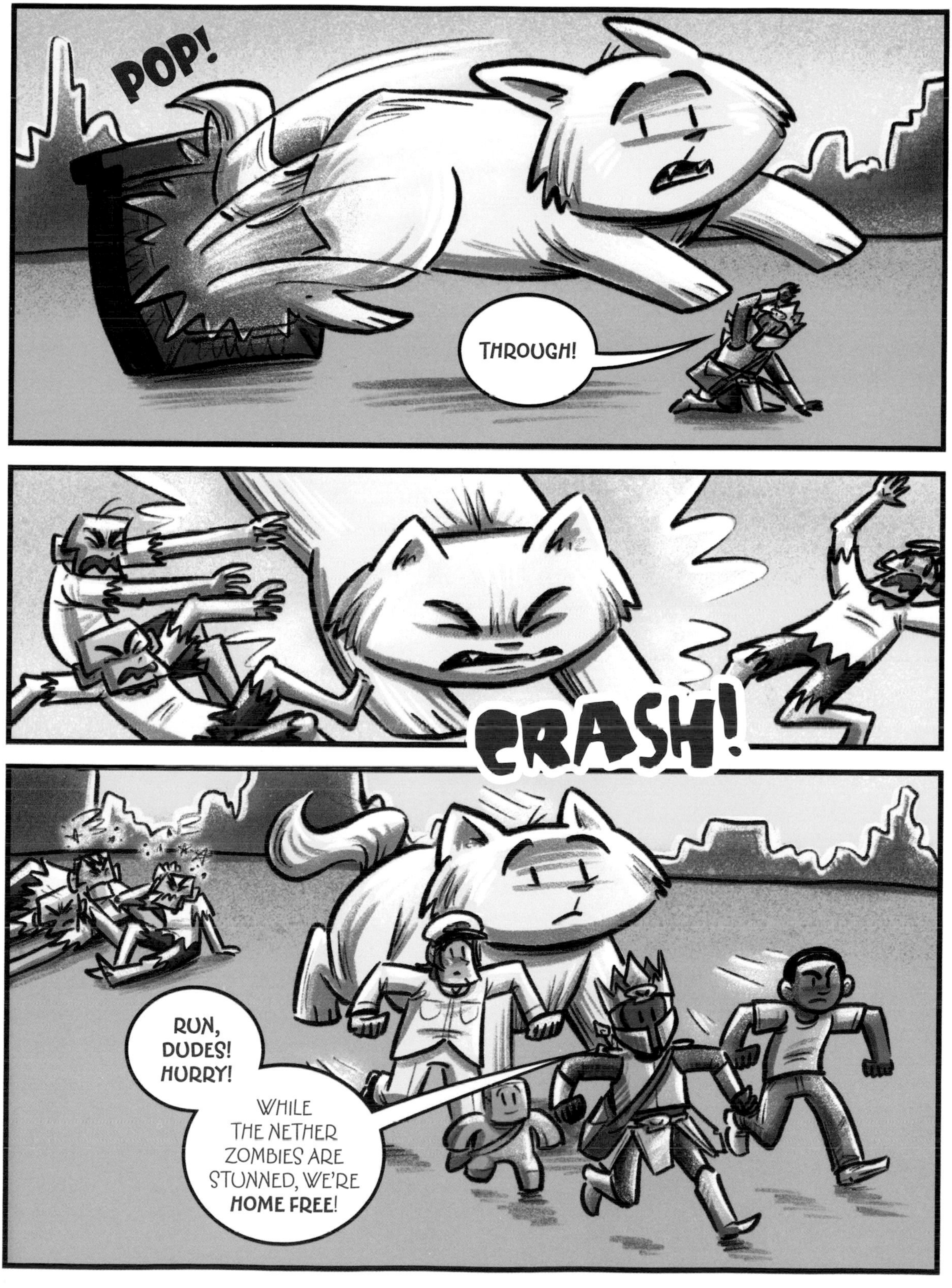
POP!
THROUGH!
CRASH!
RUN, DUDES! HURRY!
WHILE THE NETHER ZOMBIES ARE STUNNED, WE'RE HOME FREE!

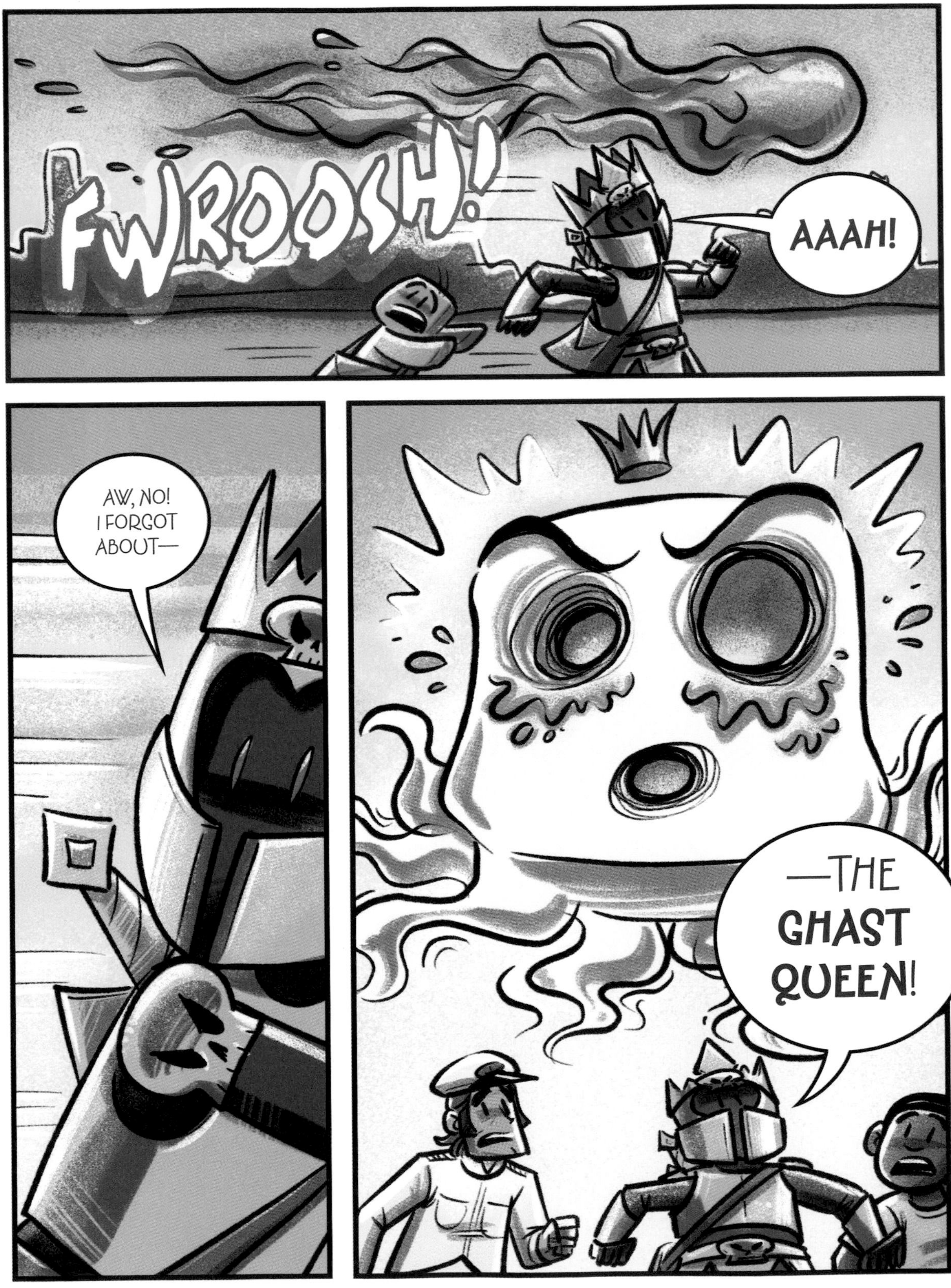
FWROOSH!
AAAH!
AW, NO! I FORGOT ABOUT—
—THE GHAST QUEEN!

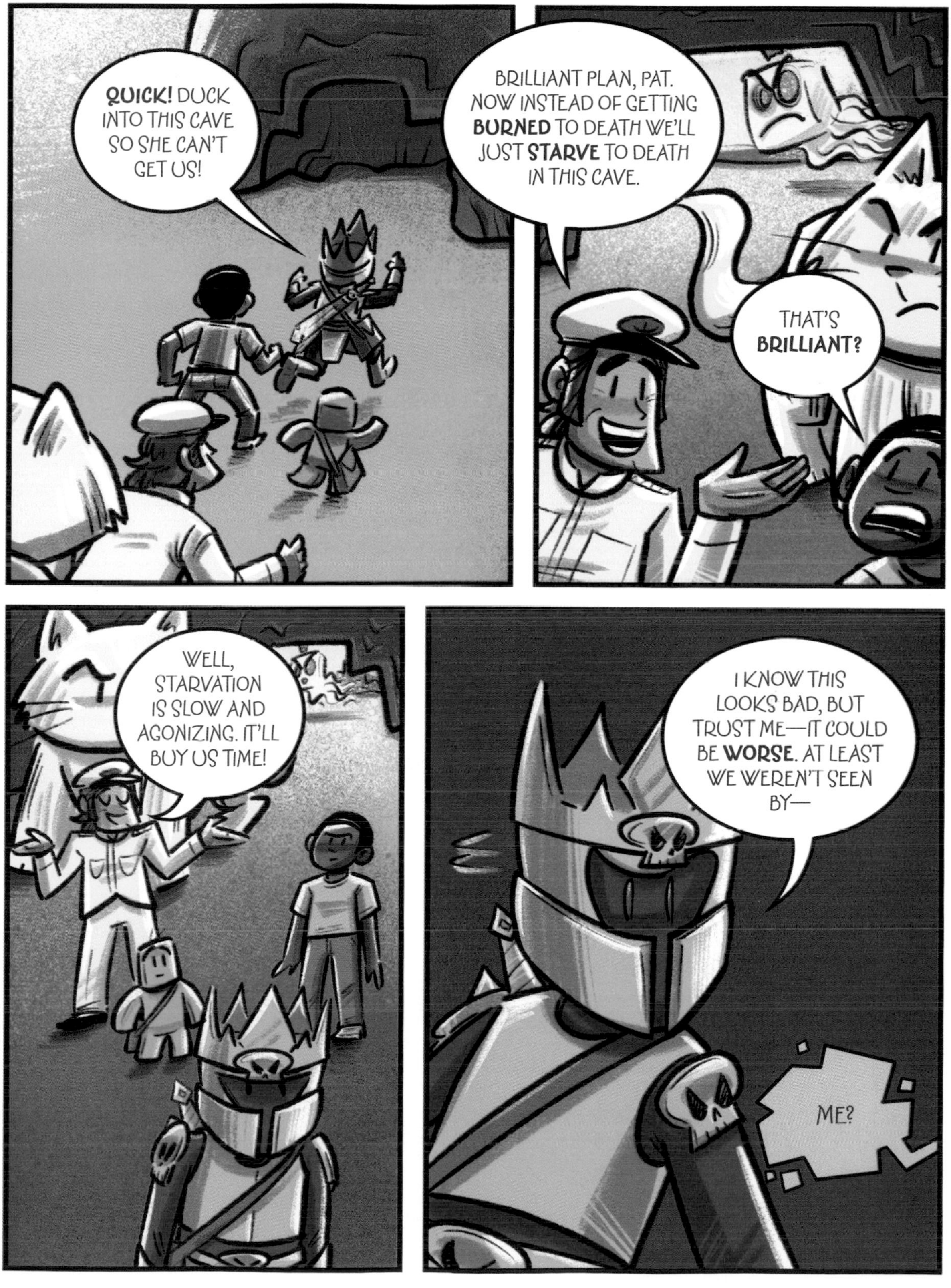
QUICK! DUCK INTO THIS CAVE SO SHE CAN'T GET US!
BRILLIANT PLAN, PAT. NOW INSTEAD OF GETTING BURNED TO DEATH WE'LL JUST STARVE TO DEATH IN THIS CAVE.
THAT'S BRILLIANT?
WELL, STARVATION IS SLOW AND AGONIZING. IT'LL BUY US TIME!
I KNOW THIS LOOKS BAD, BUT TRUST ME—IT COULD BE WORSE. AT LEAST WE WEREN'T SEEN BY—
ME?

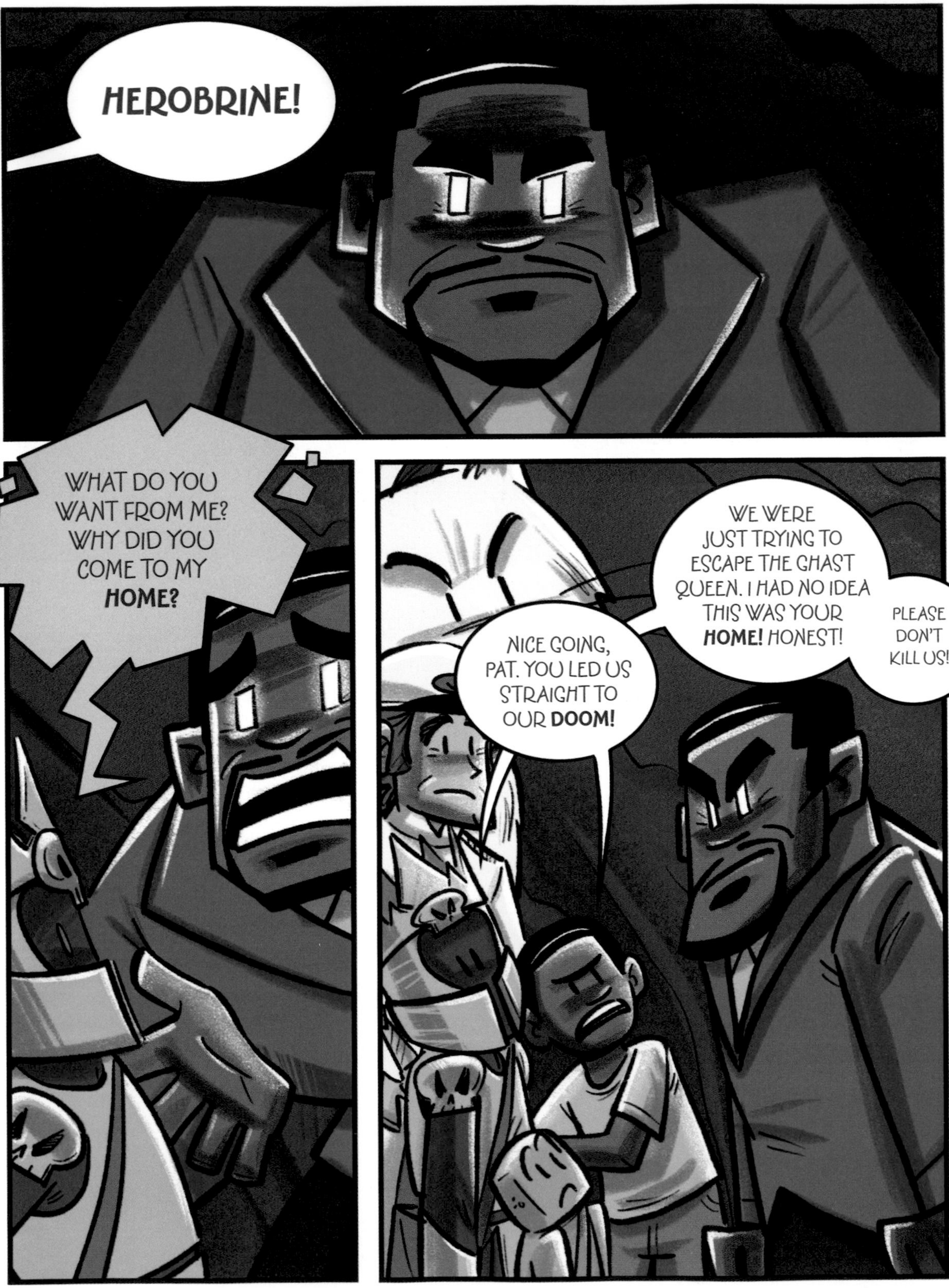
HEROBRINE!
WHAT DO YOU WANT FROM ME? WHY DID YOU COME TO MY **HOME?**
WE WERE JUST TRYING TO ESCAPE THE GHAST QUEEN. I HAD NO IDEA THIS WAS YOUR **HOME!** HONEST!
PLEASE DON'T KILL US!
NICE GOING, PAT. YOU LED US STRAIGHT TO OUR **DOOM!**

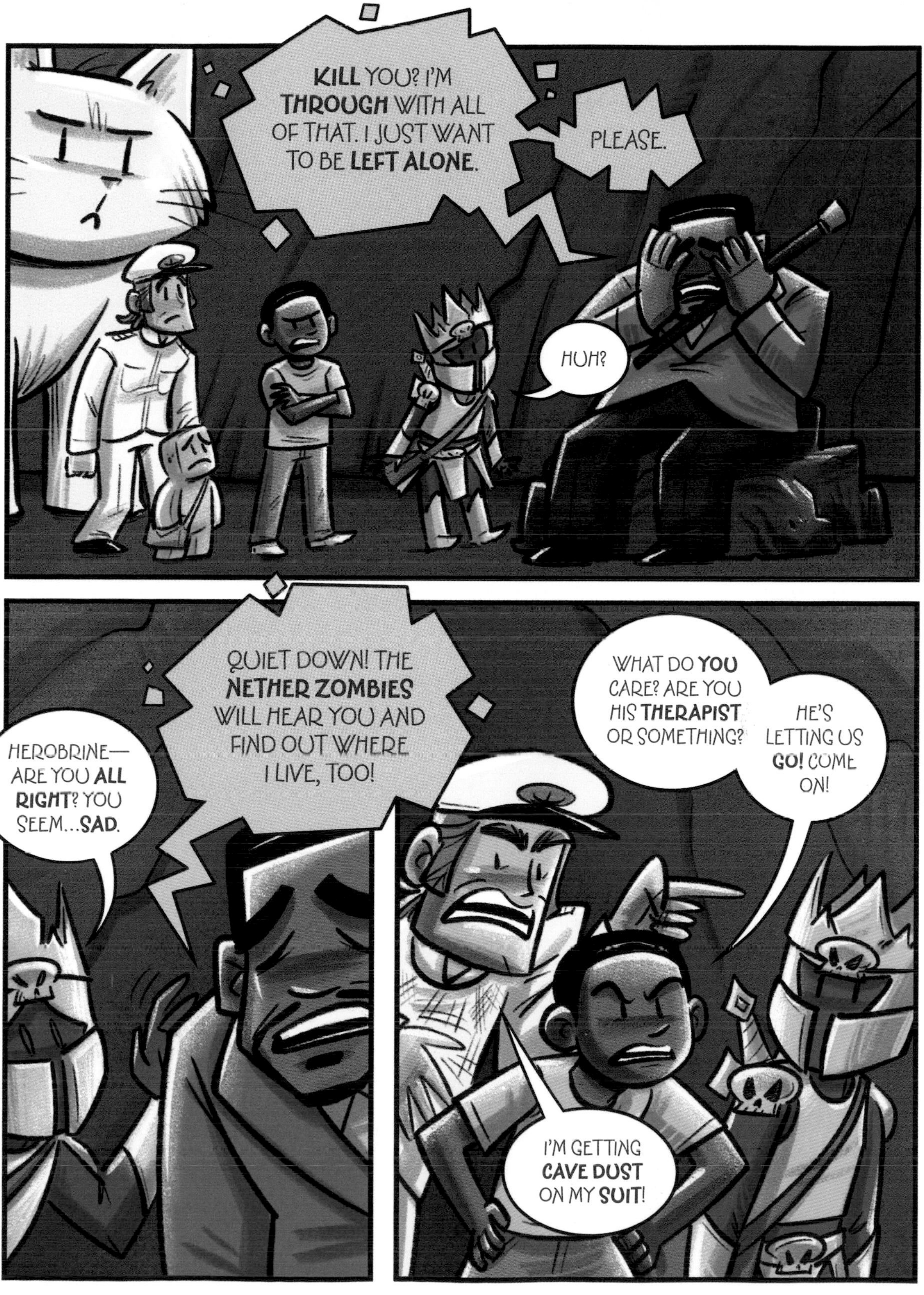
KILL YOU? I'M THROUGH WITH ALL OF THAT. I JUST WANT TO BE LEFT ALONE.
PLEASE.
HUH?
QUIET DOWN! THE NETHER ZOMBIES WILL HEAR YOU AND FIND OUT WHERE I LIVE, TOO!
HEROBRINE—ARE YOU ALL RIGHT? YOU SEEM...SAD.
WHAT DO YOU CARE? ARE YOU HIS THERAPIST OR SOMETHING?
HE'S LETTING US GO! COME ON!
I'M GETTING CAVE DUST ON MY SUIT!

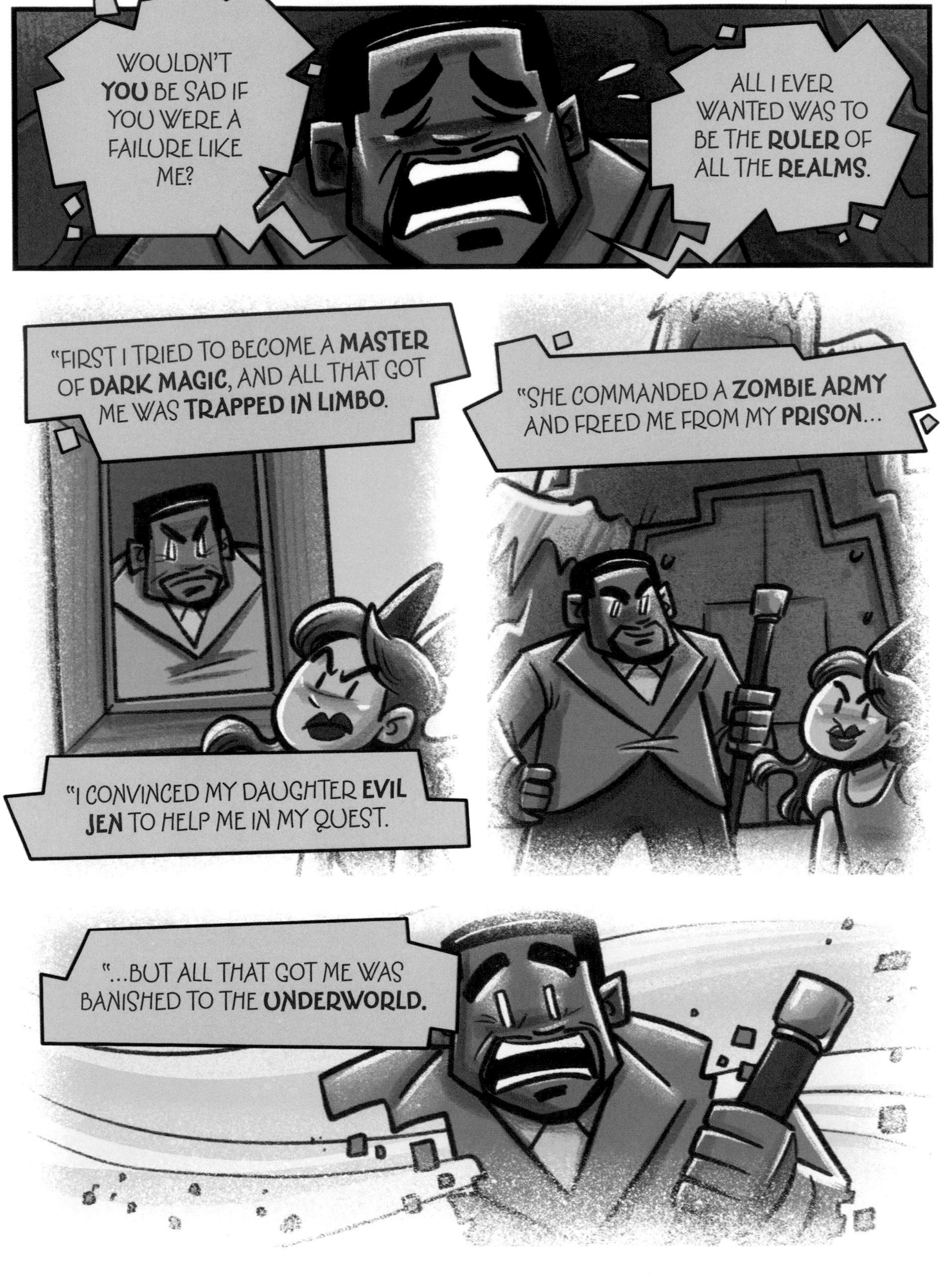

WOULDN'T **YOU** BE SAD IF YOU WERE A FAILURE LIKE ME?
ALL I EVER WANTED WAS TO BE THE **RULER** OF ALL THE **REALMS**.
"FIRST I TRIED TO BECOME A **MASTER** OF **DARK MAGIC**, AND ALL THAT GOT ME WAS **TRAPPED IN LIMBO**.
"I CONVINCED MY DAUGHTER **EVIL JEN** TO HELP ME IN MY QUEST.
"SHE COMMANDED A **ZOMBIE ARMY** AND FREED ME FROM MY **PRISON**...
"...BUT ALL THAT GOT ME WAS BANISHED TO THE **UNDERWORLD**.

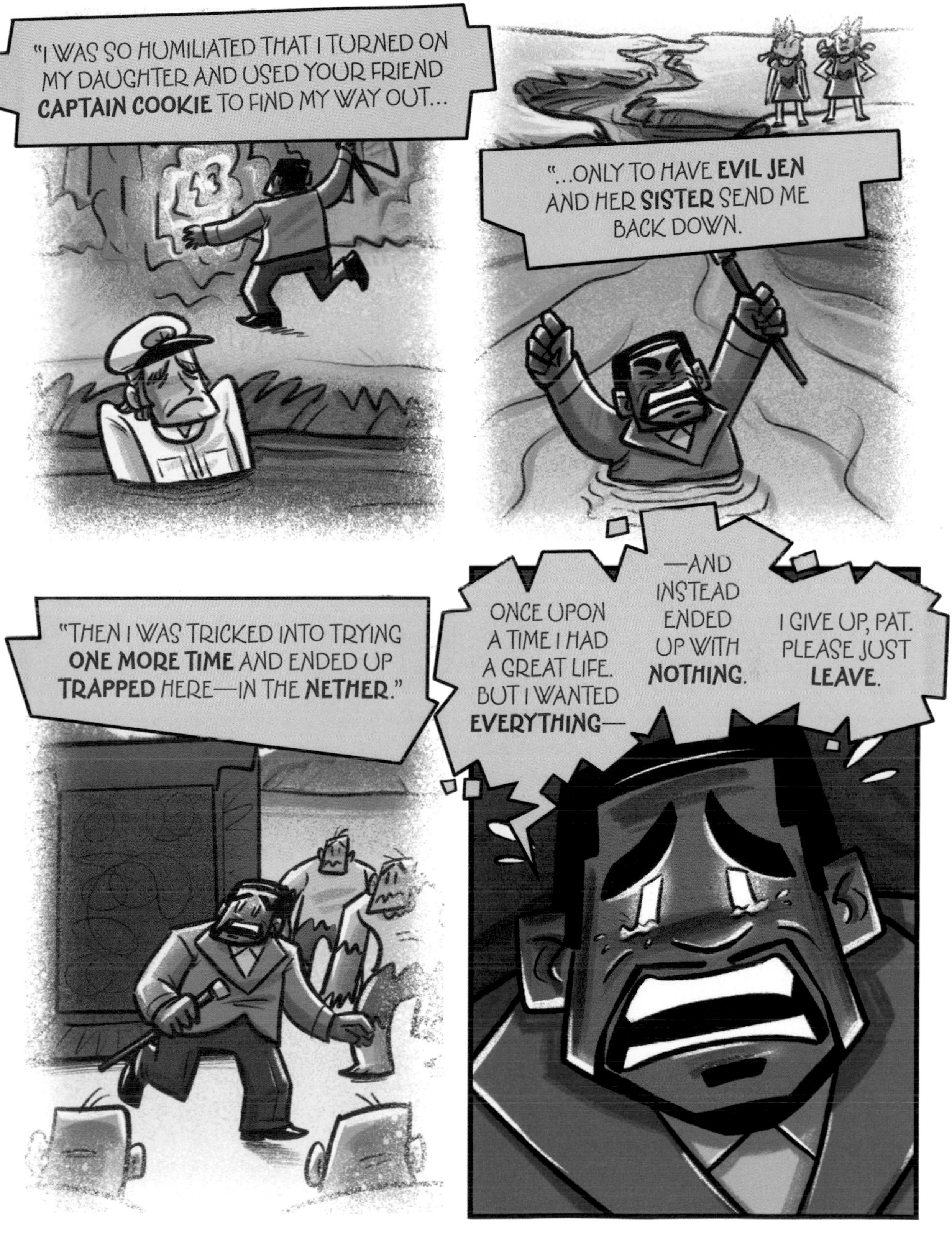
"I WAS SO HUMILIATED THAT I TURNED ON MY DAUGHTER AND USED YOUR FRIEND **CAPTAIN COOKIE** TO FIND MY WAY OUT...
"...ONLY TO HAVE **EVIL JEN** AND HER **SISTER** SEND ME BACK DOWN.
"THEN I WAS TRICKED INTO TRYING **ONE MORE TIME** AND ENDED UP **TRAPPED** HERE—IN THE **NETHER**."
ONCE UPON A TIME I HAD A GREAT LIFE. BUT I WANTED **EVERYTHING**—
—AND INSTEAD ENDED UP WITH **NOTHING**.
I GIVE UP, PAT. PLEASE JUST **LEAVE**.

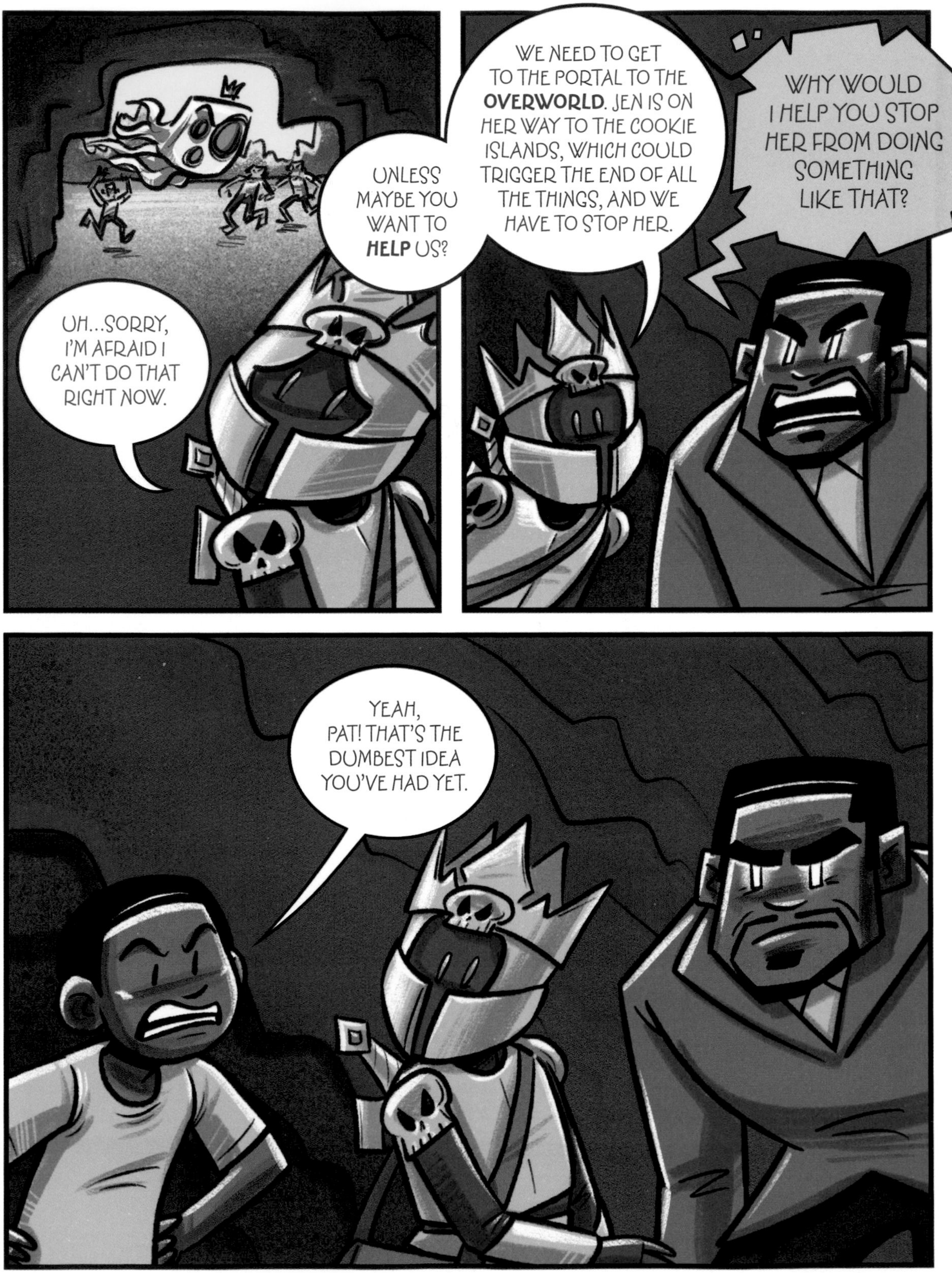
UNLESS MAYBE YOU WANT TO **HELP** US?
WE NEED TO GET TO THE PORTAL TO THE **OVERWORLD**. JEN IS ON HER WAY TO THE COOKIE ISLANDS, WHICH COULD TRIGGER THE END OF ALL THE THINGS, AND WE HAVE TO STOP HER.
UH...SORRY, I'M AFRAID I CAN'T DO THAT RIGHT NOW.
WHY WOULD I HELP YOU STOP HER FROM DOING SOMETHING LIKE THAT?
YEAH, PAT! THAT'S THE DUMBEST IDEA YOU'VE HAD YET.

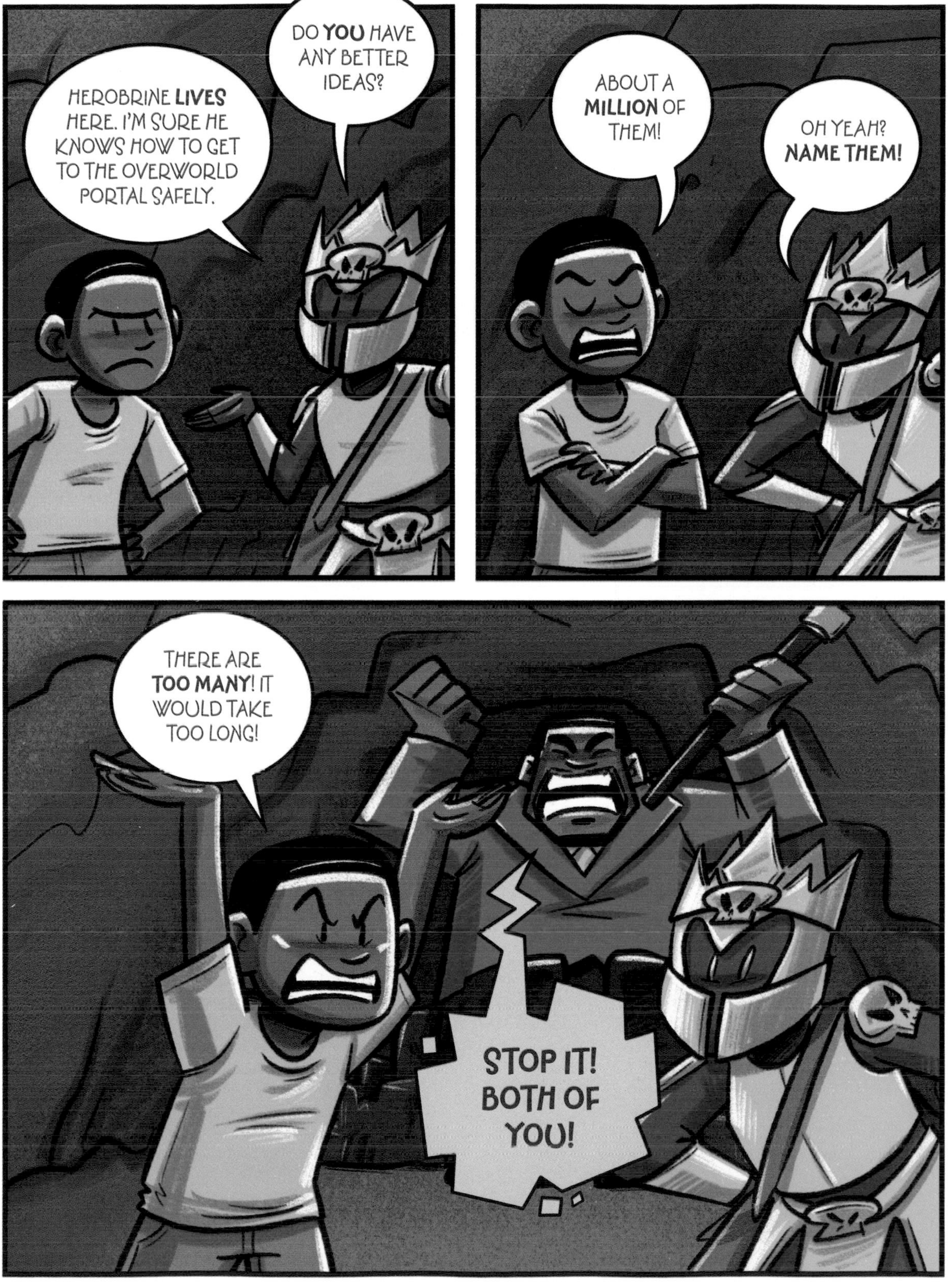
HEROBRINE **LIVES** HERE. I'M SURE HE KNOWS HOW TO GET TO THE OVERWORLD PORTAL SAFELY.
DO **YOU** HAVE ANY BETTER IDEAS?
ABOUT A **MILLION** OF THEM!
OH YEAH? **NAME THEM!**
THERE ARE **TOO MANY**! IT WOULD TAKE TOO LONG!
STOP IT! BOTH OF YOU!

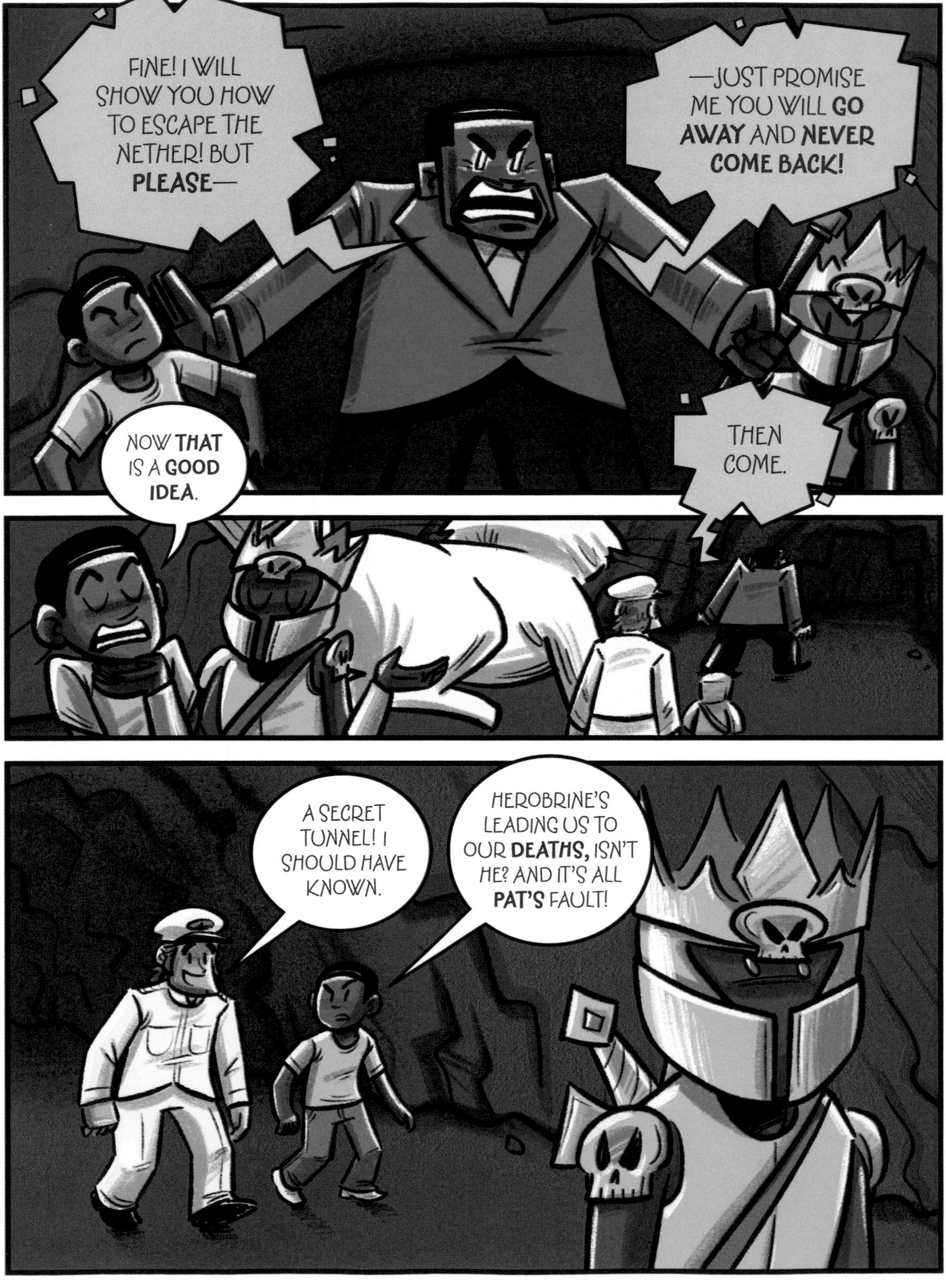
FINE! I WILL SHOW YOU HOW TO ESCAPE THE NETHER! BUT **PLEASE**—
—JUST PROMISE ME YOU WILL **GO AWAY** AND **NEVER COME BACK!**
NOW **THAT** IS A **GOOD IDEA**.
THEN COME.
A SECRET TUNNEL! I SHOULD HAVE KNOWN.
HEROBRINE'S LEADING US TO OUR **DEATHS,** ISN'T HE? AND IT'S ALL **PAT'S** FAULT!

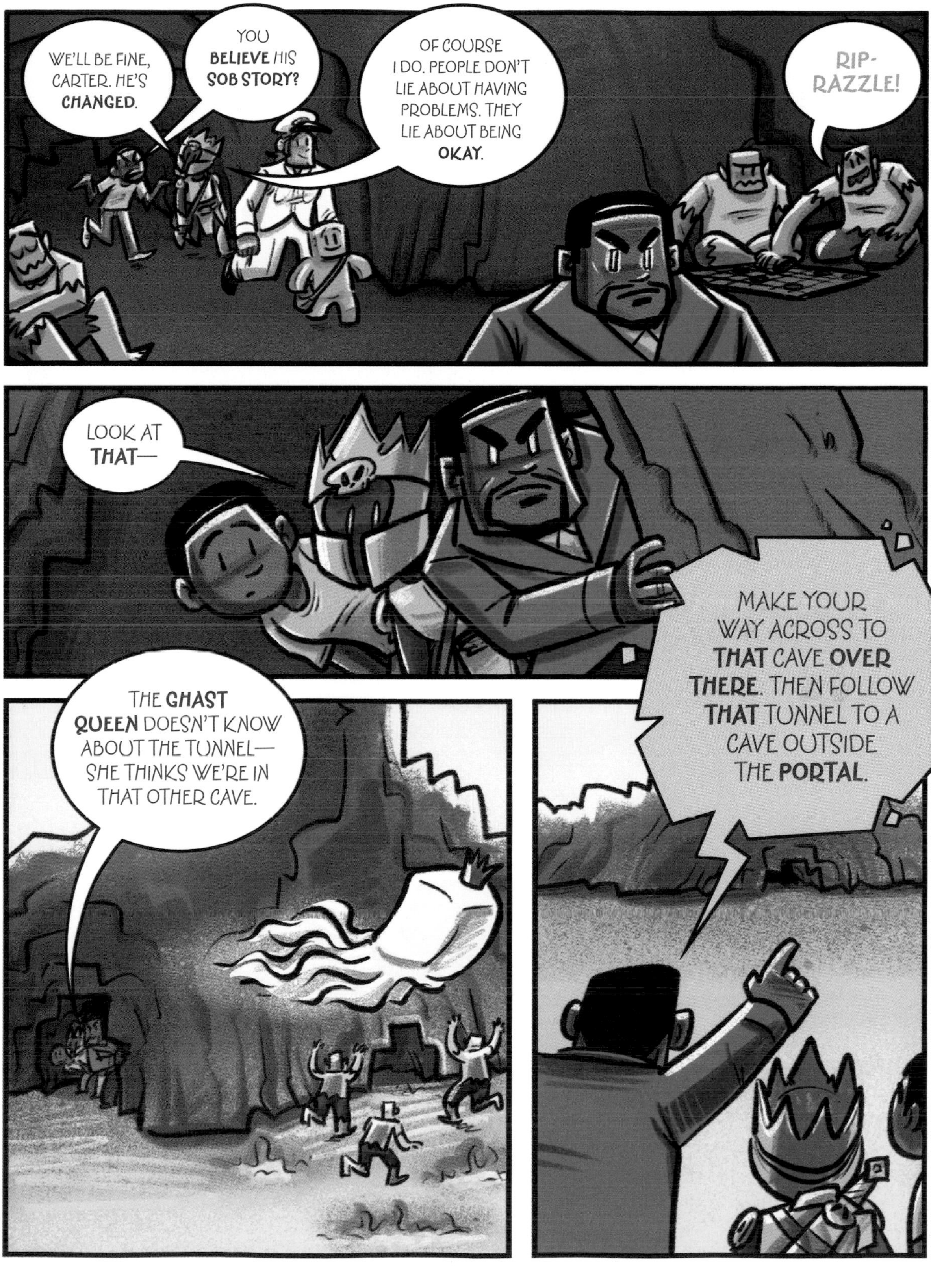
WE'LL BE FINE, CARTER. HE'S **CHANGED**.
YOU **BELIEVE** HIS **SOB STORY?**
OF COURSE I DO. PEOPLE DON'T LIE ABOUT HAVING PROBLEMS. THEY LIE ABOUT BEING **OKAY**.
RIP-RAZZLE!
LOOK AT **THAT**—
MAKE YOUR WAY ACROSS TO **THAT** CAVE **OVER THERE**. THEN FOLLOW **THAT** TUNNEL TO A CAVE OUTSIDE THE **PORTAL**.
THE **GHAST QUEEN** DOESN'T KNOW ABOUT THE TUNNEL—SHE THINKS WE'RE IN THAT OTHER CAVE.

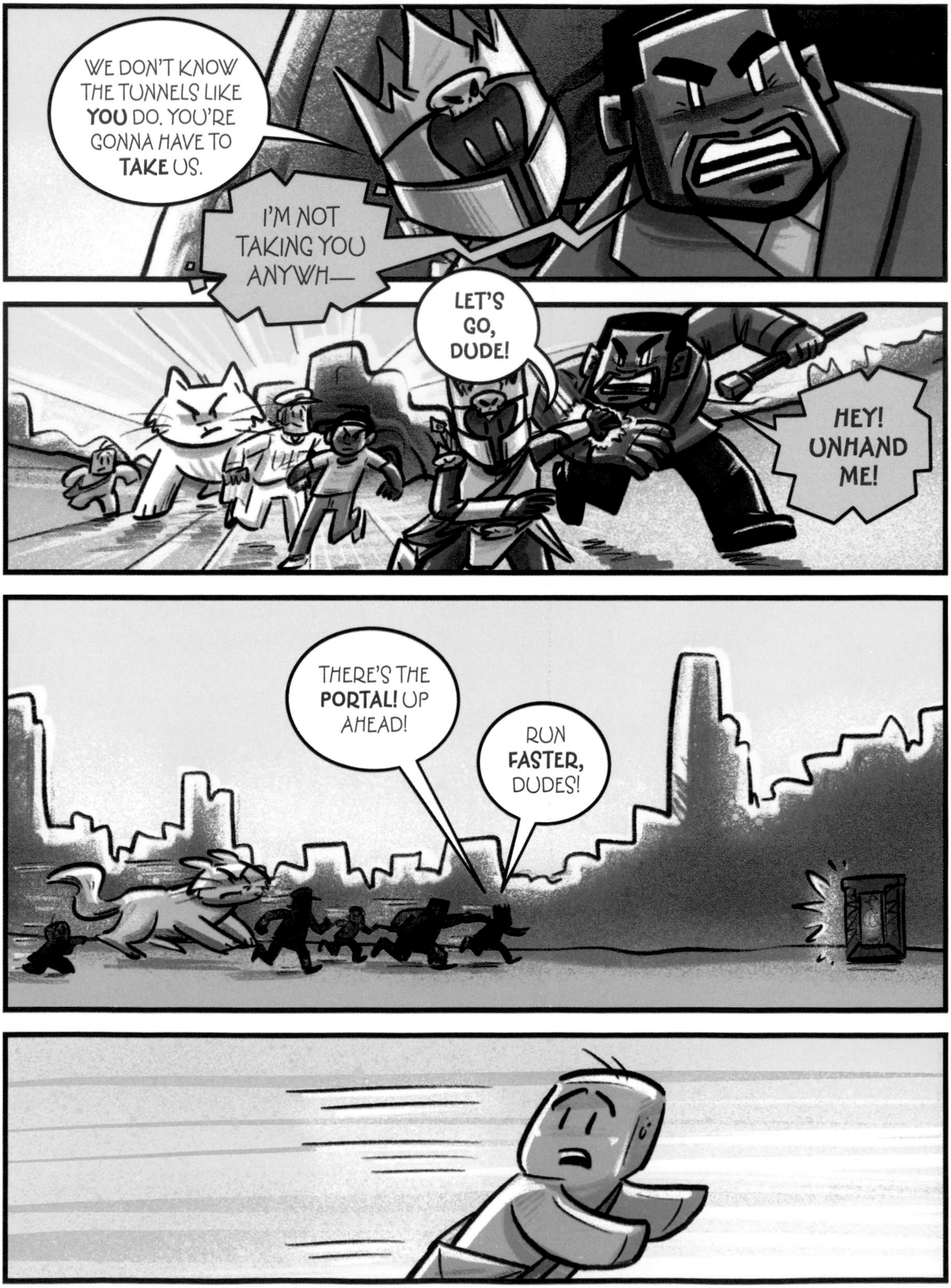
WE DON'T KNOW THE TUNNELS LIKE **YOU** DO. YOU'RE GONNA HAVE TO **TAKE** US.
I'M NOT TAKING YOU ANYWH—
LET'S GO, DUDE!
HEY! UNHAND ME!
THERE'S THE **PORTAL!** UP AHEAD!
RUN **FASTER,** DUDES!

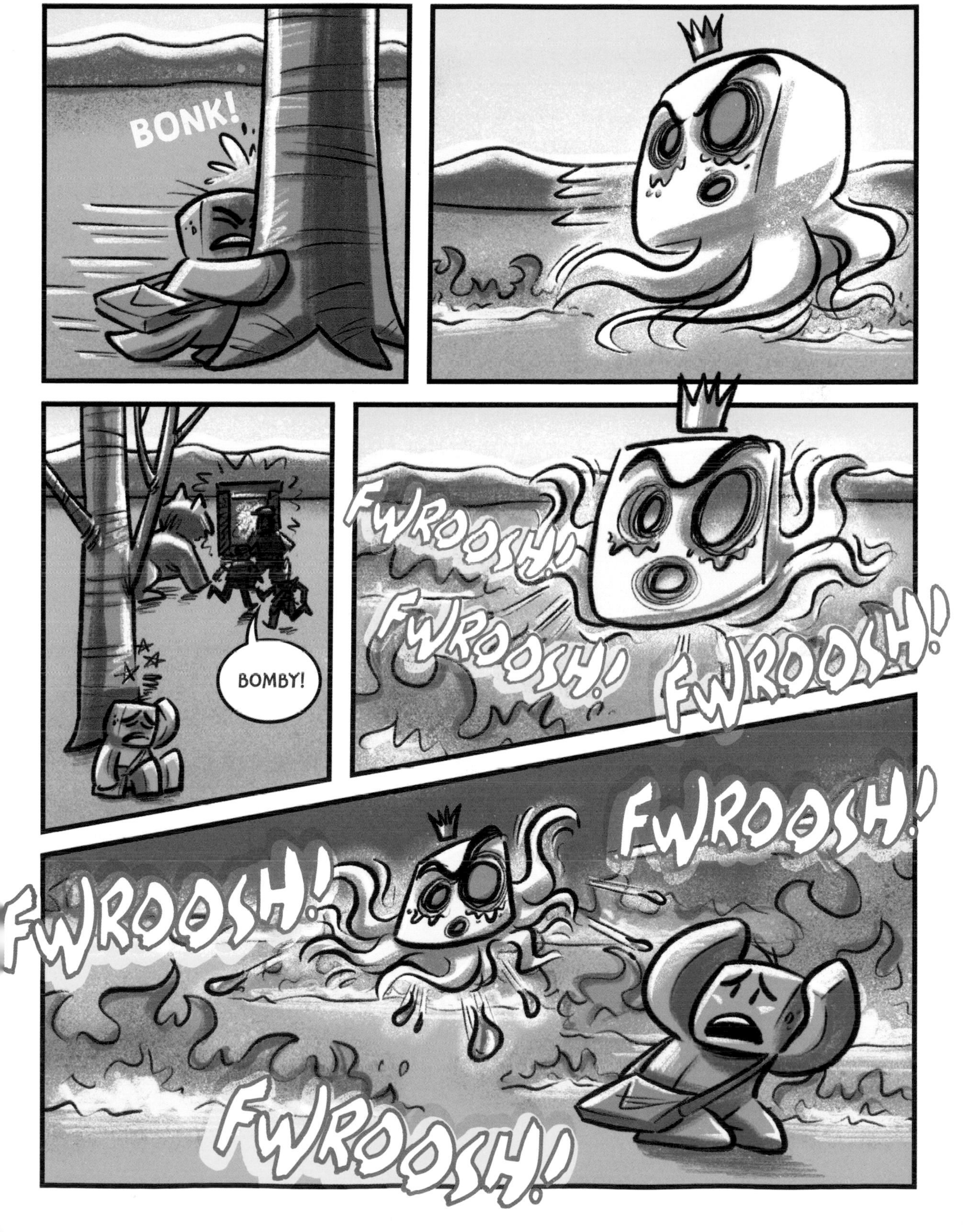
BONK!
BOMBY!
FWROOSH!
FWROOSH!
FWROOSH!
FWROOSH!
FWROOSH!
FWROOSH!

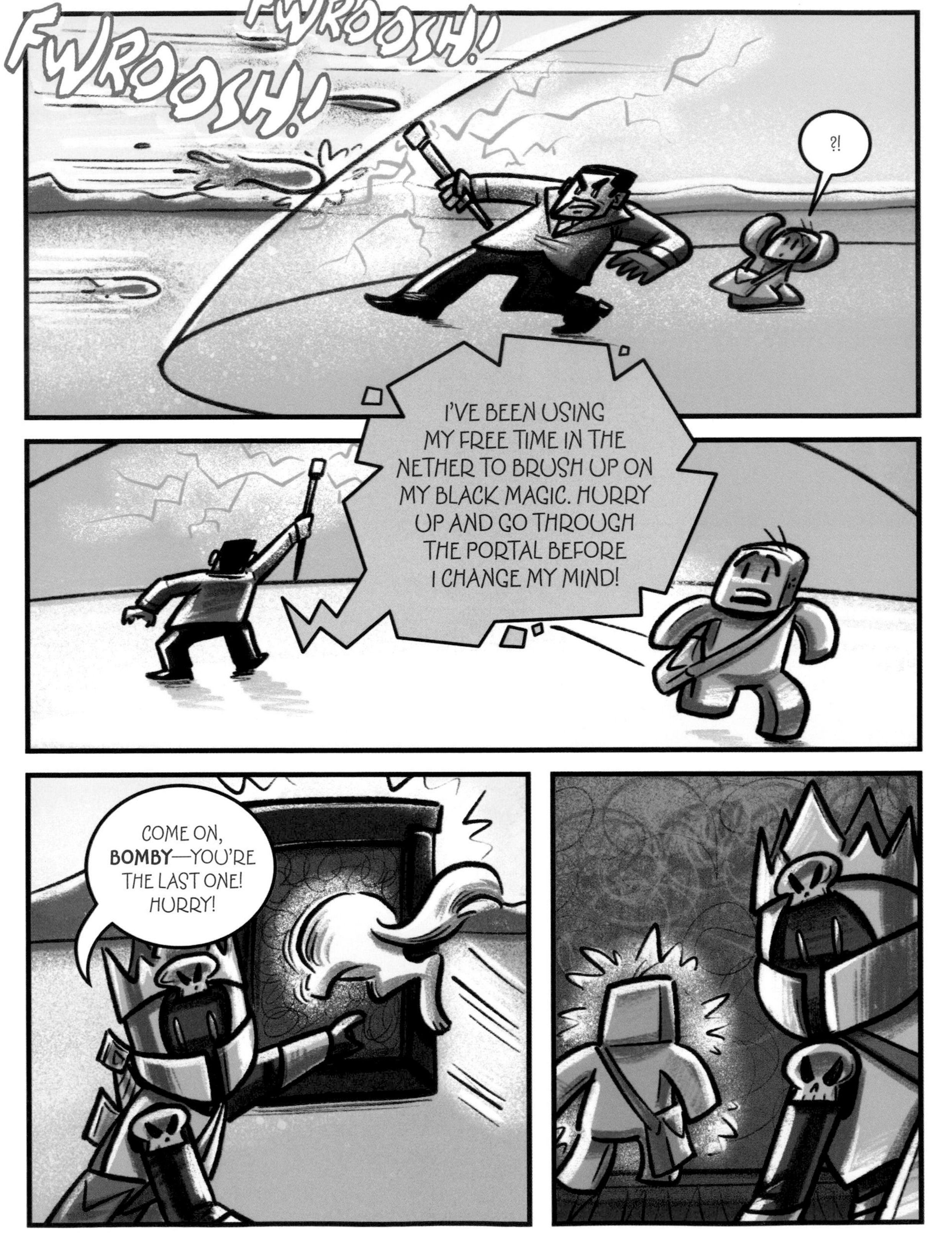
FWROOSH!
FWROOSH!
?!
I'VE BEEN USING MY FREE TIME IN THE NETHER TO BRUSH UP ON MY BLACK MAGIC. HURRY UP AND GO THROUGH THE PORTAL BEFORE I CHANGE MY MIND!
COME ON, **BOMBY**—YOU'RE THE LAST ONE! HURRY!

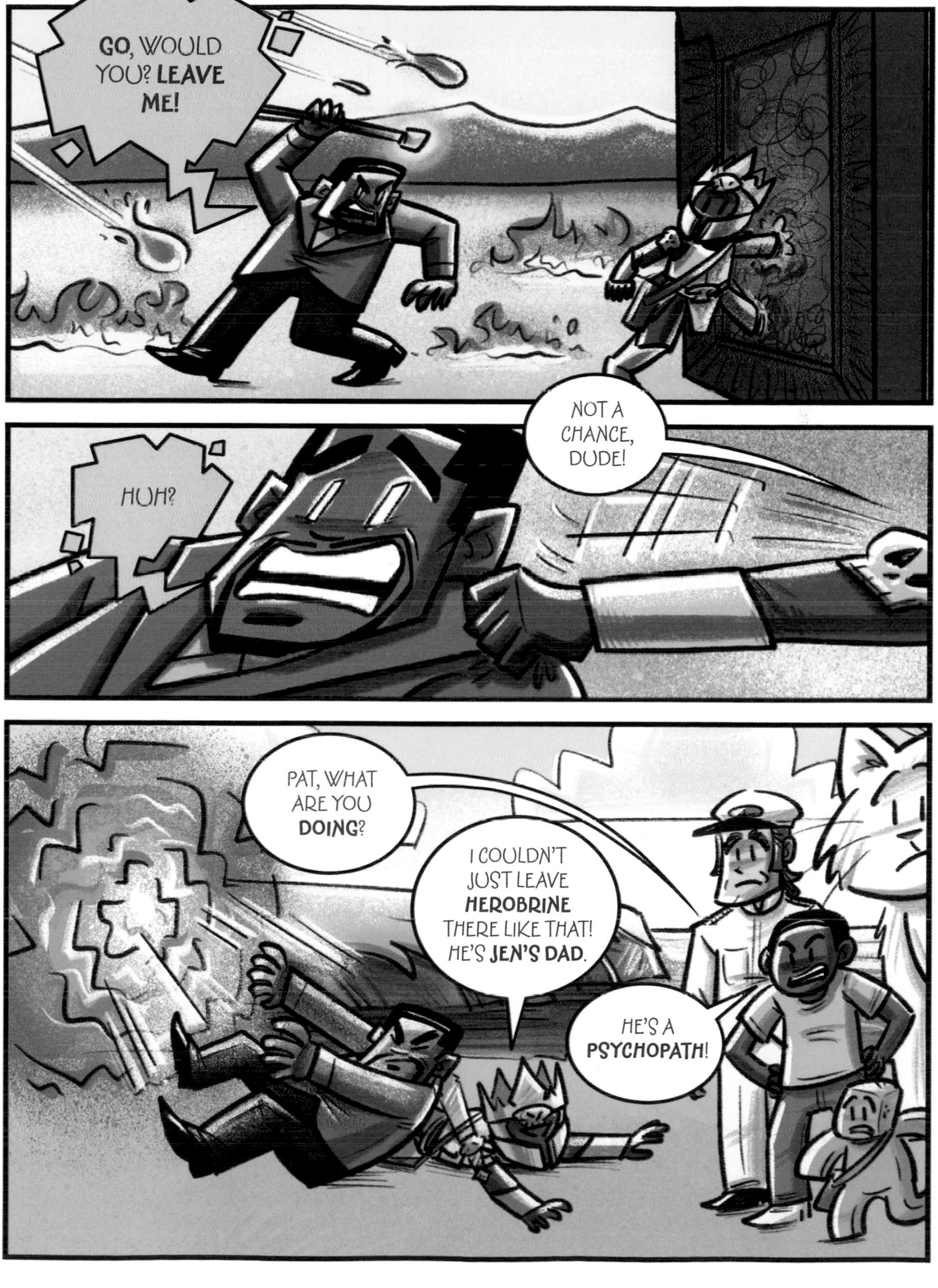
GO, WOULD YOU? **LEAVE ME!**
HUH?
NOT A CHANCE, DUDE!
PAT, WHAT ARE YOU **DOING**?
I COULDN'T JUST LEAVE **HEROBRINE** THERE LIKE THAT! HE'S **JEN'S DAD**.
HE'S A **PSYCHOPATH**!

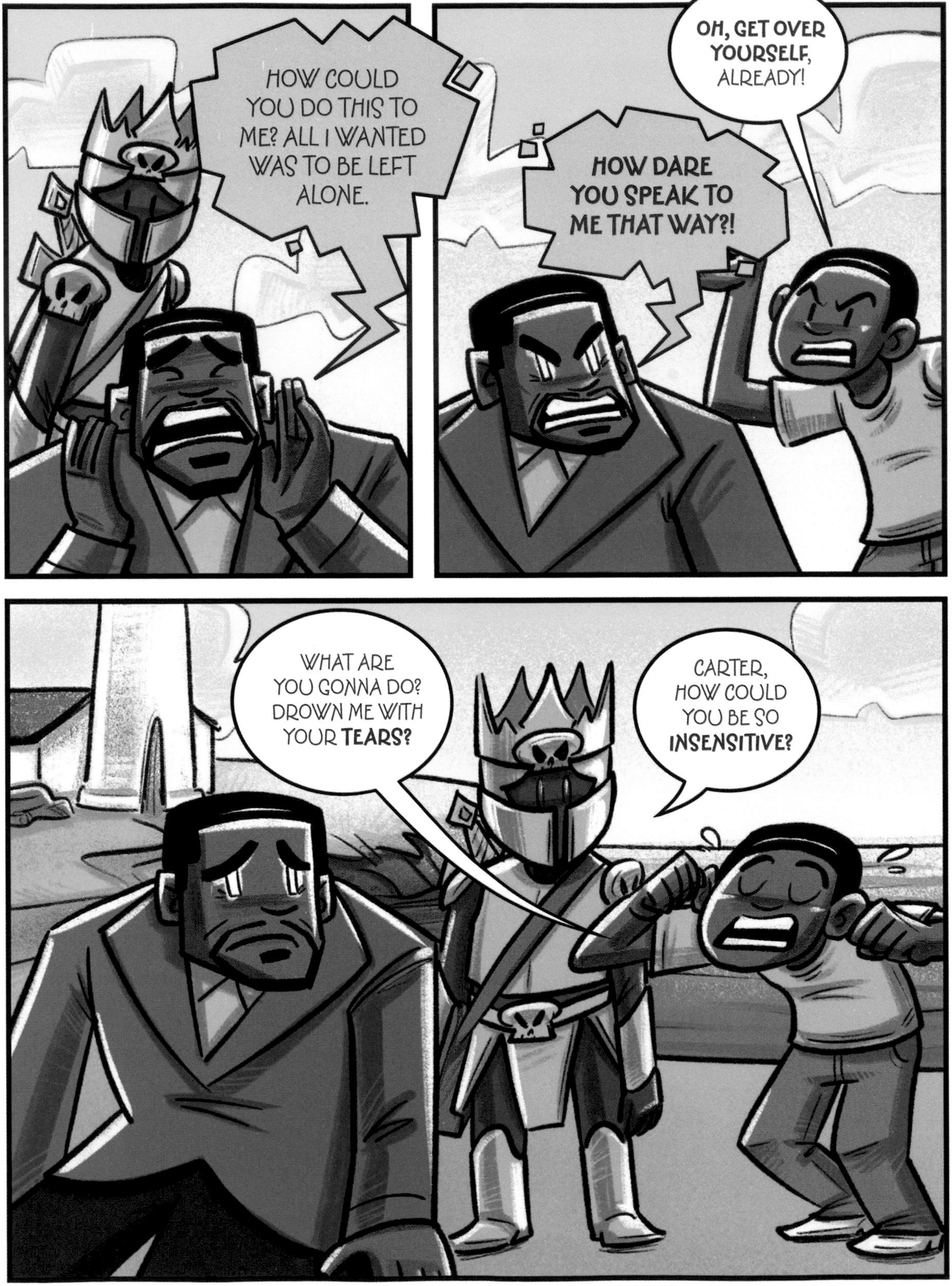
HOW COULD YOU DO THIS TO ME? ALL I WANTED WAS TO BE LEFT ALONE.
OH, GET OVER YOURSELF, ALREADY!
HOW DARE YOU SPEAK TO ME THAT WAY?!
WHAT ARE YOU GONNA DO? DROWN ME WITH YOUR **TEARS?**
CARTER, HOW COULD YOU BE SO **INSENSITIVE?**

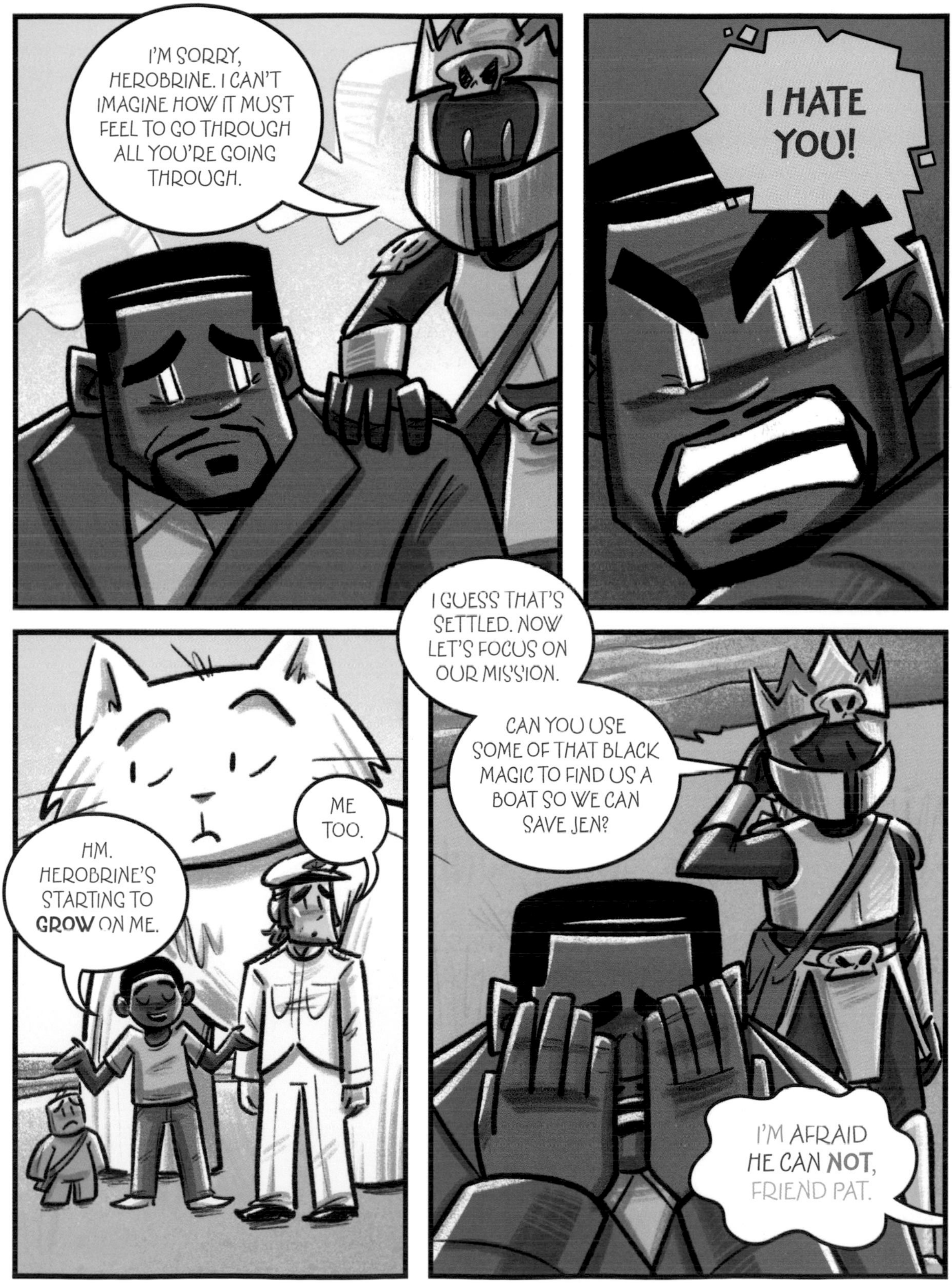
I'M SORRY, HEROBRINE. I CAN'T IMAGINE HOW IT MUST FEEL TO GO THROUGH ALL YOU'RE GOING THROUGH.
I HATE YOU!
HM. HEROBRINE'S STARTING TO **GROW** ON ME.
ME TOO.
I GUESS THAT'S SETTLED. NOW LET'S FOCUS ON OUR MISSION.
CAN YOU USE SOME OF THAT BLACK MAGIC TO FIND US A BOAT SO WE CAN SAVE JEN?
I'M AFRAID HE CAN **NOT**, FRIEND PAT.

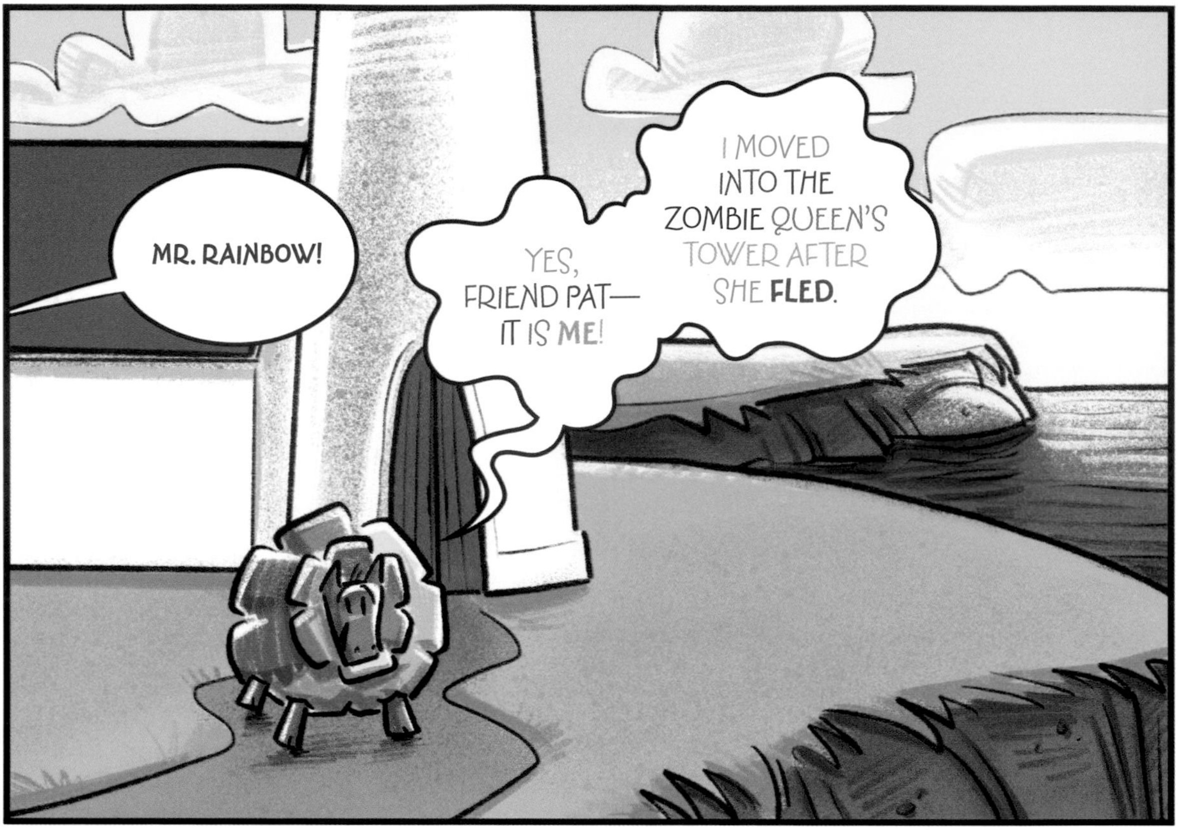
MR. RAINBOW!
YES, FRIEND PAT— IT IS ME!
I MOVED INTO THE ZOMBIE QUEEN'S TOWER AFTER SHE FLED.

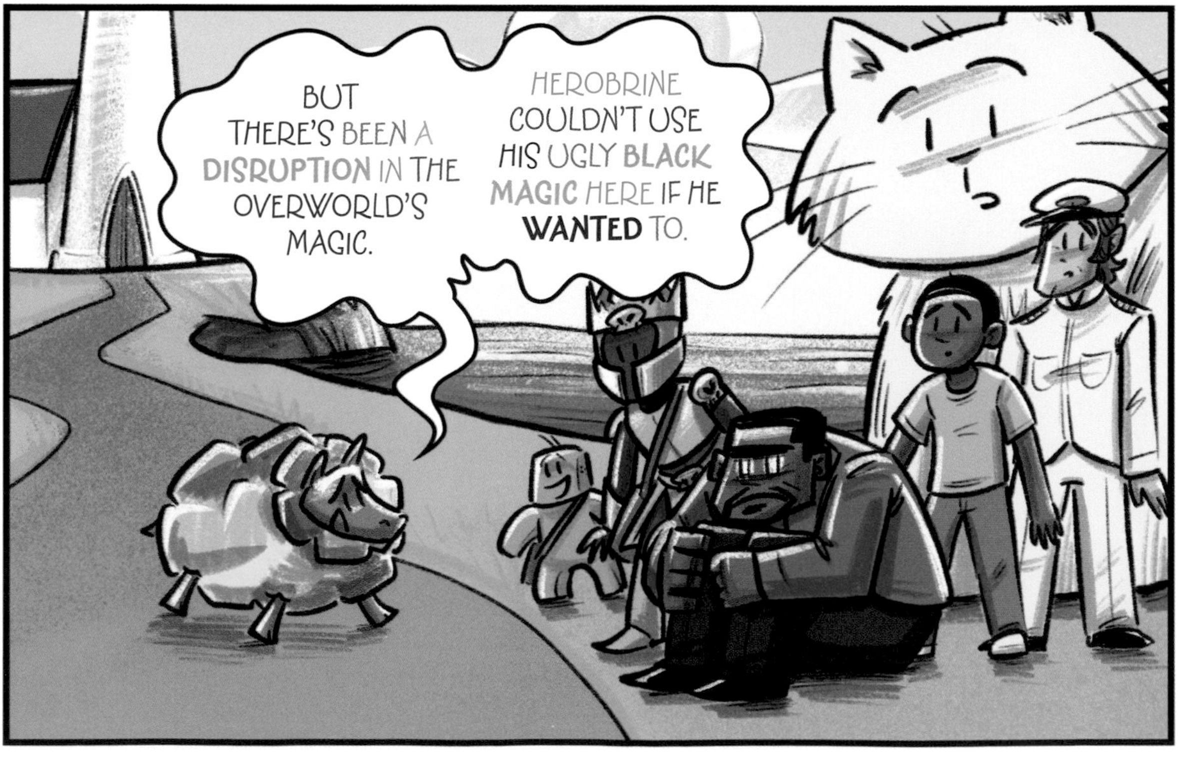
BUT THERE'S BEEN A DISRUPTION IN THE OVERWORLD'S MAGIC.
HEROBRINE COULDN'T USE HIS UGLY BLACK MAGIC HERE IF HE WANTED TO.

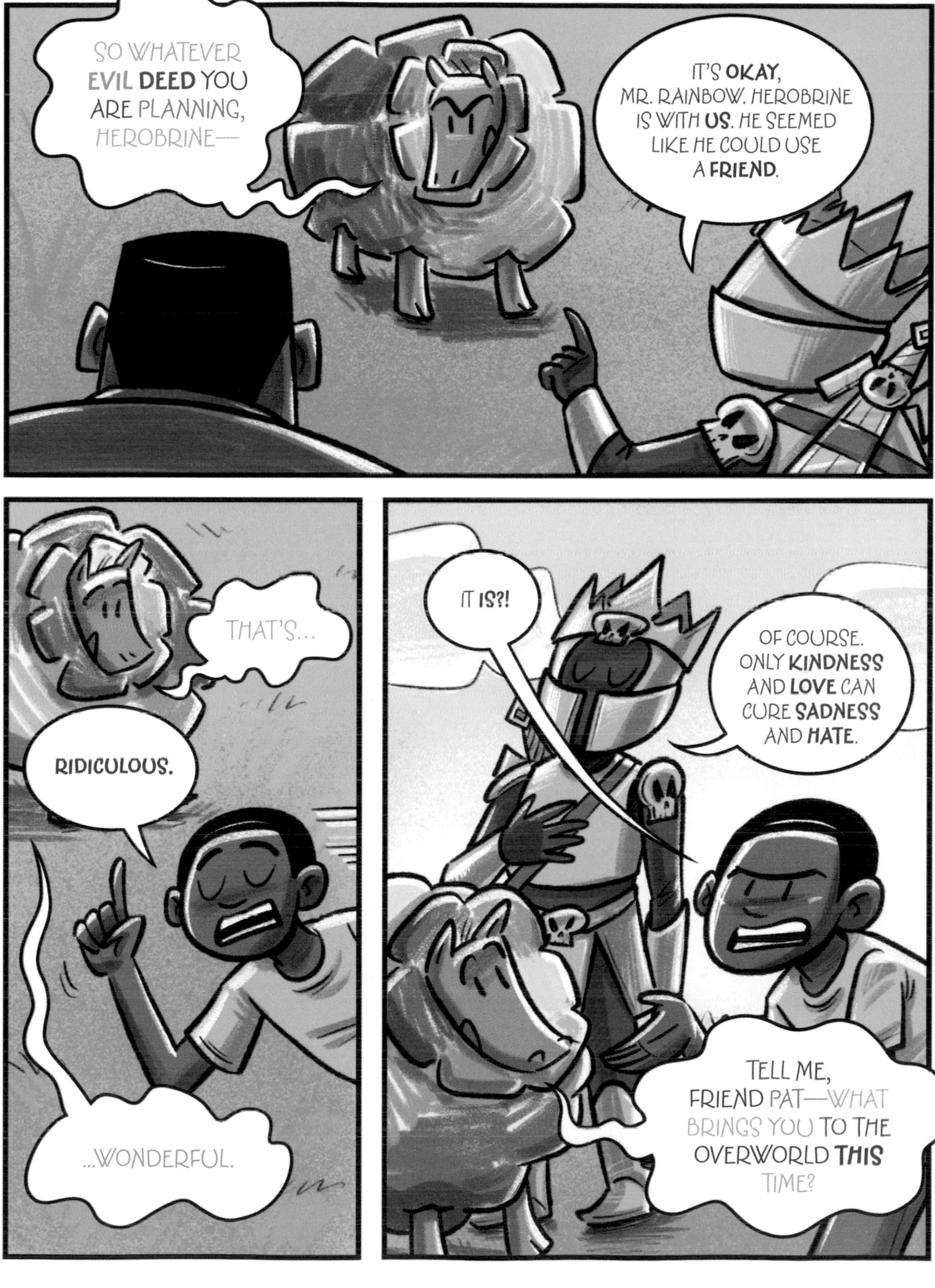
SO WHATEVER EVIL DEED YOU ARE PLANNING, HEROBRINE—
IT'S OKAY, MR. RAINBOW. HEROBRINE IS WITH US. HE SEEMED LIKE HE COULD USE A FRIEND.
THAT'S...
RIDICULOUS.
...WONDERFUL.
IT IS?!
OF COURSE. ONLY KINDNESS AND LOVE CAN CURE SADNESS AND HATE.
TELL ME, FRIEND PAT—WHAT BRINGS YOU TO THE OVERWORLD THIS TIME?

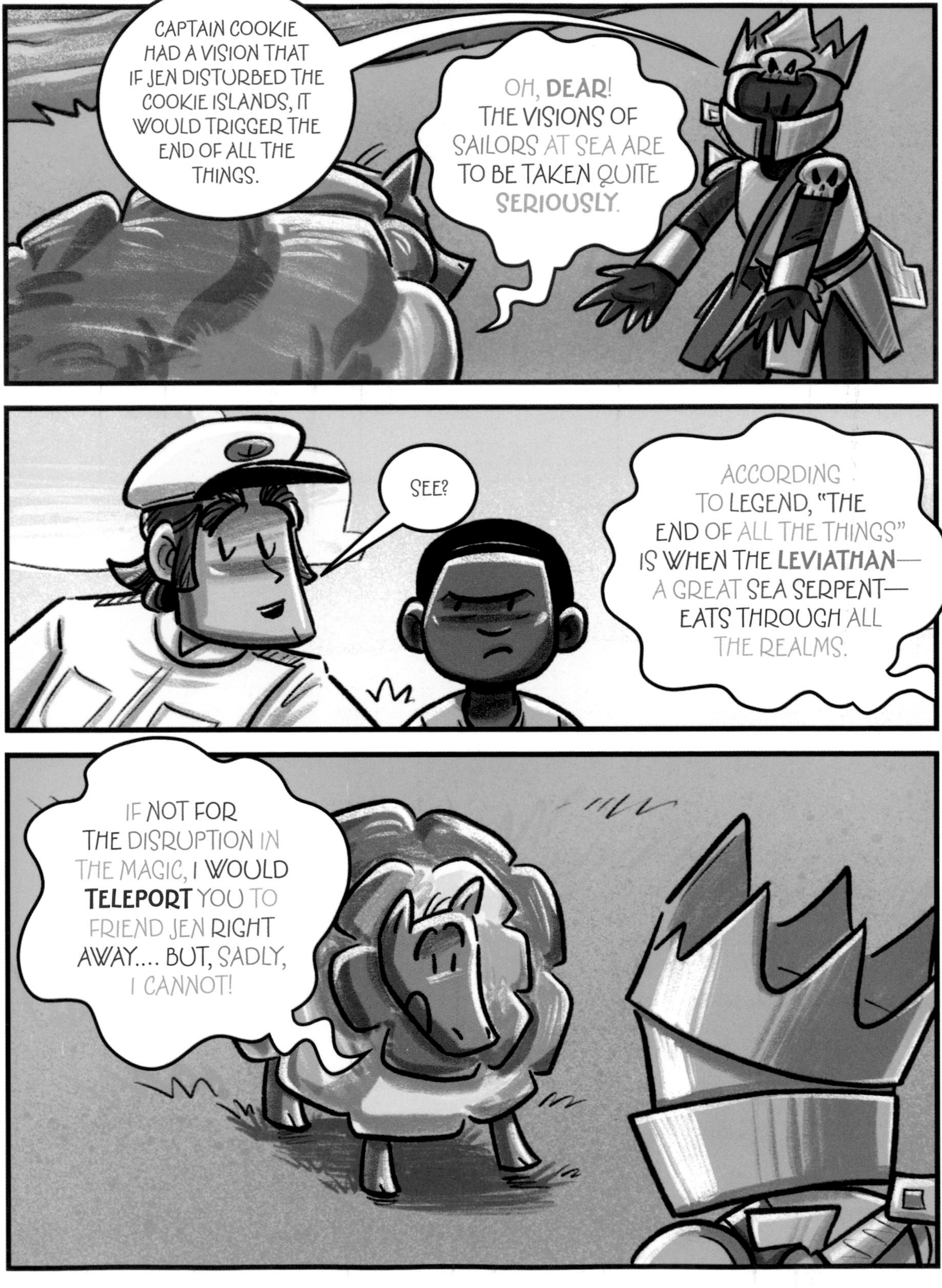
CAPTAIN COOKIE HAD A VISION THAT IF JEN DISTURBED THE COOKIE ISLANDS, IT WOULD TRIGGER THE END OF ALL THE THINGS.
OH, **DEAR**! THE VISIONS OF SAILORS AT SEA ARE TO BE TAKEN QUITE **SERIOUSLY**.
SEE?
ACCORDING TO LEGEND, "THE END OF ALL THE THINGS" IS WHEN THE **LEVIATHAN**—A GREAT SEA SERPENT—EATS THROUGH ALL THE REALMS.
IF NOT FOR THE DISRUPTION IN THE MAGIC, I WOULD **TELEPORT** YOU TO FRIEND JEN RIGHT AWAY.... BUT, SADLY, I CANNOT!

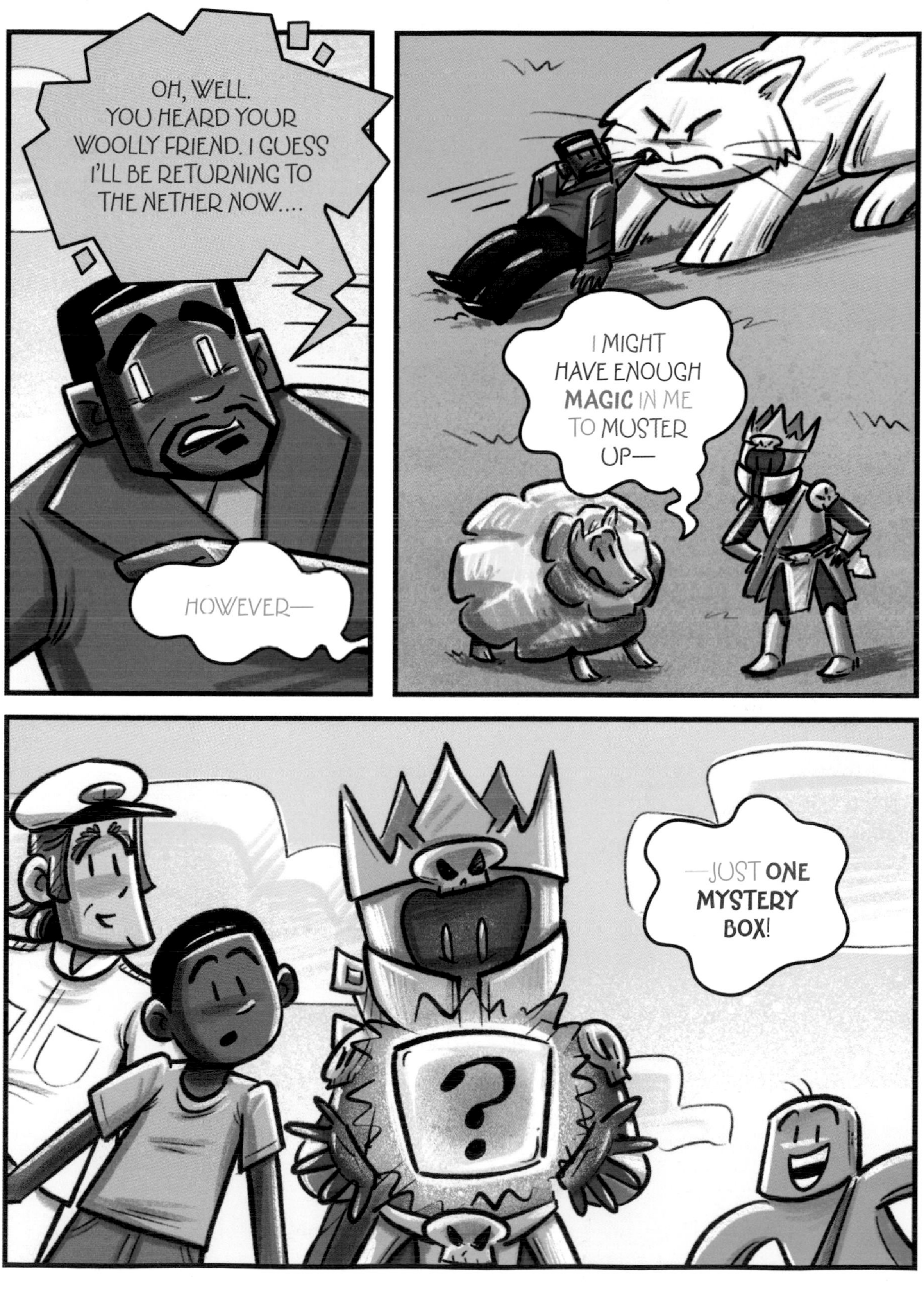
OH, WELL. YOU HEARD YOUR WOOLLY FRIEND. I GUESS I'LL BE RETURNING TO THE NETHER NOW....
HOWEVER—
I MIGHT HAVE ENOUGH MAGIC IN ME TO MUSTER UP—
—JUST ONE MYSTERY BOX!

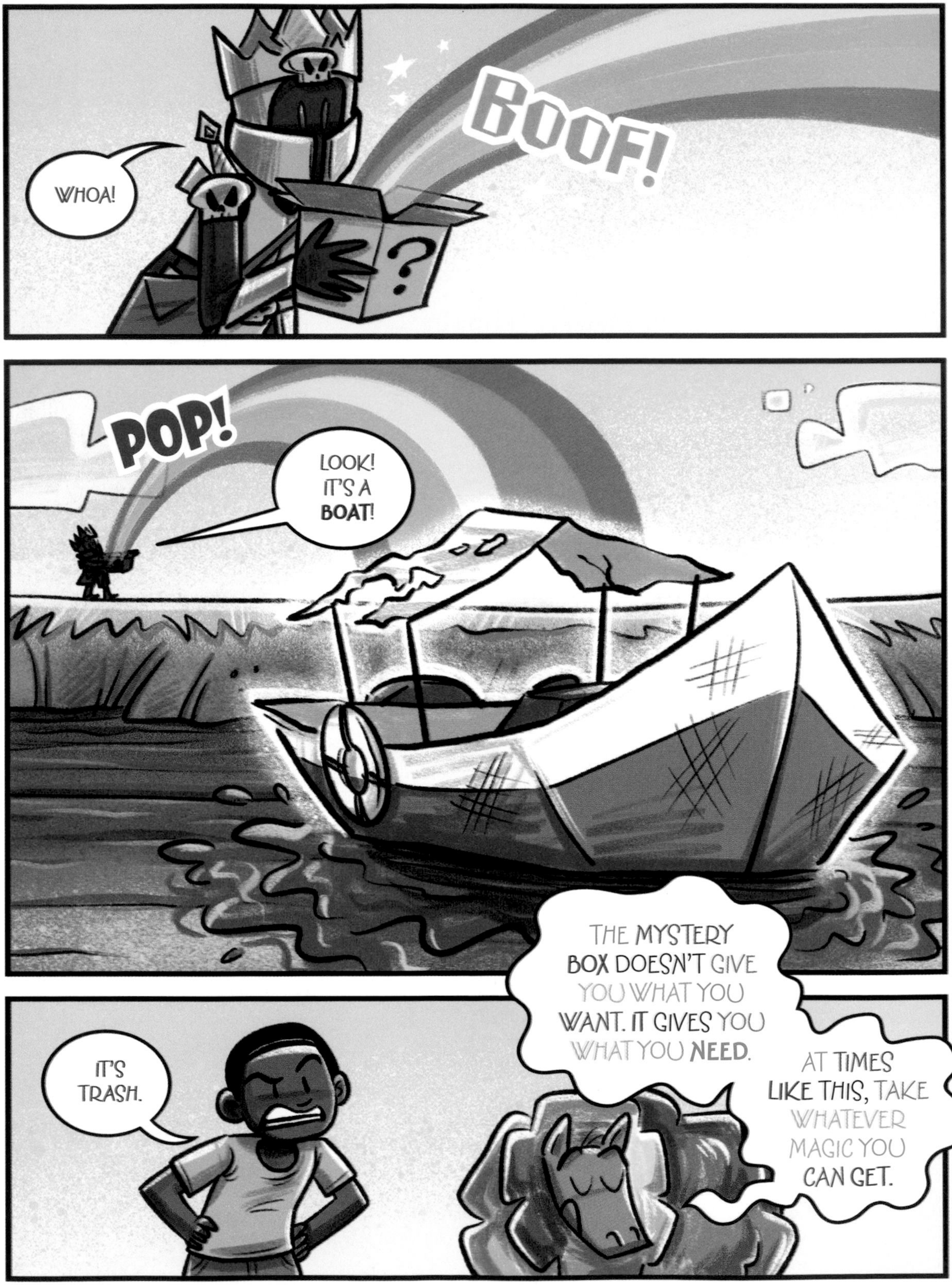
WHOA!
BOOF!
POP!
LOOK! IT'S A BOAT!
IT'S TRASH.
THE MYSTERY BOX DOESN'T GIVE YOU WHAT YOU WANT. IT GIVES YOU WHAT YOU NEED.
AT TIMES LIKE THIS, TAKE WHATEVER MAGIC YOU CAN GET.

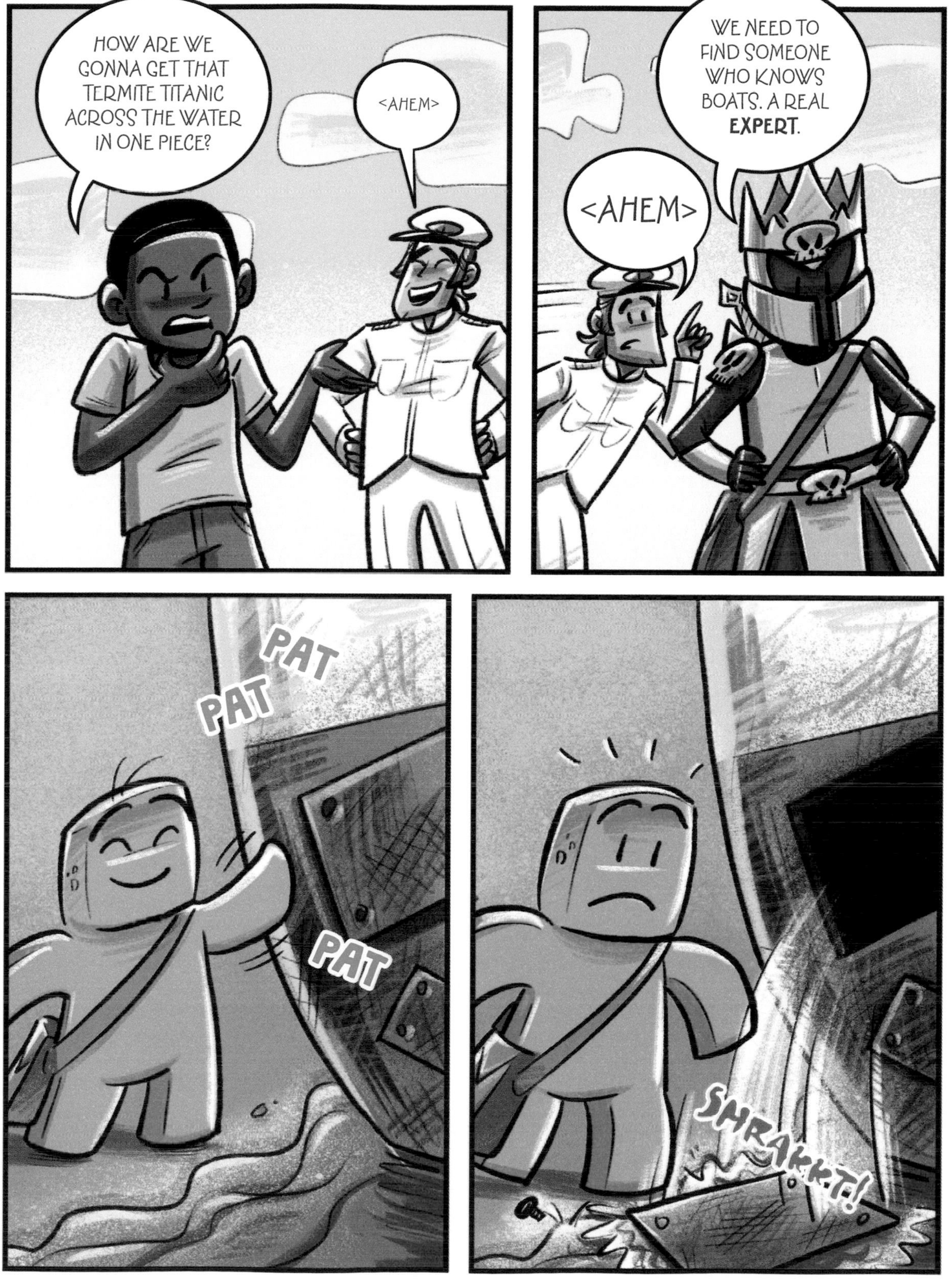
HOW ARE WE GONNA GET THAT TERMITE TITANIC ACROSS THE WATER IN ONE PIECE?
<AHEM>
<AHEM>
WE NEED TO FIND SOMEONE WHO KNOWS BOATS. A REAL **EXPERT**.
PAT
PAT
PAT
SHRAKKT!

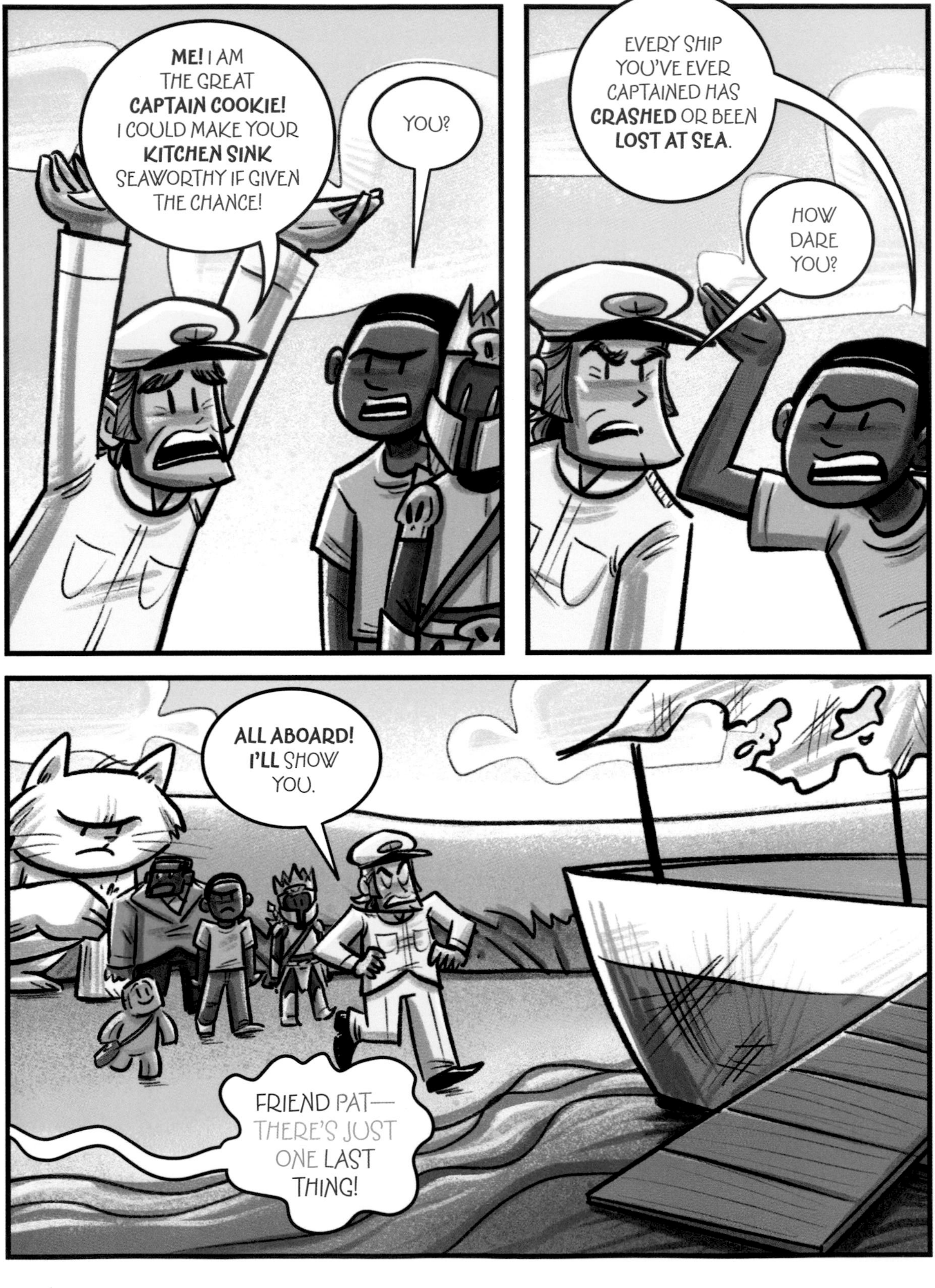
ME! I AM THE GREAT **CAPTAIN COOKIE!** I COULD MAKE YOUR **KITCHEN SINK** SEAWORTHY IF GIVEN THE CHANCE!
YOU?
EVERY SHIP YOU'VE EVER CAPTAINED HAS **CRASHED** OR BEEN **LOST AT SEA**.
HOW DARE YOU?
ALL ABOARD! I'LL SHOW YOU.
FRIEND PAT— THERE'S JUST ONE LAST THING!

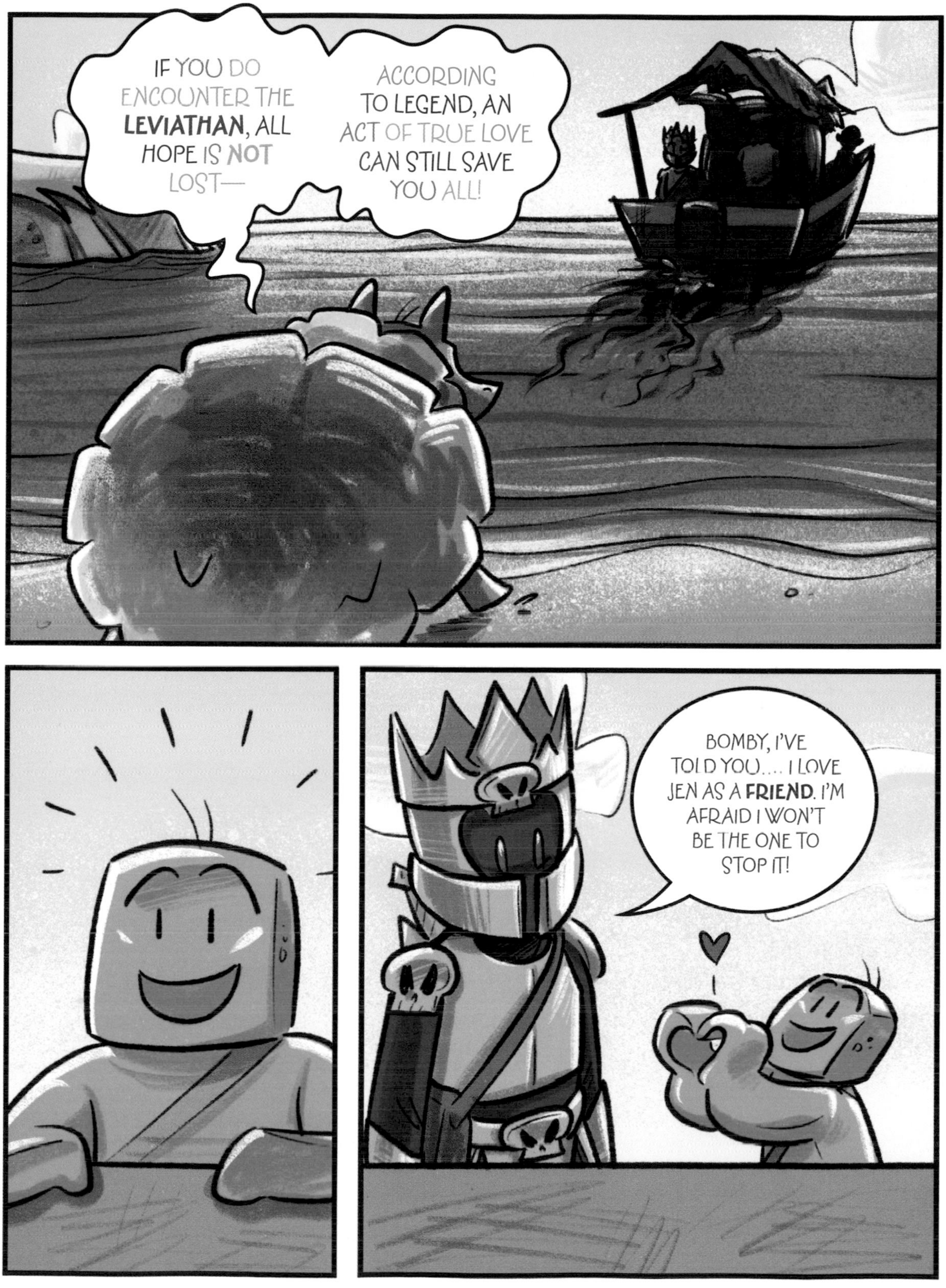
IF YOU DO ENCOUNTER THE LEVIATHAN, ALL HOPE IS NOT LOST—
ACCORDING TO LEGEND, AN ACT OF TRUE LOVE CAN STILL SAVE YOU ALL!
BOMBY, I'VE TOLD YOU.... I LOVE JEN AS A FRIEND. I'M AFRAID I WON'T BE THE ONE TO STOP IT!

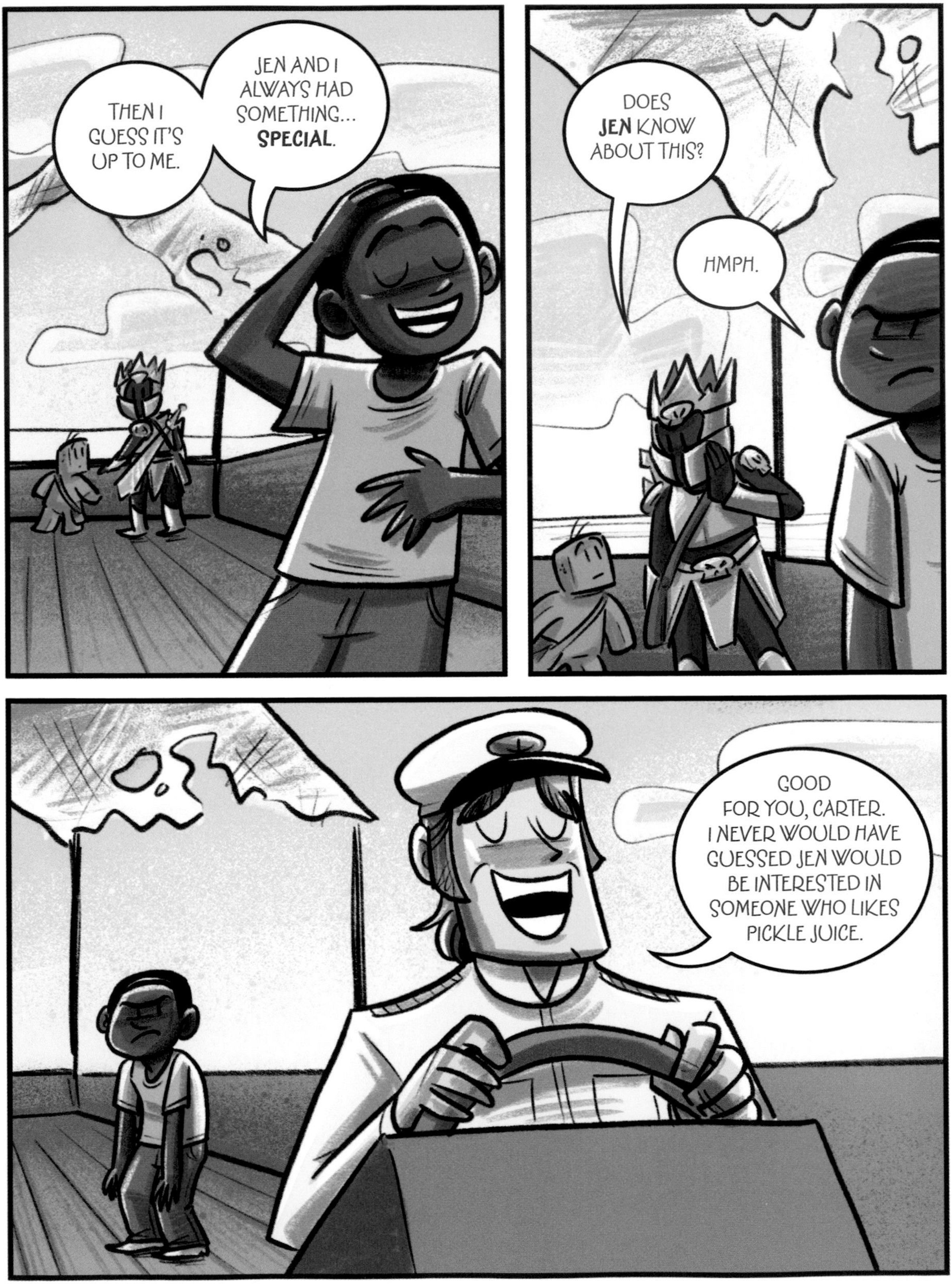
THEN I GUESS IT'S UP TO ME.
JEN AND I ALWAYS HAD SOMETHING... **SPECIAL**.
DOES **JEN** KNOW ABOUT THIS?
HMPH.
GOOD FOR YOU, CARTER. I NEVER WOULD HAVE GUESSED JEN WOULD BE INTERESTED IN SOMEONE WHO LIKES PICKLE JUICE.

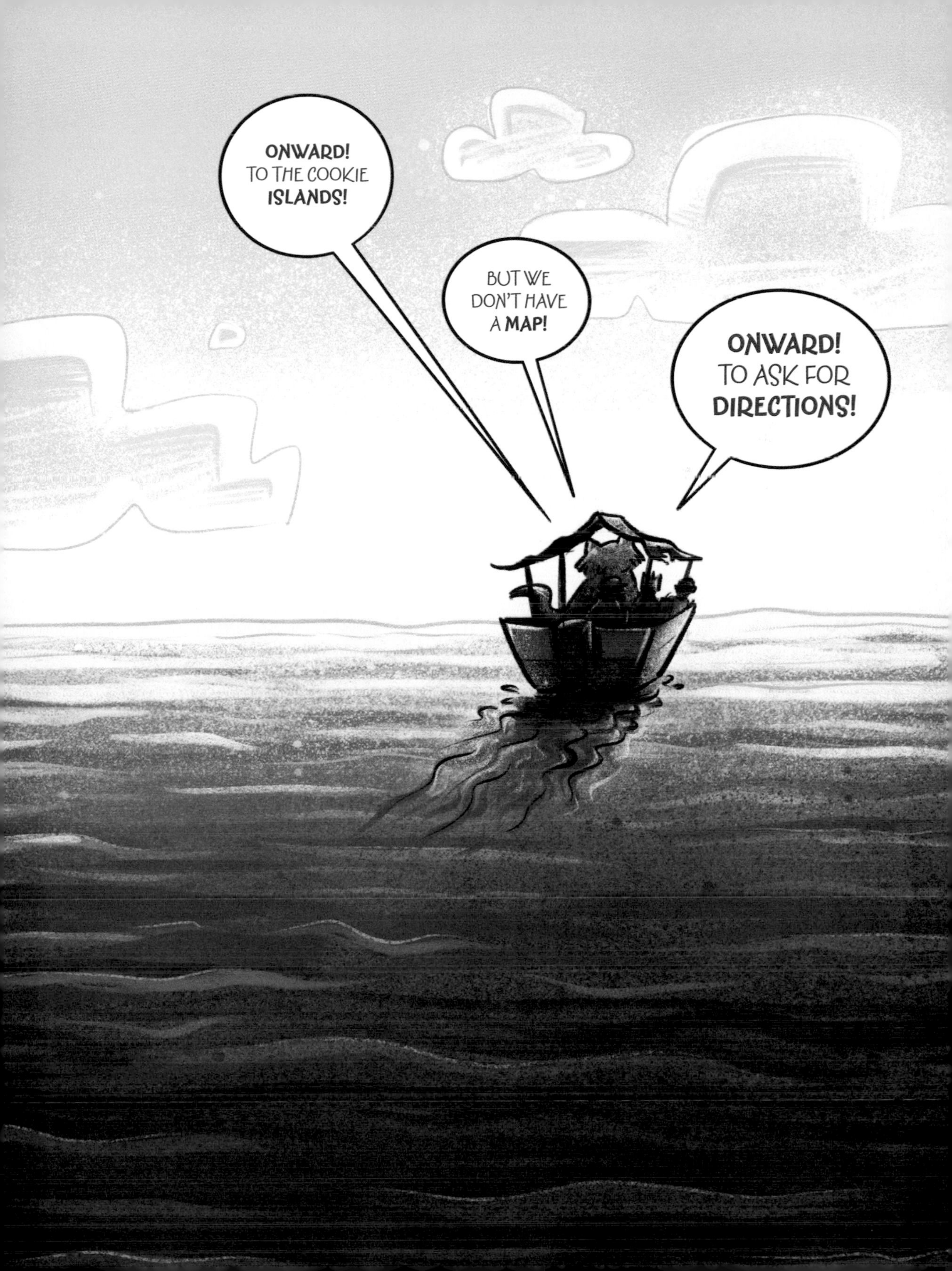

ONWARD! TO THE COOKIE ISLANDS!
BUT WE DON'T HAVE A MAP!
ONWARD! TO ASK FOR DIRECTIONS!

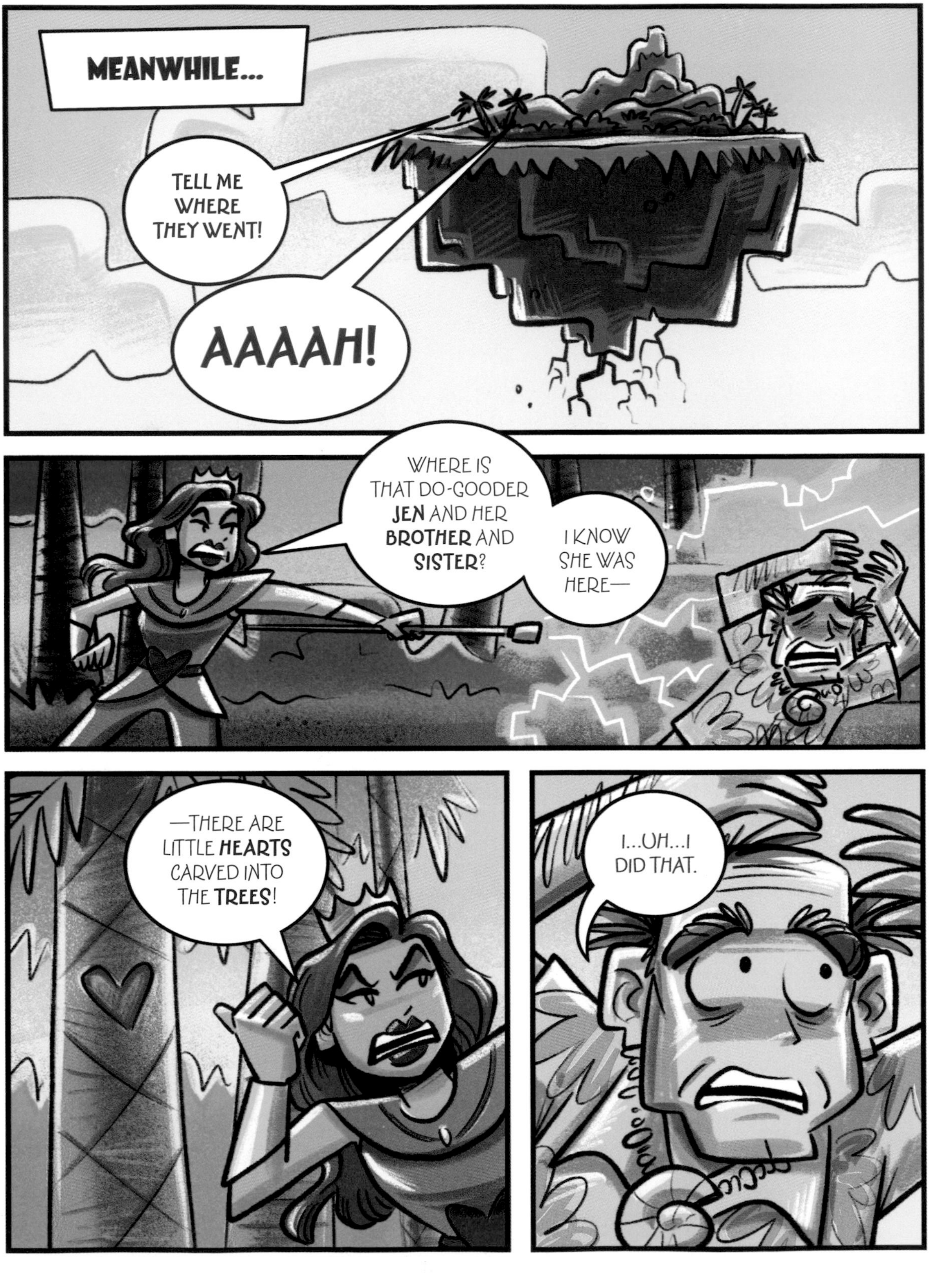
MEANWHILE...
TELL ME WHERE THEY WENT!
AAAAH!
WHERE IS THAT DO-GOODER JEN AND HER BROTHER AND SISTER?
I KNOW SHE WAS HERE—
—THERE ARE LITTLE HEARTS CARVED INTO THE TREES!
I...UH...I DID THAT.

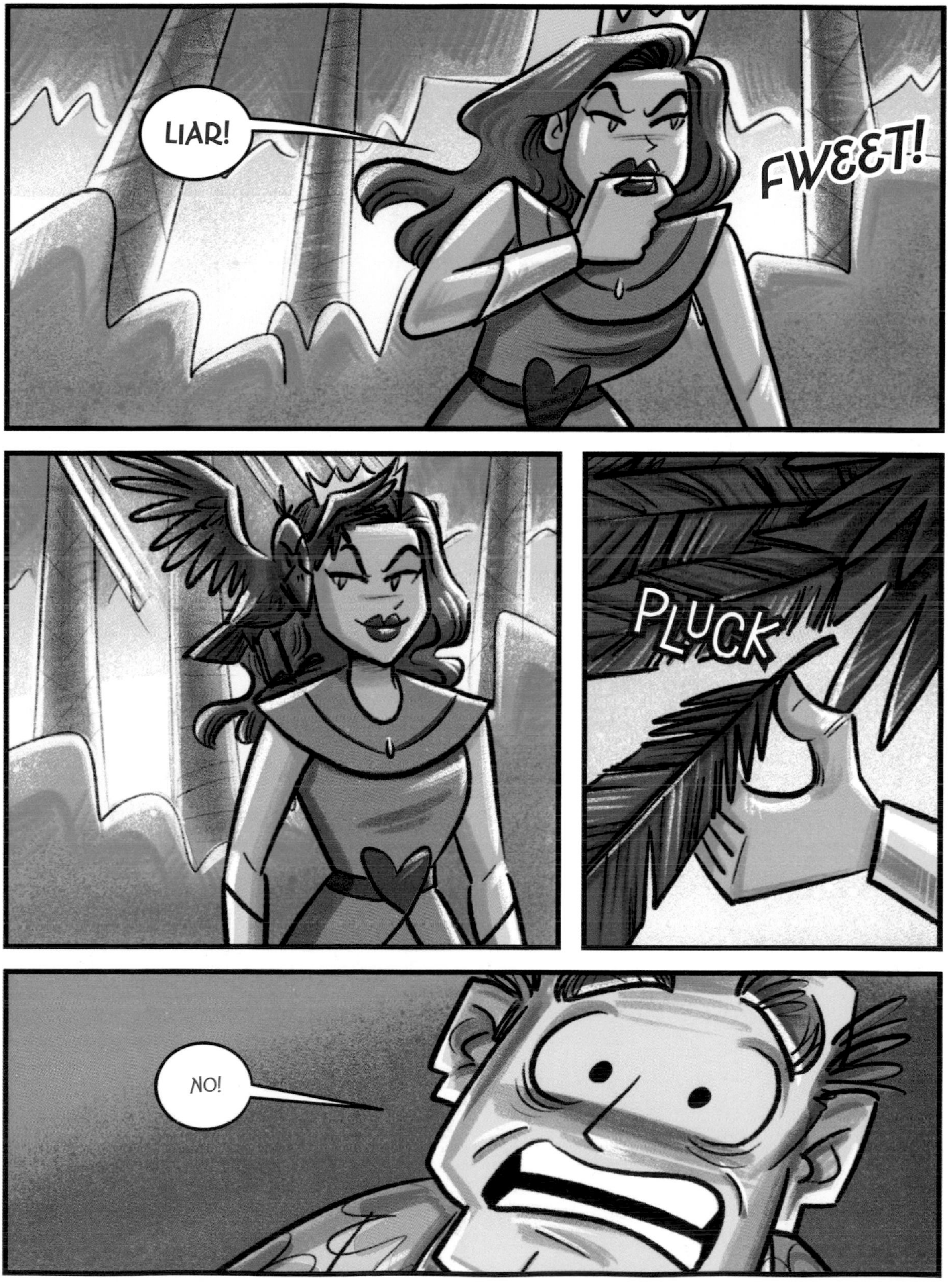
LIAR!
FWEET!
PLUCK
NO!

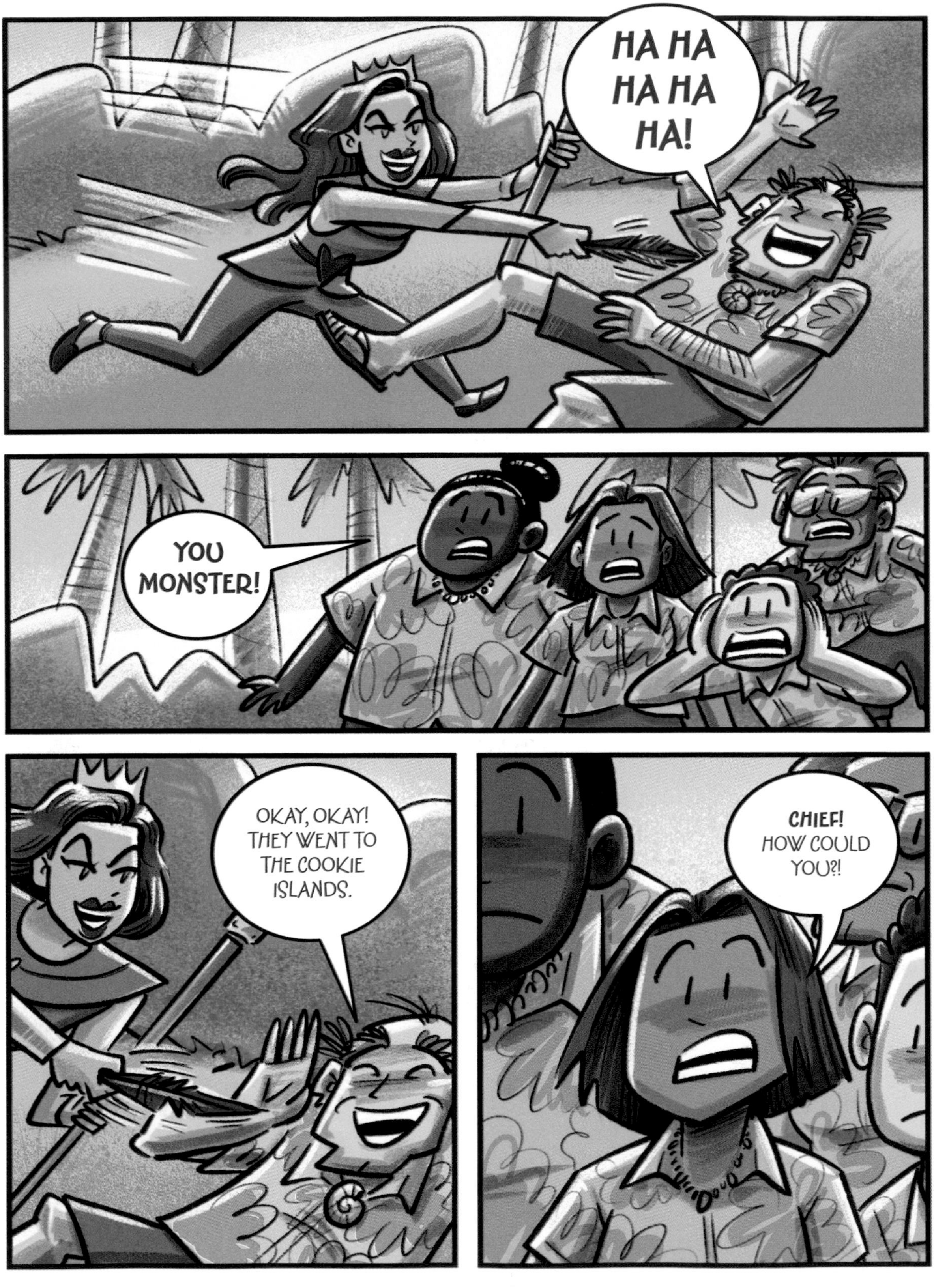
HA HA HA HA HA!
YOU MONSTER!
OKAY, OKAY! THEY WENT TO THE COOKIE ISLANDS.
CHIEF! HOW COULD YOU?!

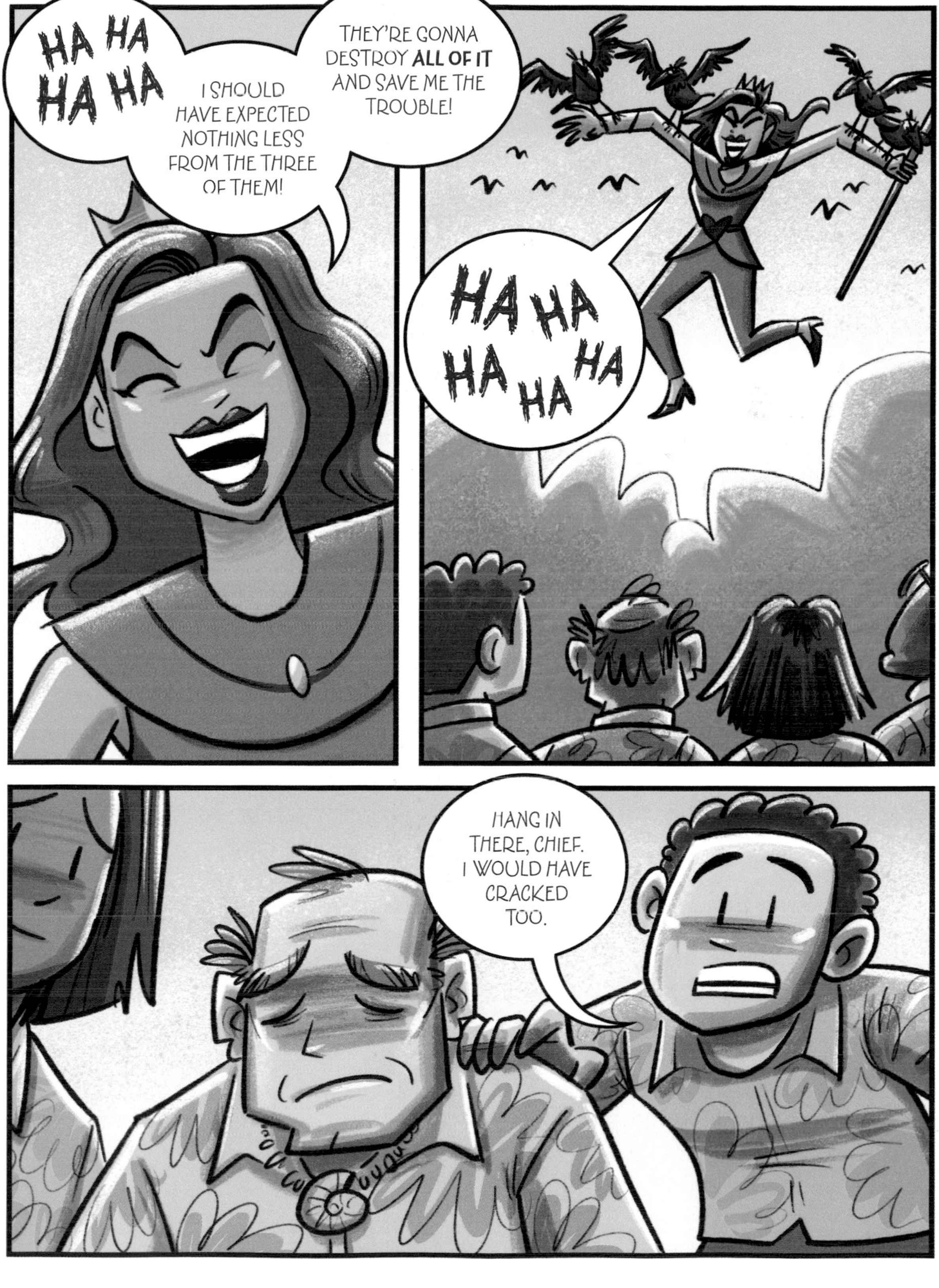
HA HA HA HA
I SHOULD HAVE EXPECTED NOTHING LESS FROM THE THREE OF THEM!
THEY'RE GONNA DESTROY **ALL OF IT** AND SAVE ME THE TROUBLE!
HA HA HA HA HA HA
HANG IN THERE, CHIEF. I WOULD HAVE CRACKED TOO.

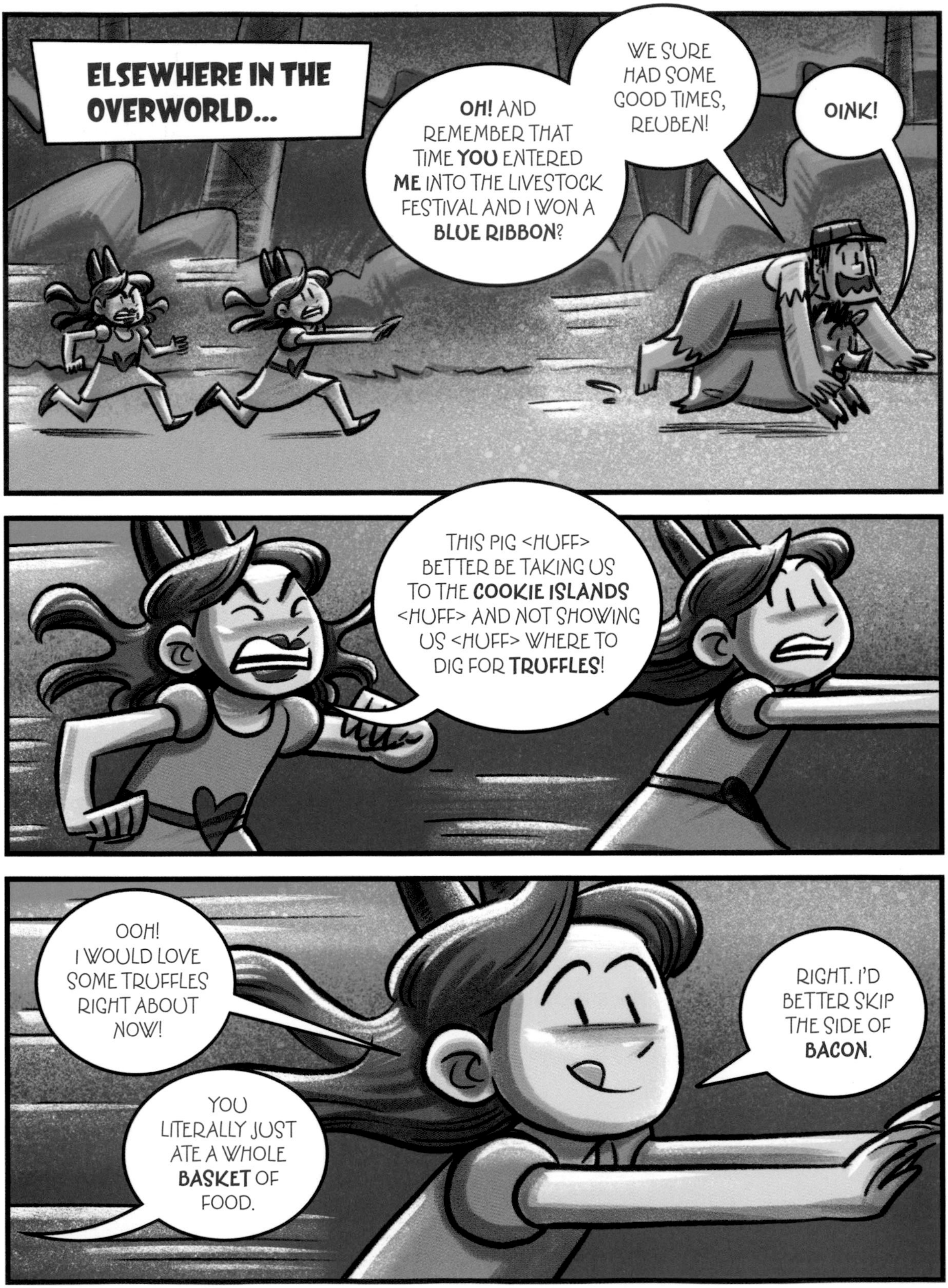
ELSEWHERE IN THE OVERWORLD...
WE SURE HAD SOME GOOD TIMES, REUBEN!
OH! AND REMEMBER THAT TIME YOU ENTERED ME INTO THE LIVESTOCK FESTIVAL AND I WON A BLUE RIBBON?
OINK!
THIS PIG <HUFF> BETTER BE TAKING US TO THE COOKIE ISLANDS <HUFF> AND NOT SHOWING US <HUFF> WHERE TO DIG FOR TRUFFLES!
OOH! I WOULD LOVE SOME TRUFFLES RIGHT ABOUT NOW!
YOU LITERALLY JUST ATE A WHOLE BASKET OF FOOD.
RIGHT. I'D BETTER SKIP THE SIDE OF BACON.

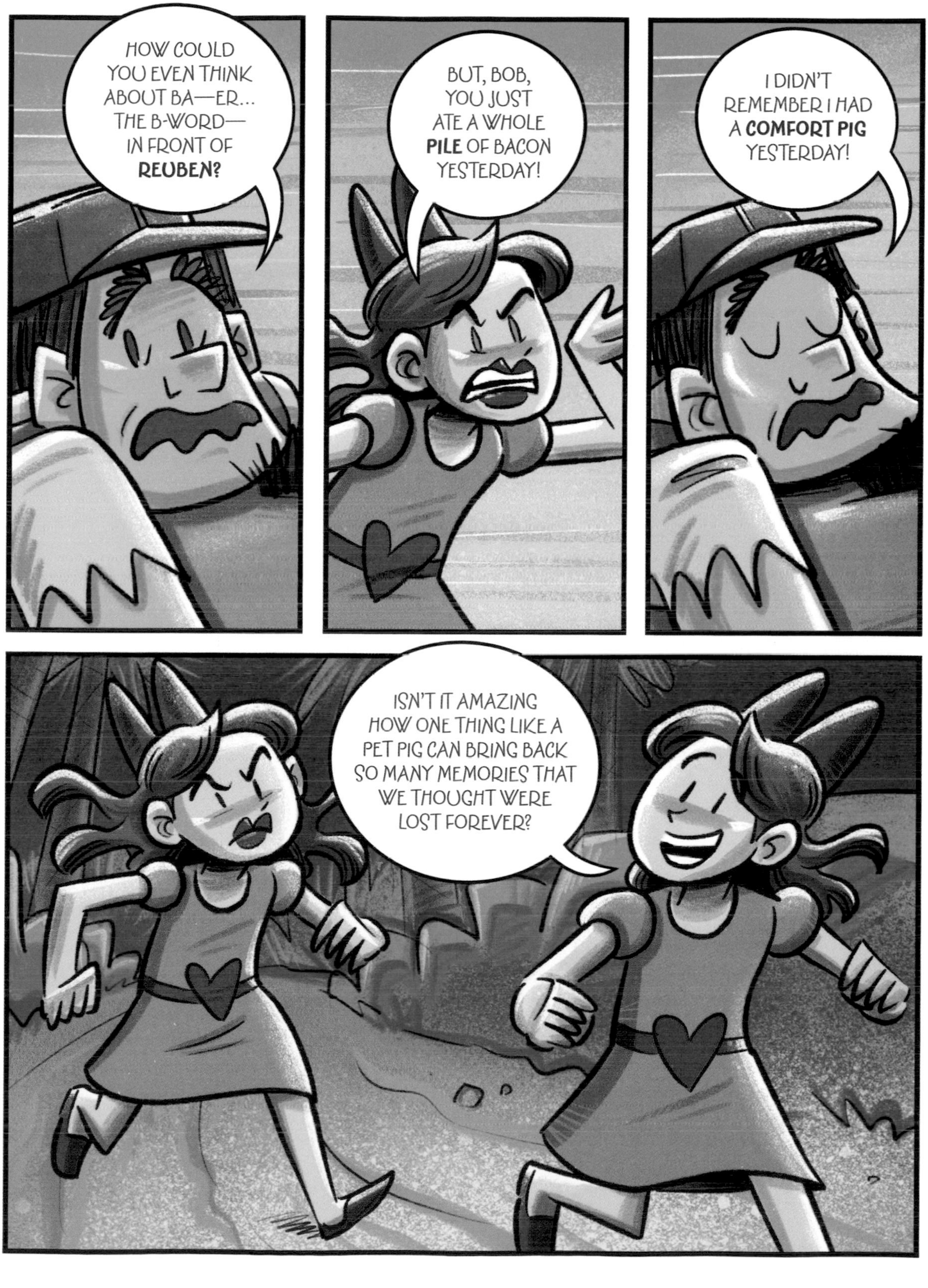

HOW COULD YOU EVEN THINK ABOUT BA—ER... THE B-WORD— IN FRONT OF **REUBEN?**
BUT, BOB, YOU JUST ATE A WHOLE **PILE** OF BACON YESTERDAY!
I DIDN'T REMEMBER I HAD A **COMFORT PIG** YESTERDAY!
ISN'T IT AMAZING HOW ONE THING LIKE A PET PIG CAN BRING BACK SO MANY MEMORIES THAT WE THOUGHT WERE LOST FOREVER?

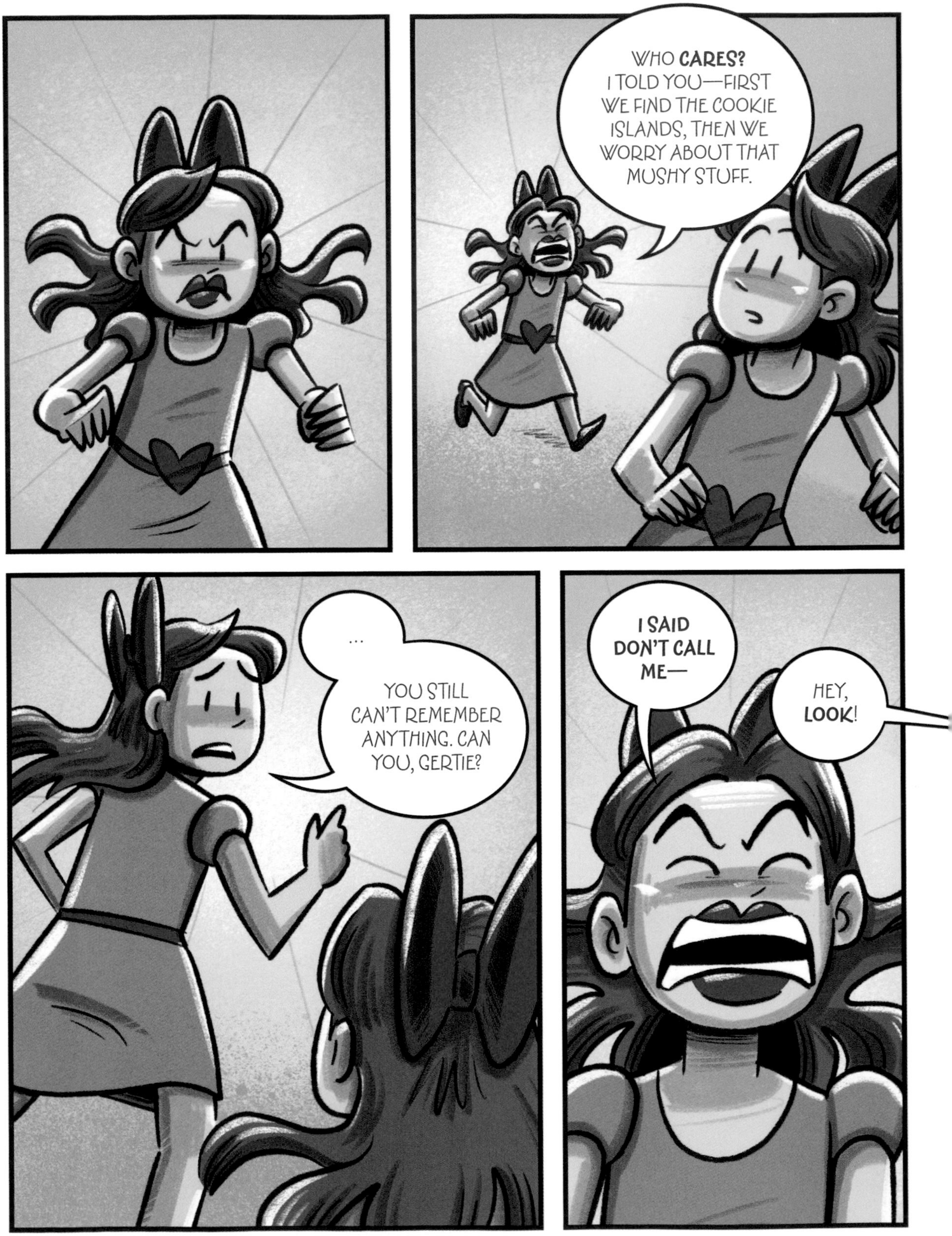
WHO **CARES?** I TOLD YOU—FIRST WE FIND THE COOKIE ISLANDS, THEN WE WORRY ABOUT THAT MUSHY STUFF.
...
YOU STILL CAN'T REMEMBER ANYTHING. CAN YOU, GERTIE?
I SAID DON'T CALL ME—
HEY, **LOOK**!

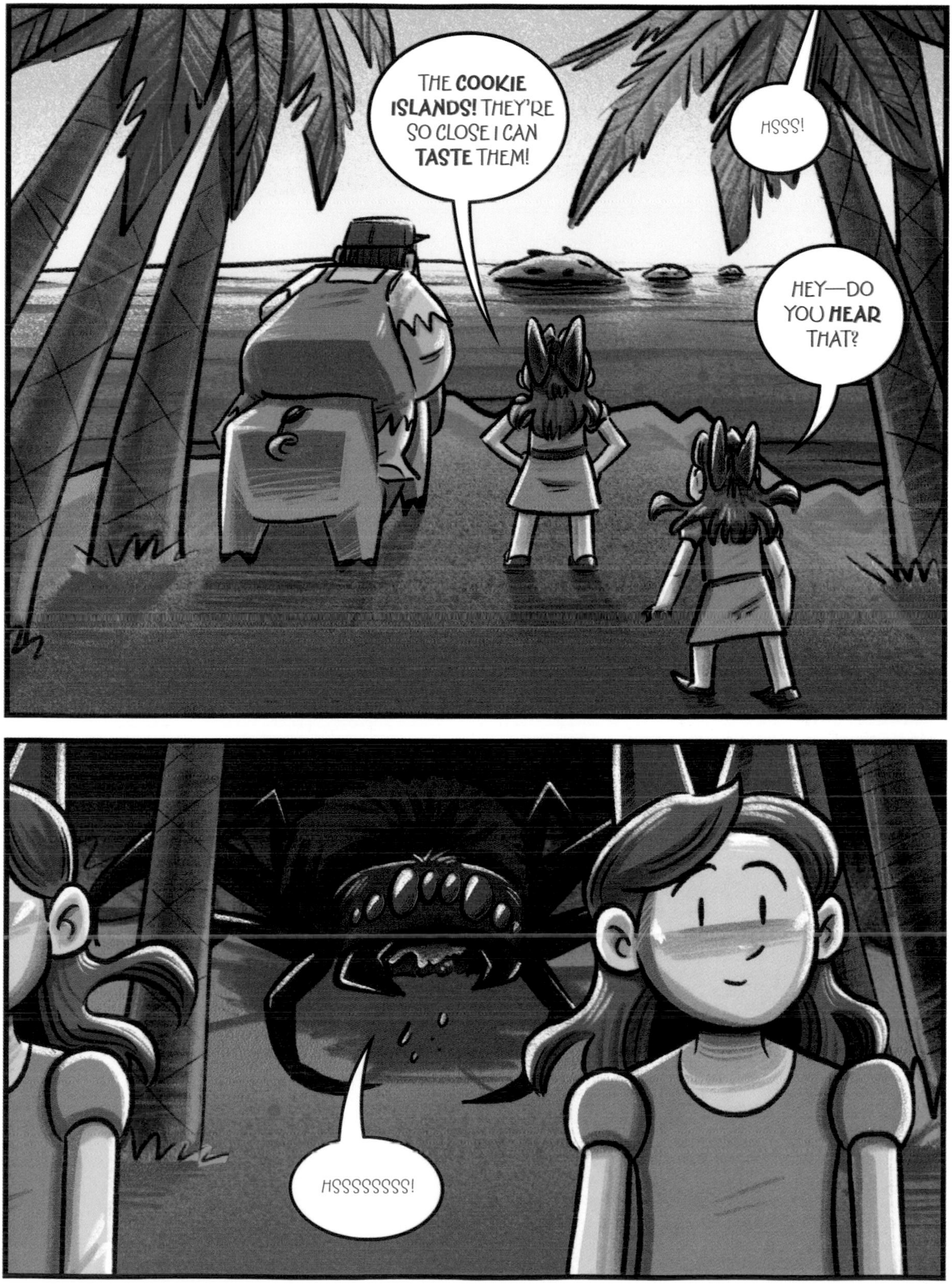
THE **COOKIE ISLANDS!** THEY'RE SO CLOSE I CAN **TASTE** THEM!
HSSS!
HEY—DO YOU **HEAR** THAT?
HSSSSSSSS!

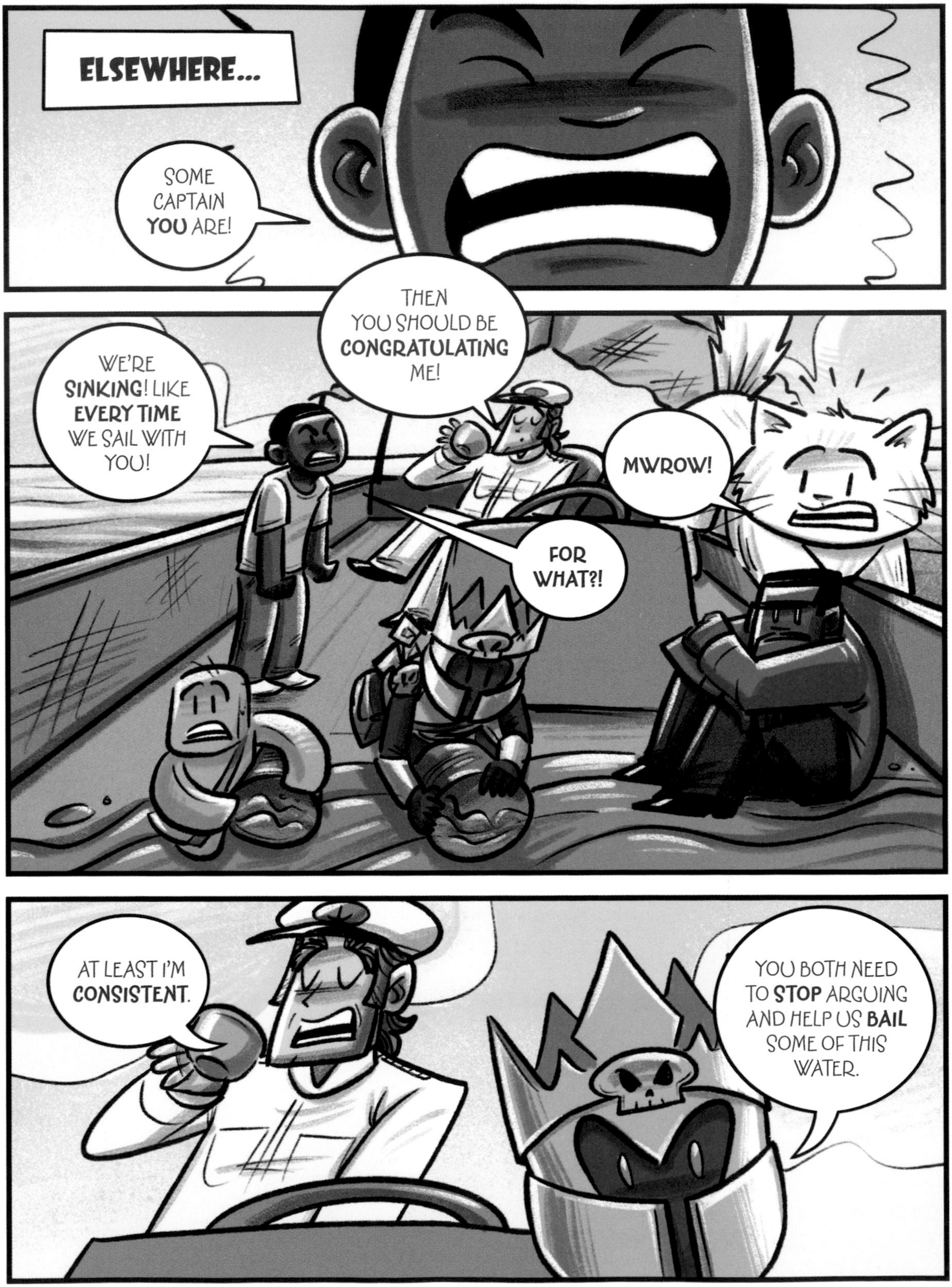
ELSEWHERE...
SOME CAPTAIN **YOU** ARE!
WE'RE **SINKING**! LIKE **EVERY TIME** WE SAIL WITH YOU!
THEN YOU SHOULD BE **CONGRATULATING** ME!
FOR WHAT?!
MWROW!
AT LEAST I'M **CONSISTENT**.
YOU BOTH NEED TO **STOP** ARGUING AND HELP US **BAIL** SOME OF THIS WATER.

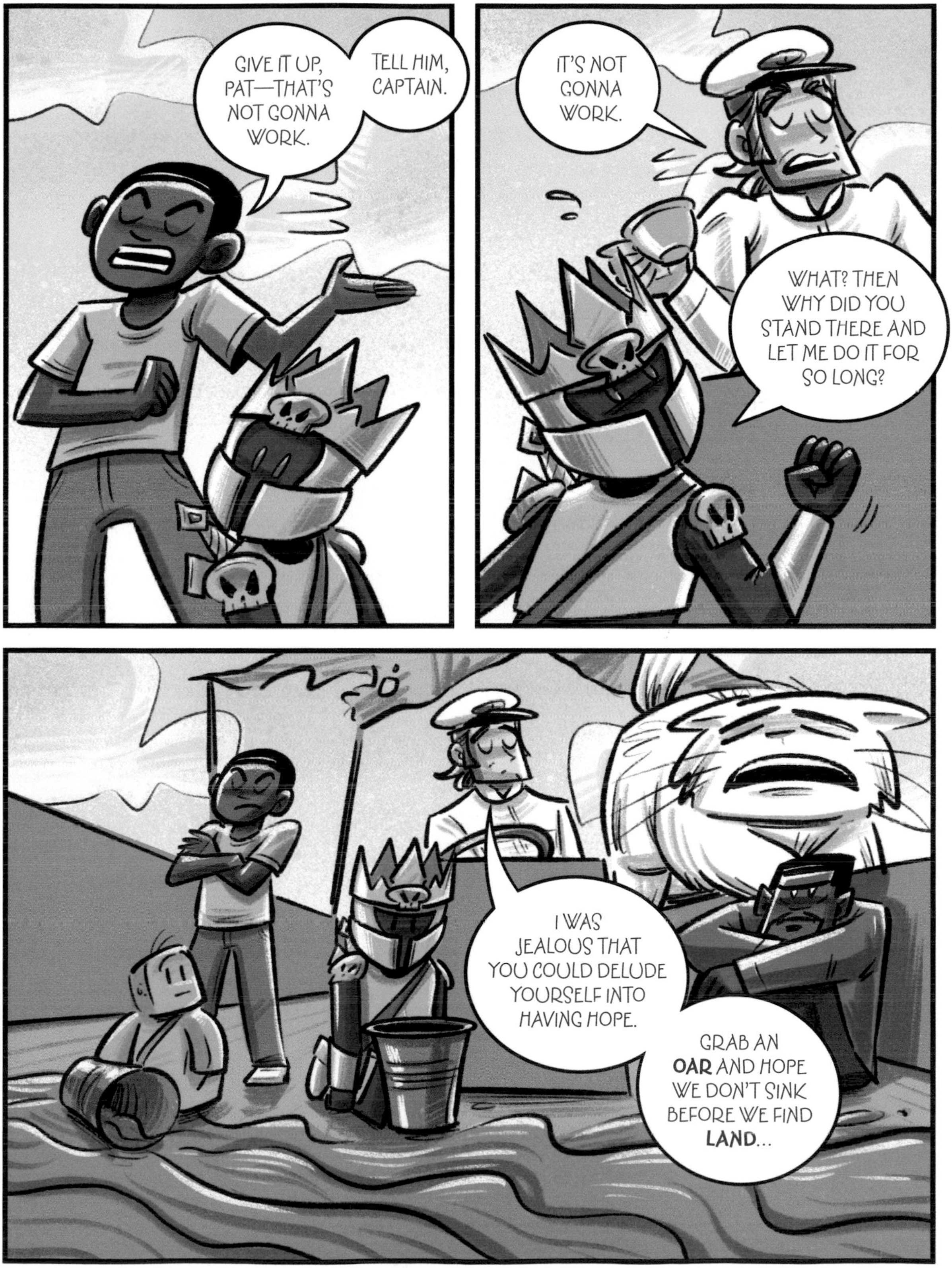
GIVE IT UP, PAT—THAT'S NOT GONNA WORK.
TELL HIM, CAPTAIN.
IT'S NOT GONNA WORK.
WHAT? THEN WHY DID YOU STAND THERE AND LET ME DO IT FOR SO LONG?
I WAS JEALOUS THAT YOU COULD DELUDE YOURSELF INTO HAVING HOPE.
GRAB AN **OAR** AND HOPE WE DON'T SINK BEFORE WE FIND **LAND**...

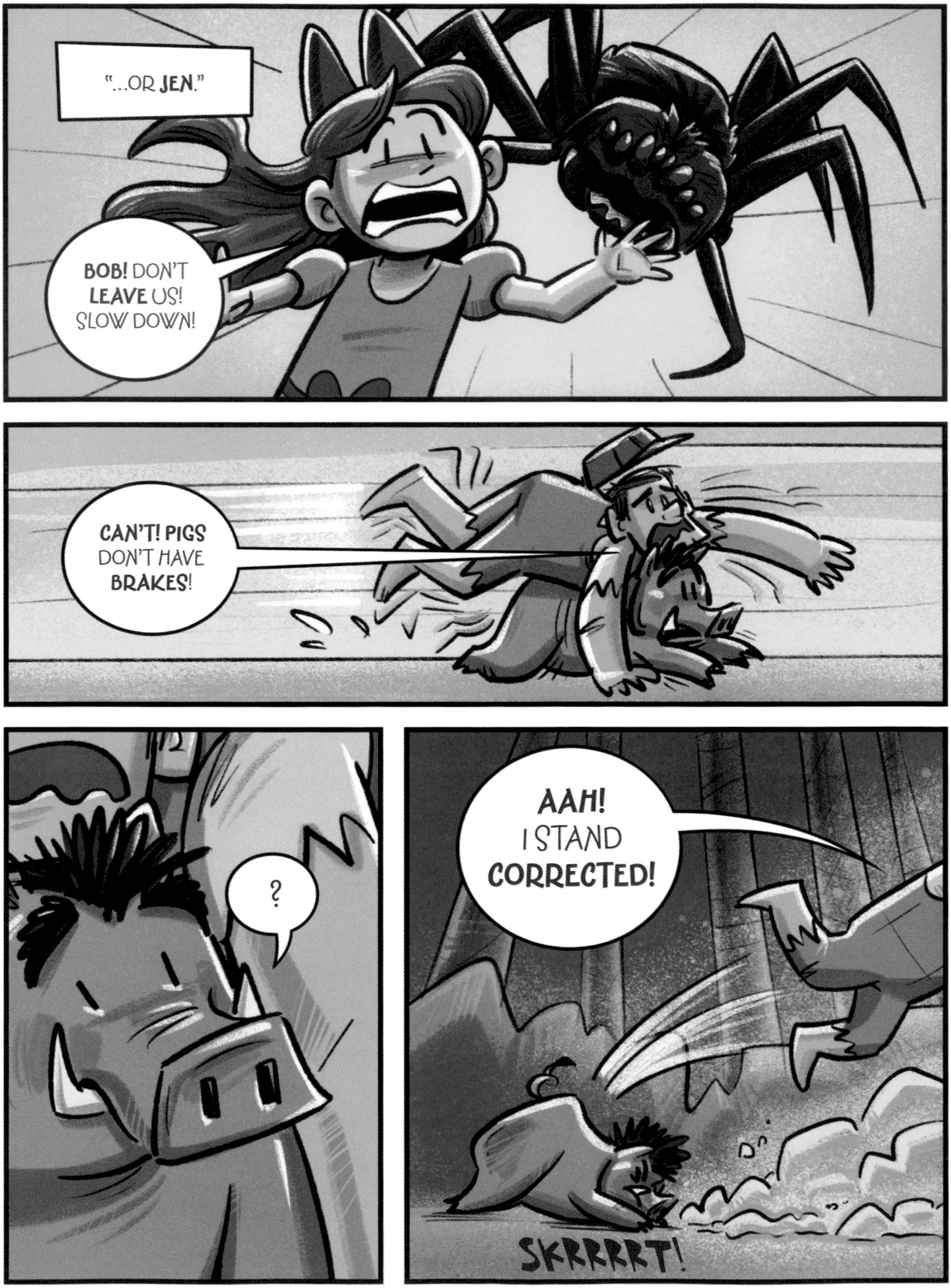

"...OR JEN."
BOB! DON'T LEAVE US! SLOW DOWN!
CAN'T! PIGS DON'T HAVE BRAKES!
?
AAH! I STAND CORRECTED!
SKRRRRT!

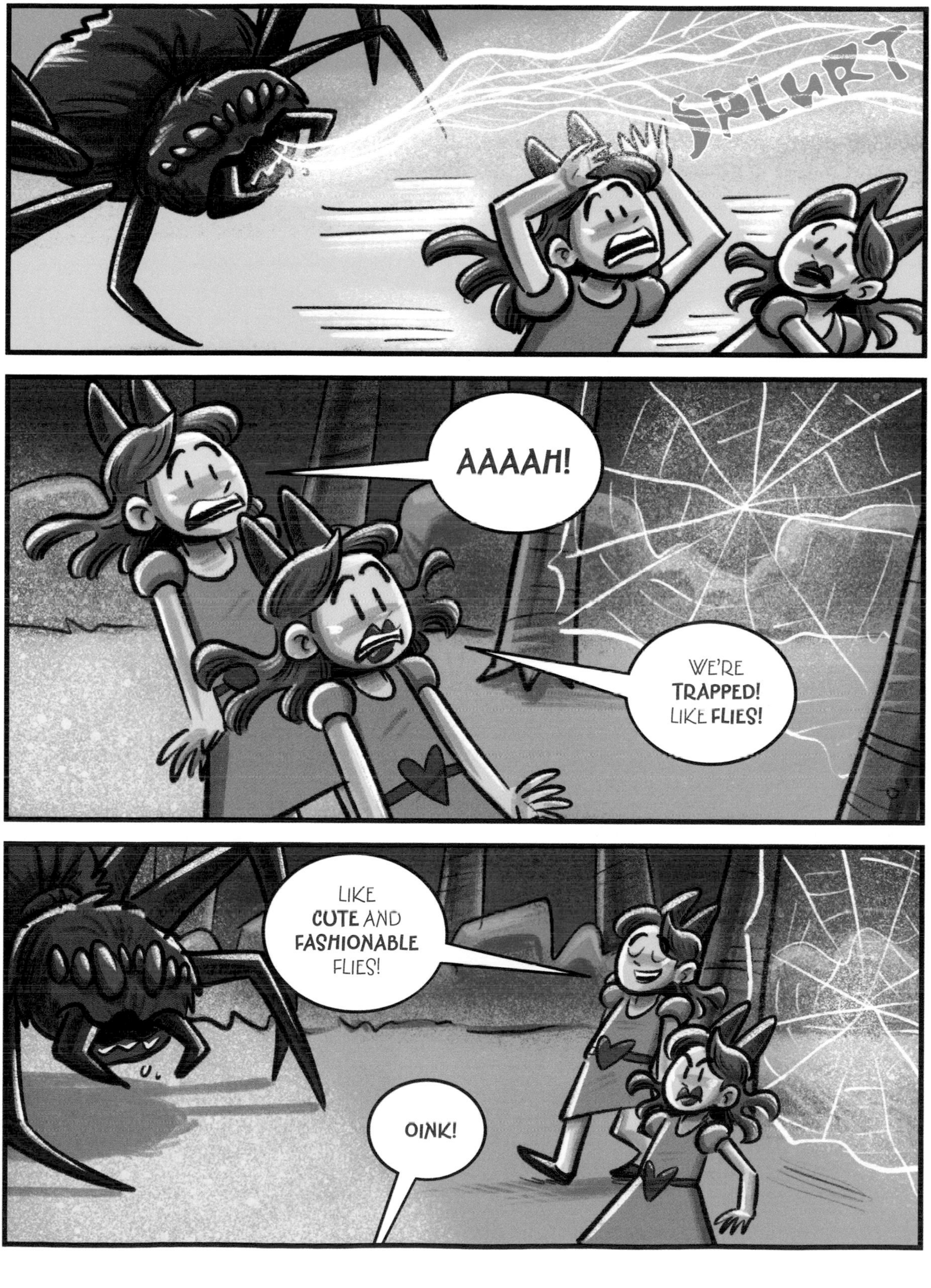
SPLURT
AAAAH!
WE'RE TRAPPED! LIKE FLIES!
LIKE CUTE AND FASHIONABLE FLIES!
OINK!

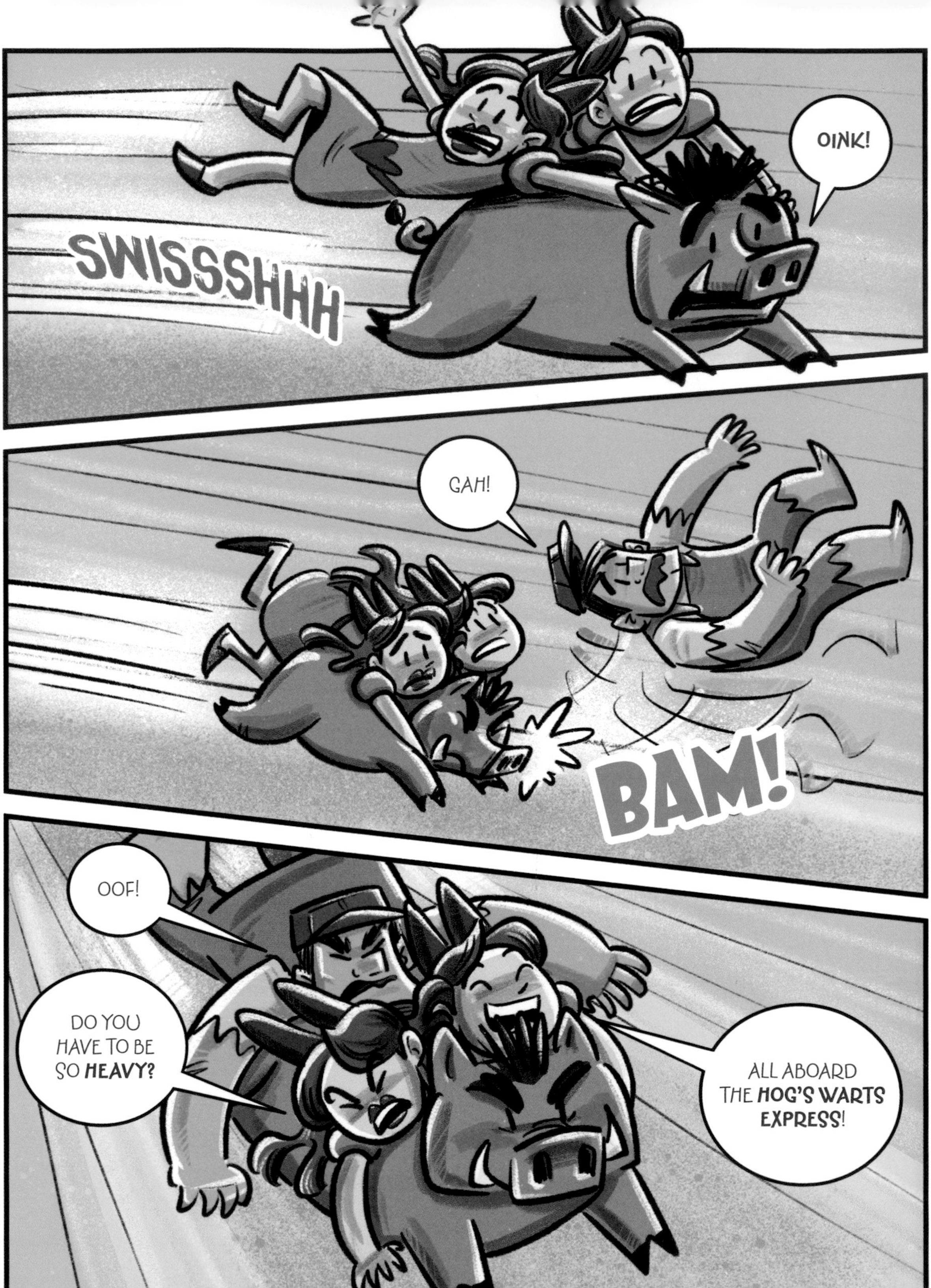
OINK!
SWISSSHHH
GAH!
BAM!
OOF!
DO YOU HAVE TO BE SO **HEAVY?**
ALL ABOARD THE **HOG'S WARTS EXPRESS!**

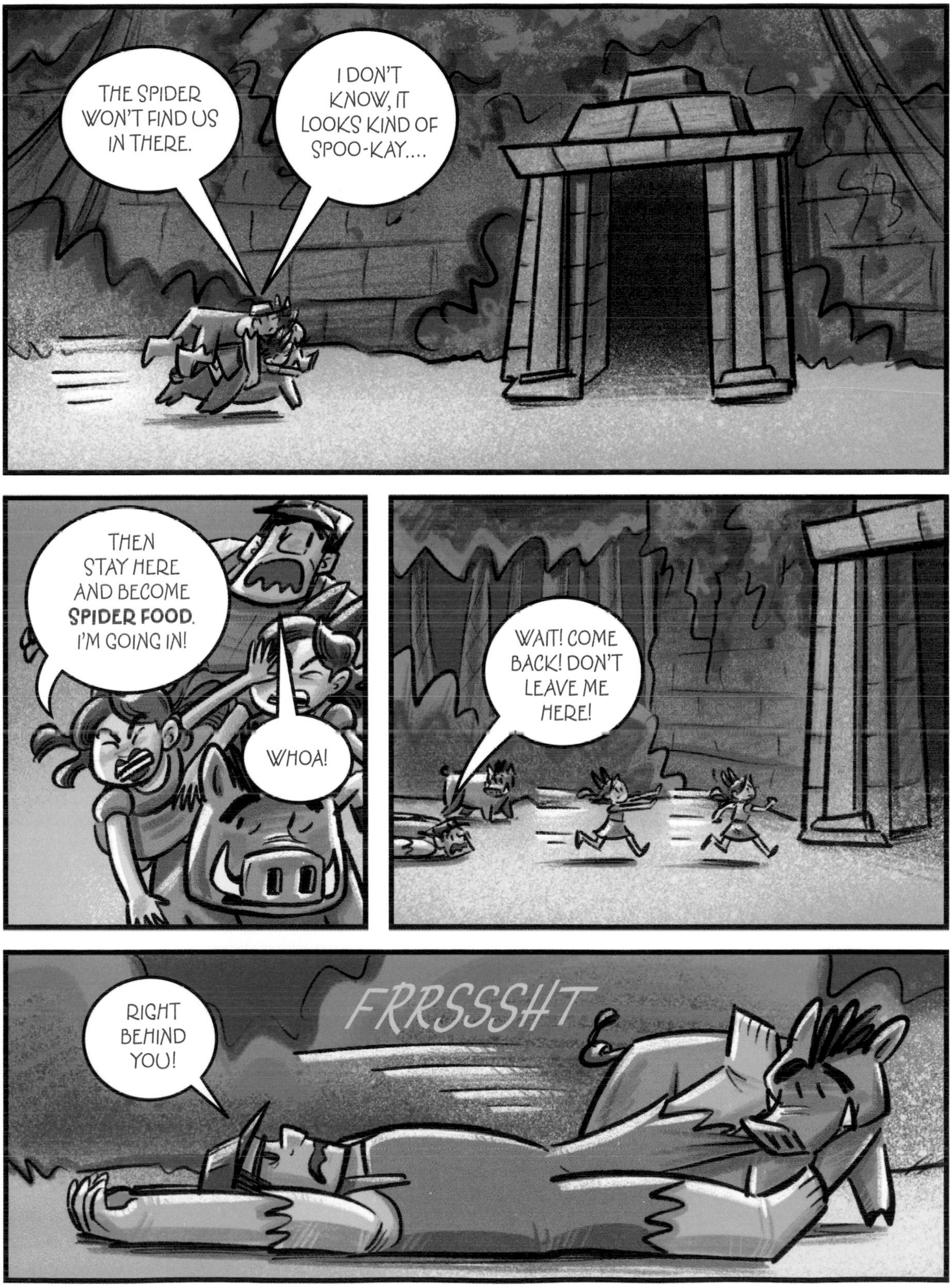
THE SPIDER WON'T FIND US IN THERE.
I DON'T KNOW, IT LOOKS KIND OF SPOO-KAY....
THEN STAY HERE AND BECOME **SPIDER FOOD**. I'M GOING IN!
WHOA!
WAIT! COME BACK! DON'T LEAVE ME HERE!
FRRSSSHT
RIGHT BEHIND YOU!

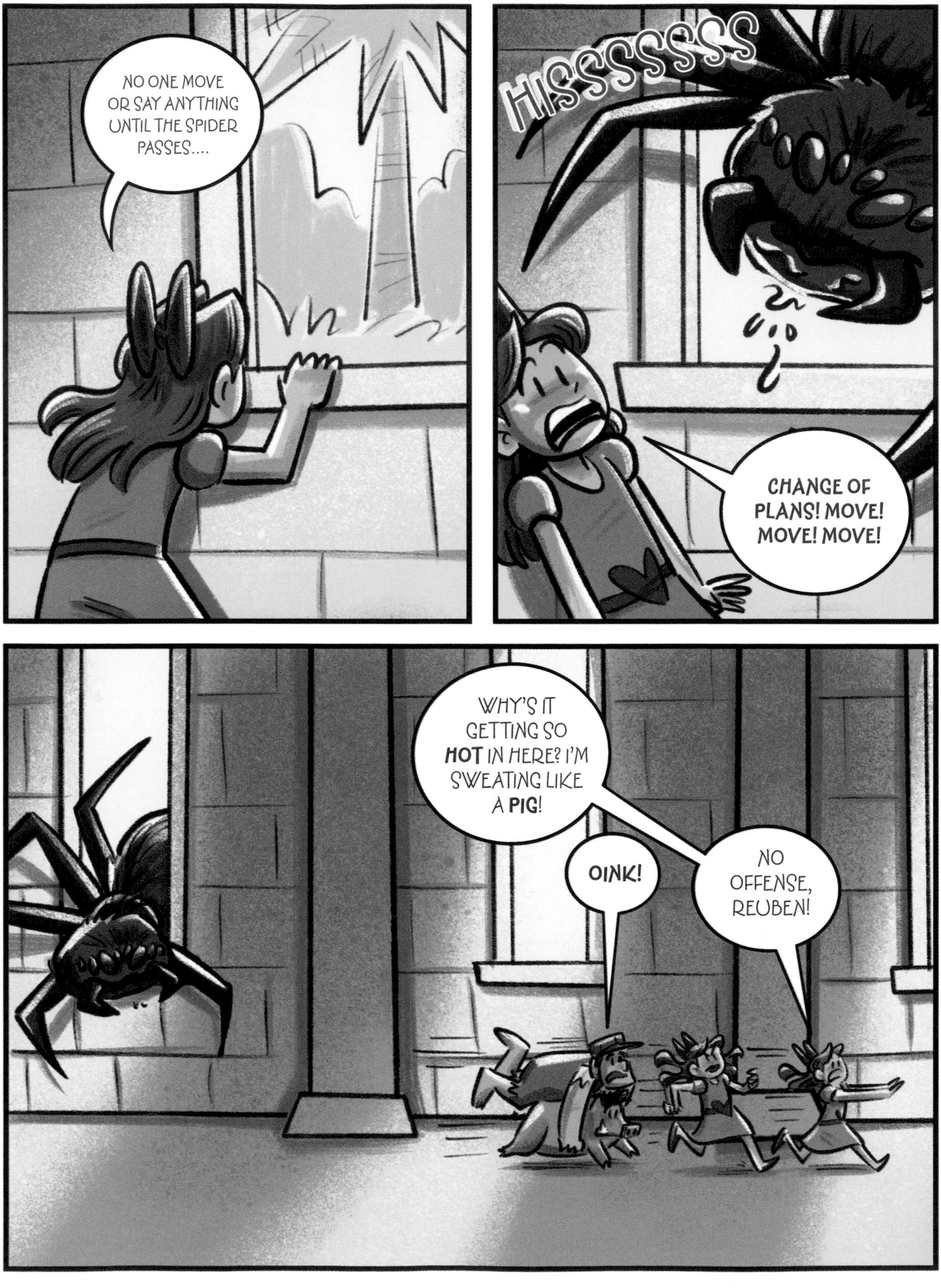
NO ONE MOVE OR SAY ANYTHING UNTIL THE SPIDER PASSES....
HISSSSSSS
CHANGE OF PLANS! MOVE! MOVE! MOVE!
WHY'S IT GETTING SO HOT IN HERE? I'M SWEATING LIKE A PIG!
OINK!
NO OFFENSE, REUBEN!

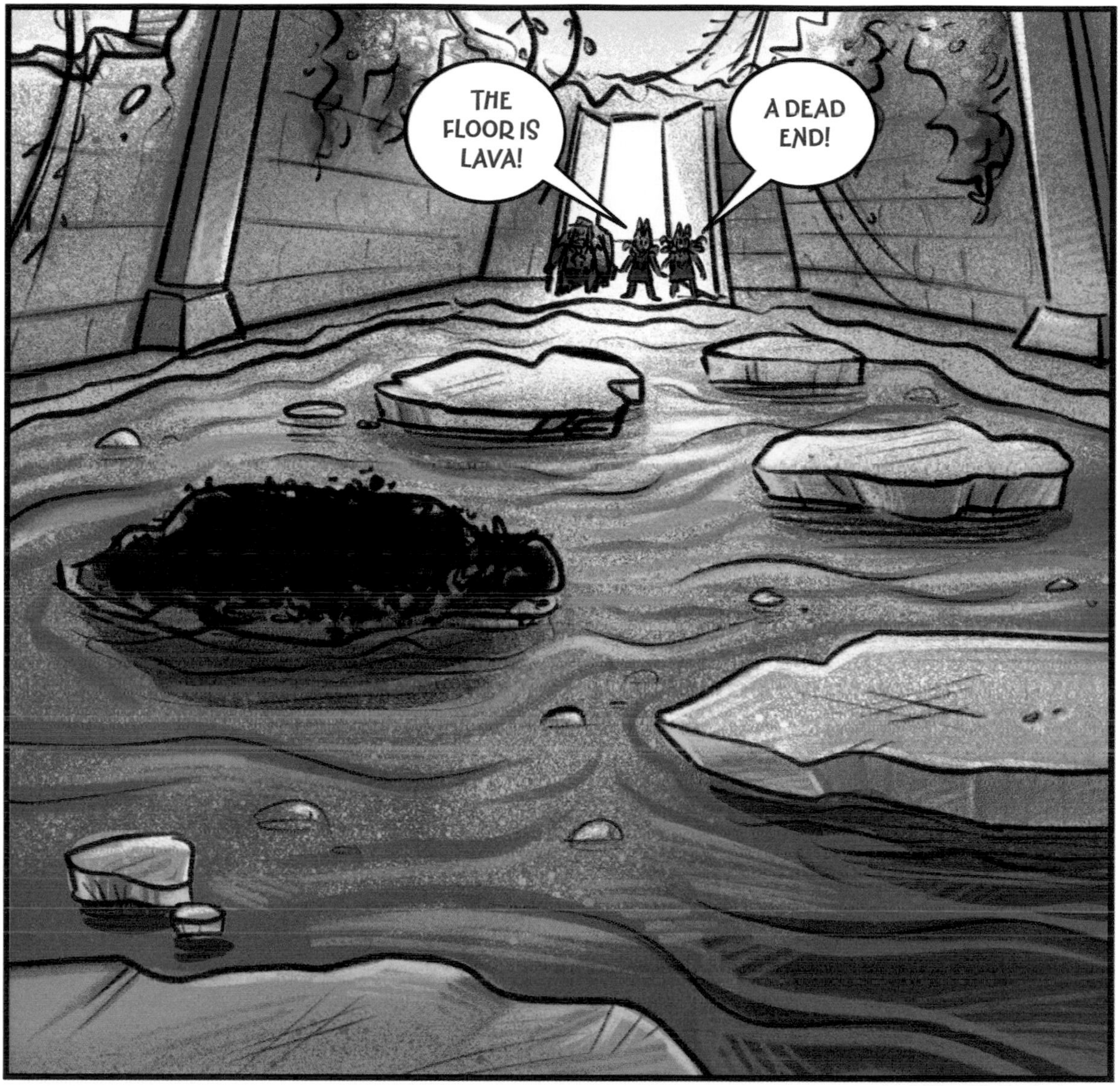
THE FLOOR IS LAVA!
A DEAD END!

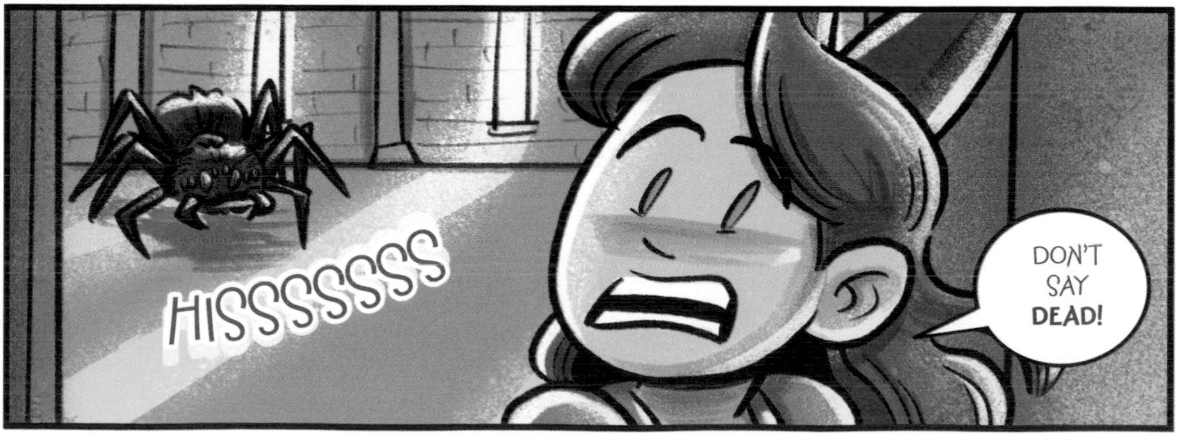
HISSSSSSS
DON'T SAY DEAD!

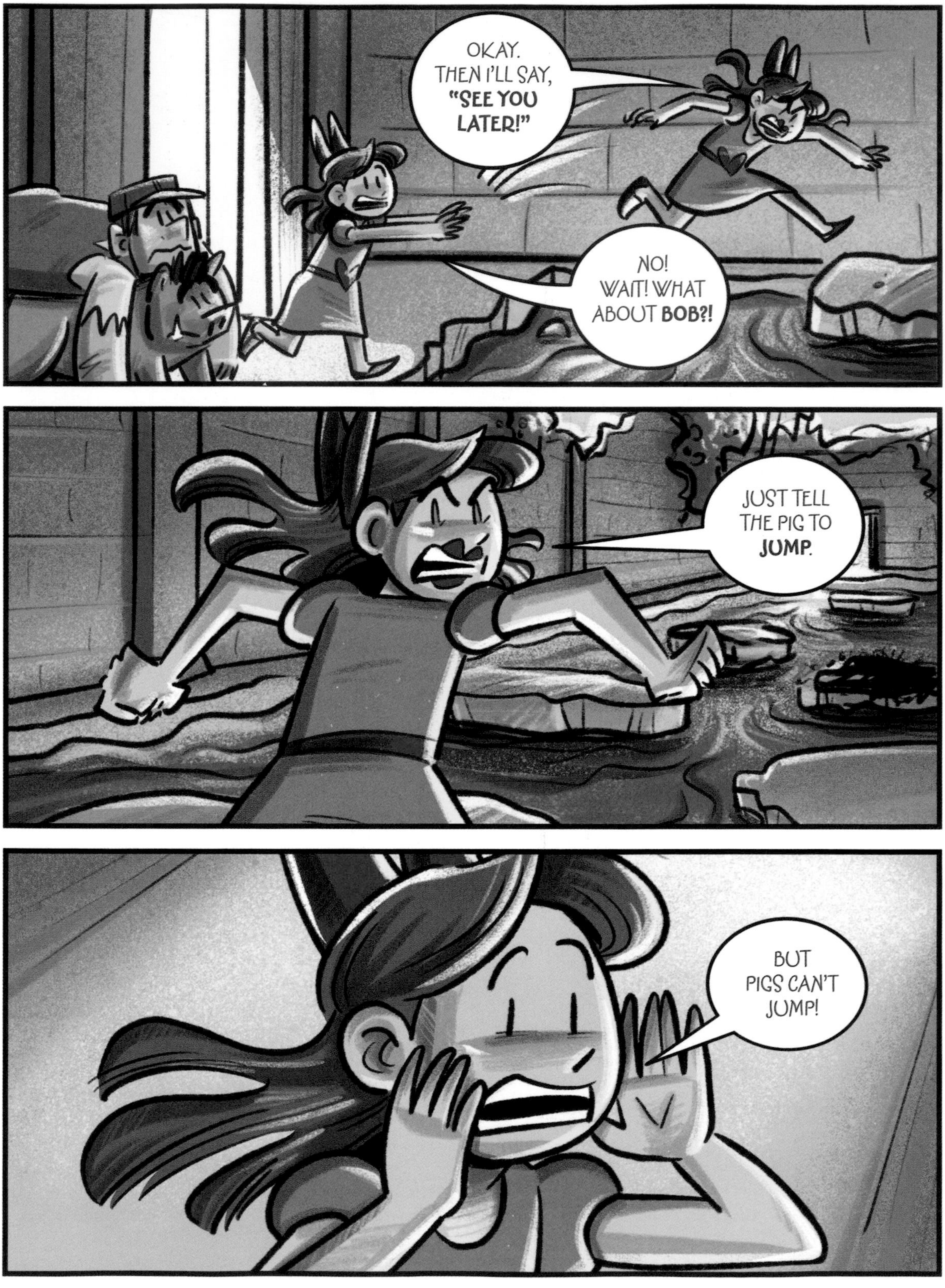
OKAY. THEN I'LL SAY, **"SEE YOU LATER!"**
NO! WAIT! WHAT ABOUT **BOB?!**
JUST TELL THE PIG TO **JUMP**.
BUT PIGS CAN'T JUMP!

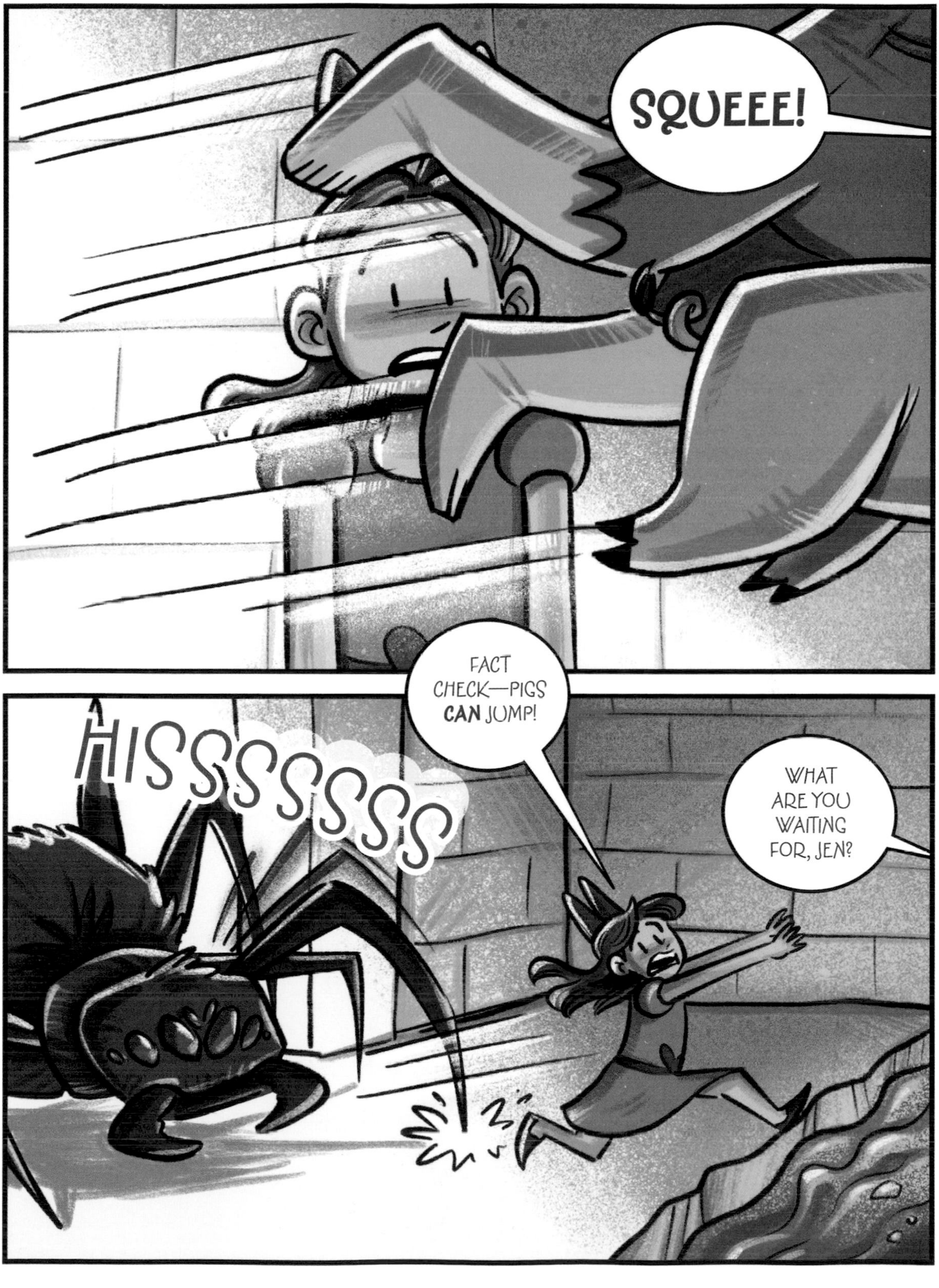
SQUEEE!
HISSSSSSS
FACT CHECK—PIGS CAN JUMP!
WHAT ARE YOU WAITING FOR, JEN?

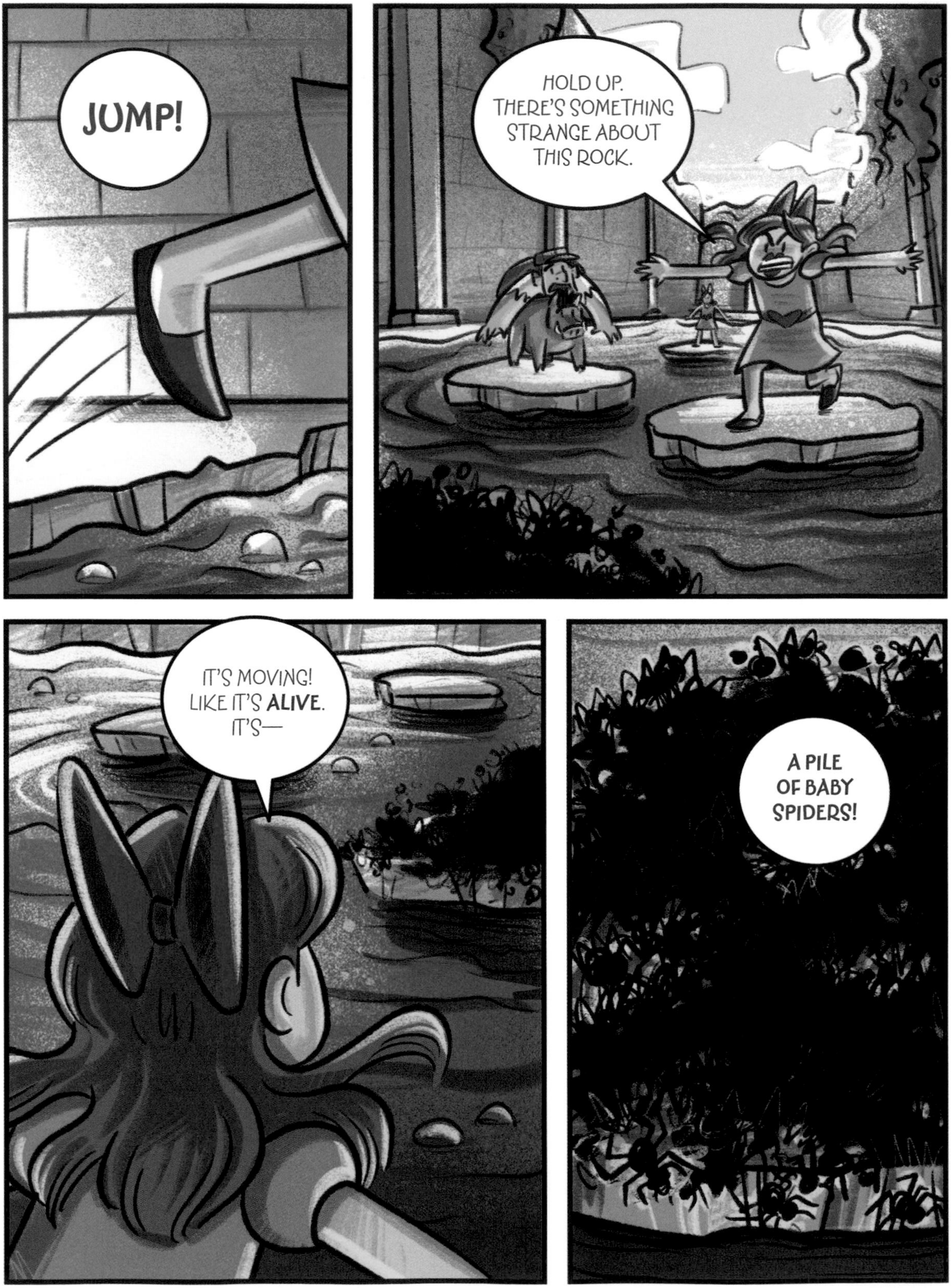
JUMP!
HOLD UP. THERE'S SOMETHING STRANGE ABOUT THIS ROCK.
IT'S MOVING! LIKE IT'S **ALIVE**. IT'S—
A PILE OF BABY SPIDERS!

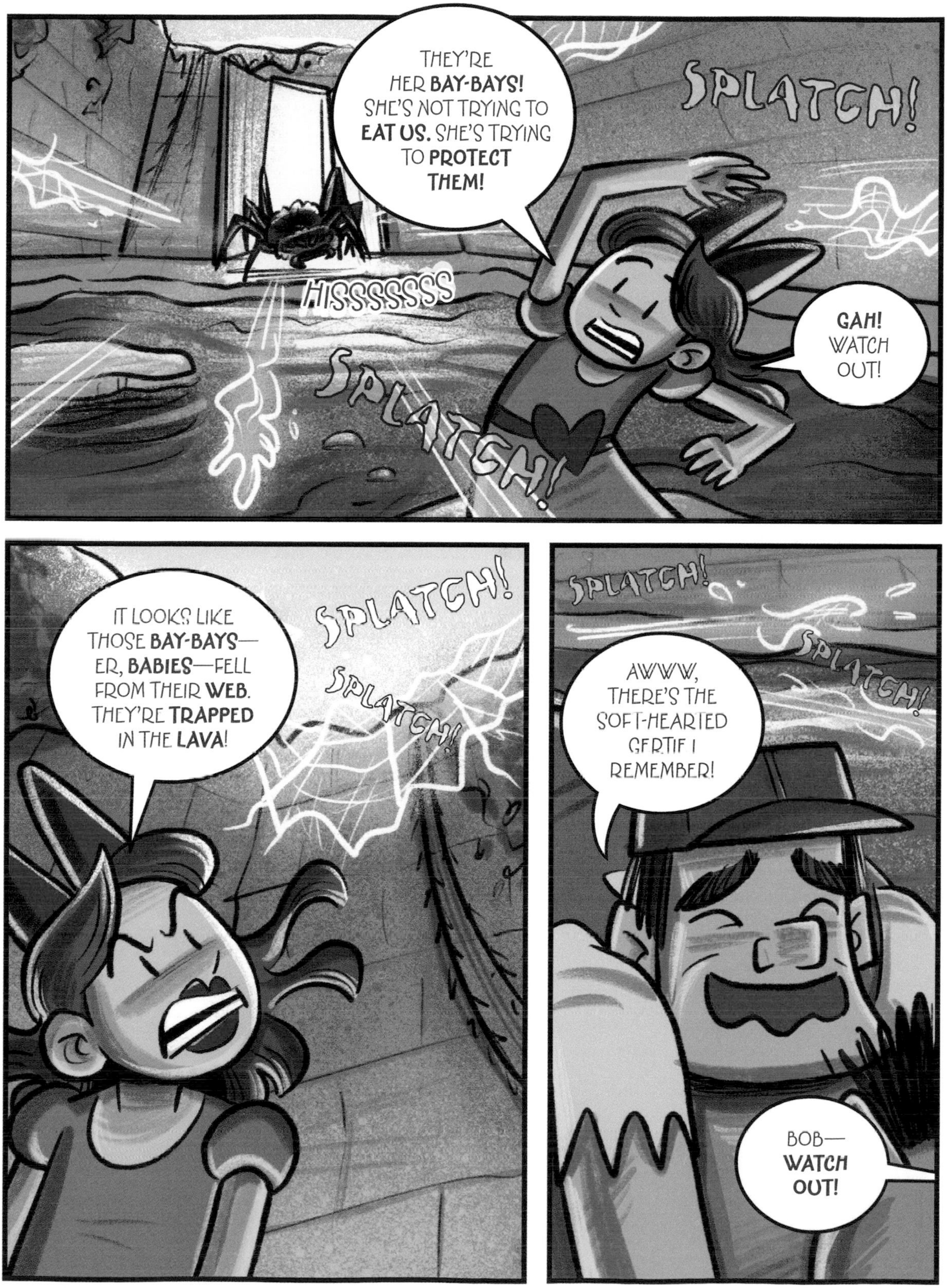
THEY'RE HER BAY-BAYS! SHE'S NOT TRYING TO EAT US. SHE'S TRYING TO PROTECT THEM!
SPLATCH!
HISSSSSSS
SPLATCH!
GAH! WATCH OUT!
IT LOOKS LIKE THOSE BAY-BAYS— ER, BABIES—FELL FROM THEIR WEB. THEY'RE TRAPPED IN THE LAVA!
SPLATCH!
SPLATCH!
SPLATCH!
SPLATCH!
AWWW, THERE'S THE SOFT-HEARTED GERTIE I REMEMBER!
BOB— WATCH OUT!

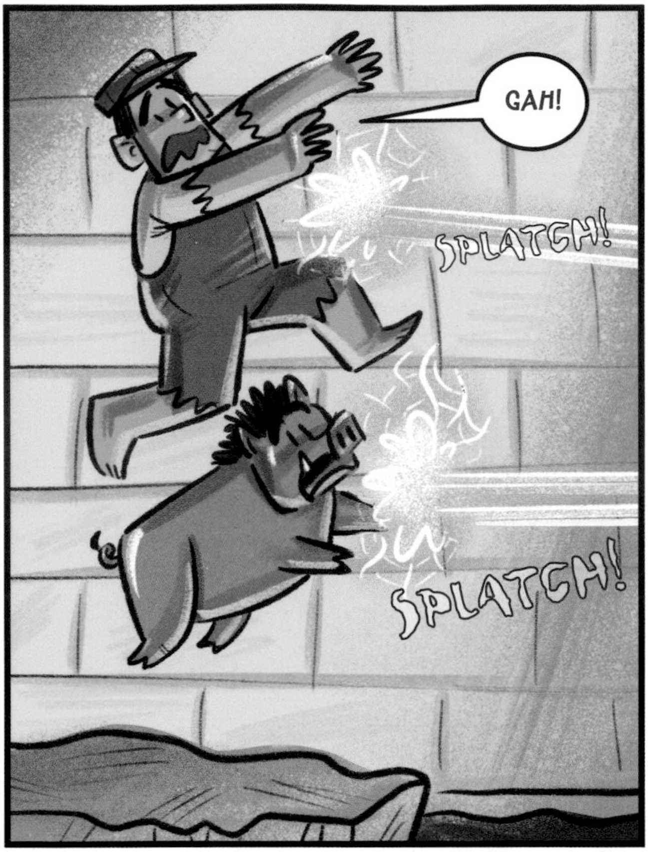
GAH!
SPLATCH!
SPLATCH!

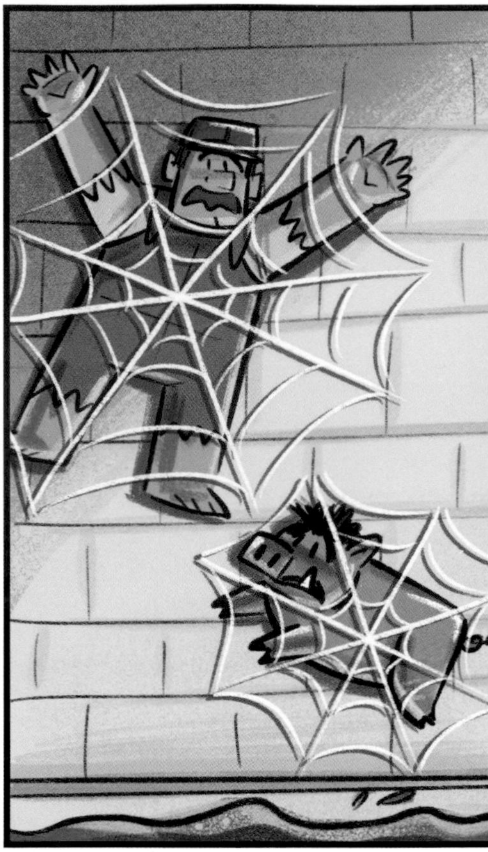

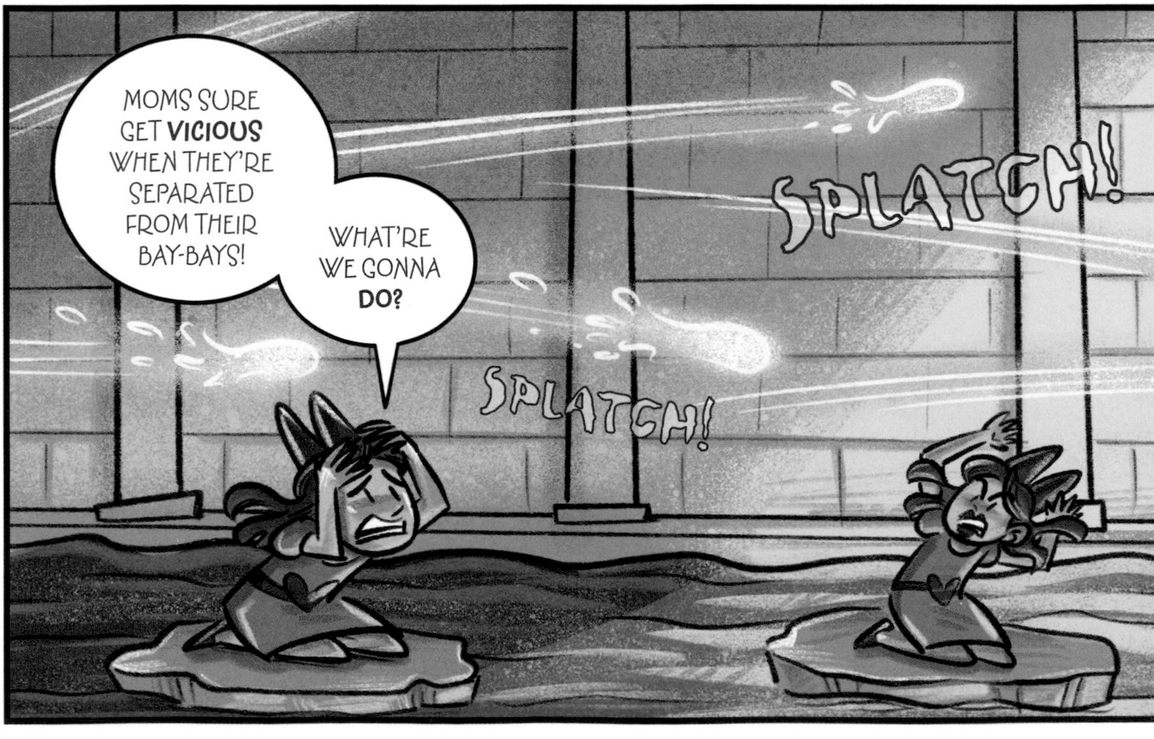
MOMS SURE GET **VICIOUS** WHEN THEY'RE SEPARATED FROM THEIR BAY-BAYS!
SPLATCH!
WHAT'RE WE GONNA **DO?**
SPLATCH!

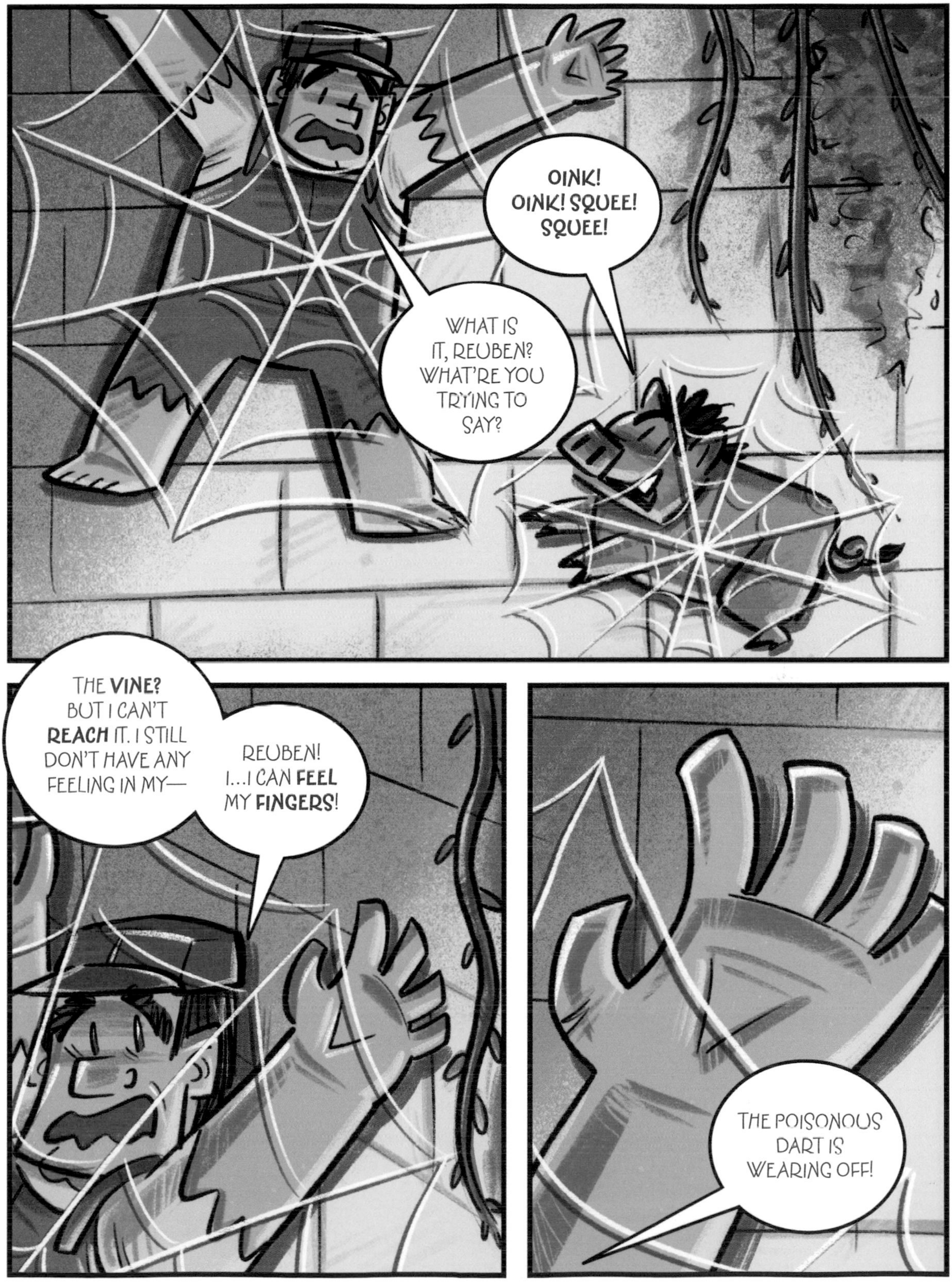
OINK! OINK! SQUEE! SQUEE!
WHAT IS IT, REUBEN? WHAT'RE YOU TRYING TO SAY?
THE VINE? BUT I CAN'T REACH IT. I STILL DON'T HAVE ANY FEELING IN MY—
REUBEN! I...I CAN FEEL MY FINGERS!
THE POISONOUS DART IS WEARING OFF!

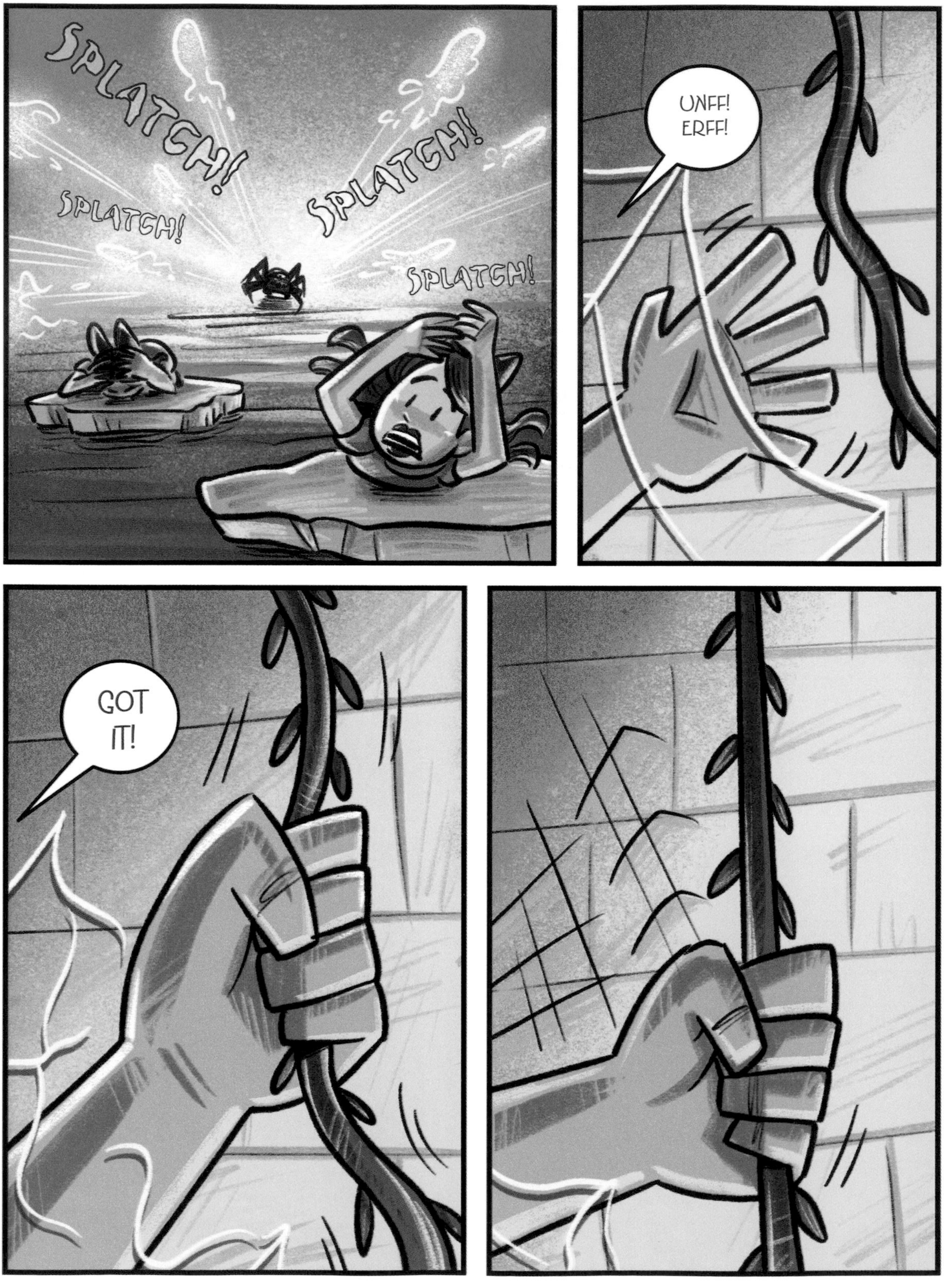
SPLATCH!
SPLATCH!
SPLATCH!
SPLATCH!
UNFF! ERFF!
GOT IT!

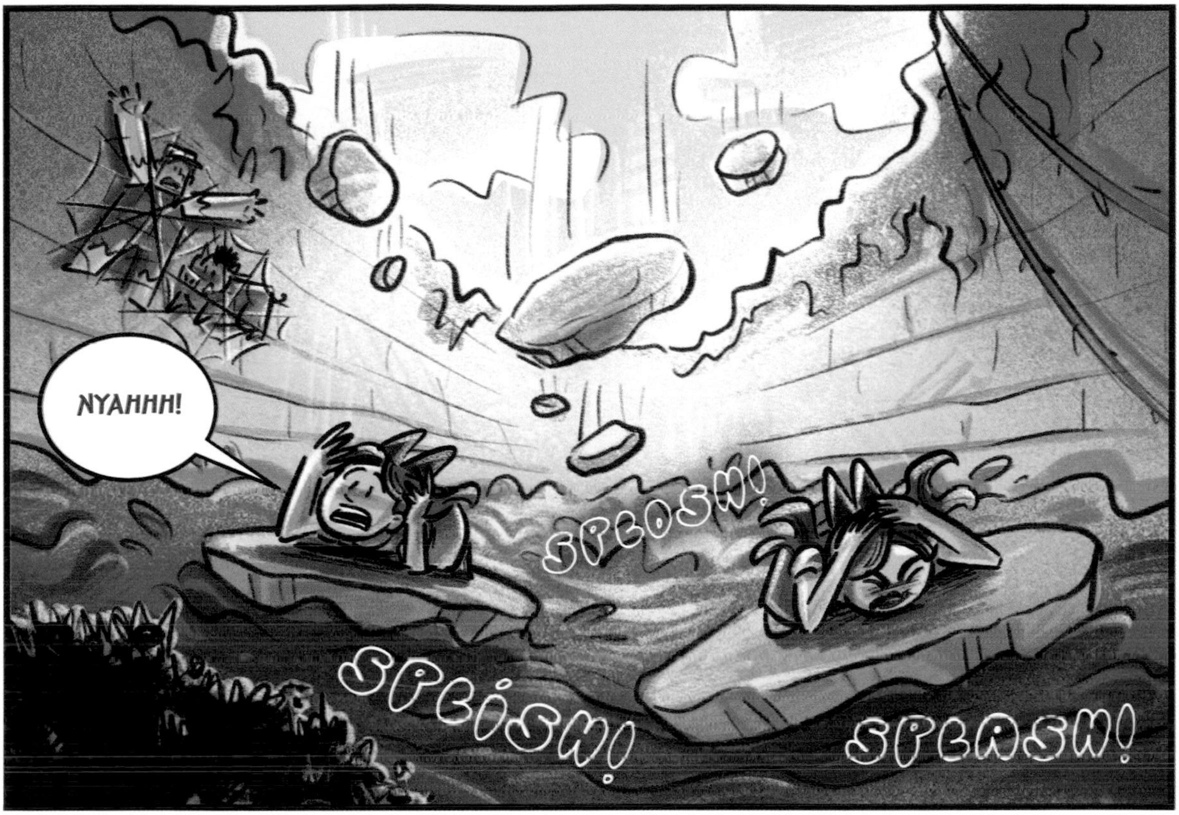
NYAHHH!
SPLOOSH!
SPLISH!
SPLASH!

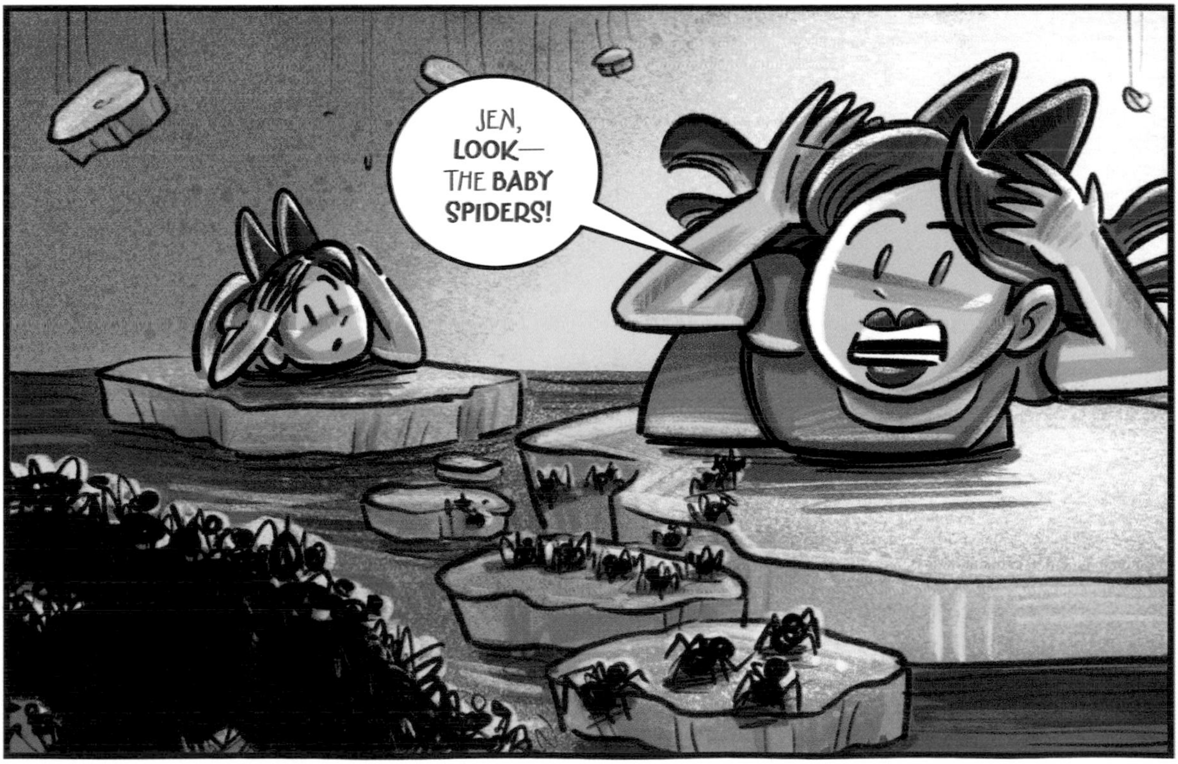
JEN, LOOK— THE BABY SPIDERS!

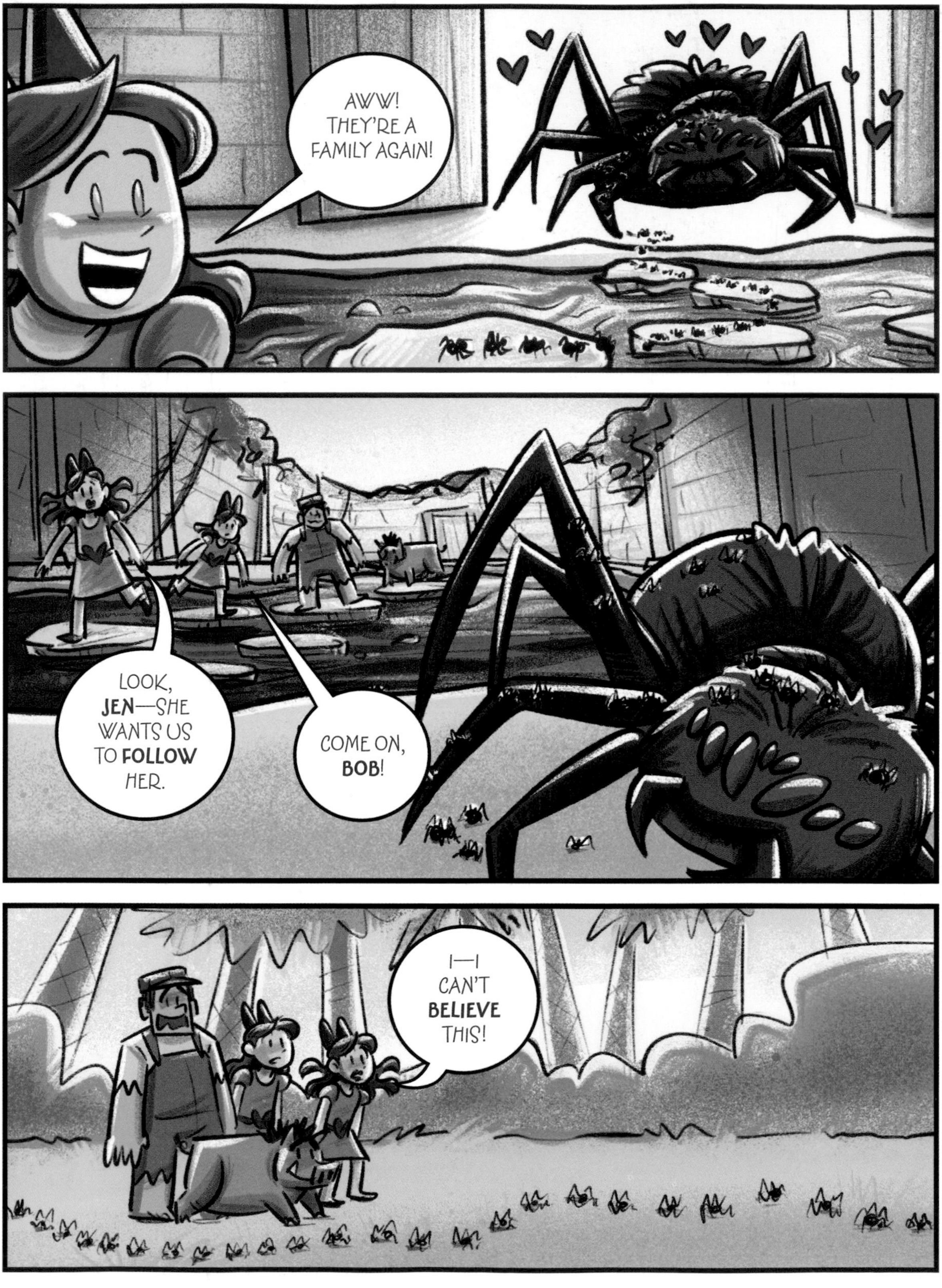
AWW! THEY'RE A FAMILY AGAIN!
LOOK, **JEN**—SHE WANTS US TO **FOLLOW** HER.
COME ON, **BOB**!
I—I CAN'T **BELIEVE** THIS!

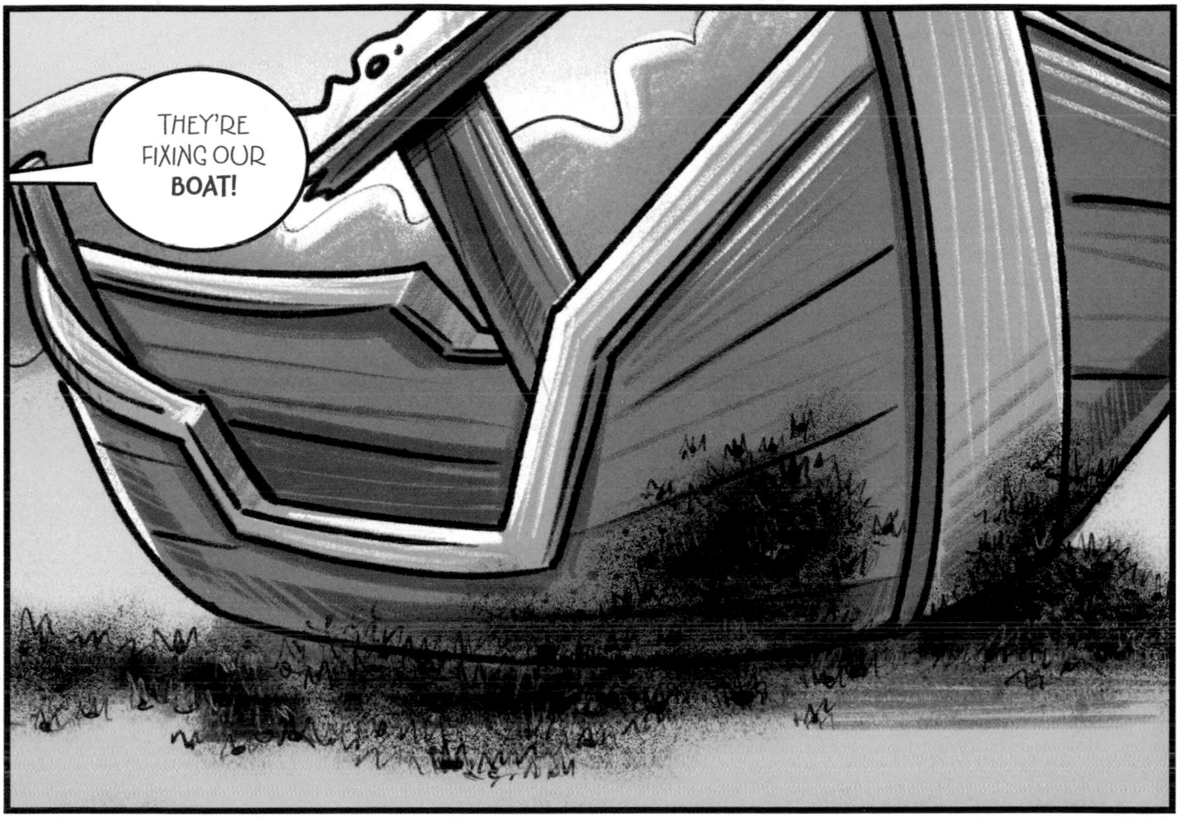
THEY'RE FIXING OUR **BOAT!**

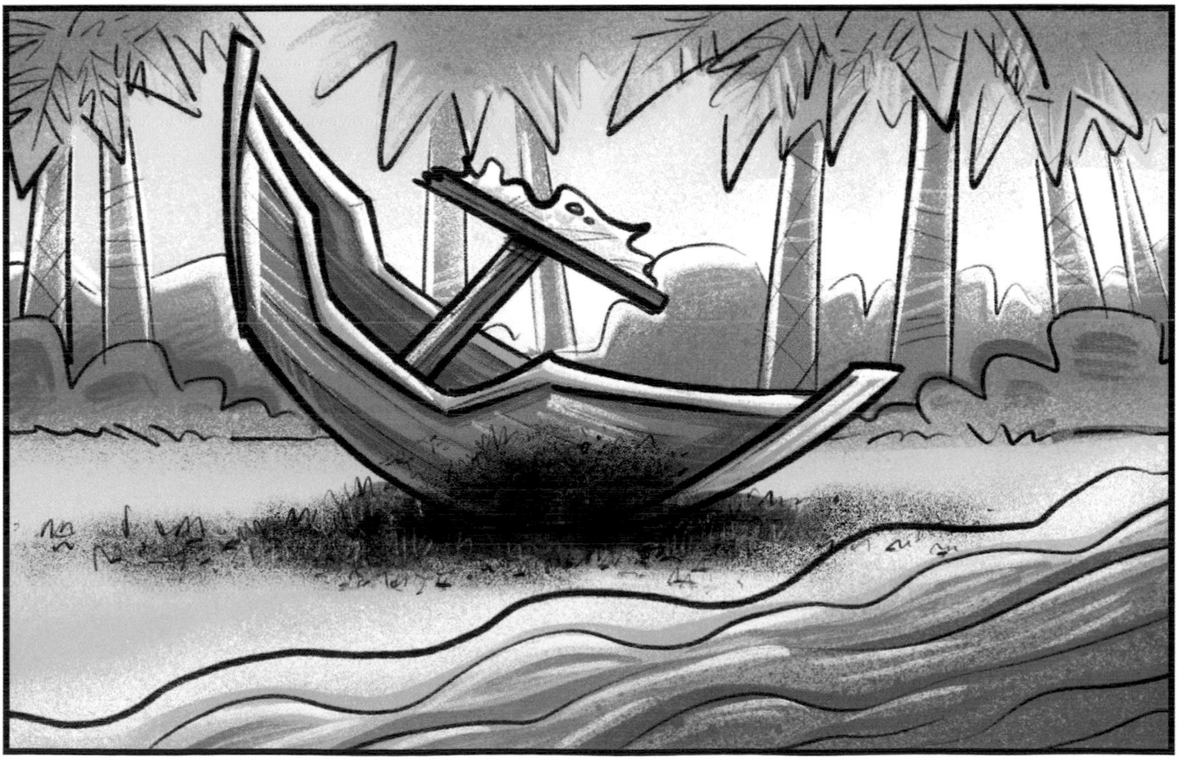

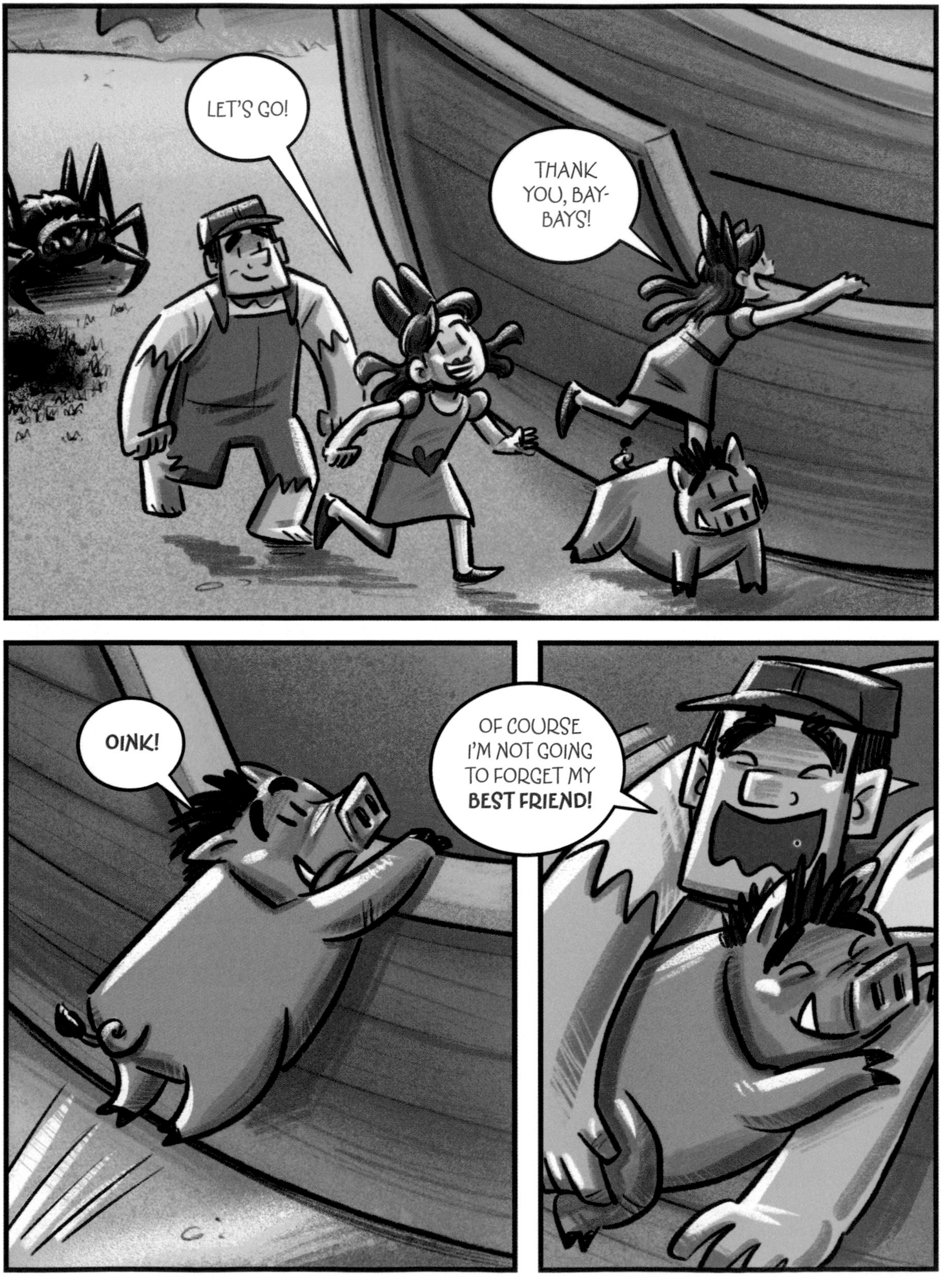
LET'S GO!
THANK YOU, BAY-BAYS!
OINK!
OF COURSE I'M NOT GOING TO FORGET MY **BEST FRIEND!**

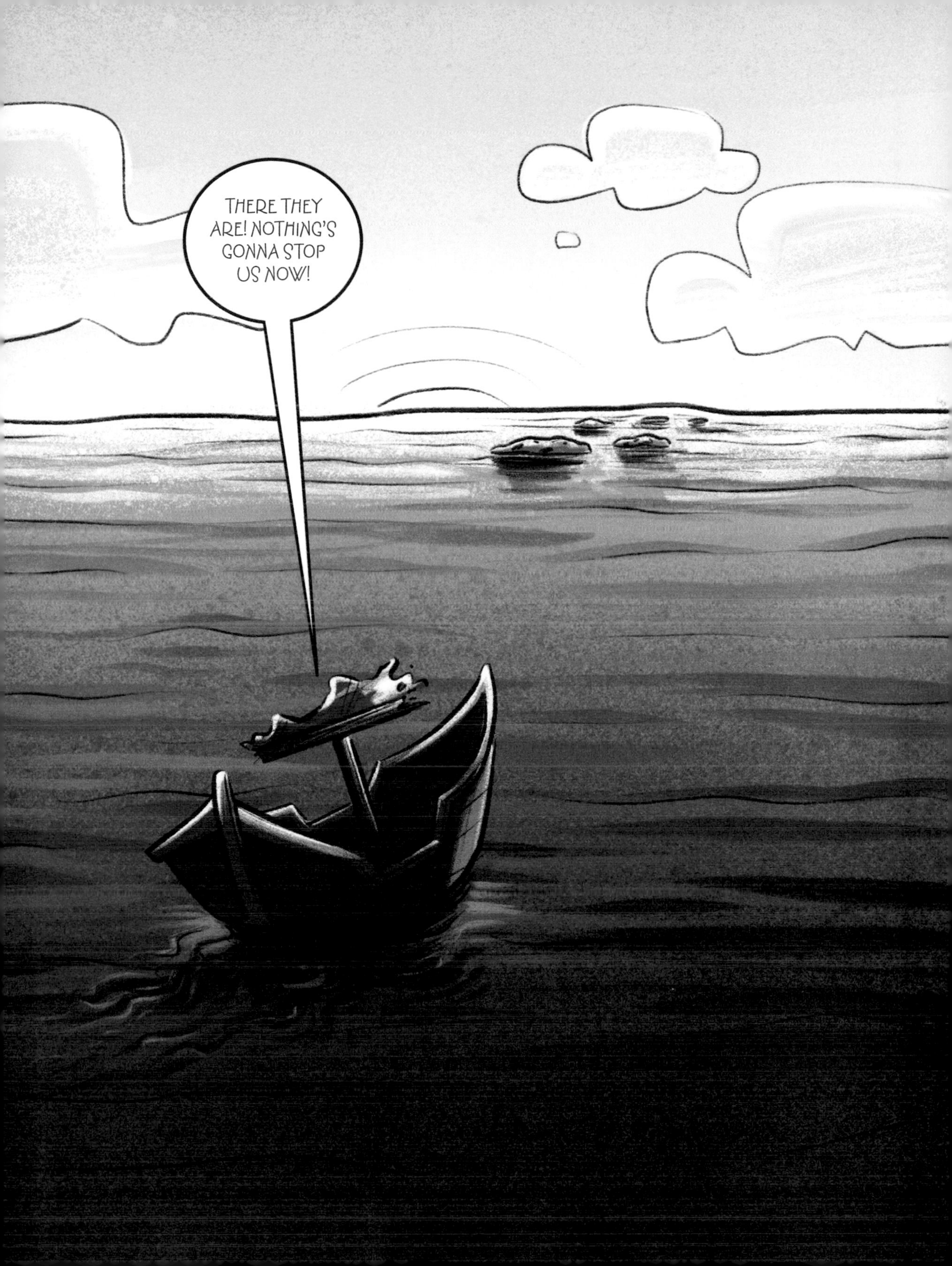
THERE THEY ARE! NOTHING'S GONNA STOP US NOW!

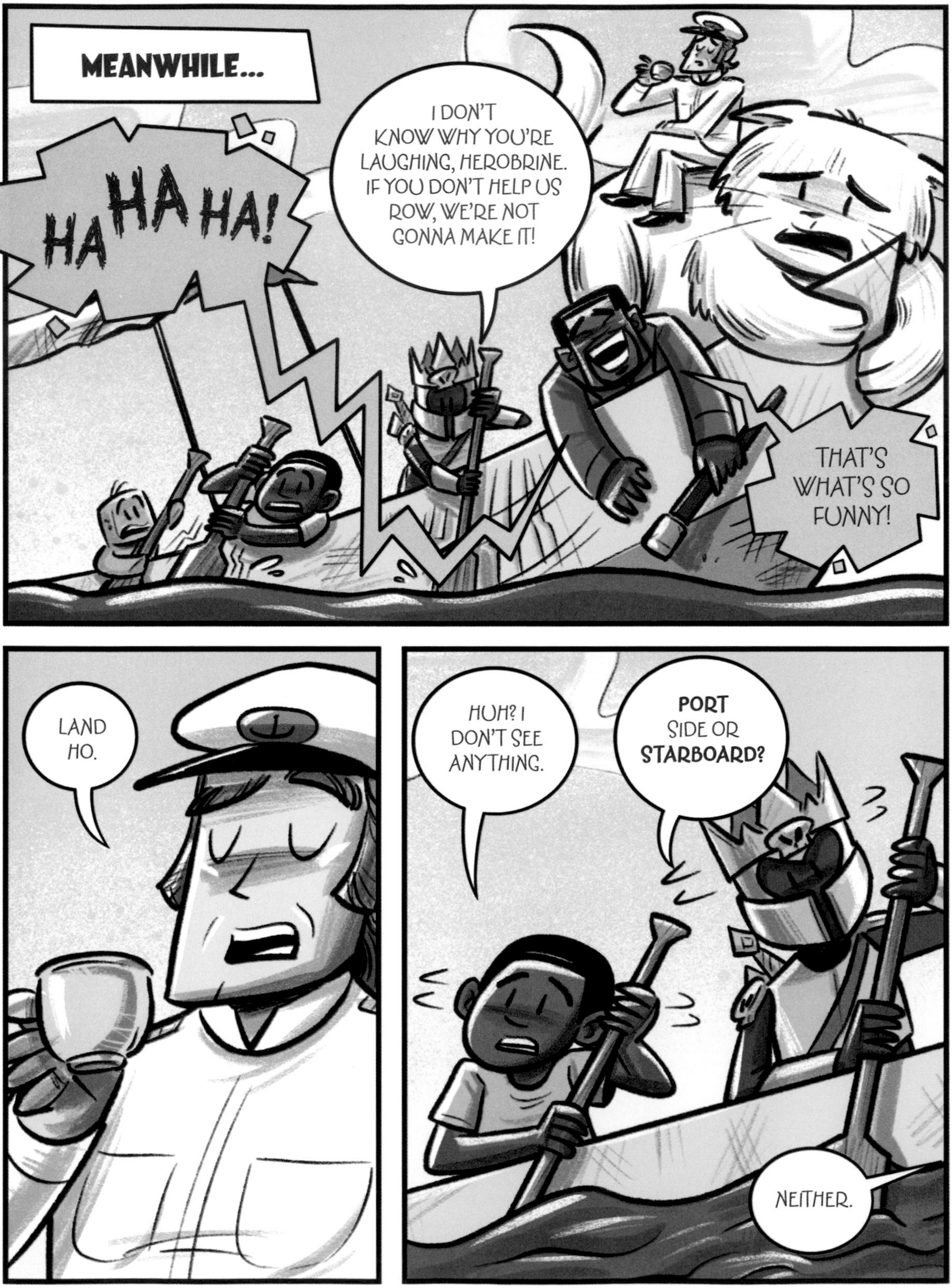
MEANWHILE...
HA HA HA!
I DON'T KNOW WHY YOU'RE LAUGHING, HEROBRINE. IF YOU DON'T HELP US ROW, WE'RE NOT GONNA MAKE IT!
THAT'S WHAT'S SO FUNNY!
LAND HO.
HUH? I DON'T SEE ANYTHING.
PORT SIDE OR STARBOARD?
NEITHER.

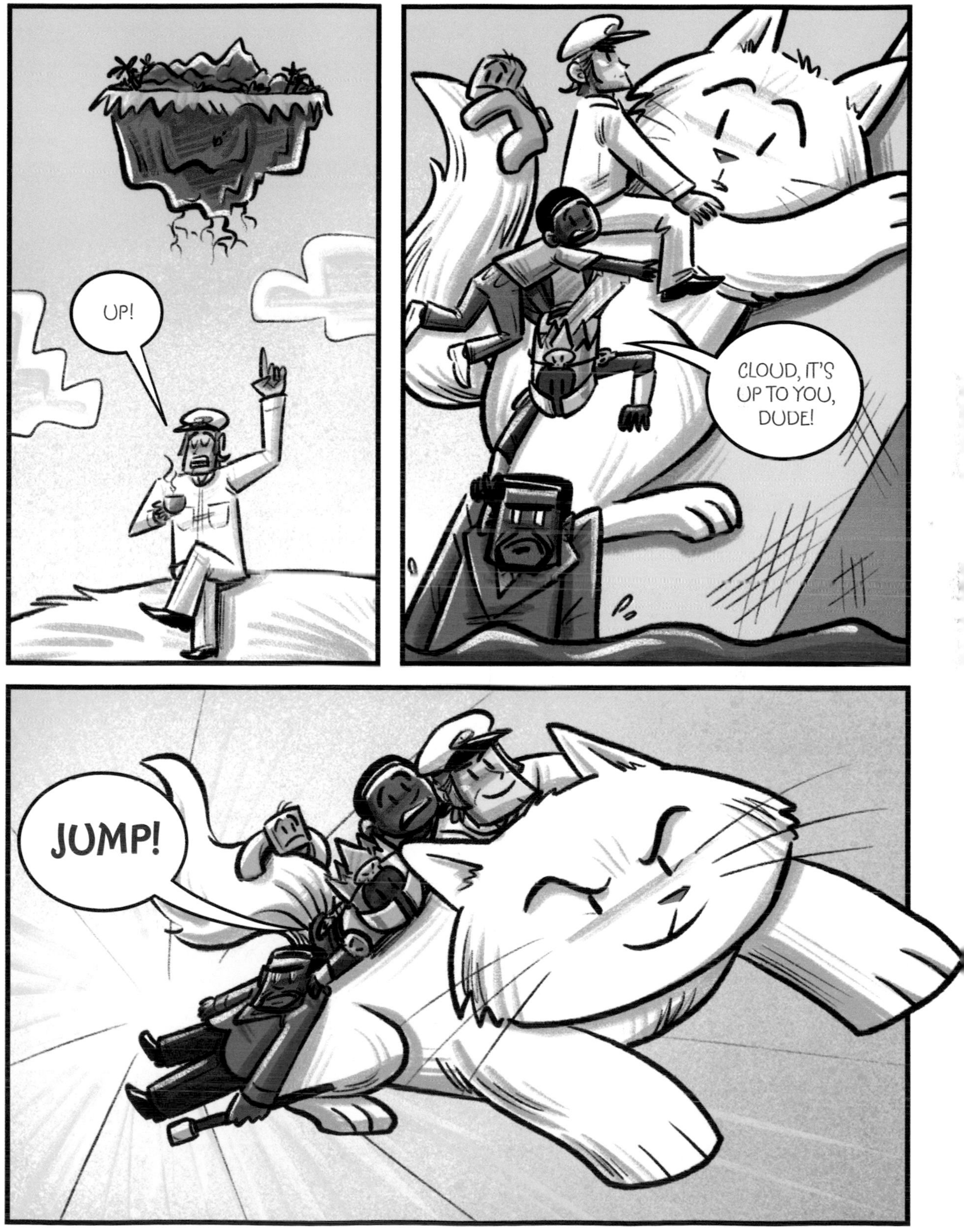
UP!
CLOUD, IT'S UP TO YOU, DUDE!
JUMP!

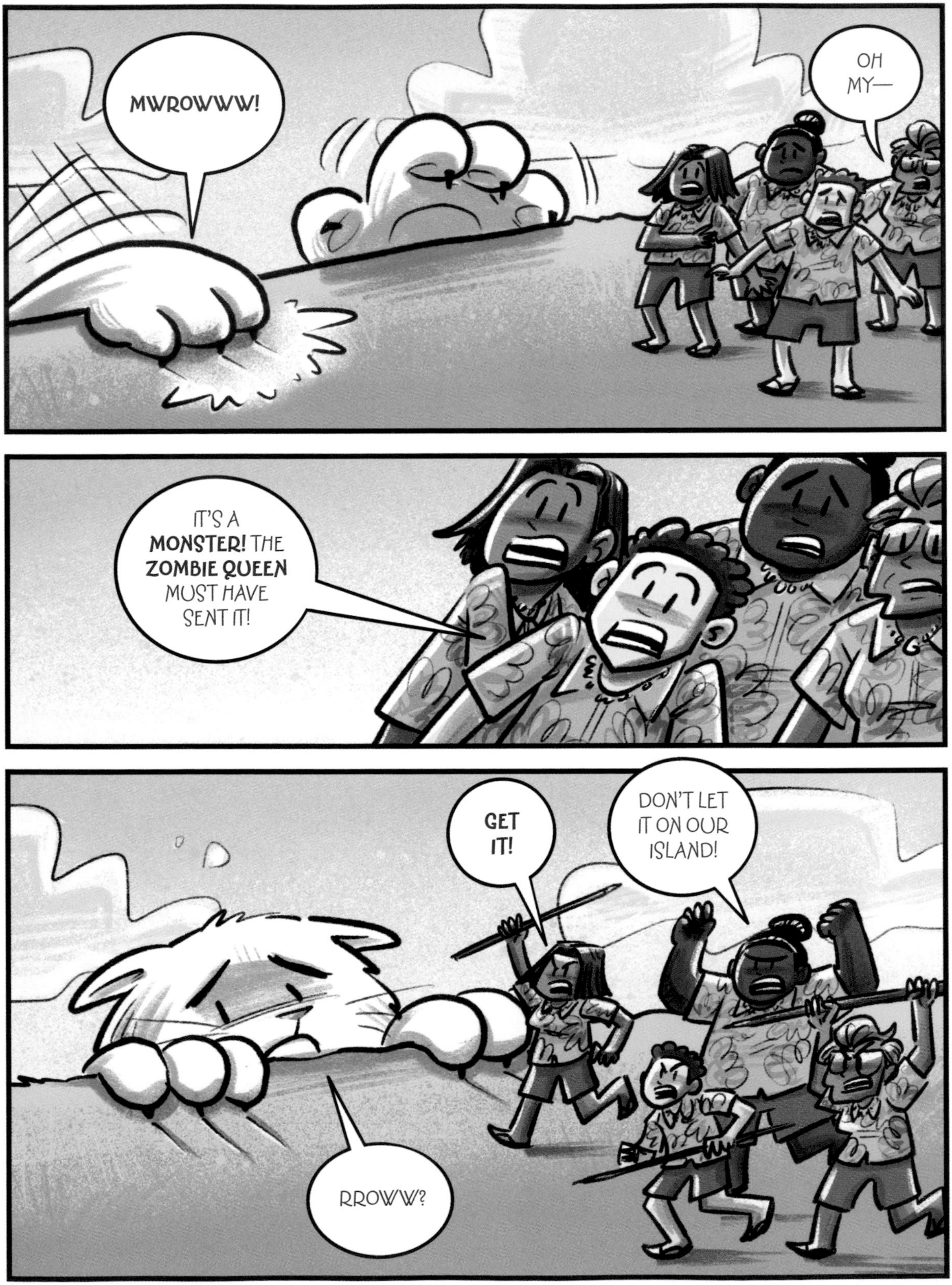
MWROWWW!
OH MY—
IT'S A **MONSTER!** THE **ZOMBIE QUEEN** MUST HAVE SENT IT!
GET IT!
DON'T LET IT ON OUR ISLAND!
RROWW?

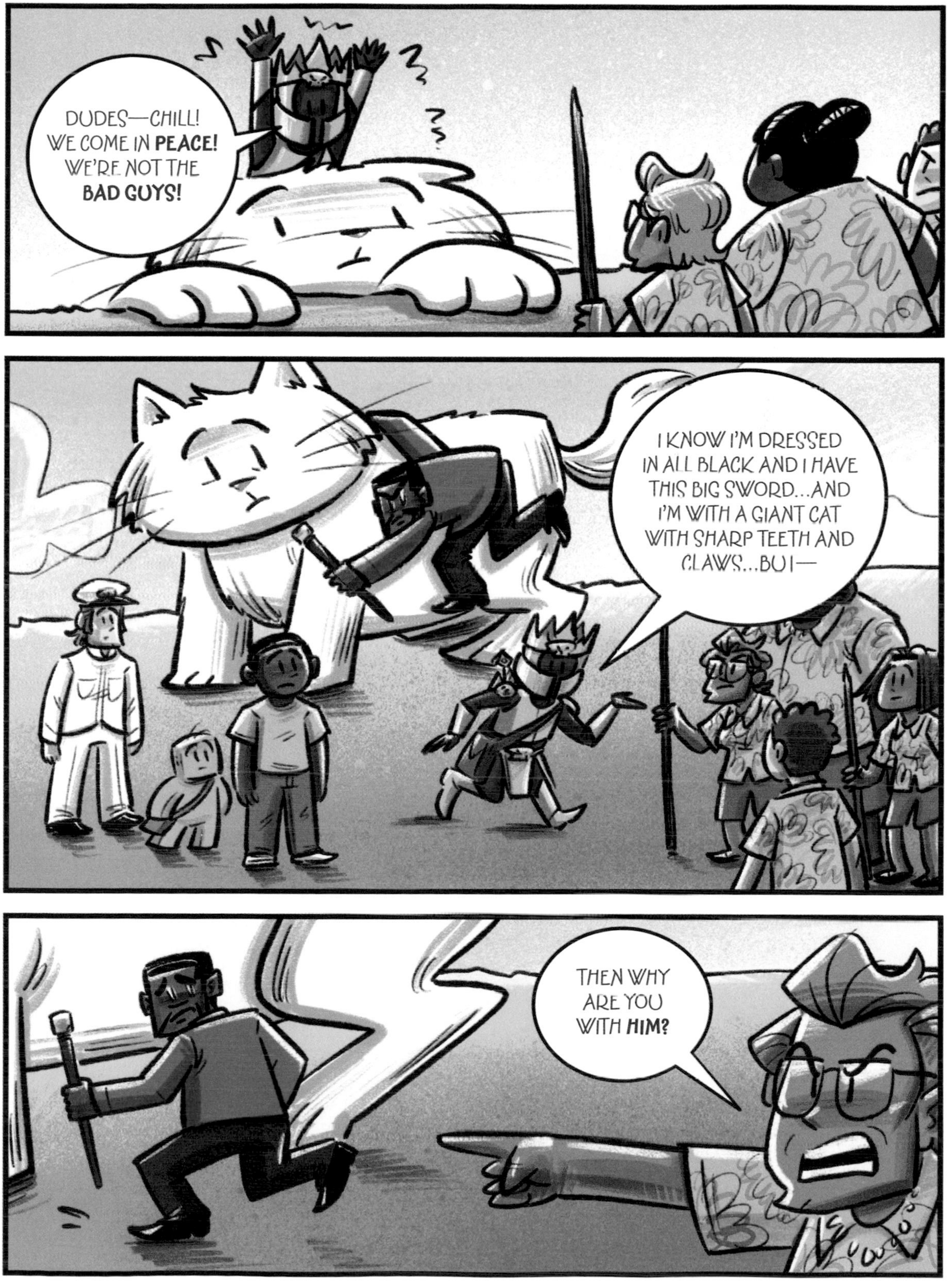
DUDES—CHILL! WE COME IN **PEACE!** WE'RE NOT THE **BAD GUYS!**
I KNOW I'M DRESSED IN ALL BLACK AND I HAVE THIS BIG SWORD...AND I'M WITH A GIANT CAT WITH SHARP TEETH AND CLAWS...BUT—
THEN WHY ARE YOU WITH **HIM?**

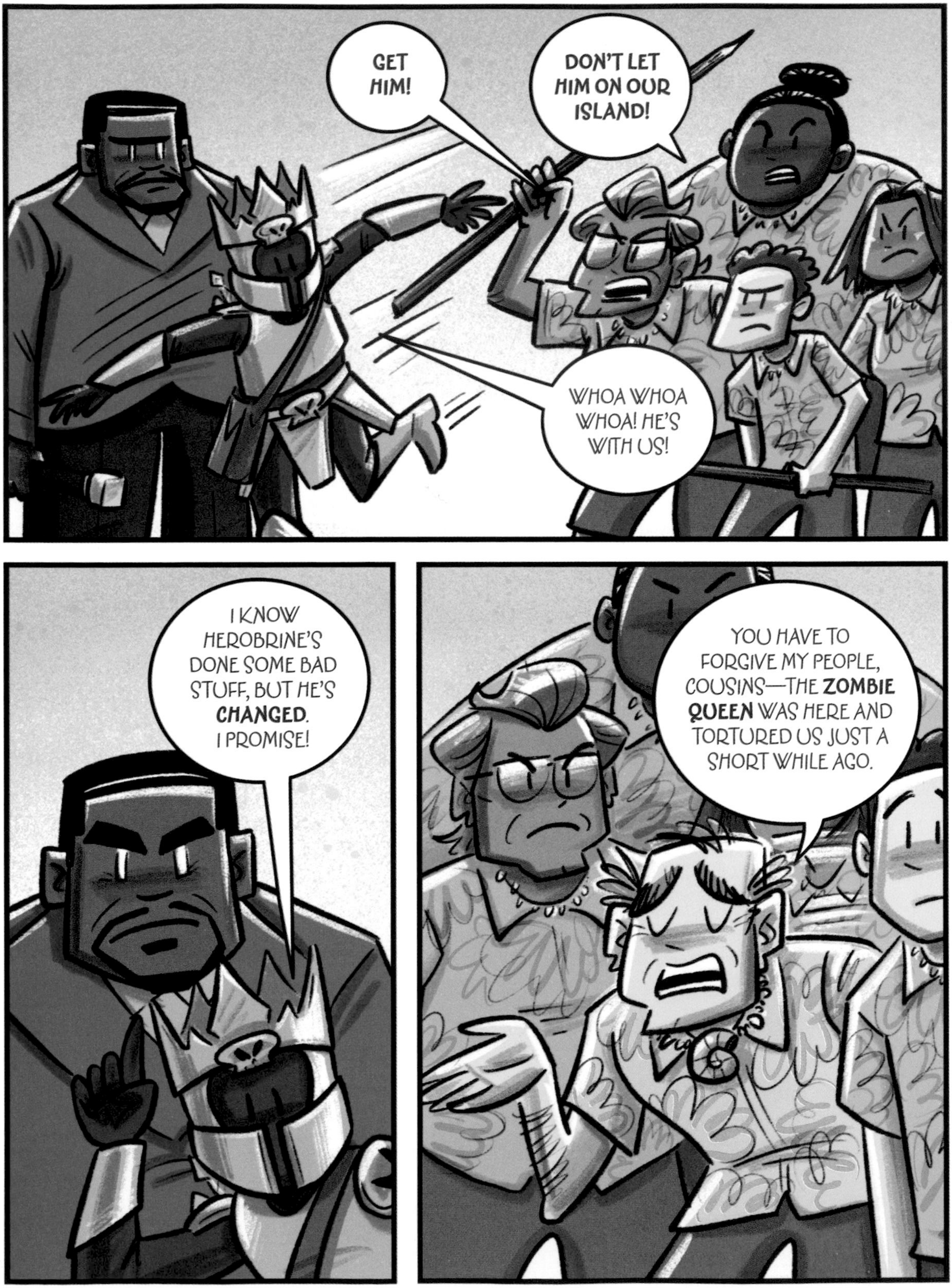
GET HIM!
DON'T LET HIM ON OUR ISLAND!
WHOA WHOA WHOA! HE'S WITH US!
I KNOW HEROBRINE'S DONE SOME BAD STUFF, BUT HE'S **CHANGED**. I PROMISE!
YOU HAVE TO FORGIVE MY PEOPLE, COUSINS—THE **ZOMBIE QUEEN** WAS HERE AND TORTURED US JUST A SHORT WHILE AGO.

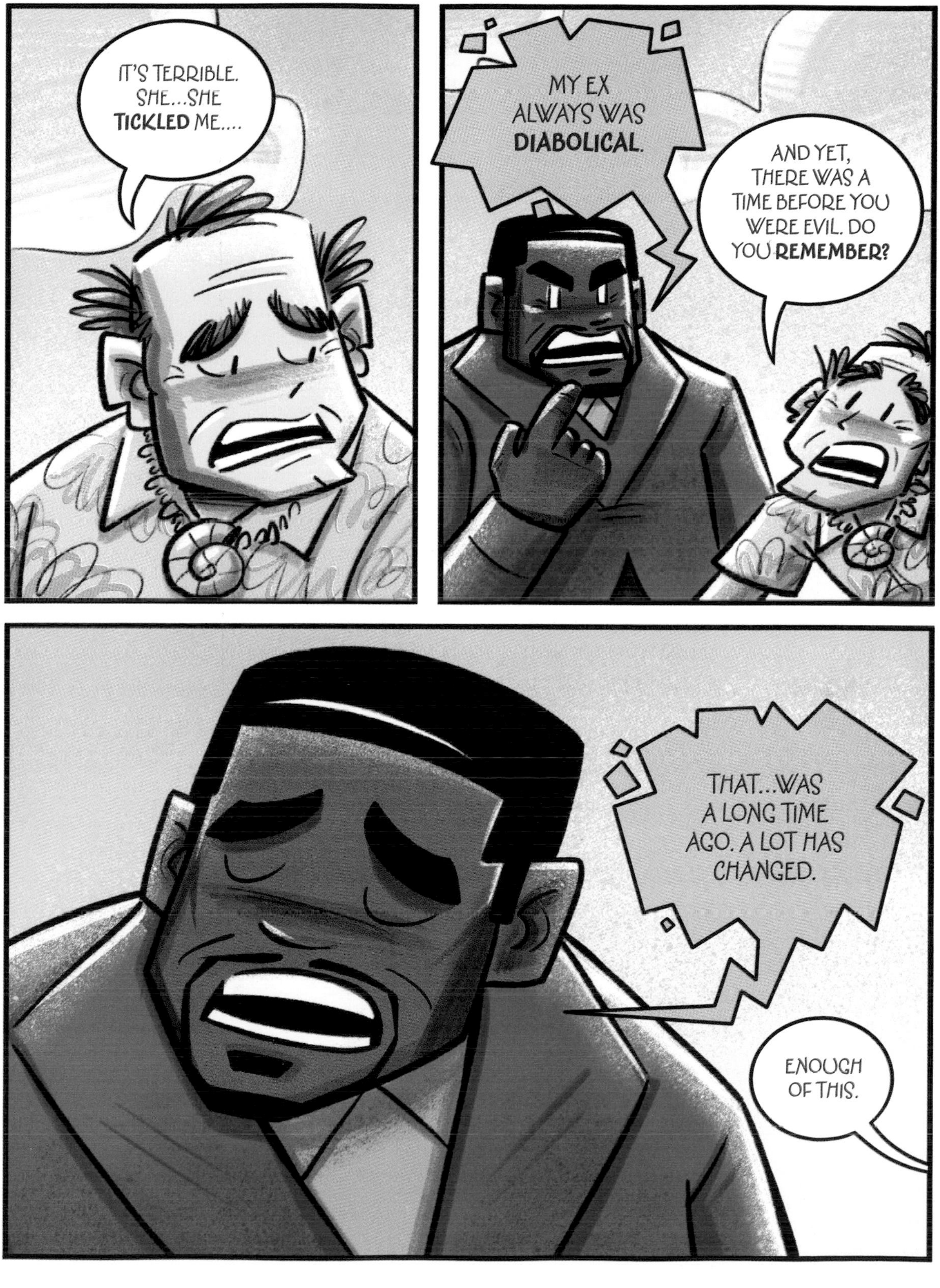
IT'S TERRIBLE. SHE...SHE **TICKLED** ME....
MY EX ALWAYS WAS **DIABOLICAL**.
AND YET, THERE WAS A TIME BEFORE YOU WERE EVIL. DO YOU **REMEMBER?**
THAT...WAS A LONG TIME AGO. A LOT HAS CHANGED.
ENOUGH OF THIS.

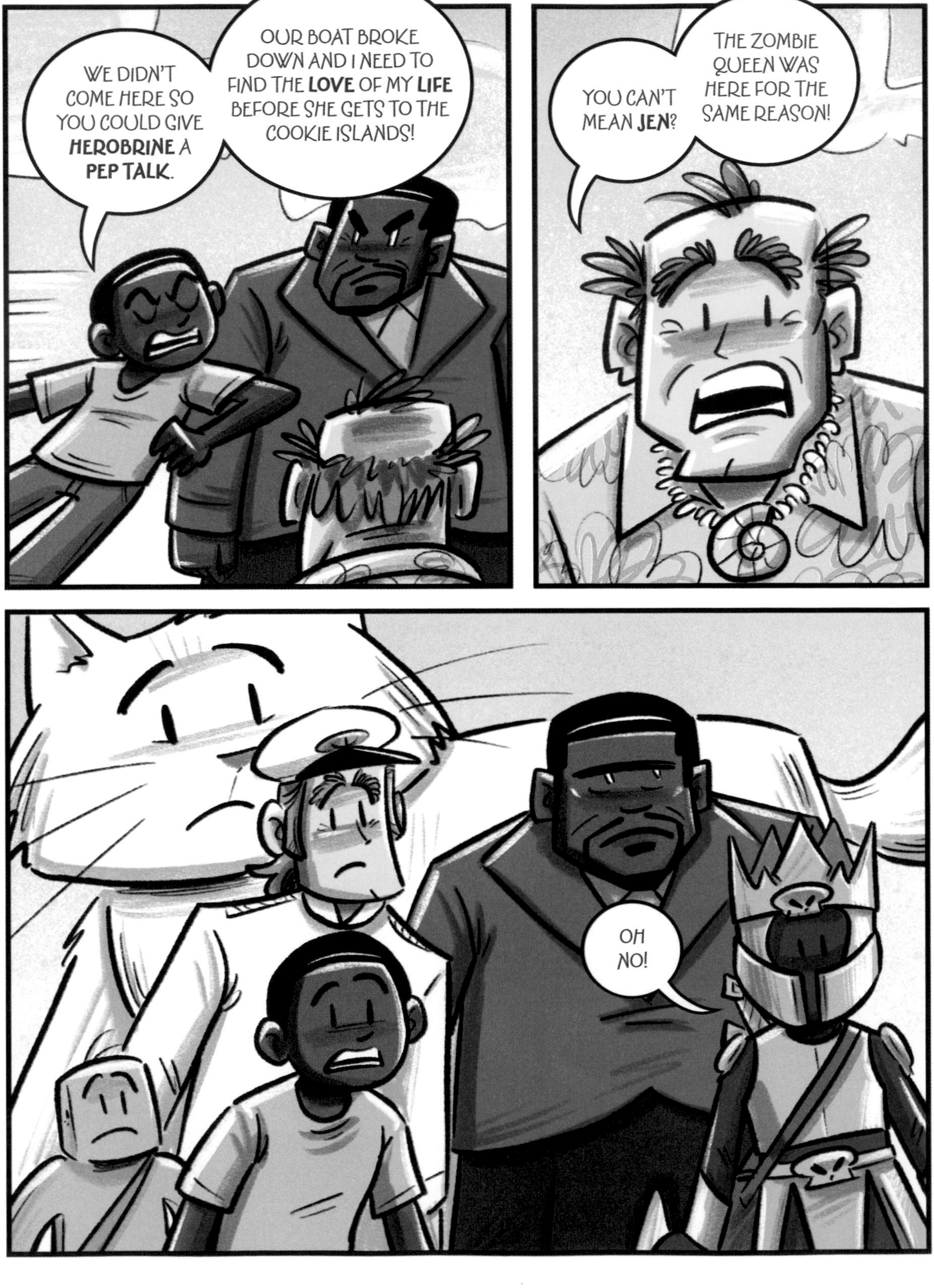
WE DIDN'T COME HERE SO YOU COULD GIVE **HEROBRINE** A **PEP TALK**.
OUR BOAT BROKE DOWN AND I NEED TO FIND THE **LOVE** OF MY **LIFE** BEFORE SHE GETS TO THE COOKIE ISLANDS!
YOU CAN'T MEAN **JEN**?
THE ZOMBIE QUEEN WAS HERE FOR THE SAME REASON!
OH NO!

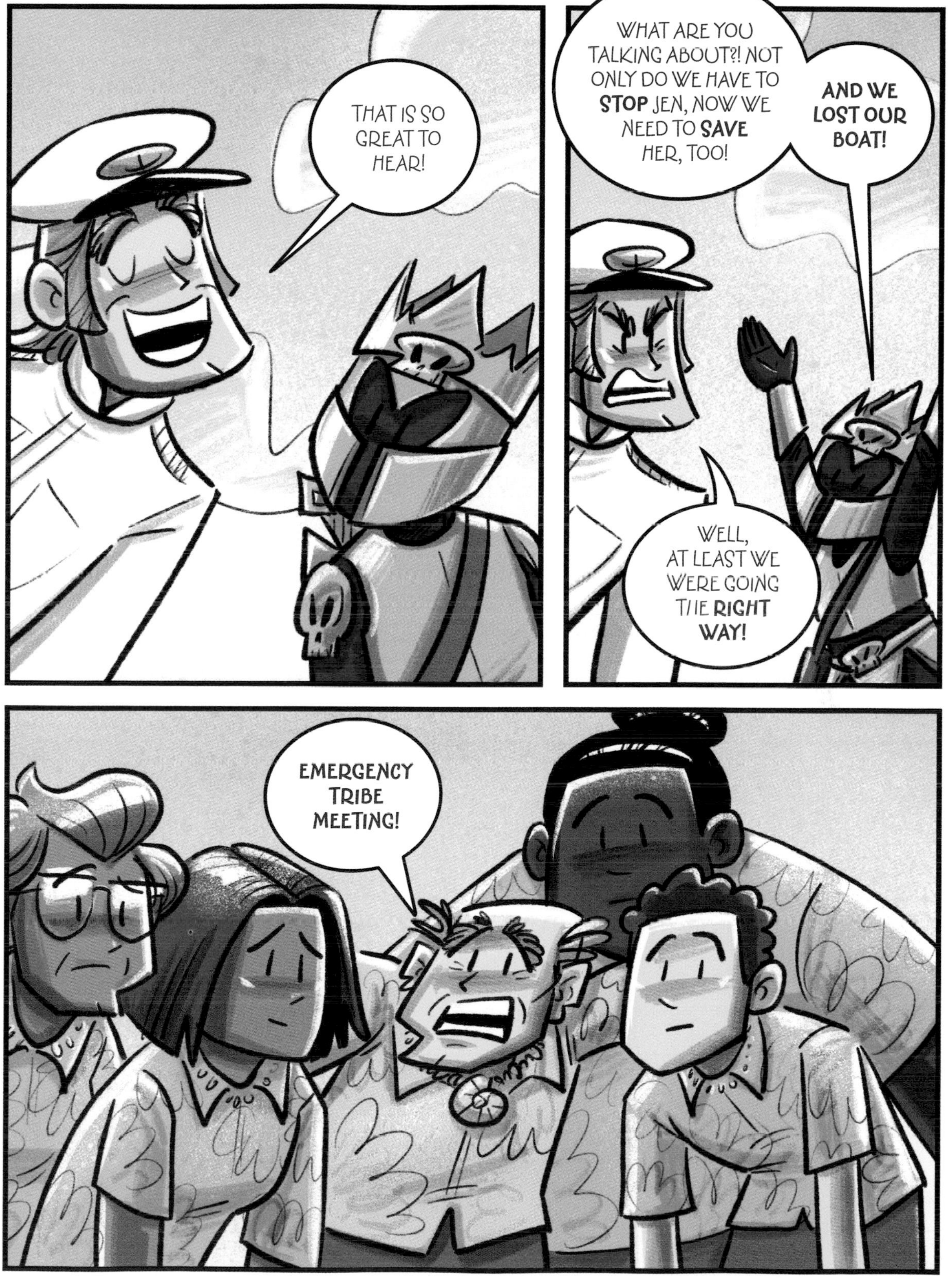
THAT IS SO GREAT TO HEAR!
WHAT ARE YOU TALKING ABOUT?! NOT ONLY DO WE HAVE TO STOP JEN, NOW WE NEED TO SAVE HER, TOO!
AND WE LOST OUR BOAT!
WELL, AT LEAST WE WERE GOING THE RIGHT WAY!
EMERGENCY TRIBE MEETING!

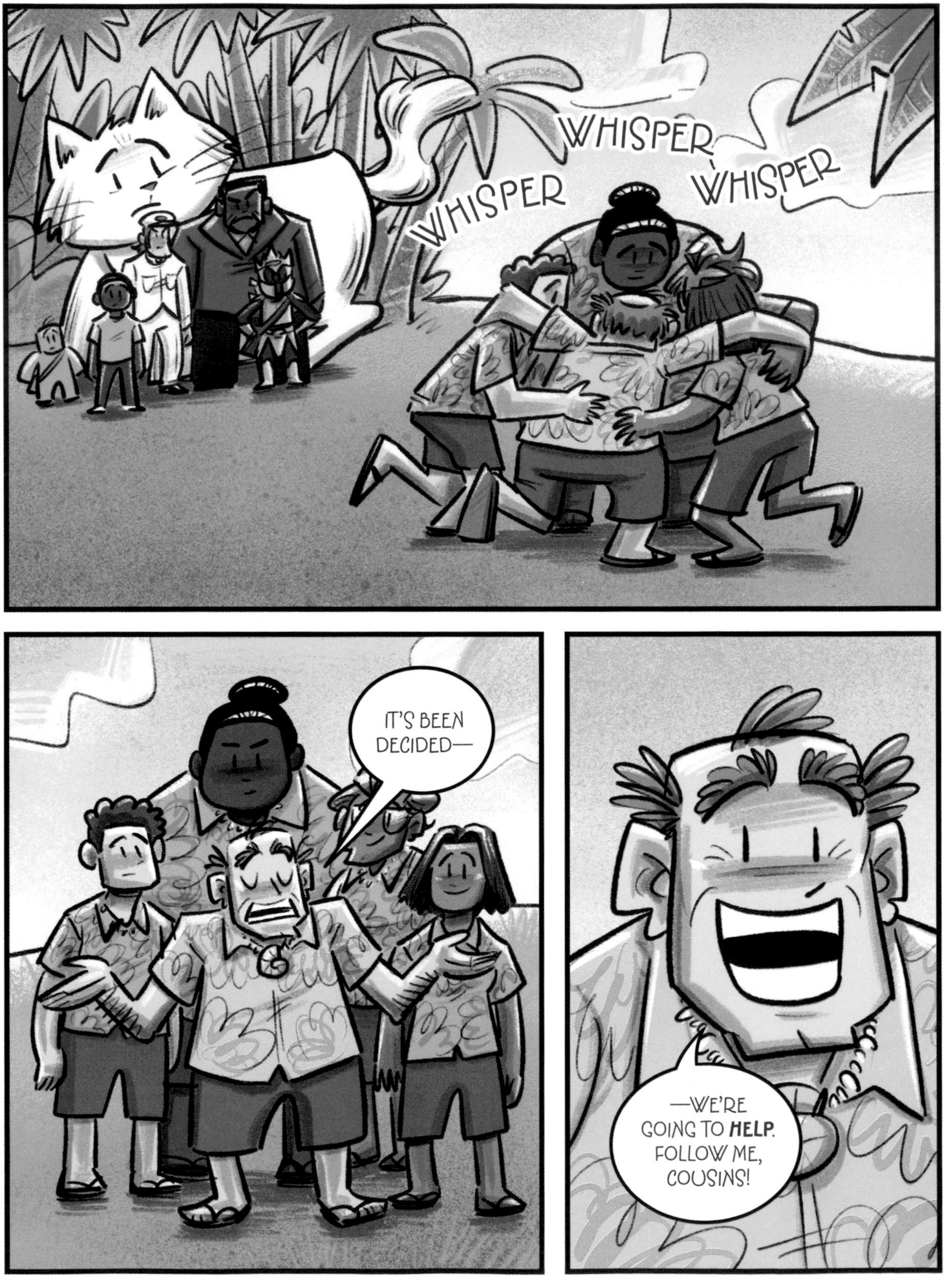
WHISPER
WHISPER
WHISPER
IT'S BEEN DECIDED—
—WE'RE GOING TO **HELP**. FOLLOW ME, COUSINS!

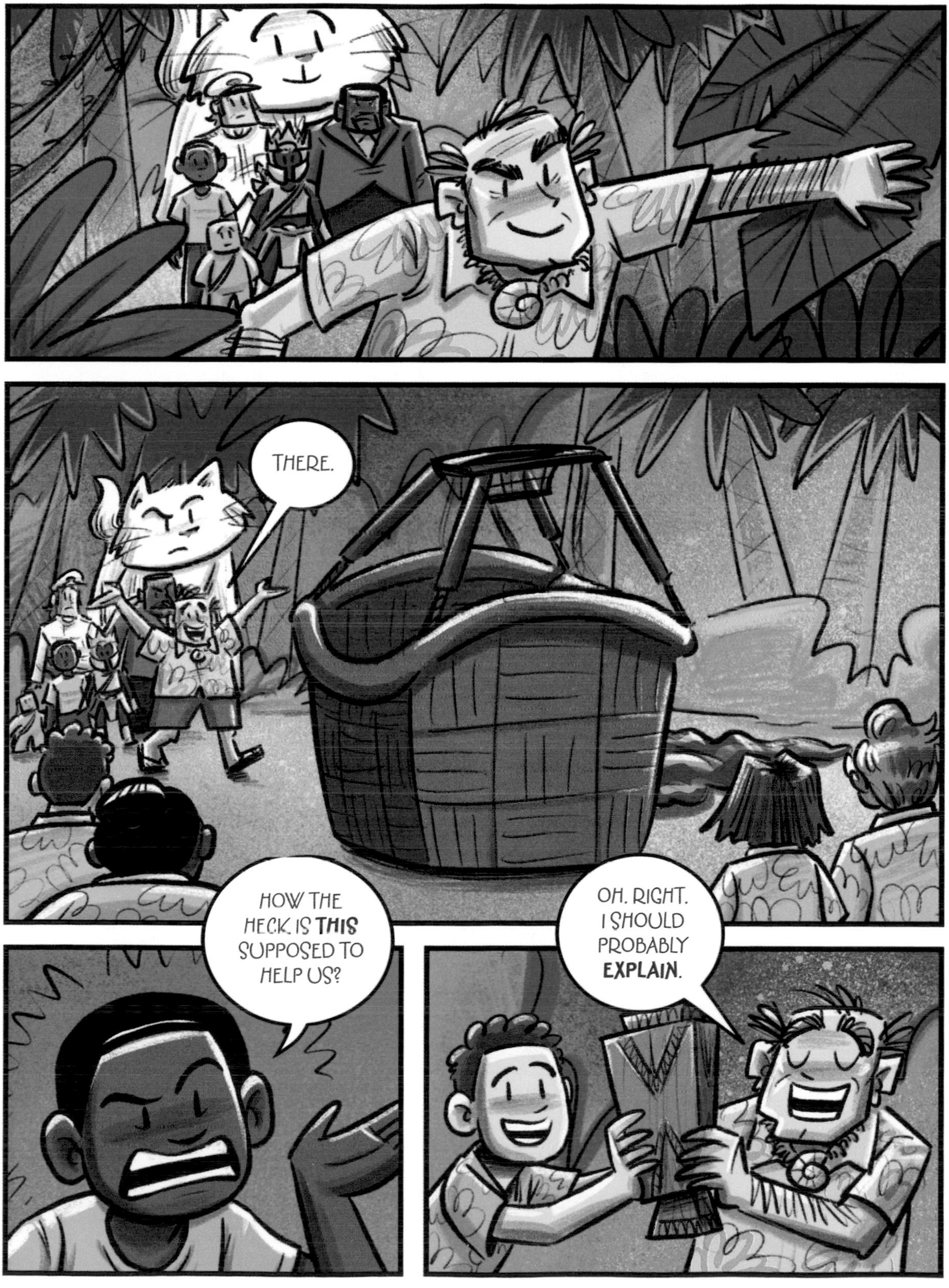
THERE.
HOW THE HECK IS **THIS** SUPPOSED TO HELP US?
OH. RIGHT. I SHOULD PROBABLY **EXPLAIN**.

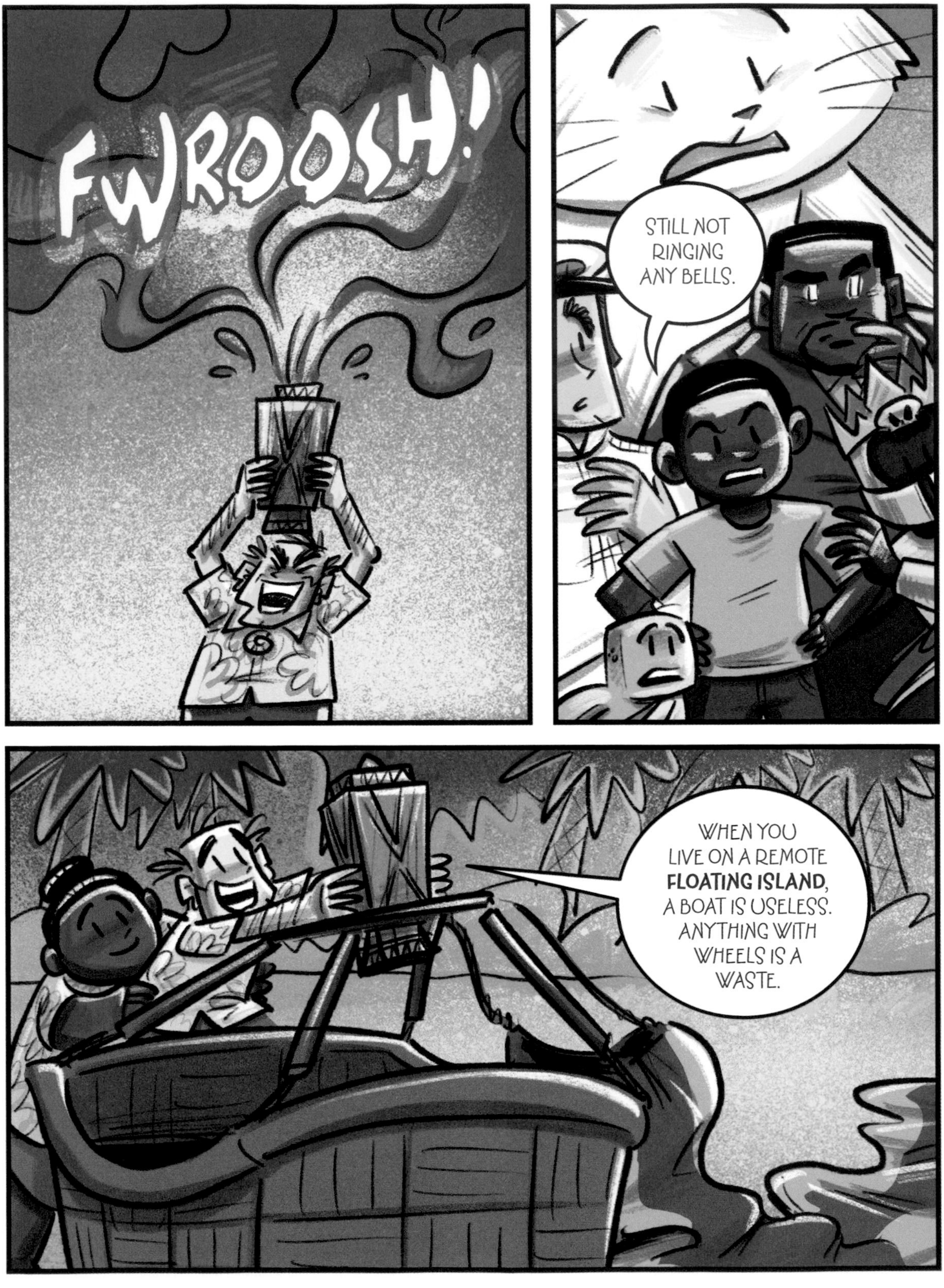
FWROOSH!
STILL NOT RINGING ANY BELLS.
WHEN YOU LIVE ON A REMOTE **FLOATING ISLAND,** A BOAT IS USELESS. ANYTHING WITH WHEELS IS A WASTE.

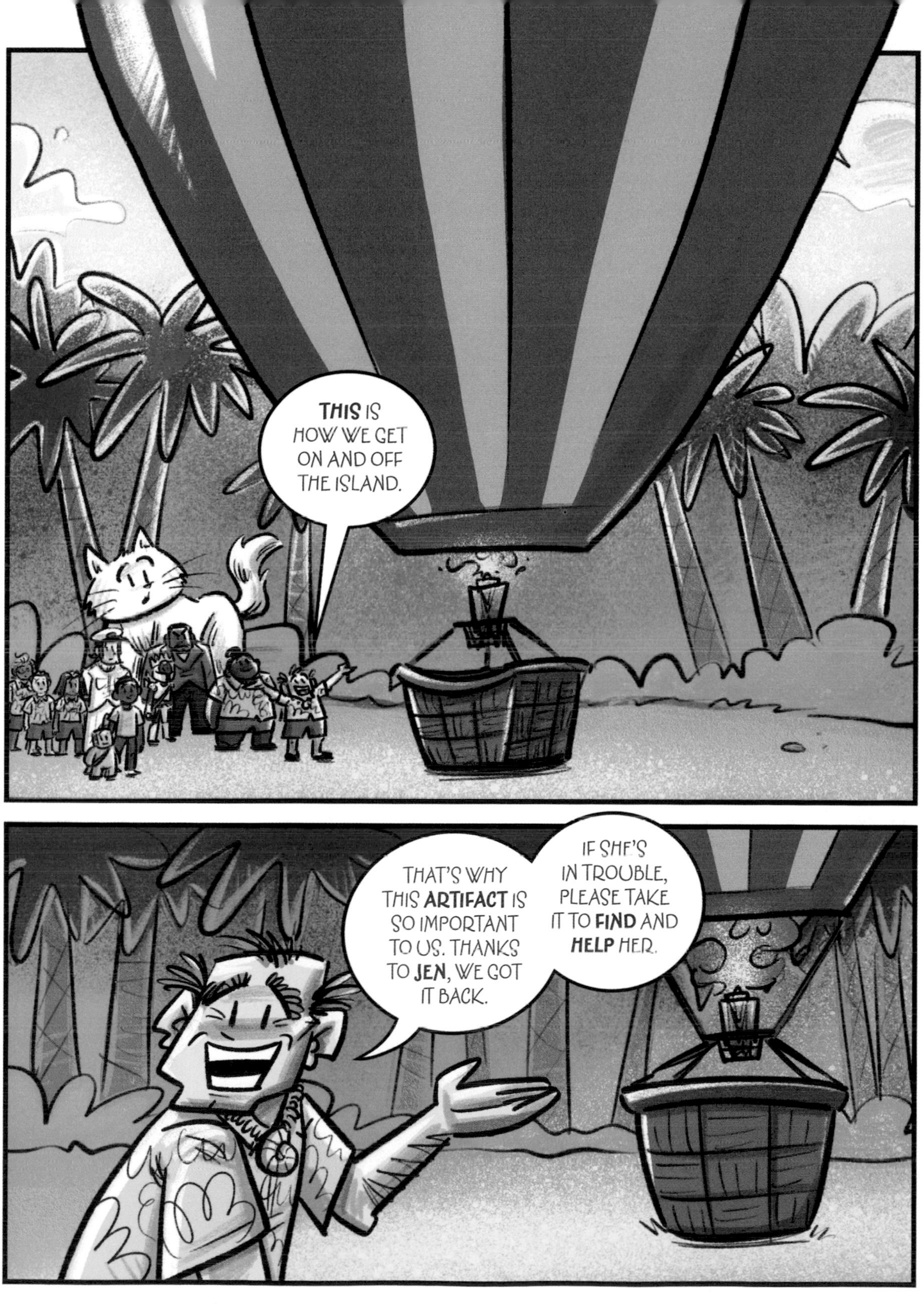
THIS IS HOW WE GET ON AND OFF THE ISLAND.
THAT'S WHY THIS ARTIFACT IS SO IMPORTANT TO US. THANKS TO JEN, WE GOT IT BACK.
IF SHE'S IN TROUBLE, PLEASE TAKE IT TO FIND AND HELP HER.

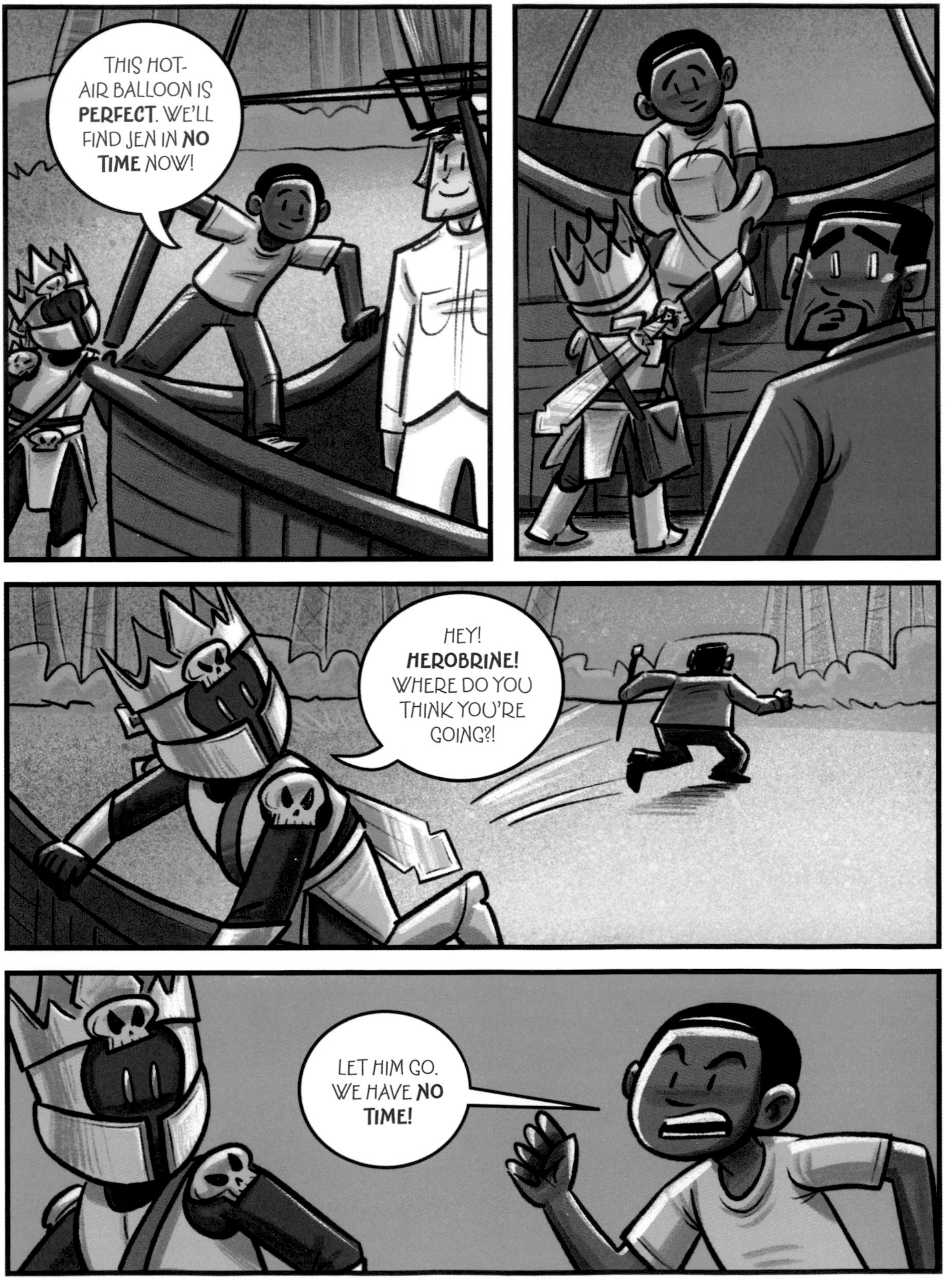
THIS HOT-AIR BALLOON IS **PERFECT**. WE'LL FIND JEN IN **NO TIME** NOW!
HEY! **HEROBRINE!** WHERE DO YOU THINK YOU'RE GOING?!
LET HIM GO. WE HAVE **NO TIME!**

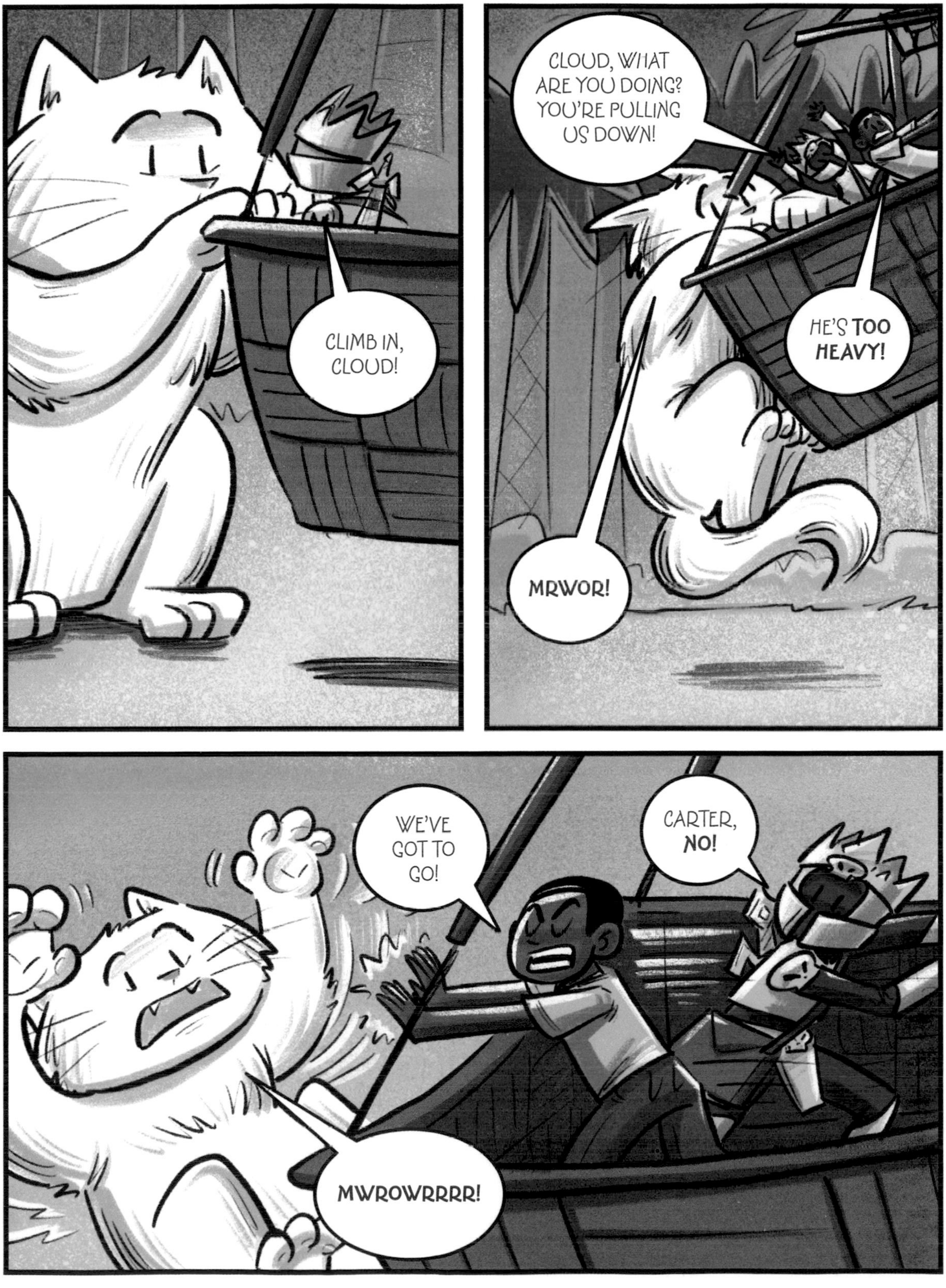
CLIMB IN, CLOUD!
CLOUD, WHAT ARE YOU DOING? YOU'RE PULLING US DOWN!
HE'S TOO HEAVY!
MRWOR!
WE'VE GOT TO GO!
CARTER, NO!
MWROWRRRR!

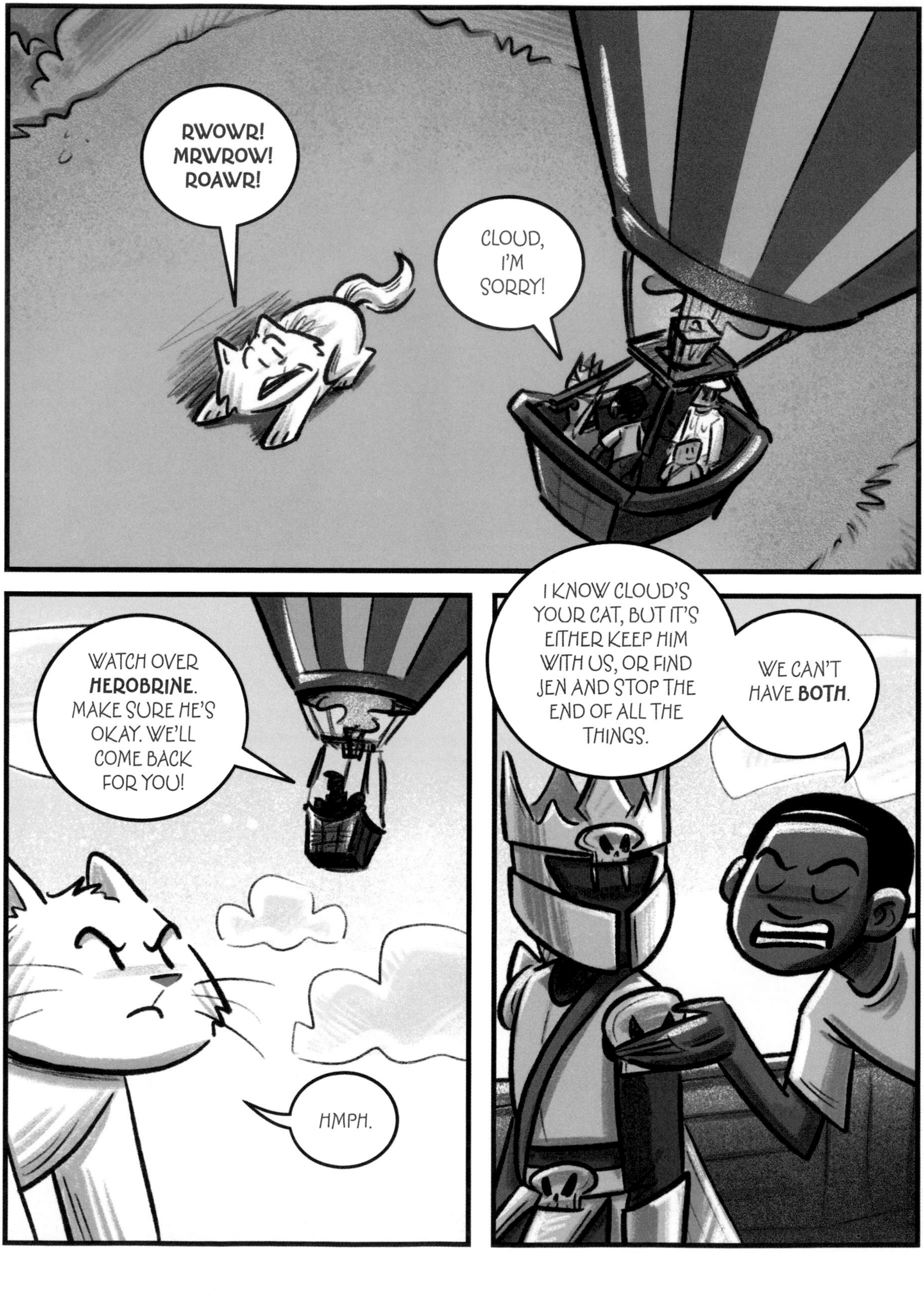
RWOWR! MRWROW! ROAWR!
CLOUD, I'M SORRY!
WATCH OVER **HEROBRINE**. MAKE SURE HE'S OKAY. WE'LL COME BACK FOR YOU!
HMPH.
I KNOW CLOUD'S YOUR CAT, BUT IT'S EITHER KEEP HIM WITH US, OR FIND JEN AND STOP THE END OF ALL THE THINGS.
WE CAN'T HAVE **BOTH**.

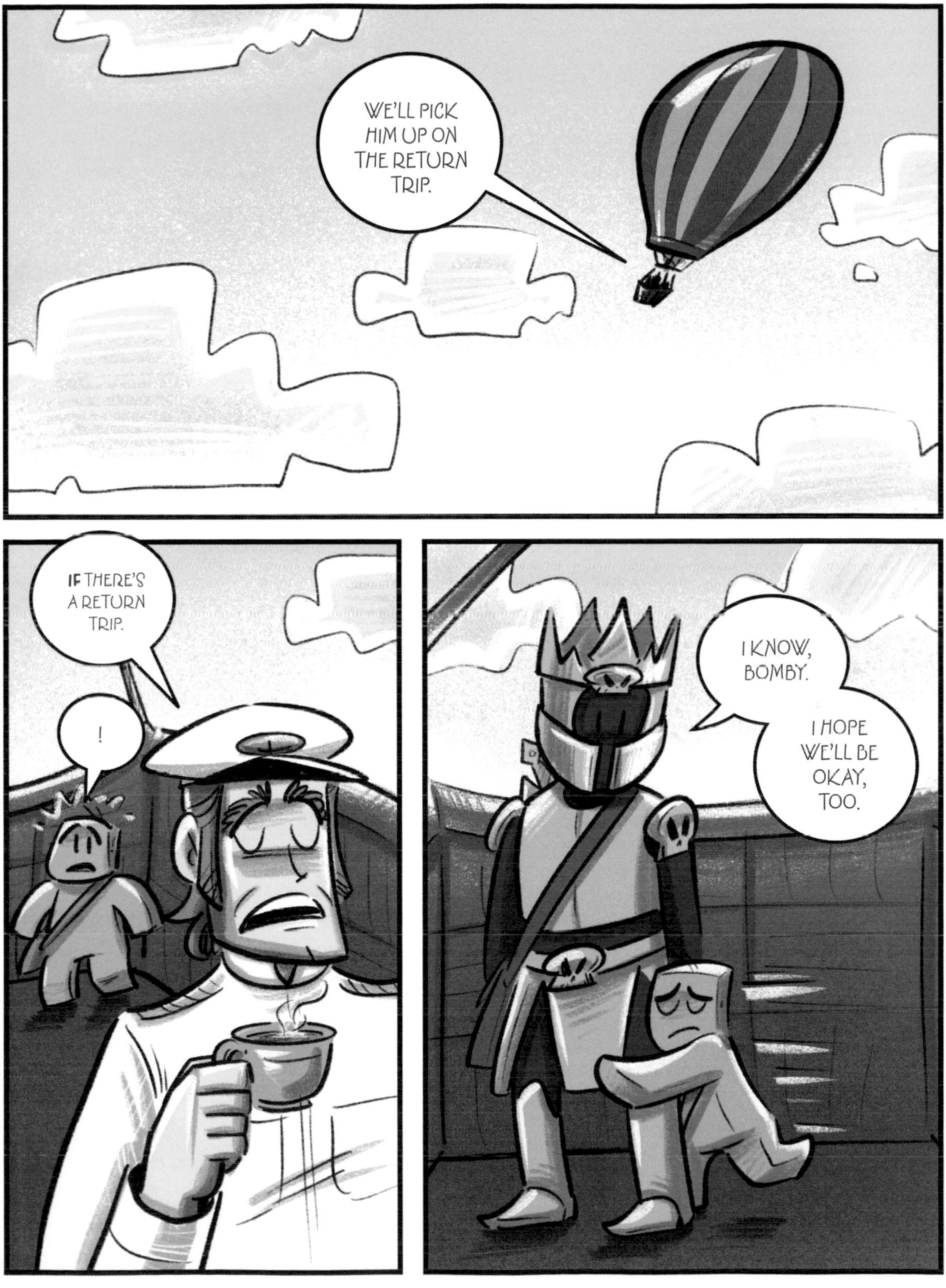
WE'LL PICK HIM UP ON THE RETURN TRIP.
IF THERE'S A RETURN TRIP.
!
I KNOW, BOMBY.
I HOPE WE'LL BE OKAY, TOO.

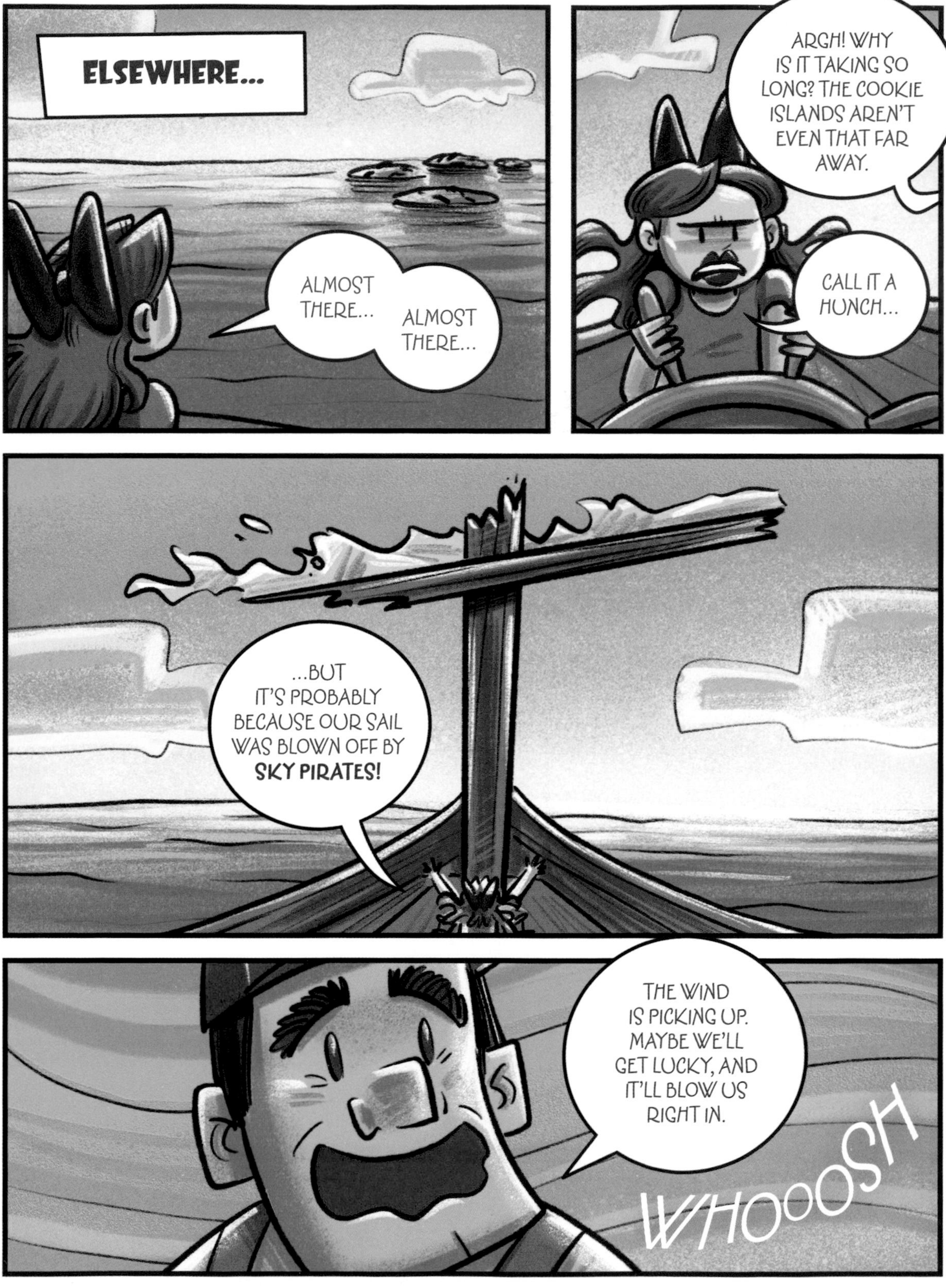
ELSEWHERE...
ALMOST THERE...
ALMOST THERE...
ARGH! WHY IS IT TAKING SO LONG? THE COOKIE ISLANDS AREN'T EVEN THAT FAR AWAY.
CALL IT A HUNCH...
...BUT IT'S PROBABLY BECAUSE OUR SAIL WAS BLOWN OFF BY **SKY PIRATES!**
THE WIND IS PICKING UP. MAYBE WE'LL GET LUCKY, AND IT'LL BLOW US RIGHT IN.
WHOOOOSH

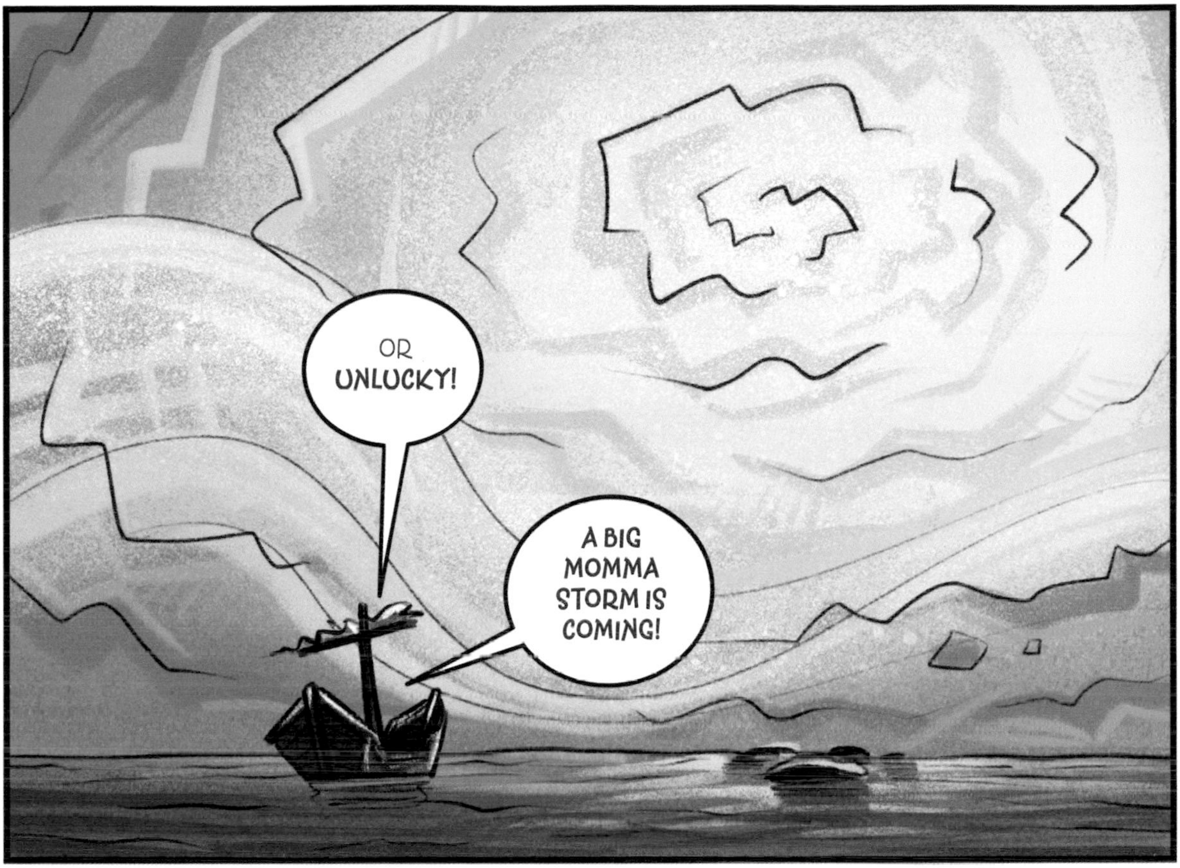
OR UNLUCKY!
A BIG MOMMA STORM IS COMING!

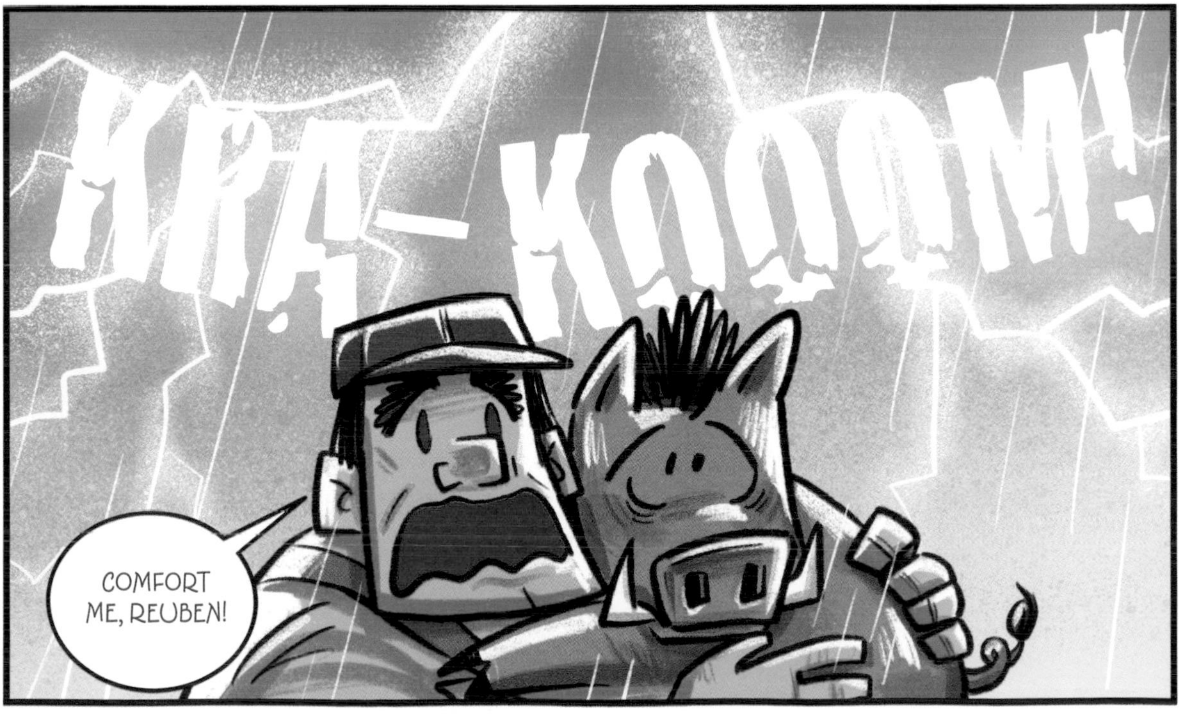
KRA-KOOOM!
COMFORT ME, REUBEN!

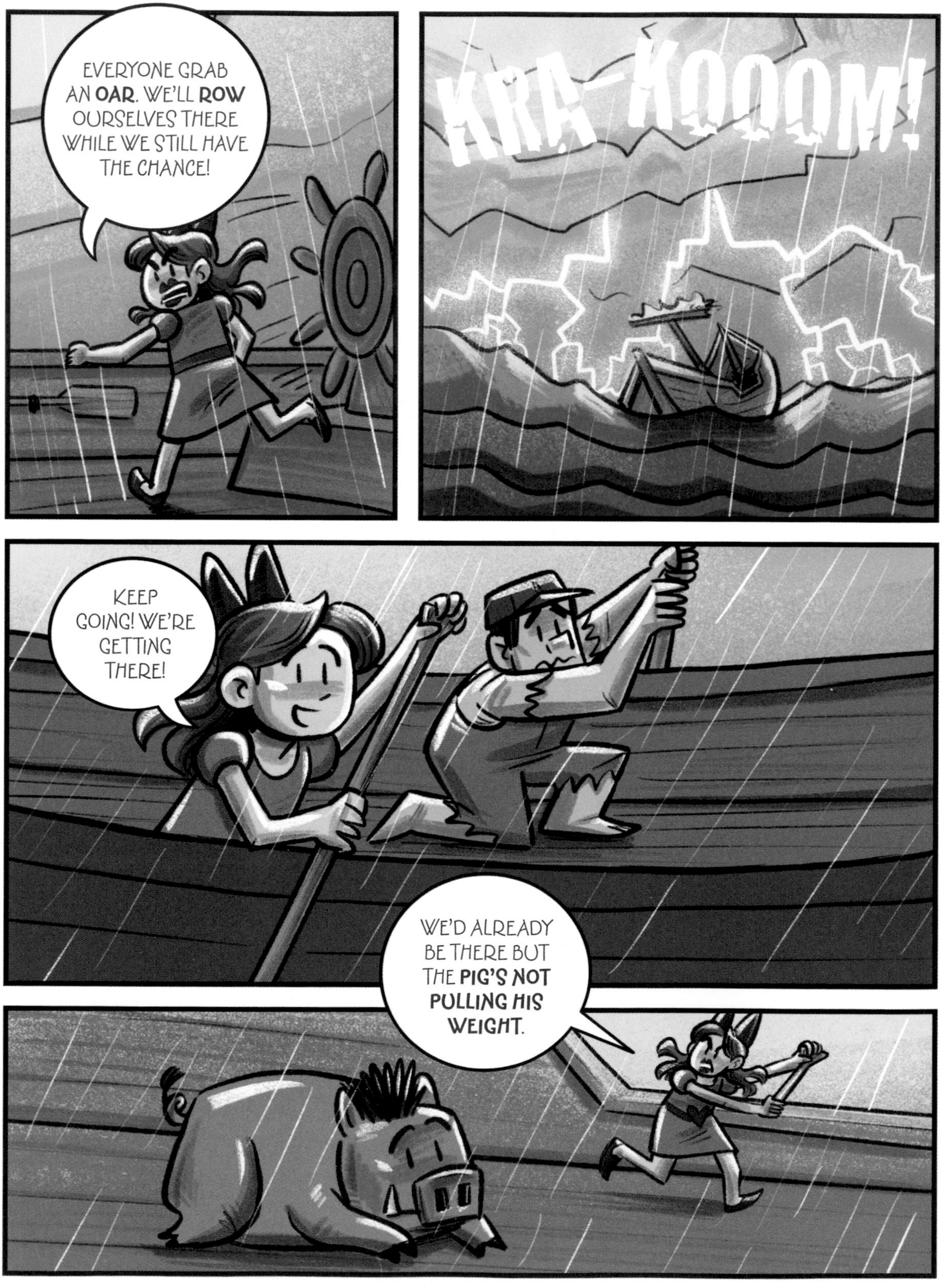
EVERYONE GRAB AN **OAR**. WE'LL **ROW** OURSELVES THERE WHILE WE STILL HAVE THE CHANCE!
KRA-KOOOM!
KEEP GOING! WE'RE GETTING THERE!
WE'D ALREADY BE THERE BUT THE **PIG'S NOT PULLING HIS WEIGHT**.

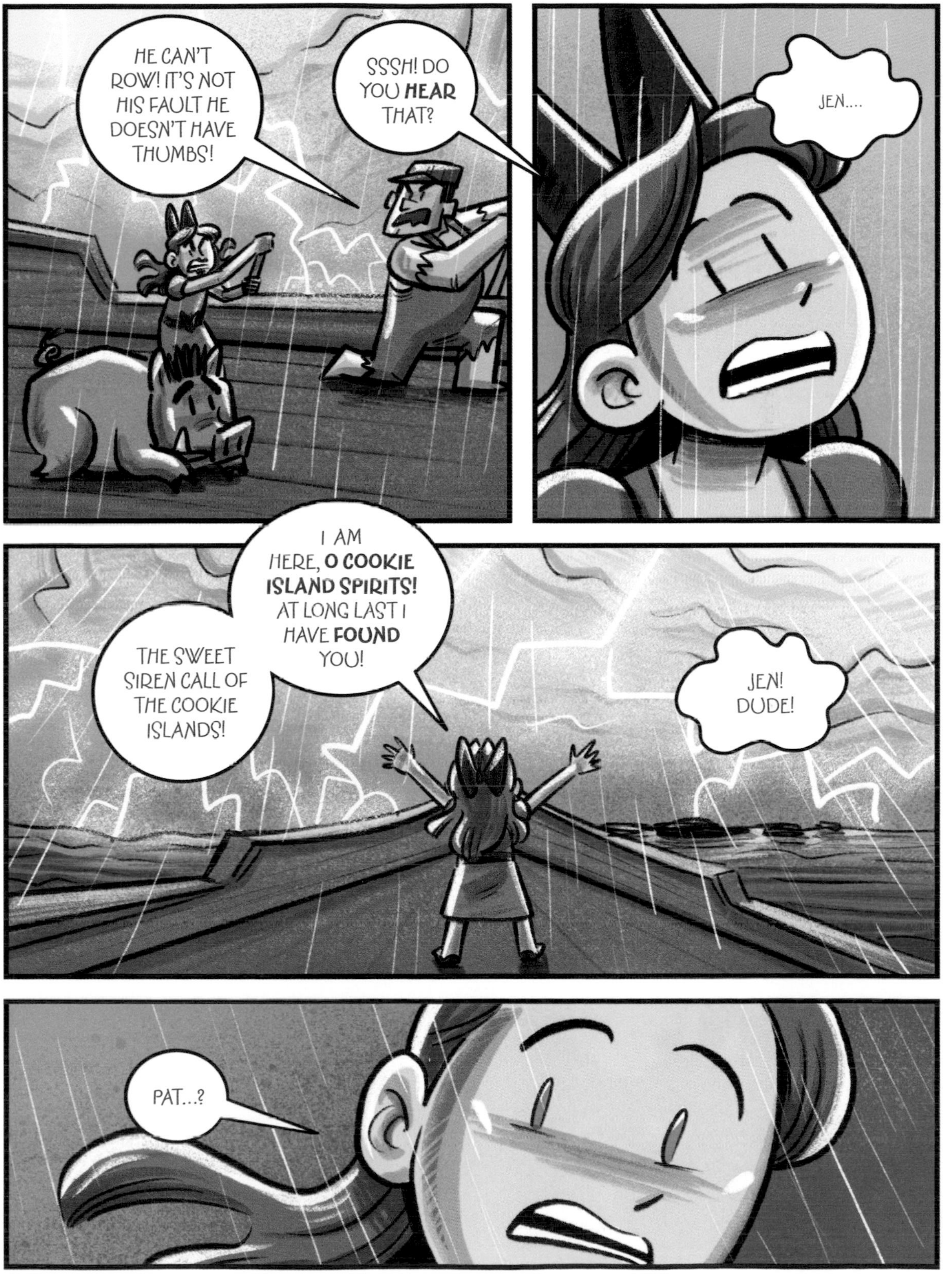
HE CAN'T ROW! IT'S NOT HIS FAULT HE DOESN'T HAVE THUMBS!
SSSH! DO YOU **HEAR** THAT?
JEN....
THE SWEET SIREN CALL OF THE COOKIE ISLANDS!
I AM HERE, **O COOKIE ISLAND SPIRITS!** AT LONG LAST I HAVE **FOUND** YOU!
JEN! DUDE!
PAT...?

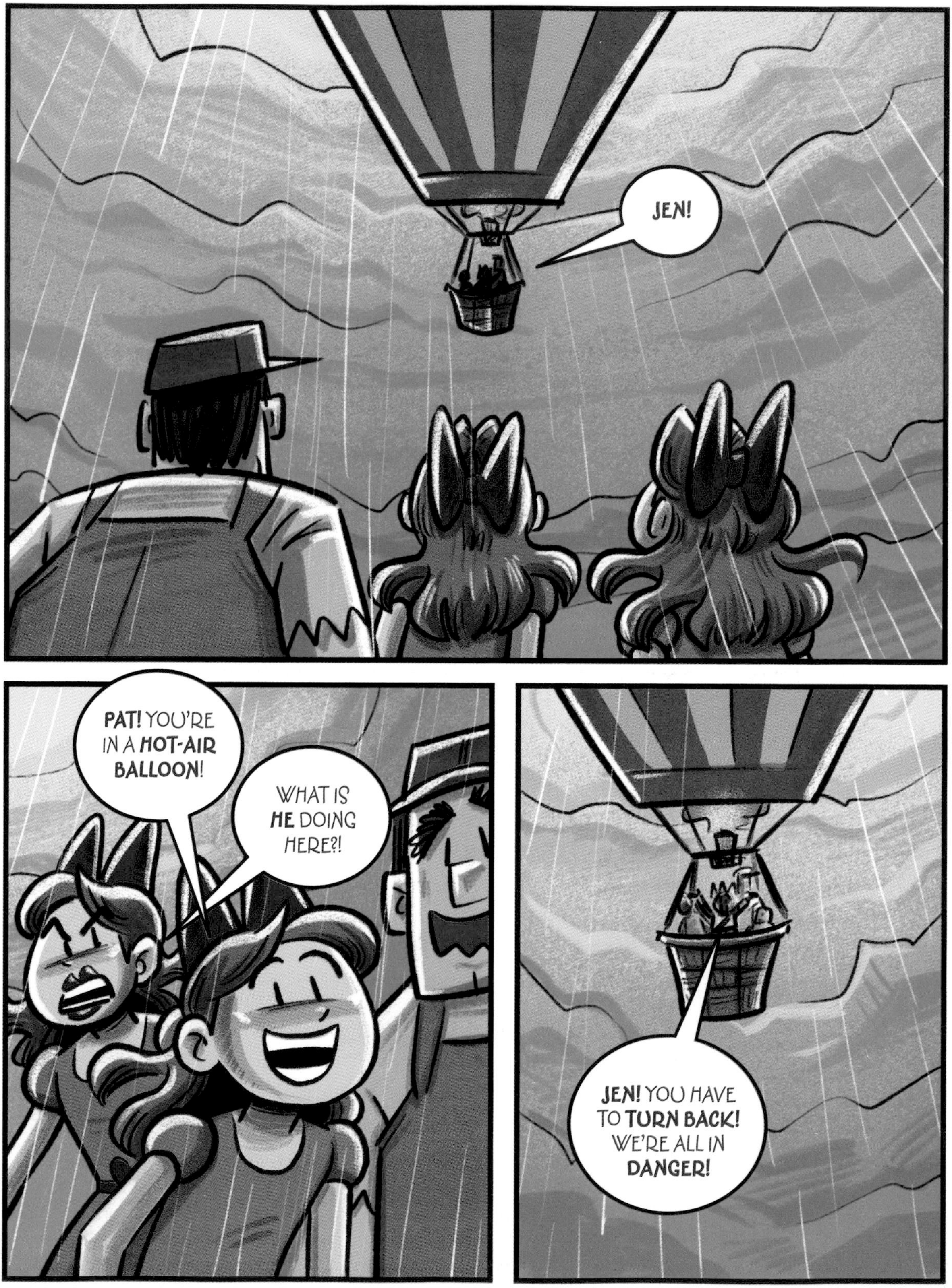
JEN!
PAT! YOU'RE IN A HOT-AIR BALLOON!
WHAT IS HE DOING HERE?!
JEN! YOU HAVE TO TURN BACK! WE'RE ALL IN DANGER!

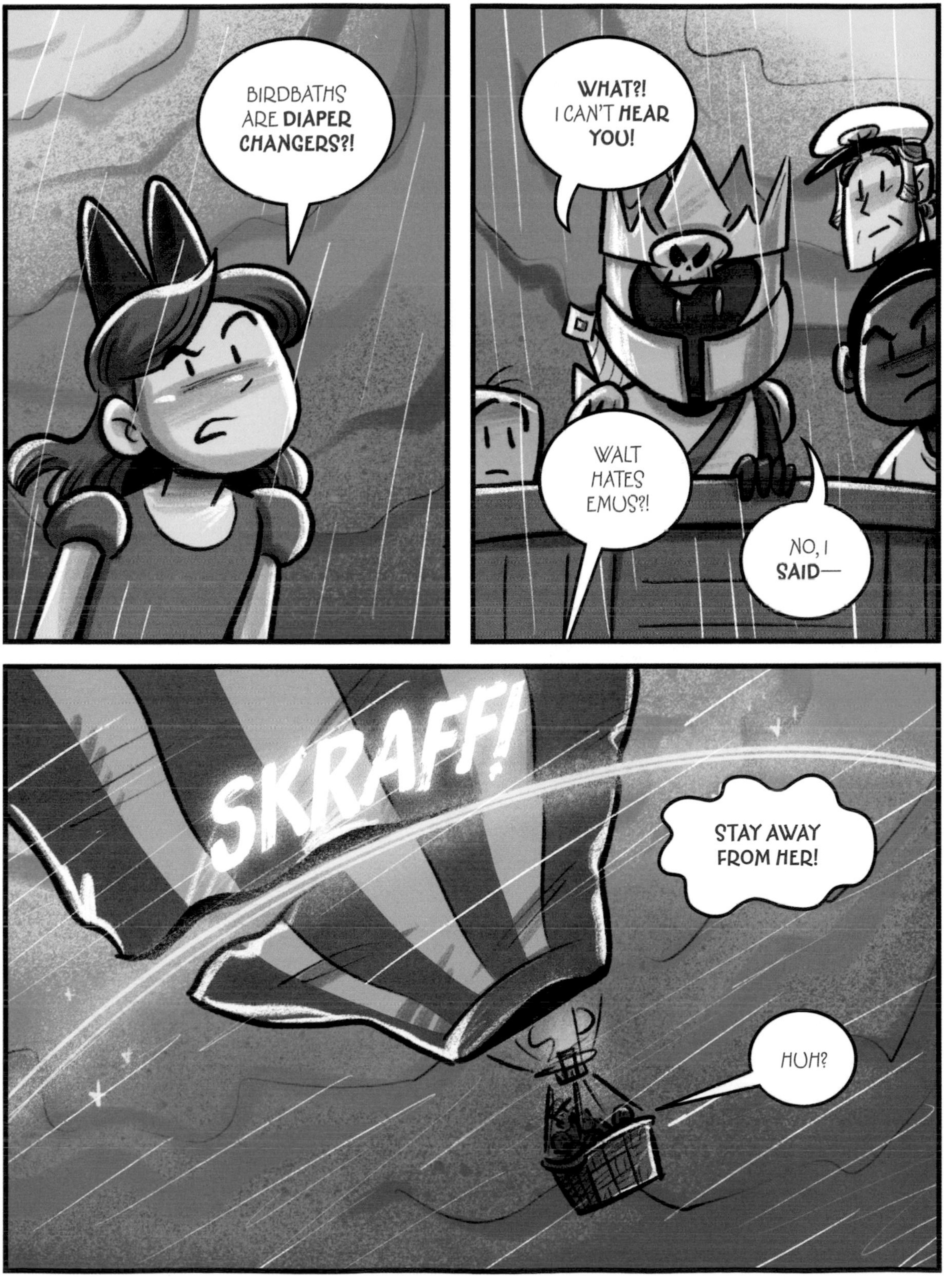
BIRDBATHS ARE DIAPER CHANGERS?!
WHAT?! I CAN'T HEAR YOU!
WALT HATES EMUS?!
NO, I SAID—
SKRAFF!
STAY AWAY FROM HER!
HUH?

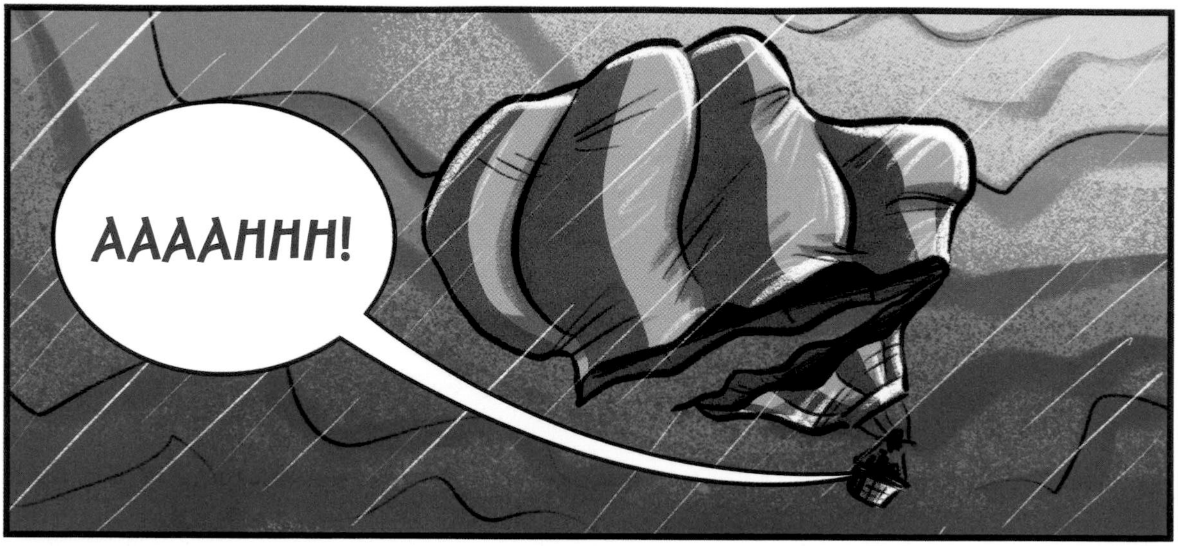
AAAAHHH!

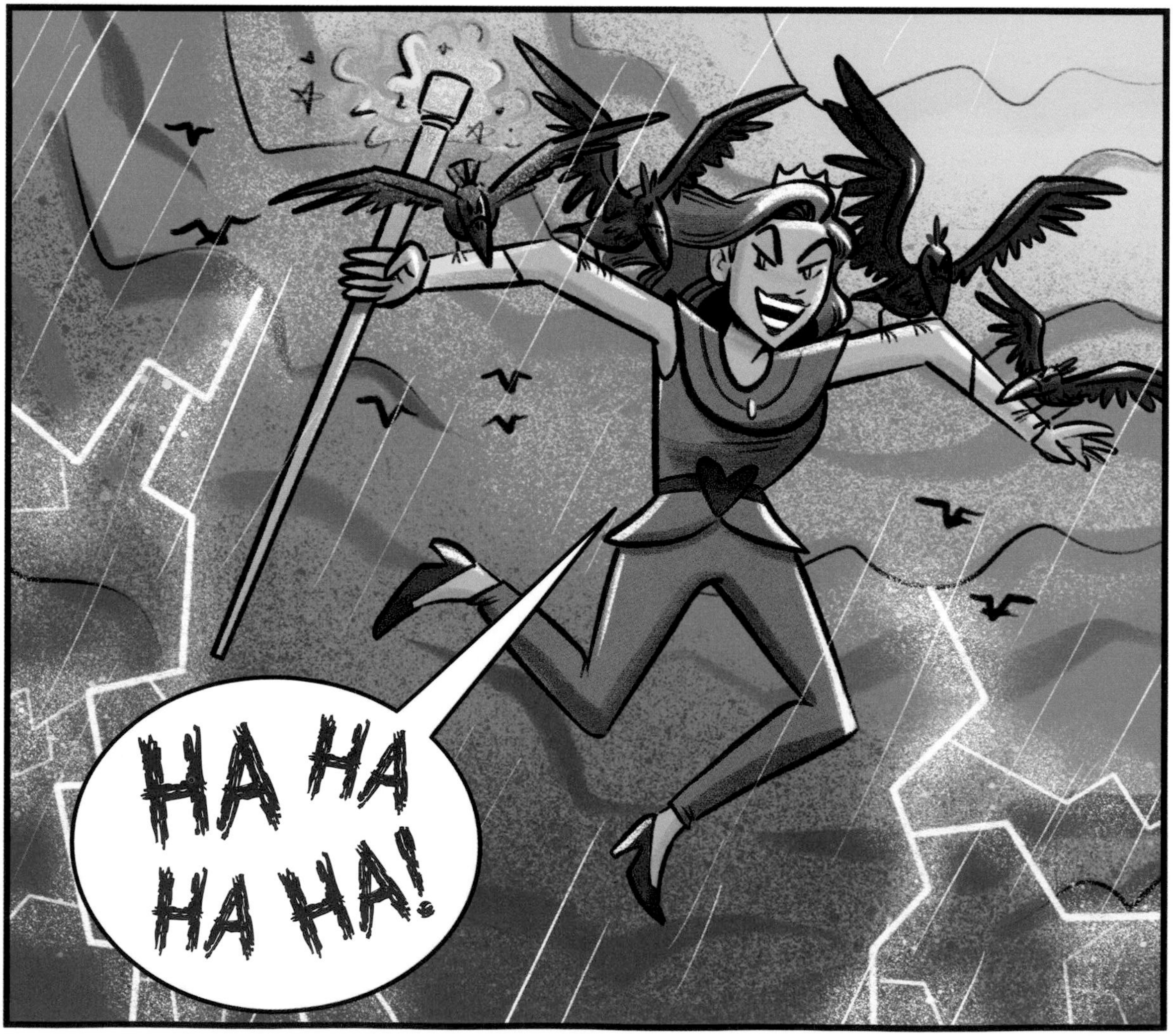
HA HA HA HA!

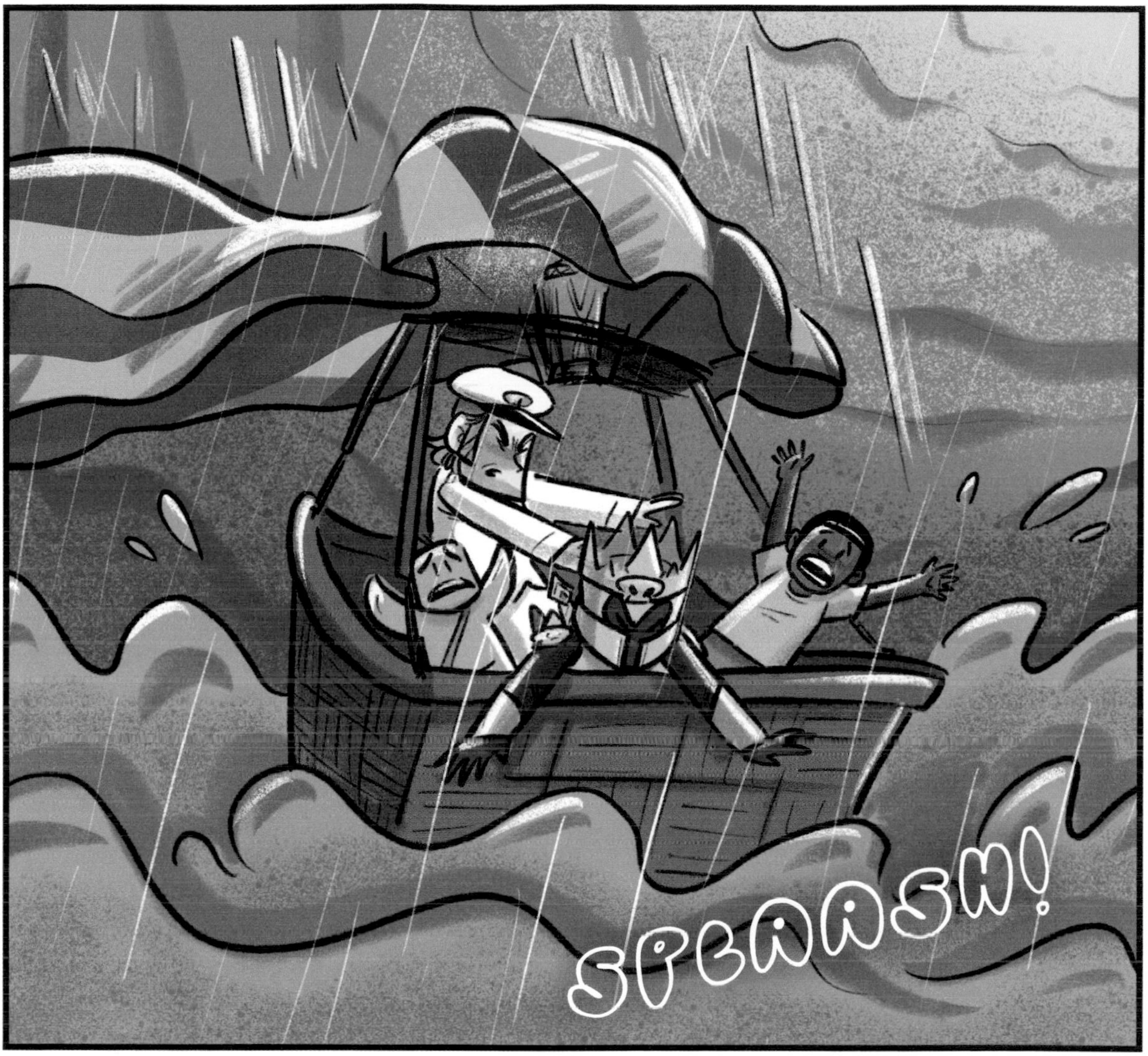
SPLAASH!

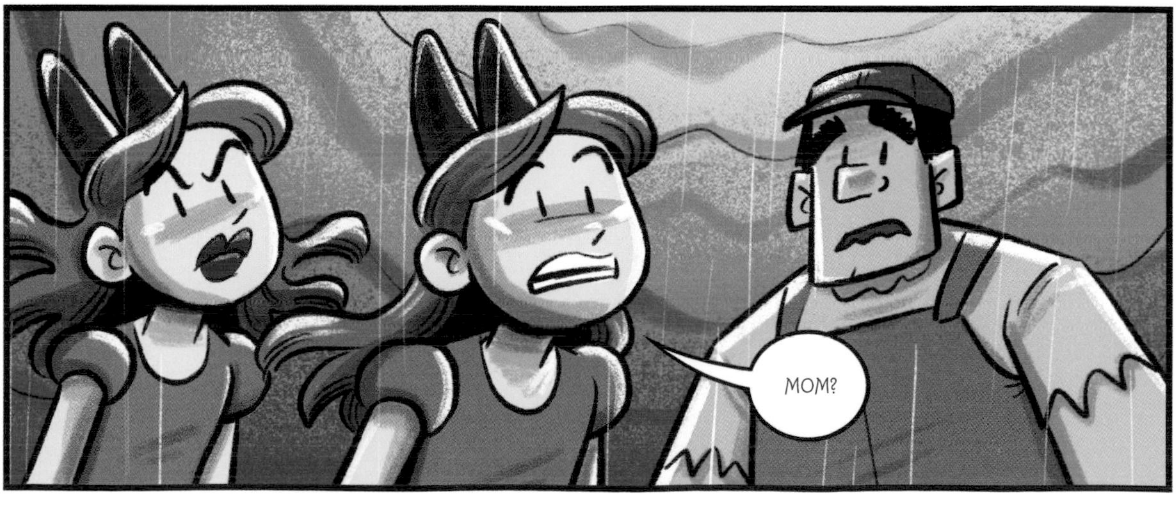
MOM?

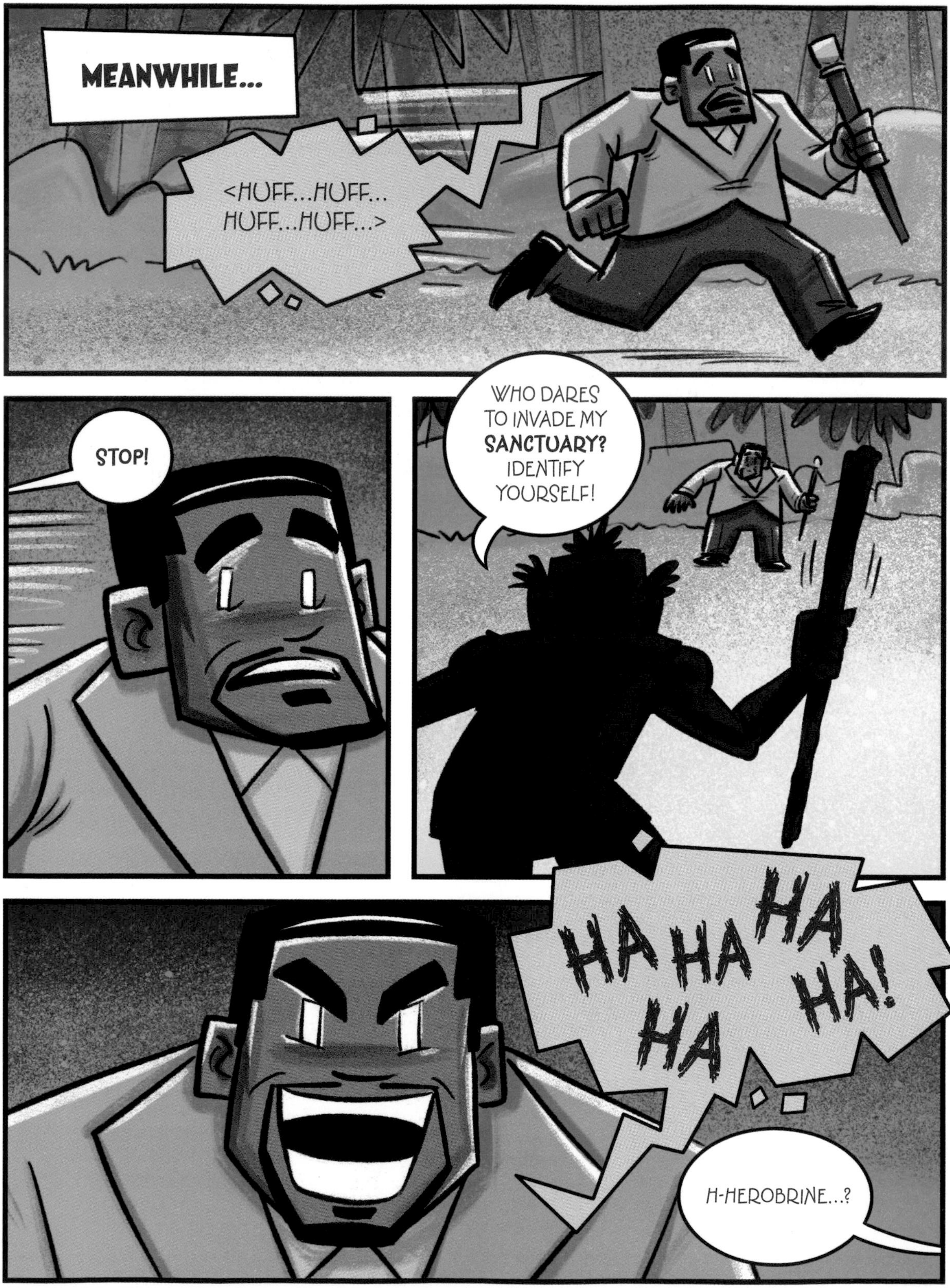
MEANWHILE...
<HUFF...HUFF...
HUFF...HUFF...>
STOP!
WHO DARES TO INVADE MY **SANCTUARY?** IDENTIFY YOURSELF!
HA HA HA HA HA HA!
H-HEROBRINE...?

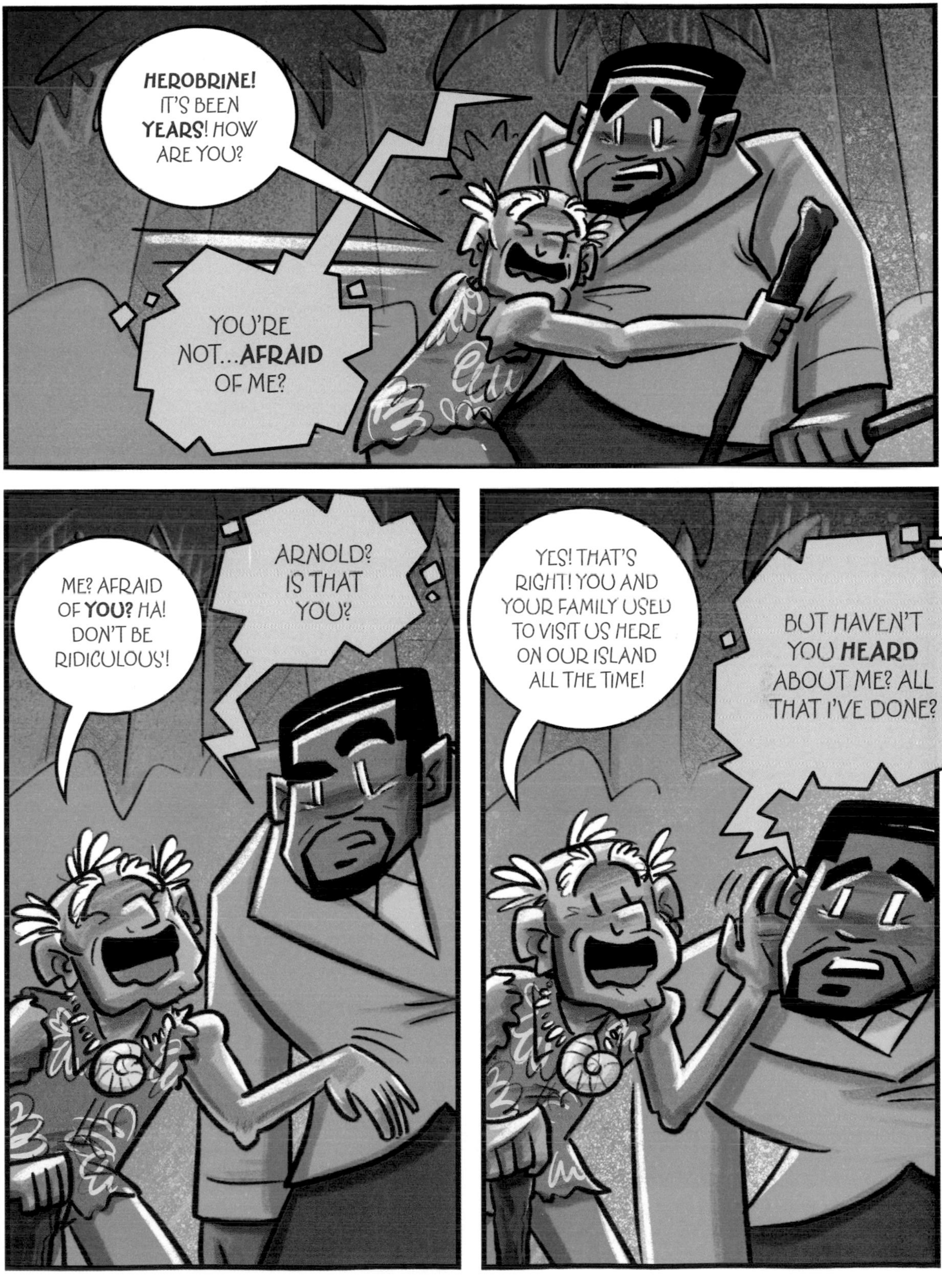
HEROBRINE! IT'S BEEN YEARS! HOW ARE YOU?
YOU'RE NOT...AFRAID OF ME?
ME? AFRAID OF YOU? HA! DON'T BE RIDICULOUS!
ARNOLD? IS THAT YOU?
YES! THAT'S RIGHT! YOU AND YOUR FAMILY USED TO VISIT US HERE ON OUR ISLAND ALL THE TIME!
BUT HAVEN'T YOU HEARD ABOUT ME? ALL THAT I'VE DONE?

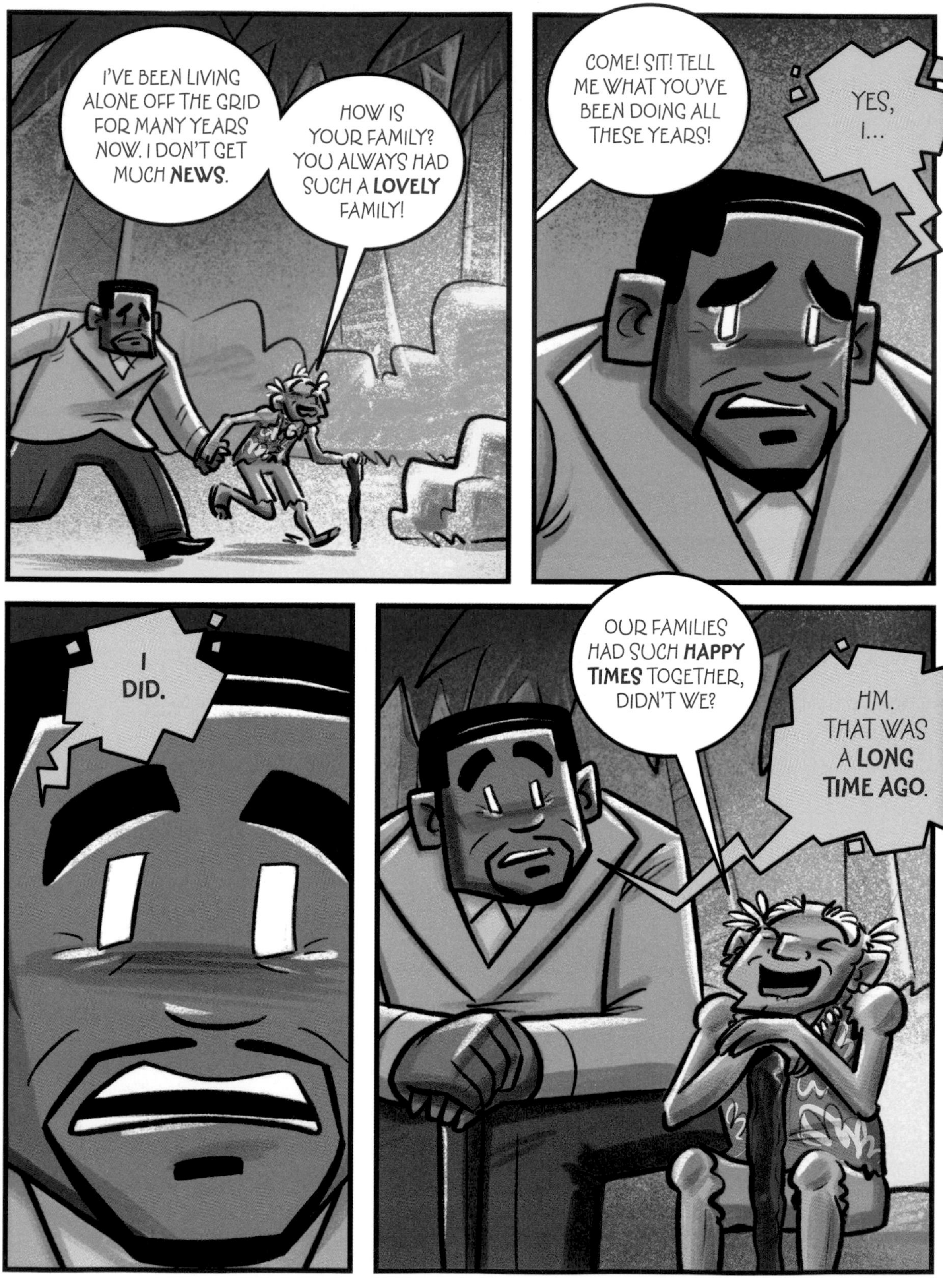
I'VE BEEN LIVING ALONE OFF THE GRID FOR MANY YEARS NOW. I DON'T GET MUCH **NEWS**.
HOW IS YOUR FAMILY? YOU ALWAYS HAD SUCH A **LOVELY** FAMILY!
COME! SIT! TELL ME WHAT YOU'VE BEEN DOING ALL THESE YEARS!
YES, I...
I DID.
OUR FAMILIES HAD SUCH **HAPPY TIMES** TOGETHER, DIDN'T WE?
HM. THAT WAS A **LONG TIME AGO**.

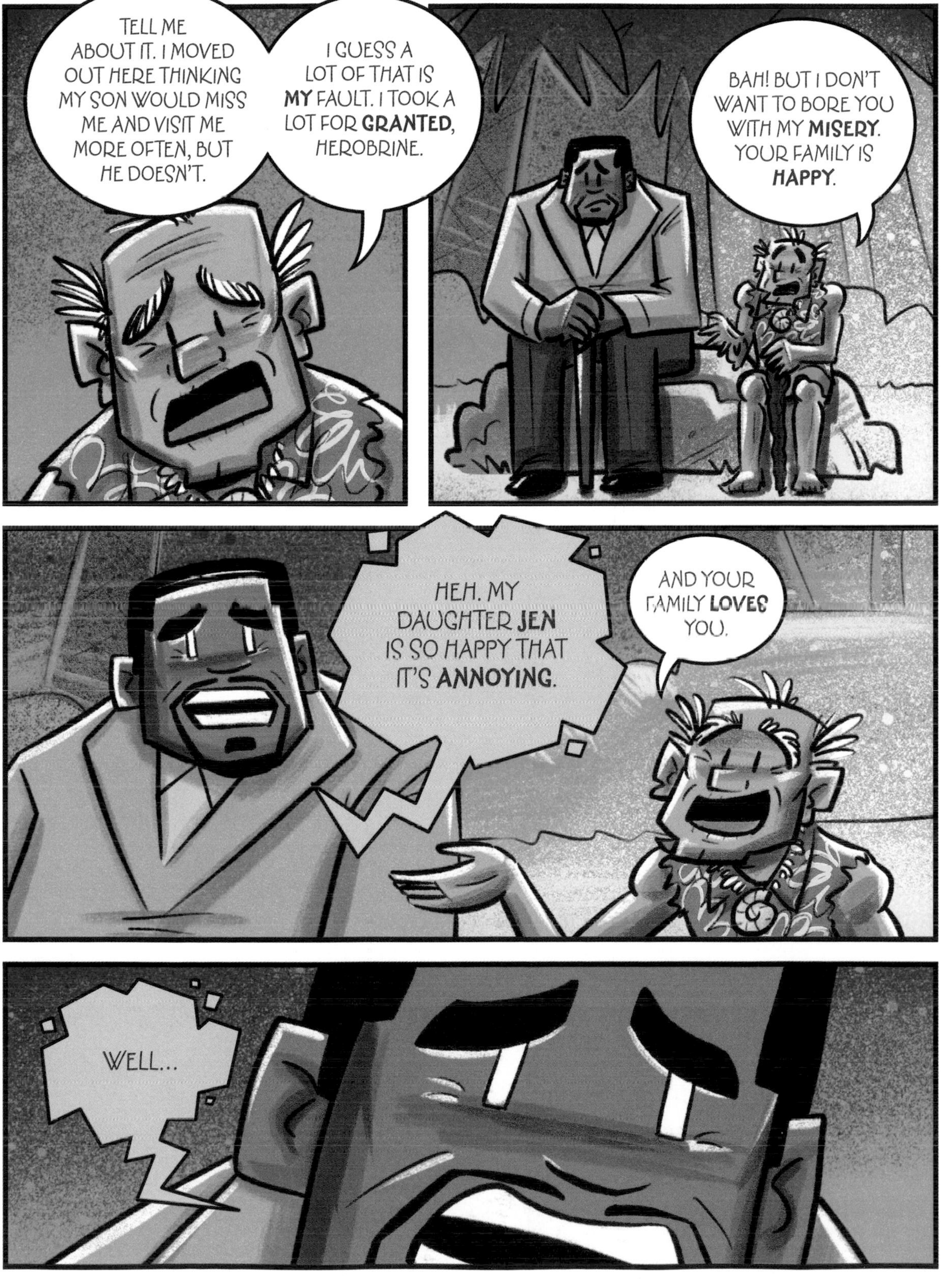
TELL ME ABOUT IT. I MOVED OUT HERE THINKING MY SON WOULD MISS ME AND VISIT ME MORE OFTEN, BUT HE DOESN'T.
I GUESS A LOT OF THAT IS **MY** FAULT. I TOOK A LOT FOR **GRANTED**, HEROBRINE.
BAH! BUT I DON'T WANT TO BORE YOU WITH MY **MISERY**. YOUR FAMILY IS **HAPPY**.
HEH. MY DAUGHTER **JEN** IS SO HAPPY THAT IT'S **ANNOYING**.
AND YOUR FAMILY **LOVES** YOU.
WELL...

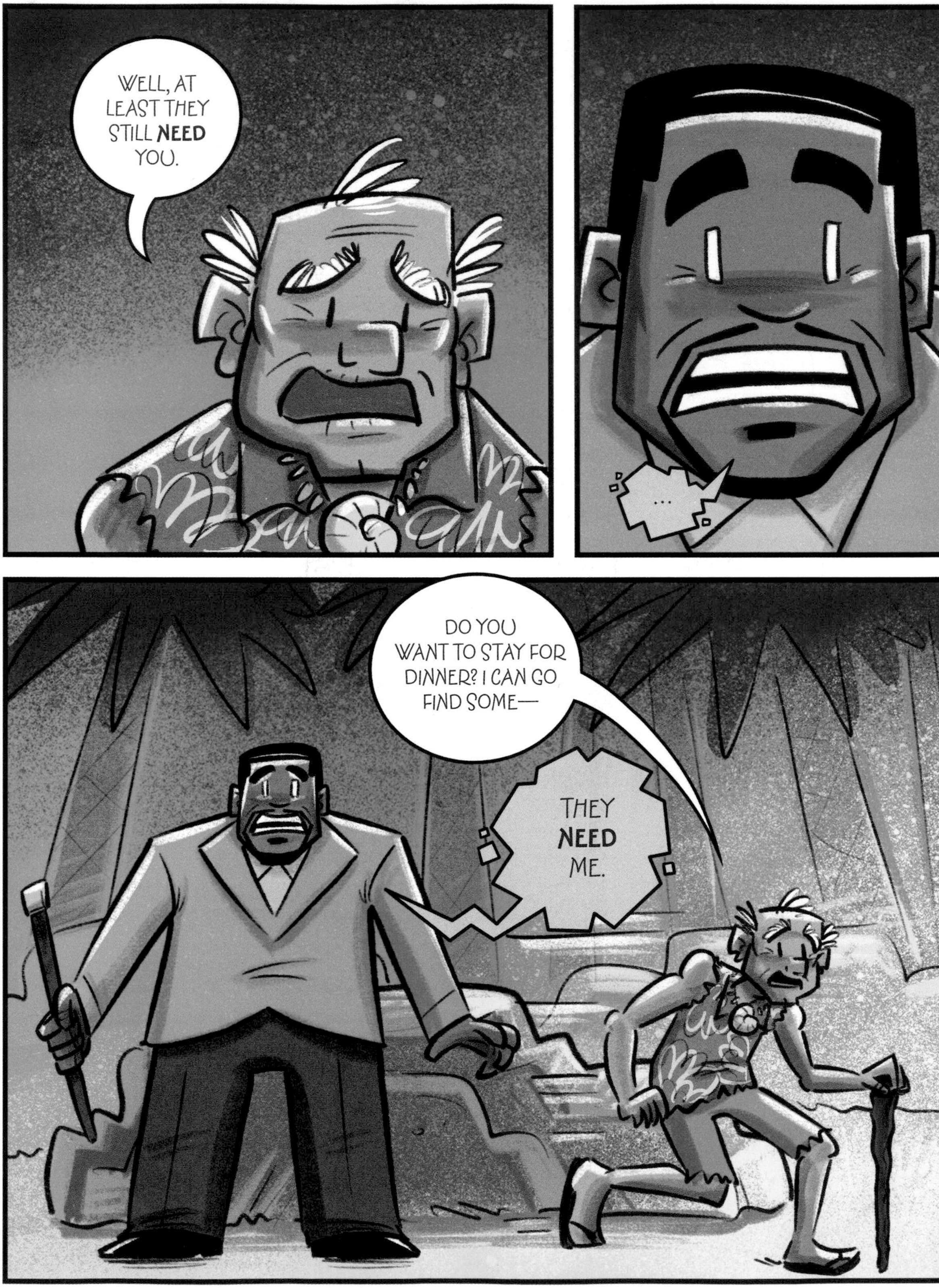
WELL, AT LEAST THEY STILL **NEED** YOU.
...
DO YOU WANT TO STAY FOR DINNER? I CAN GO FIND SOME—
THEY **NEED** ME.

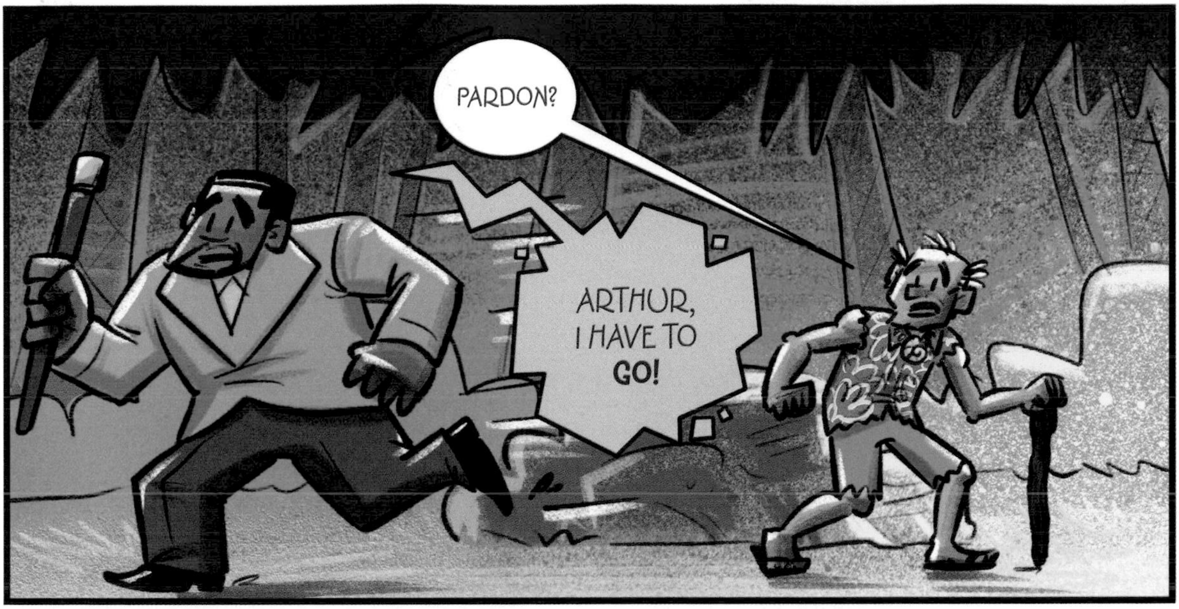
PARDON?
ARTHUR, I HAVE TO GO!

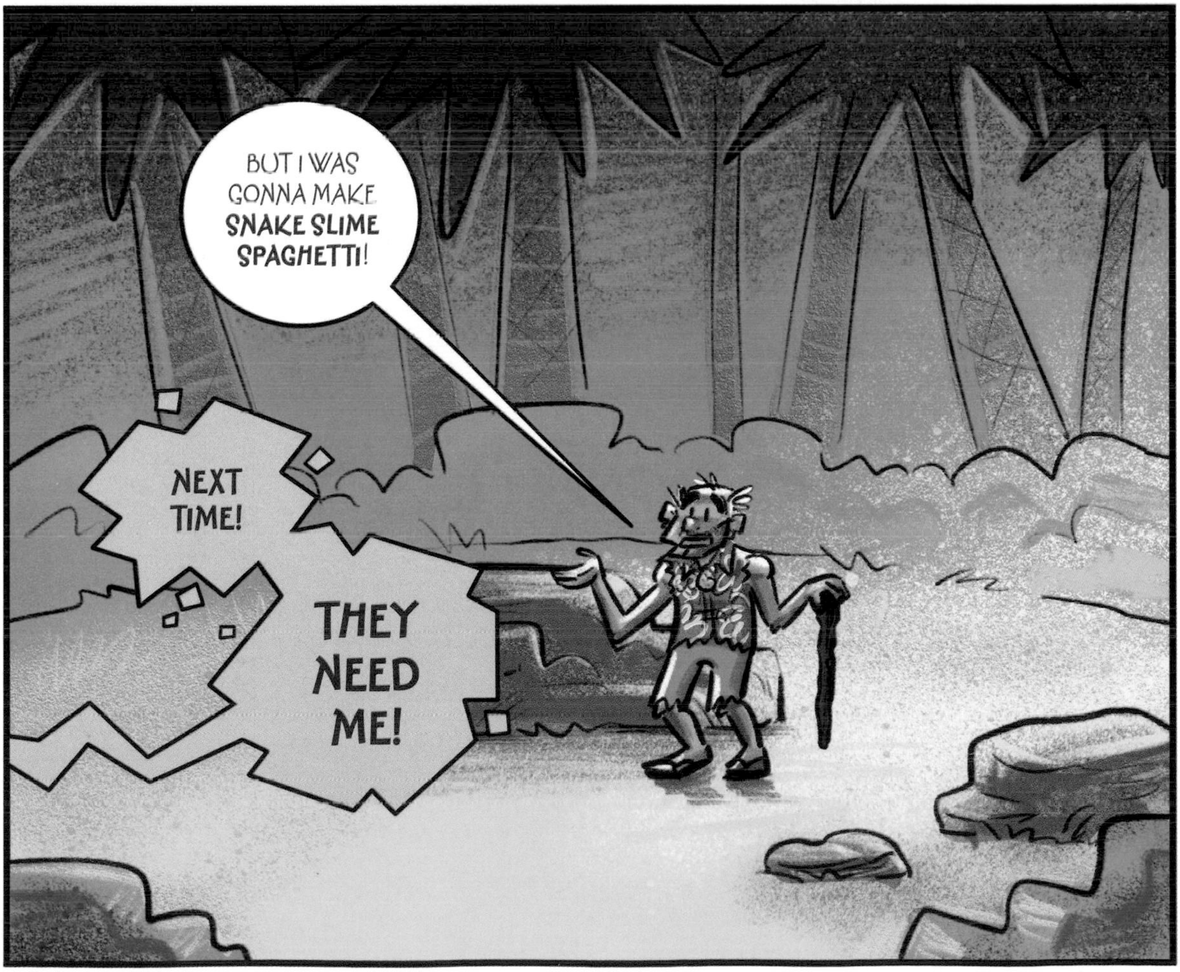
BUT I WAS GONNA MAKE SNAKE SLIME SPAGHETTI!
NEXT TIME!
THEY NEED ME!

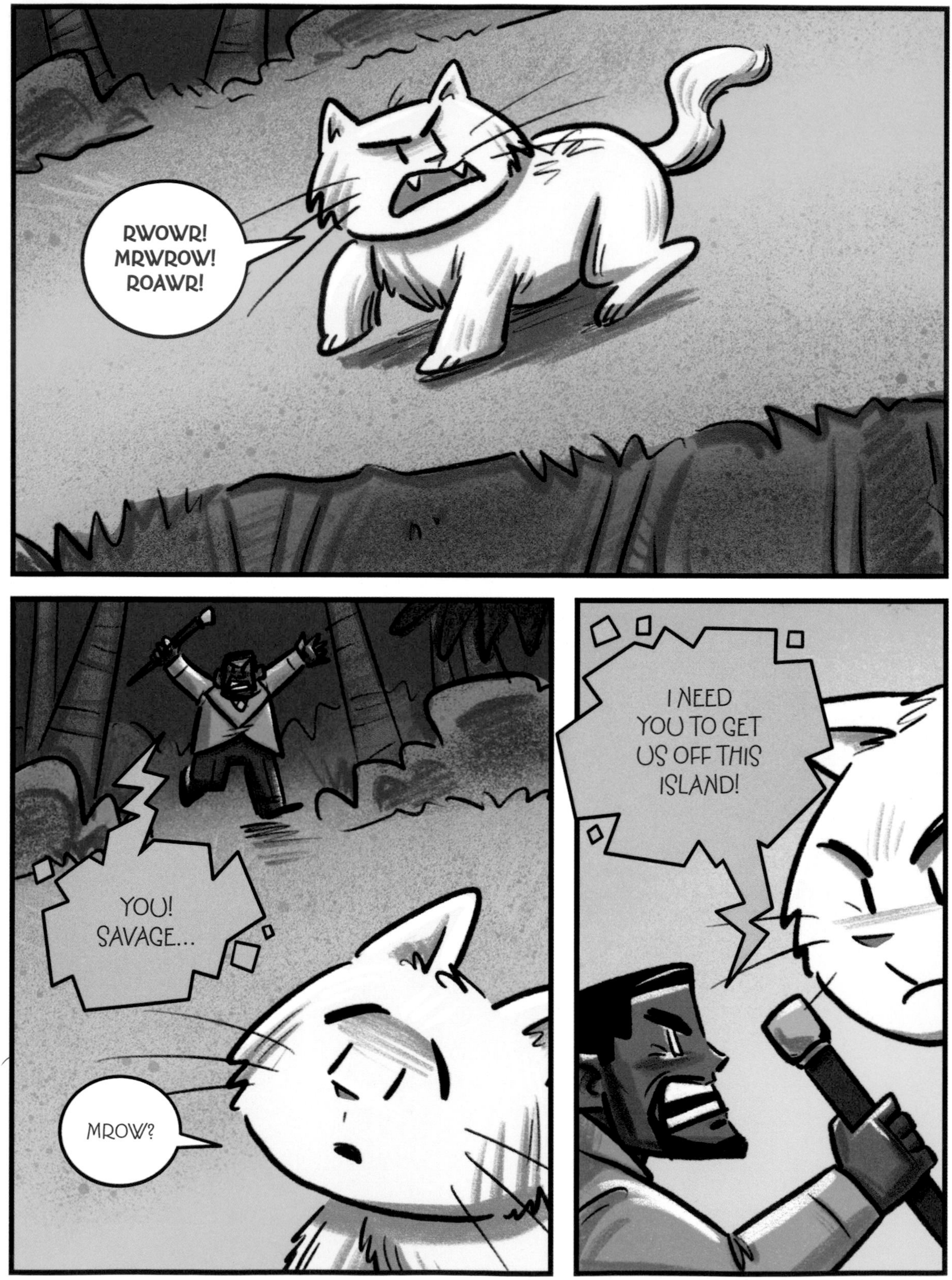
RWOWR! MRWROW! ROAWR!
YOU! SAVAGE...
MROW?
I NEED YOU TO GET US OFF THIS ISLAND!

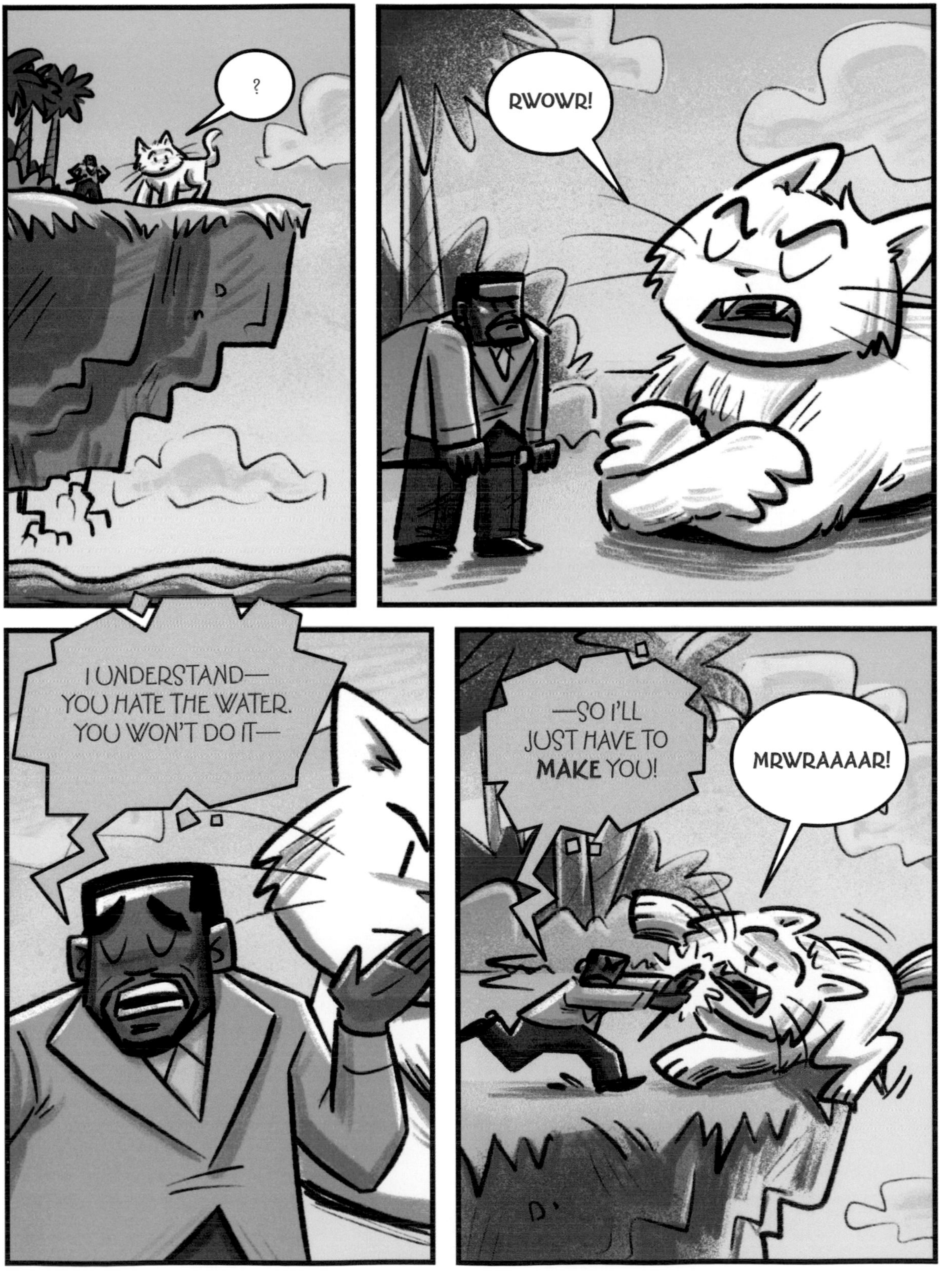
?
RWOWR!
I UNDERSTAND— YOU HATE THE WATER. YOU WON'T DO IT—
—SO I'LL JUST HAVE TO MAKE YOU!
MRWRAAAAR!

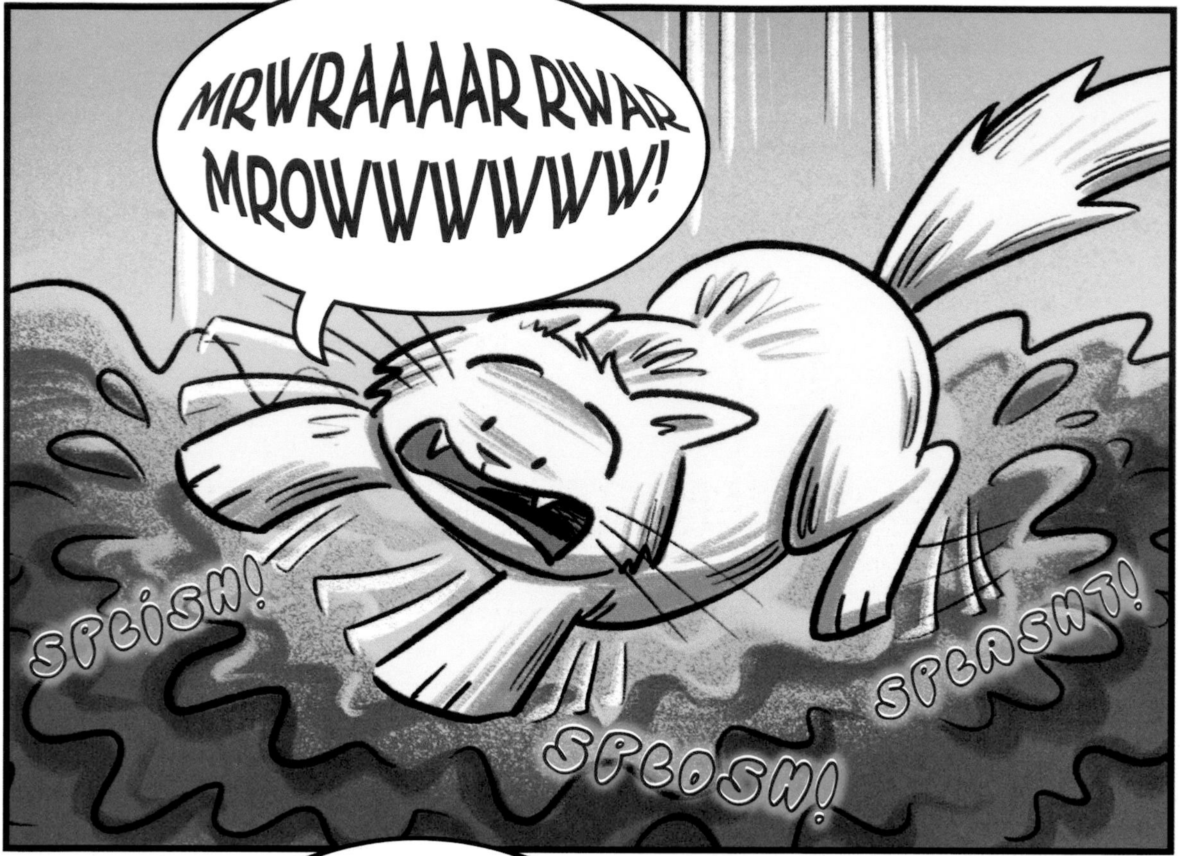
MRWRAAAAR RWAR MROWWWWWW!
SPLISH!
SPLOSH!
SPLASHT!

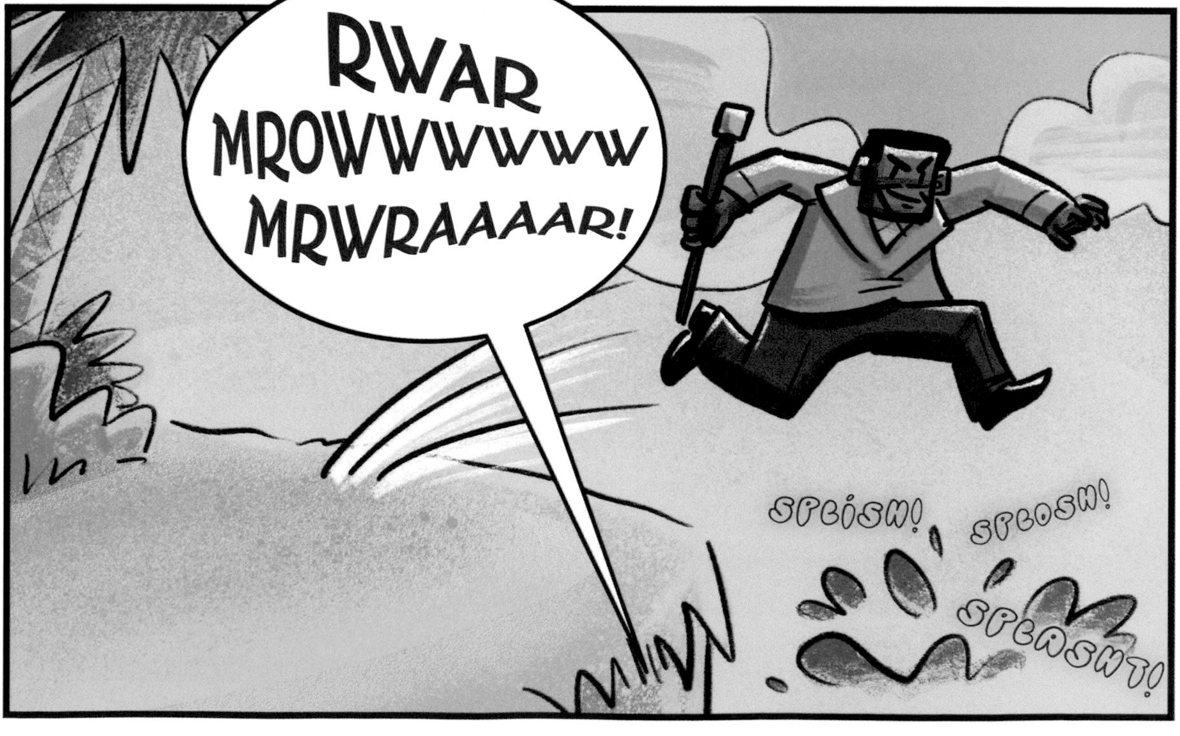
RWAR MROWWWWWW MRWRAAAAR!
SPLISH!
SPLOSH!
SPLASHT!

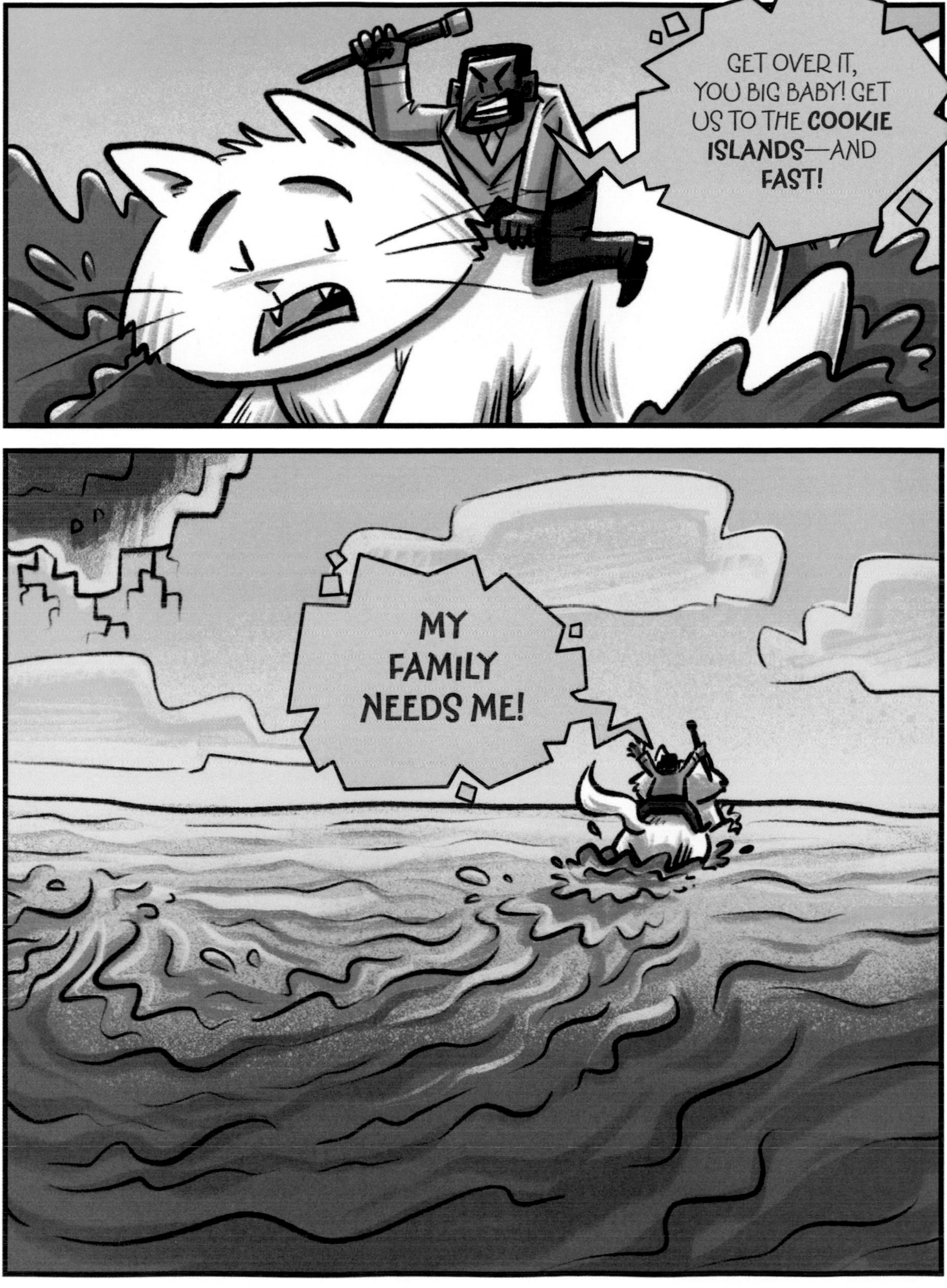
GET OVER IT, YOU BIG BABY! GET US TO THE **COOKIE ISLANDS**—AND **FAST!**
MY FAMILY NEEDS ME!

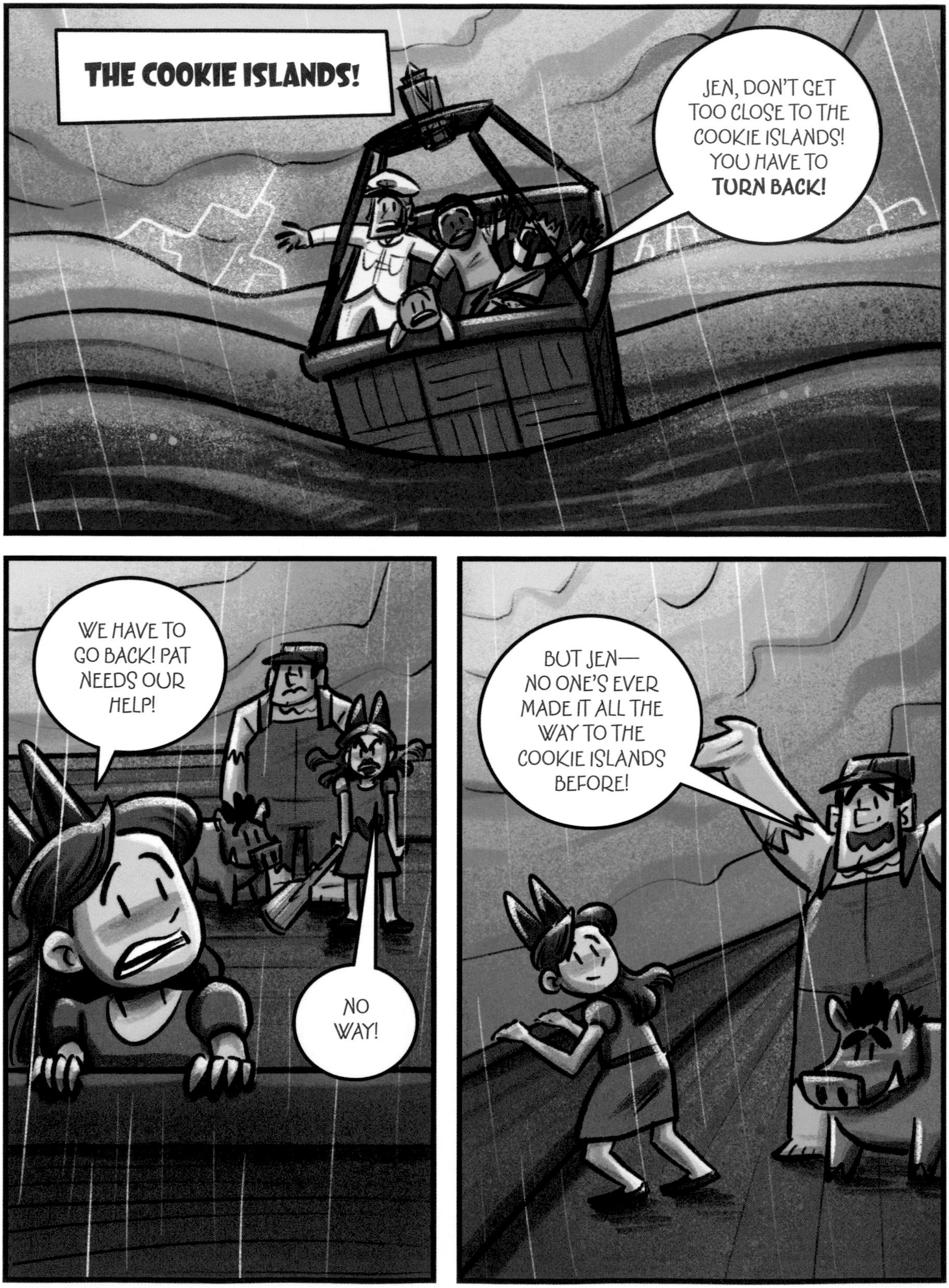
THE COOKIE ISLANDS!
JEN, DON'T GET TOO CLOSE TO THE COOKIE ISLANDS! YOU HAVE TO TURN BACK!
WE HAVE TO GO BACK! PAT NEEDS OUR HELP!
NO WAY!
BUT JEN— NO ONE'S EVER MADE IT ALL THE WAY TO THE COOKIE ISLANDS BEFORE!

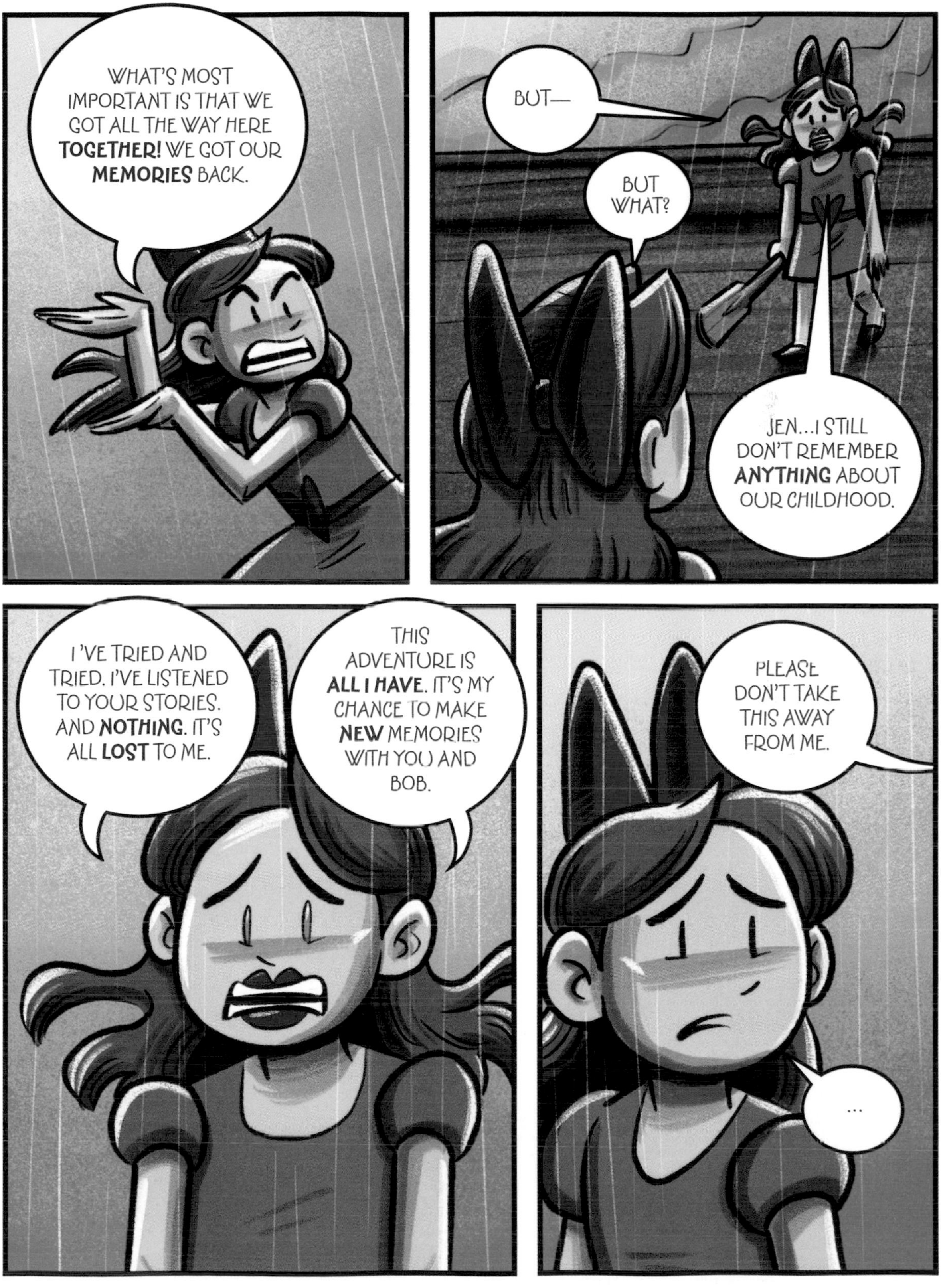
WHAT'S MOST IMPORTANT IS THAT WE GOT ALL THE WAY HERE **TOGETHER!** WE GOT OUR **MEMORIES** BACK.
BUT—
BUT WHAT?
JEN...I STILL DON'T REMEMBER **ANYTHING** ABOUT OUR CHILDHOOD.
I'VE TRIED AND TRIED. I'VE LISTENED TO YOUR STORIES. AND **NOTHING**. IT'S ALL **LOST** TO ME.
THIS ADVENTURE IS **ALL I HAVE**. IT'S MY CHANCE TO MAKE **NEW** MEMORIES WITH YOU AND BOB.
PLEASE DON'T TAKE THIS AWAY FROM ME.
...

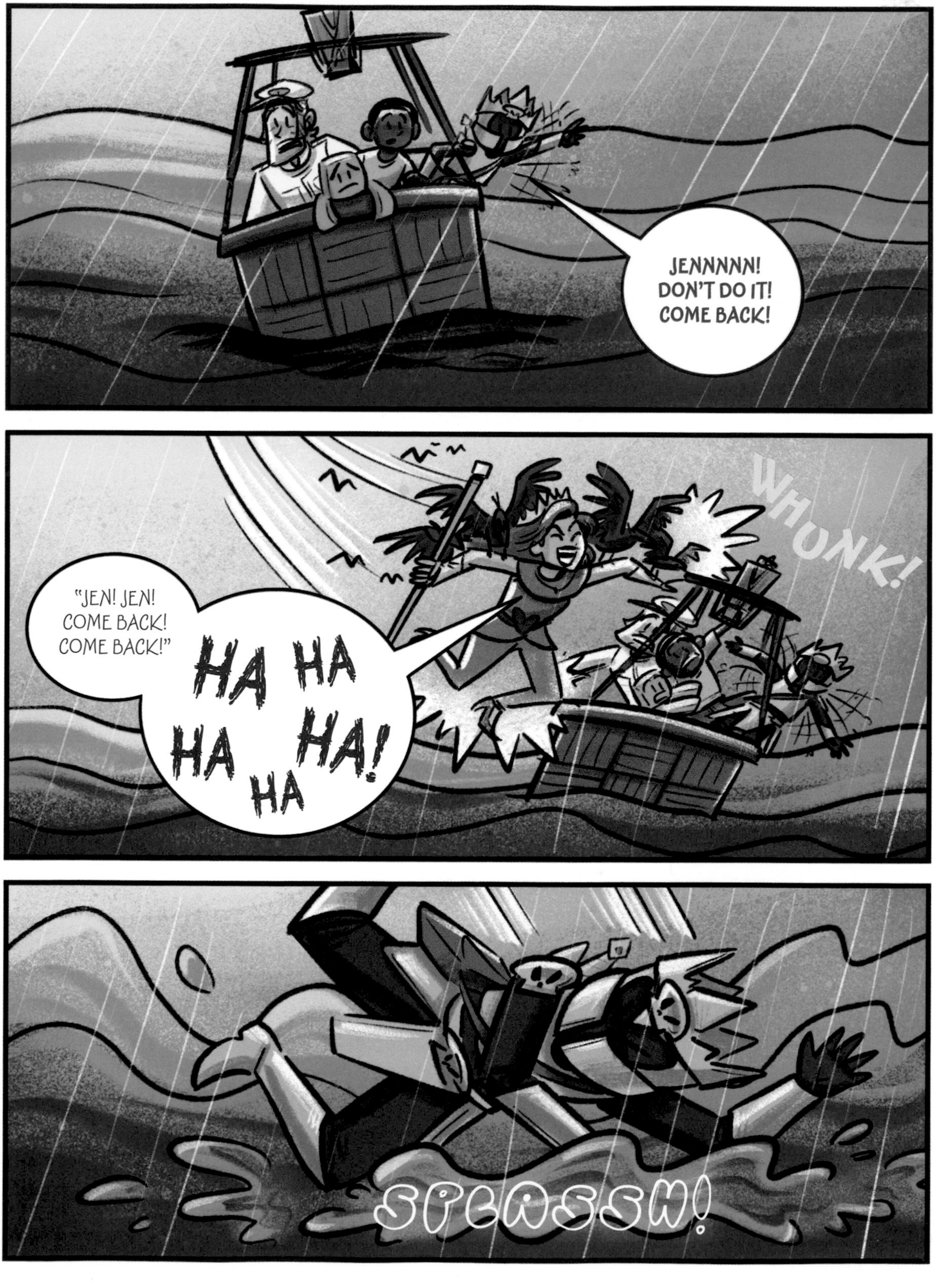
JENNNNN! DON'T DO IT! COME BACK!
WHONK!
"JEN! JEN! COME BACK! COME BACK!"
HA HA HA HA HA!
SPLASSH!

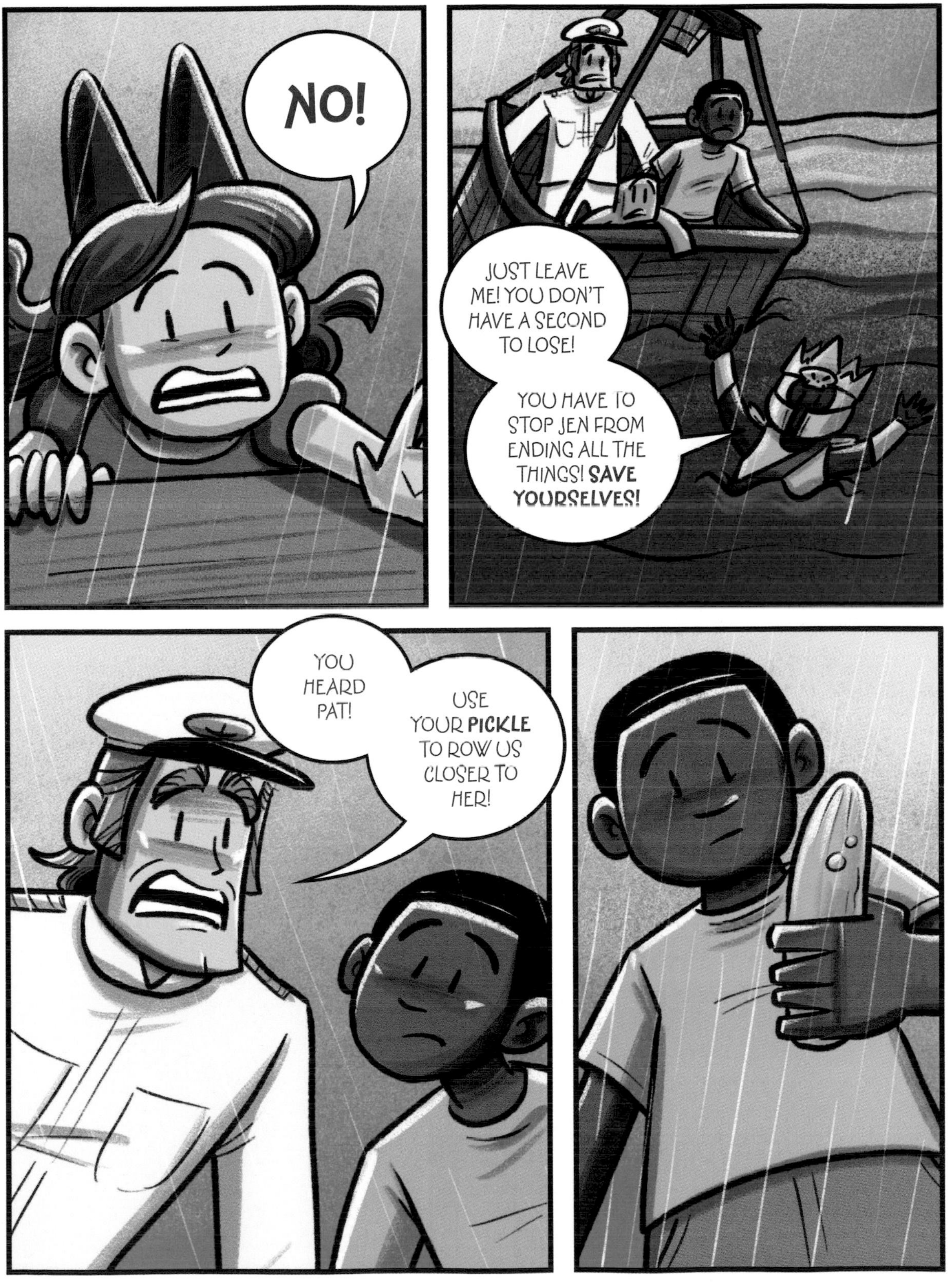
NO!
JUST LEAVE ME! YOU DON'T HAVE A SECOND TO LOSE!
YOU HAVE TO STOP JEN FROM ENDING ALL THE THINGS! SAVE YOURSELVES!
YOU HEARD PAT!
USE YOUR PICKLE TO ROW US CLOSER TO HER!

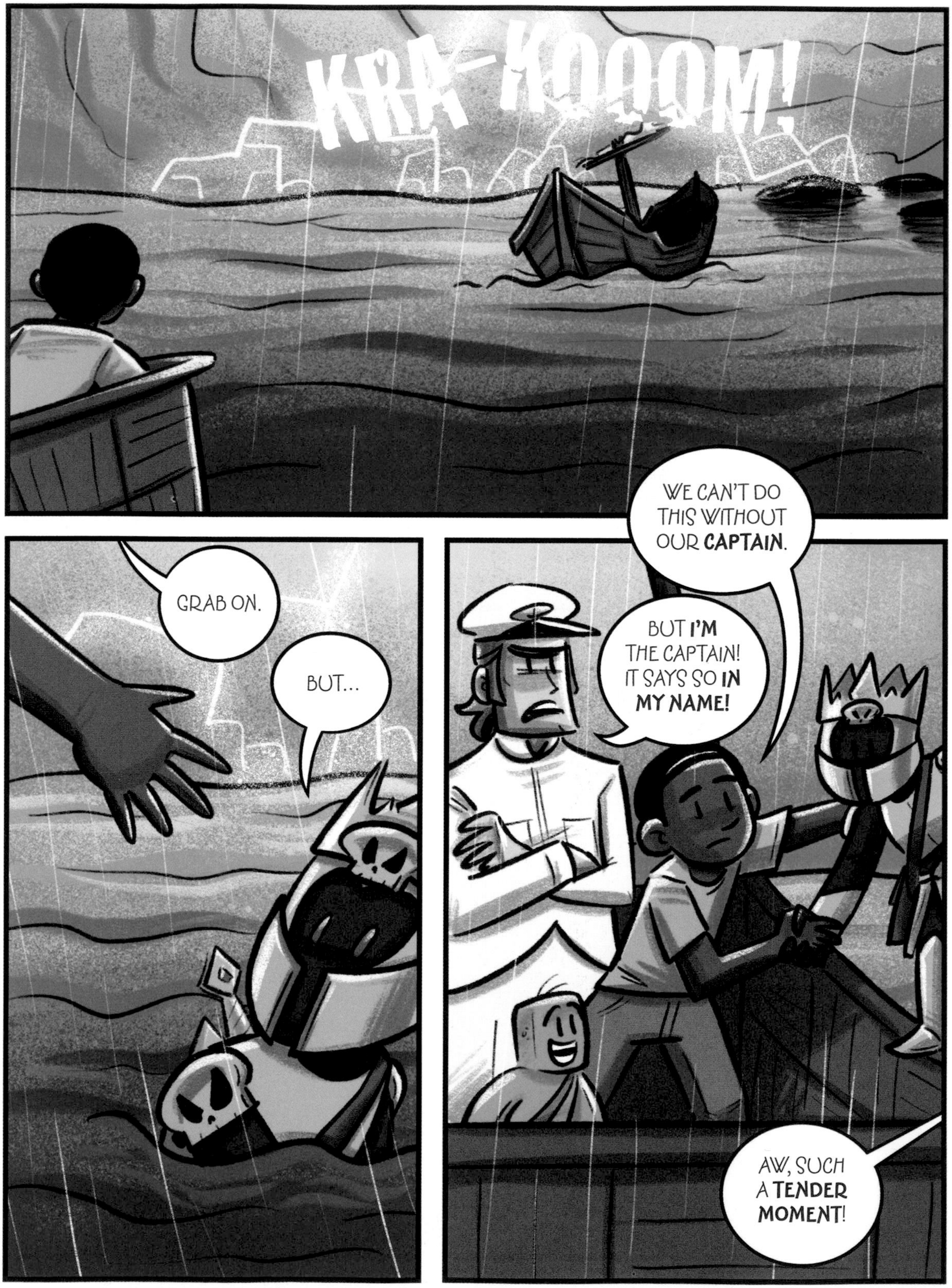
KRA-KOOOM!
GRAB ON.
BUT...
WE CAN'T DO THIS WITHOUT OUR **CAPTAIN**.
BUT **I'M** THE CAPTAIN! IT SAYS SO **IN MY NAME!**
AW, SUCH A **TENDER MOMENT**!

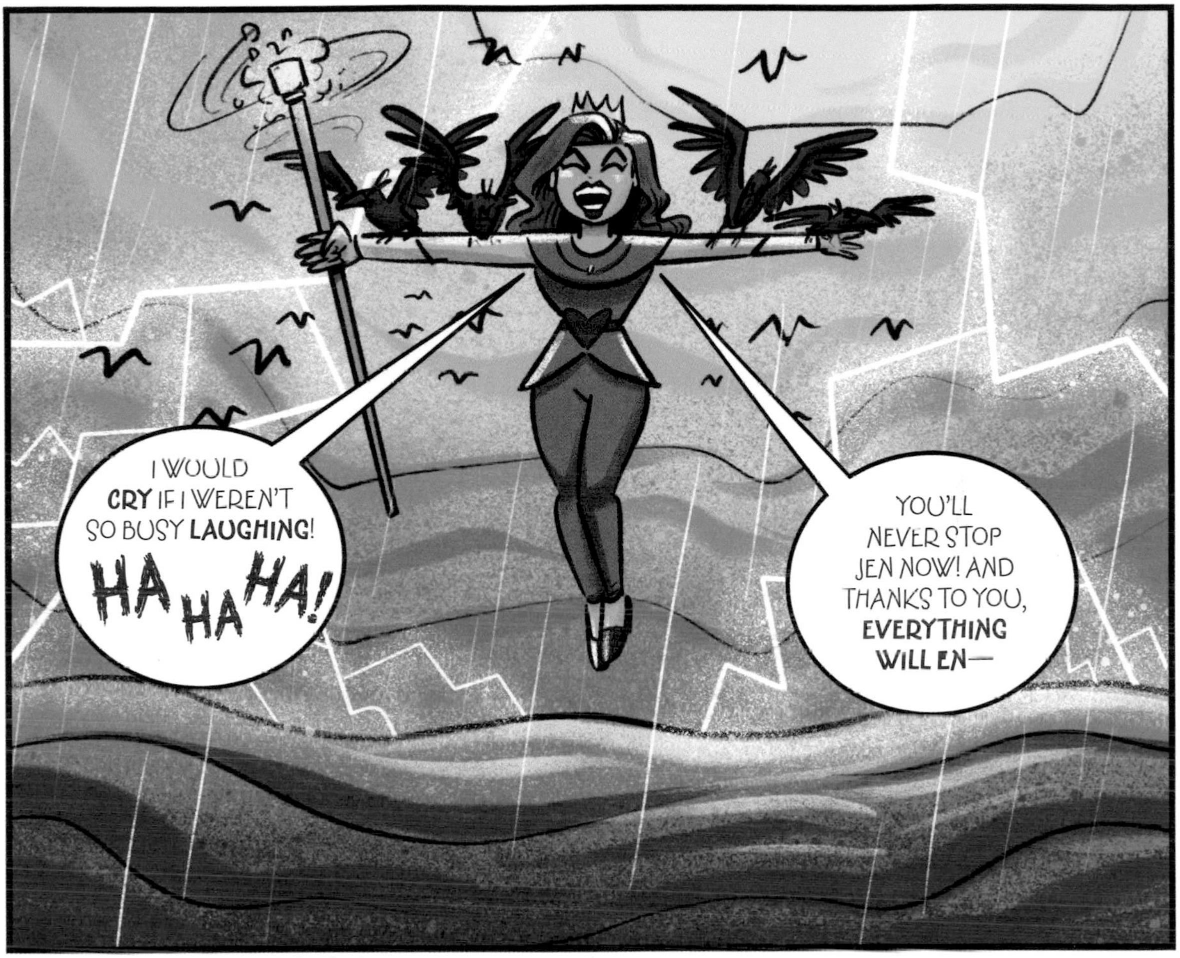
I WOULD CRY IF I WEREN'T SO BUSY LAUGHING!
HA HA HA!
YOU'LL NEVER STOP JEN NOW! AND THANKS TO YOU, EVERYTHING WILL EN—

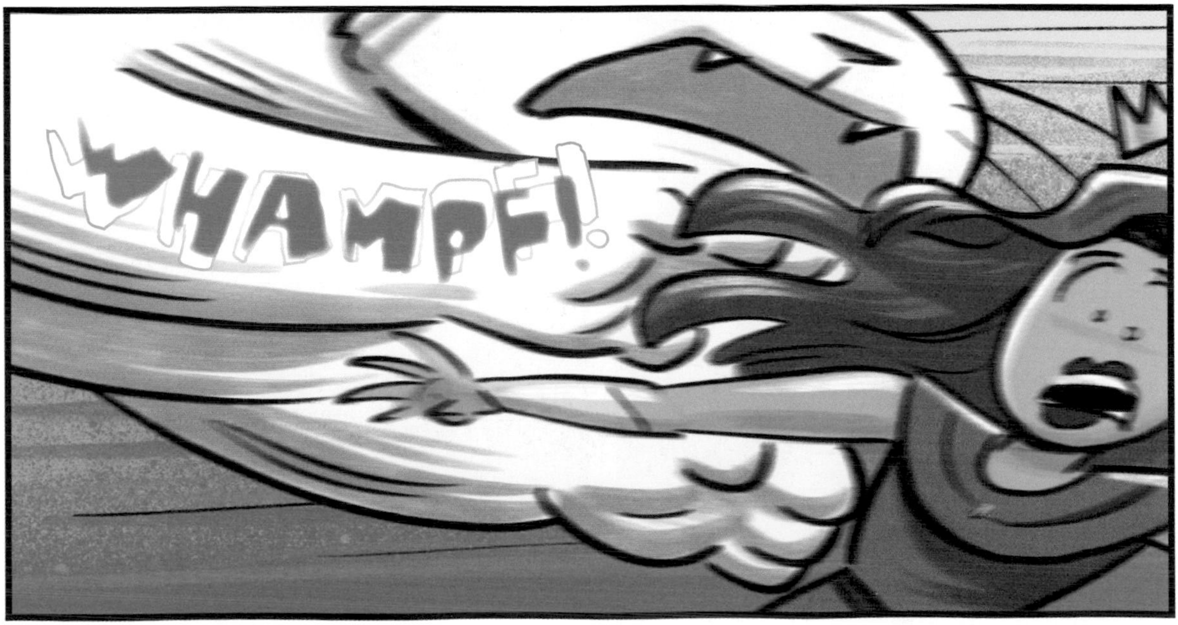
WHAMPF!

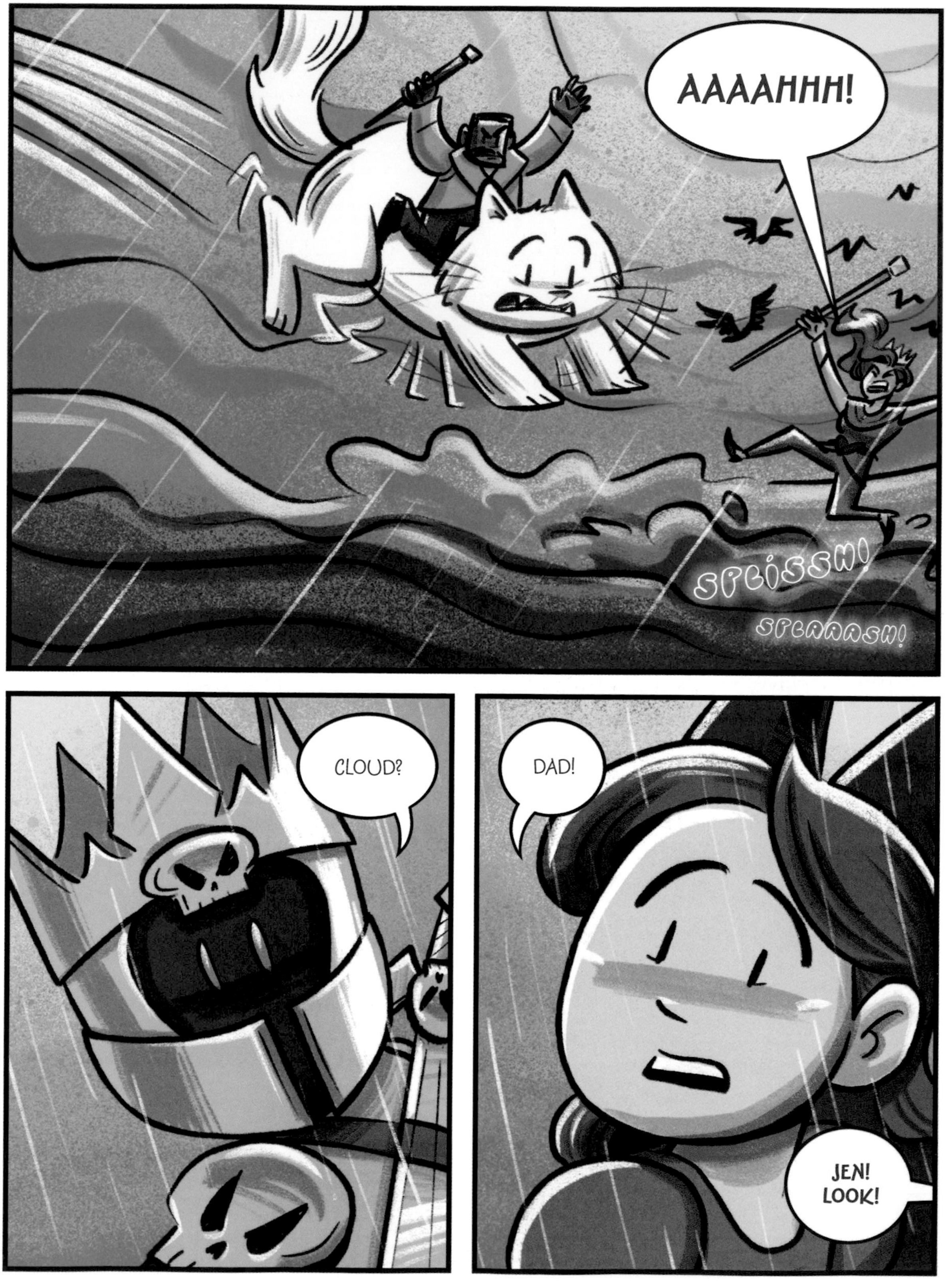
AAAAHHH!
SPLISSH!
SPLAAASH!
CLOUD?
DAD!
JEN! LOOK!

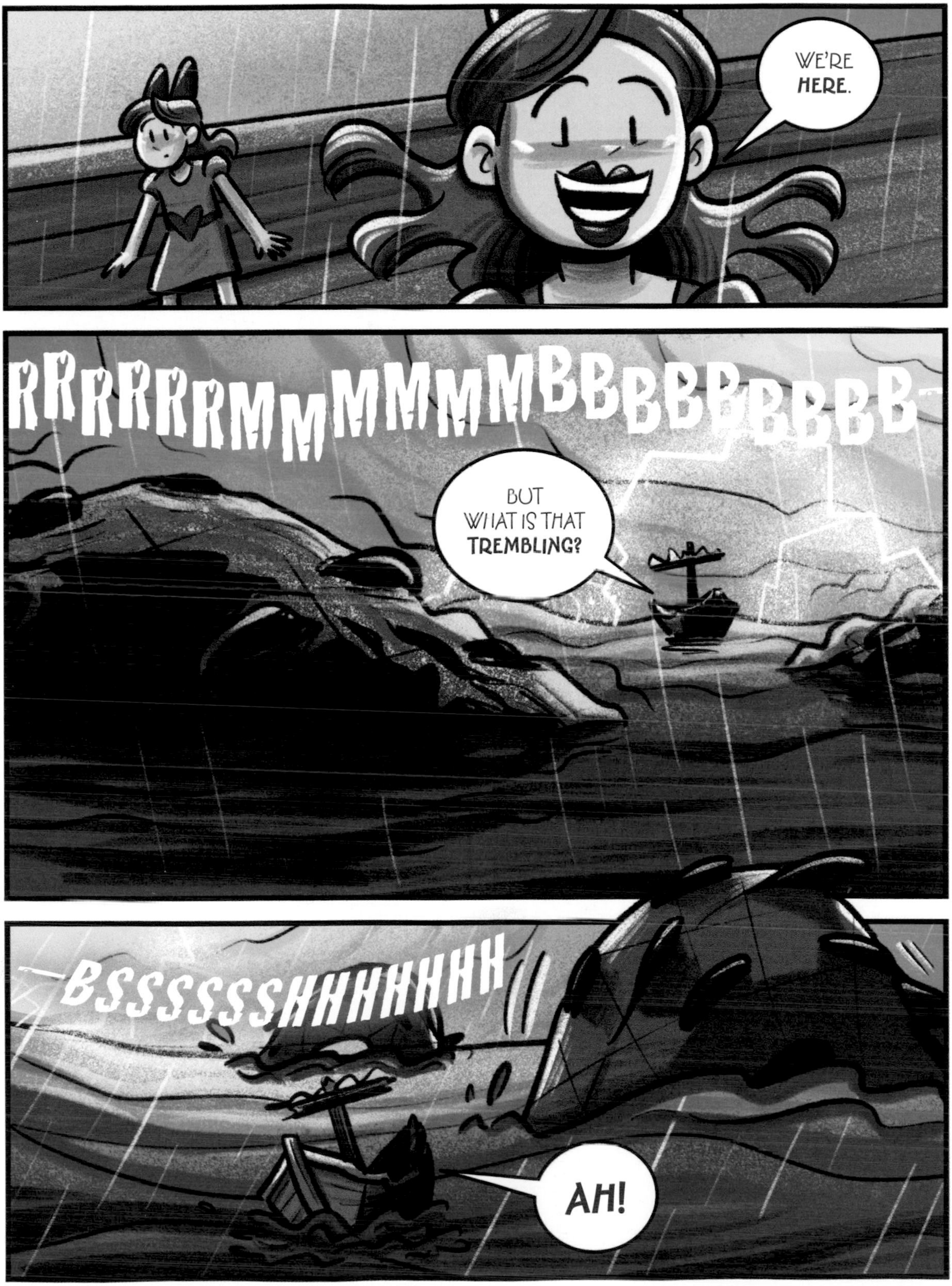
WE'RE HERE.
RRRRRRRMMMMMMMBBBBBBBBBB-
BUT WHAT IS THAT TREMBLING?
-BSSSSSSHHHHHHHH
AH!

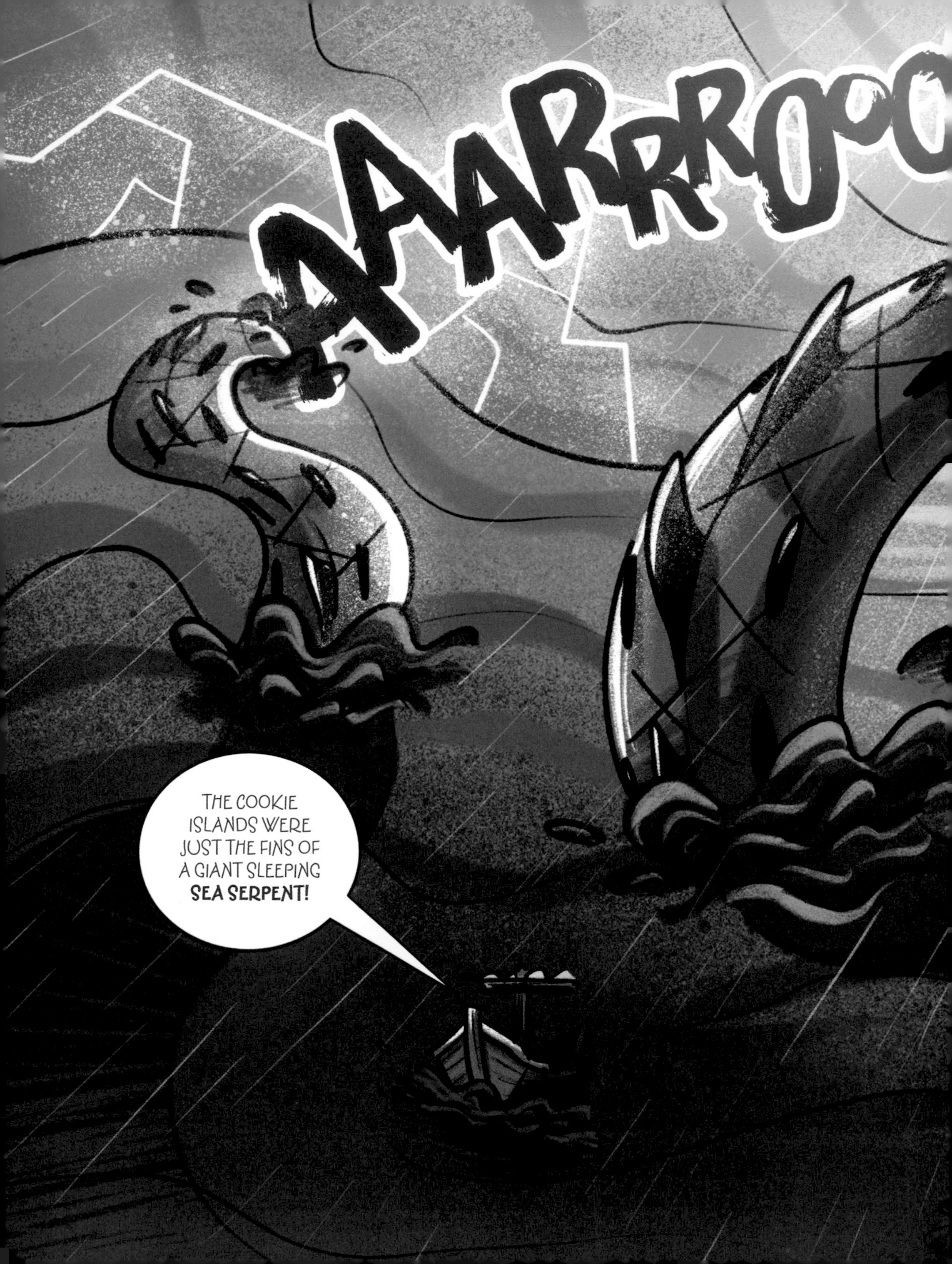
AAARRROOO
THE COOKIE ISLANDS WERE JUST THE FINS OF A GIANT SLEEPING **SEA SERPENT!**

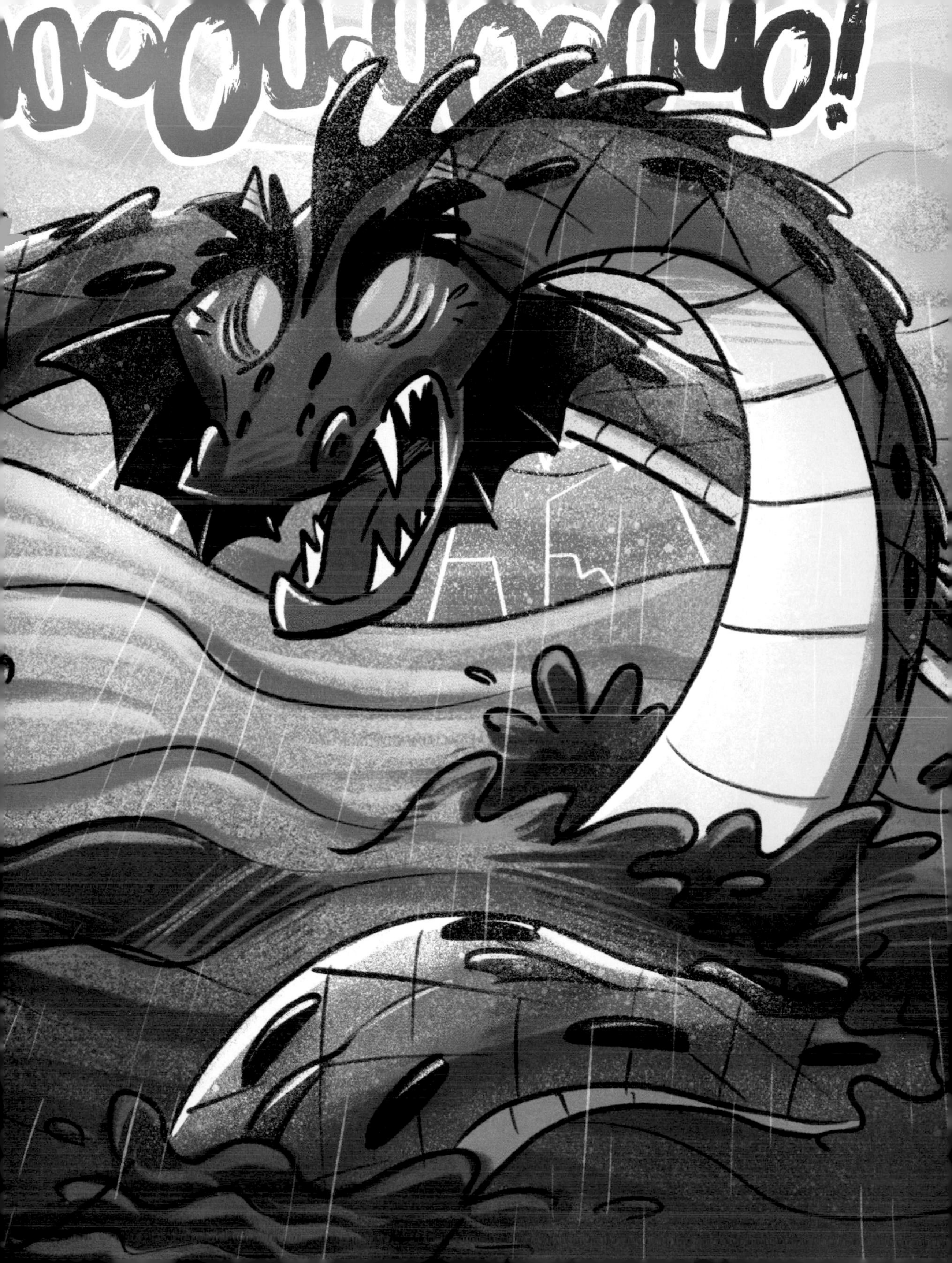

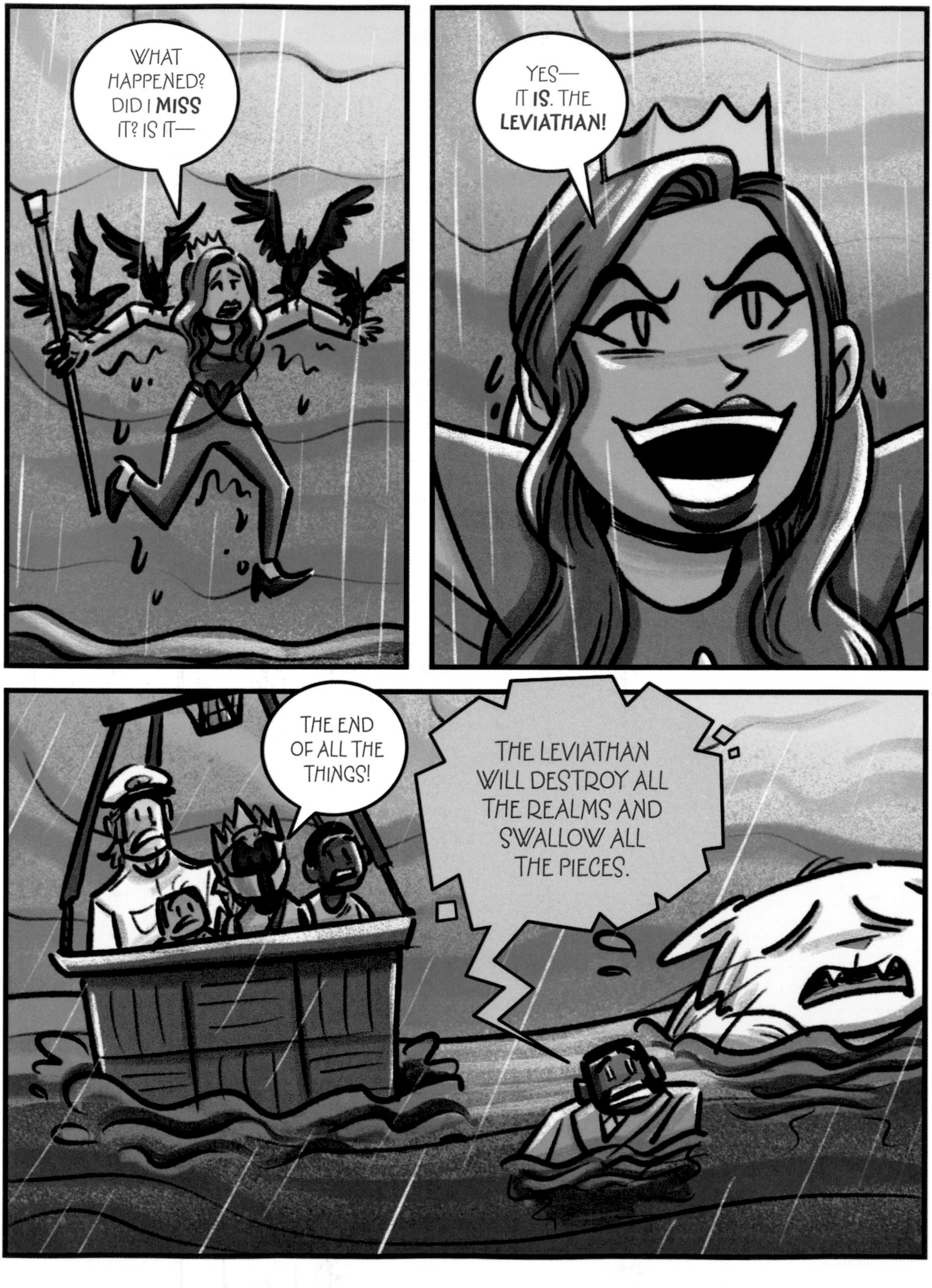
WHAT HAPPENED? DID I **MISS** IT? IS IT—
YES— IT **IS**. THE **LEVIATHAN!**
THE END OF ALL THE THINGS!
THE LEVIATHAN WILL DESTROY ALL THE REALMS AND SWALLOW ALL THE PIECES.

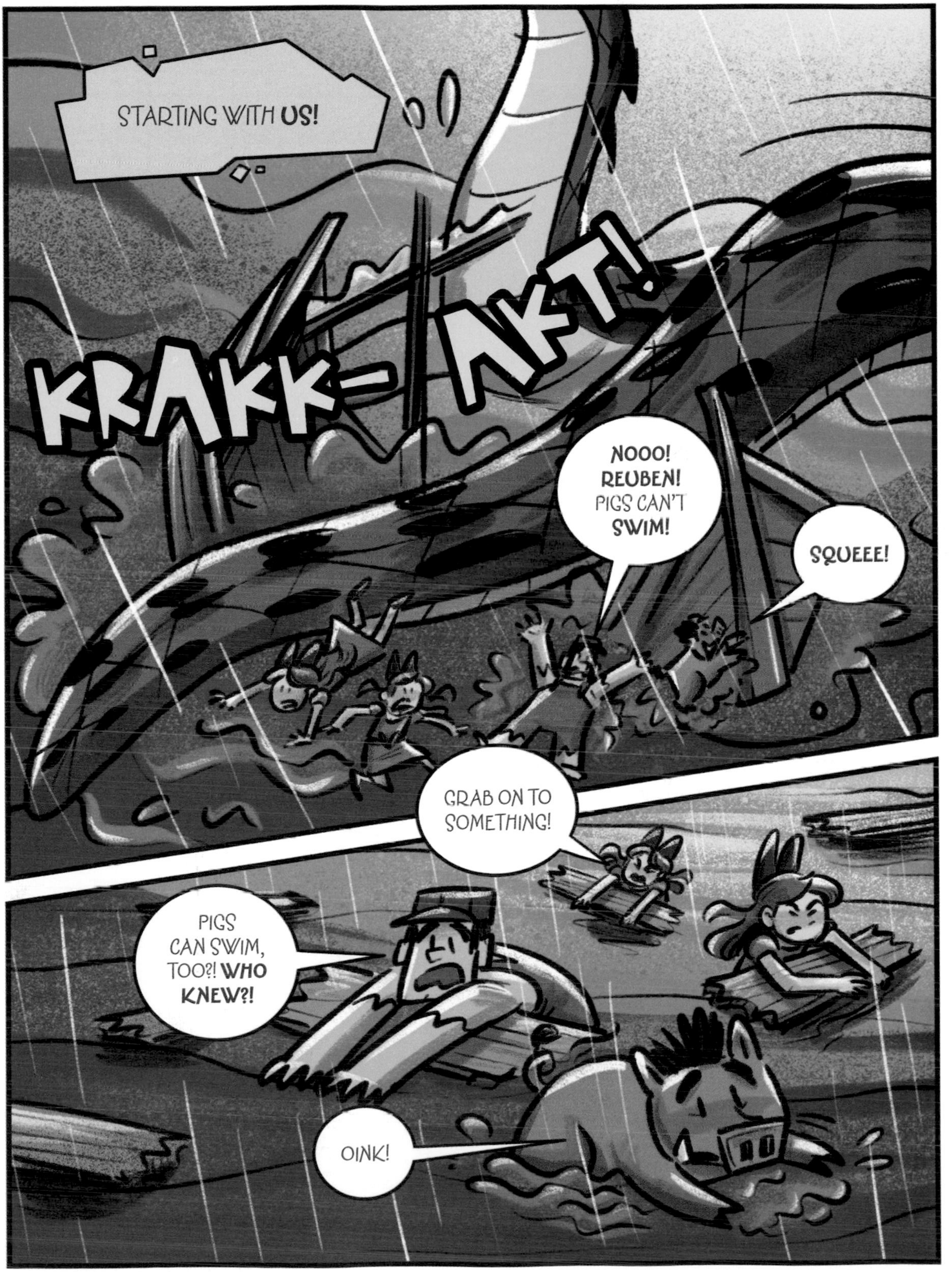
STARTING WITH **US**!
KRAKK-AKT!
NOOO! REUBEN! PIGS CAN'T **SWIM!**
SQUEEE!
GRAB ON TO SOMETHING!
PIGS CAN SWIM, TOO?! **WHO KNEW?!**
OINK!

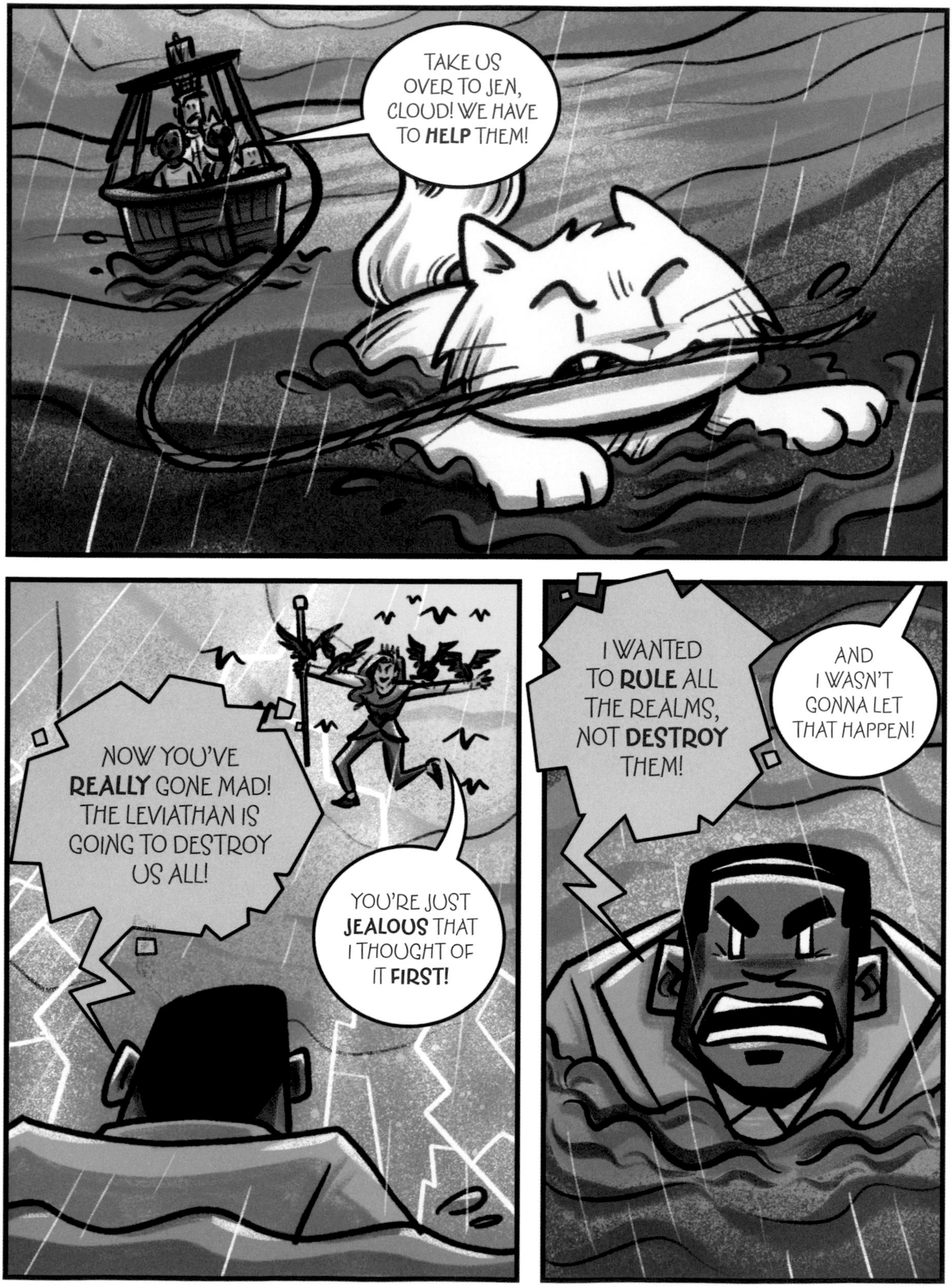
TAKE US OVER TO JEN, CLOUD! WE HAVE TO **HELP** THEM!
NOW YOU'VE **REALLY** GONE MAD! THE LEVIATHAN IS GOING TO DESTROY US ALL!
YOU'RE JUST **JEALOUS** THAT I THOUGHT OF IT **FIRST!**
I WANTED TO **RULE** ALL THE REALMS, NOT **DESTROY** THEM!
AND I WASN'T GONNA LET THAT HAPPEN!

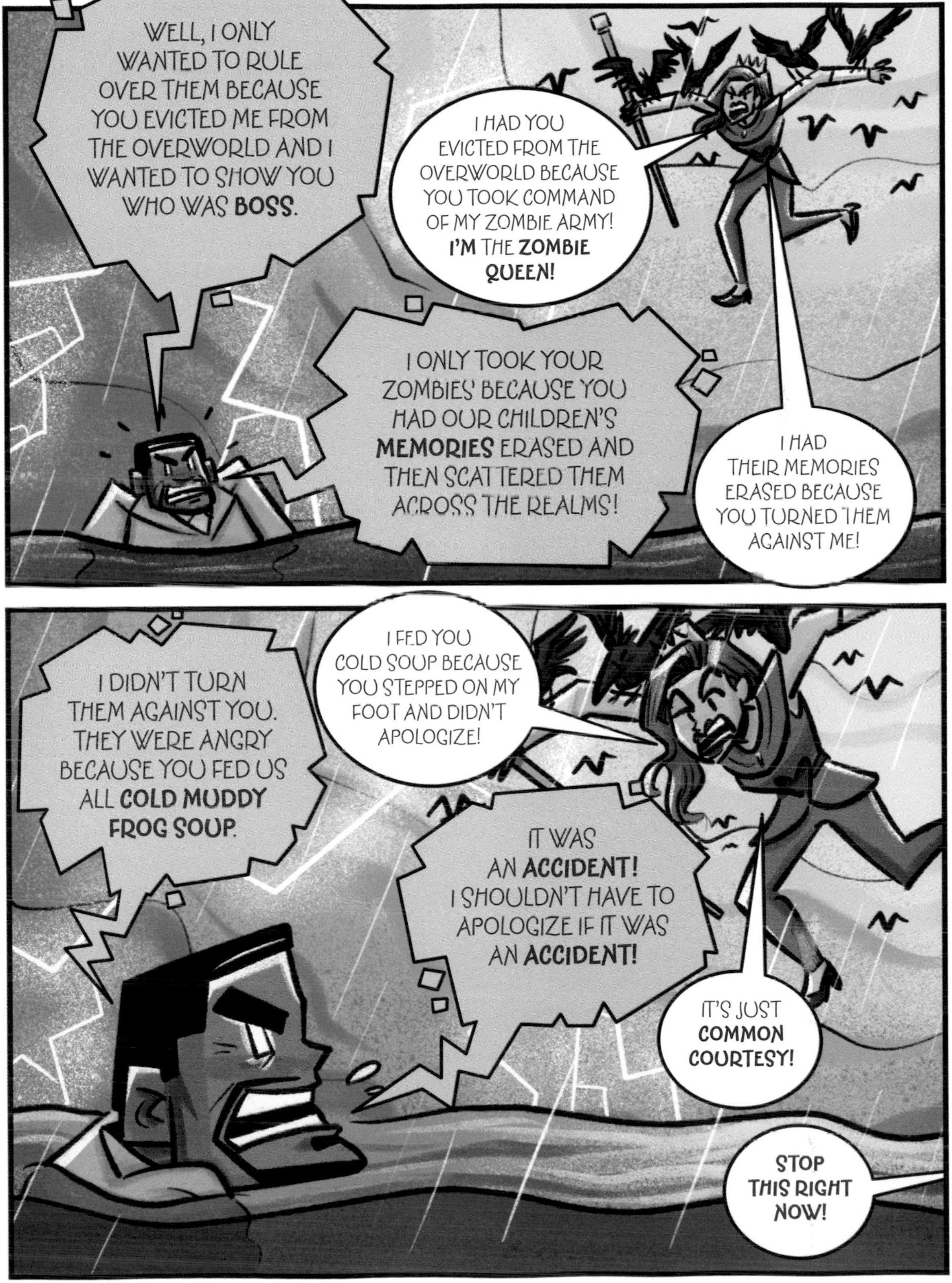
WELL, I ONLY WANTED TO RULE OVER THEM BECAUSE YOU EVICTED ME FROM THE OVERWORLD AND I WANTED TO SHOW YOU WHO WAS **BOSS**.
I HAD YOU EVICTED FROM THE OVERWORLD BECAUSE YOU TOOK COMMAND OF MY ZOMBIE ARMY! **I'M** THE **ZOMBIE QUEEN!**
I ONLY TOOK YOUR ZOMBIES' BECAUSE YOU HAD OUR CHILDREN'S **MEMORIES** ERASED AND THEN SCATTERED THEM ACROSS THE REALMS!
I HAD THEIR MEMORIES ERASED BECAUSE YOU TURNED THEM AGAINST ME!
I DIDN'T TURN THEM AGAINST YOU. THEY WERE ANGRY BECAUSE YOU FED US ALL **COLD MUDDY FROG SOUP**.
I FED YOU COLD SOUP BECAUSE YOU STEPPED ON MY FOOT AND DIDN'T APOLOGIZE!
IT WAS AN **ACCIDENT!** I SHOULDN'T HAVE TO APOLOGIZE IF IT WAS AN **ACCIDENT!**
IT'S JUST **COMMON COURTESY!**
STOP THIS RIGHT NOW!

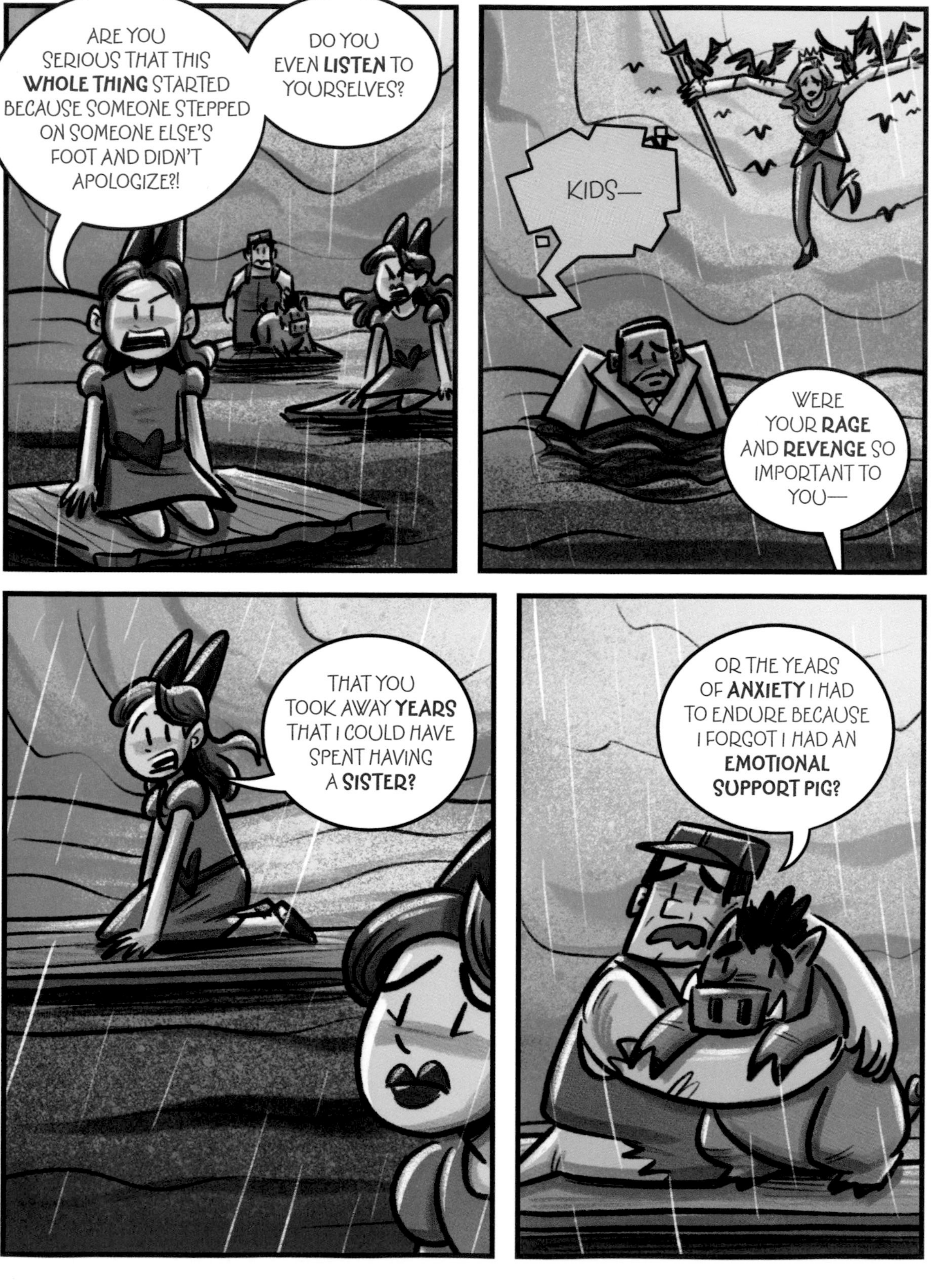
ARE YOU SERIOUS THAT THIS **WHOLE THING** STARTED BECAUSE SOMEONE STEPPED ON SOMEONE ELSE'S FOOT AND DIDN'T APOLOGIZE?!
DO YOU EVEN **LISTEN** TO YOURSELVES?
KIDS—
WERE YOUR **RAGE** AND **REVENGE** SO IMPORTANT TO YOU—
THAT YOU TOOK AWAY **YEARS** THAT I COULD HAVE SPENT HAVING A **SISTER**?
OR THE YEARS OF **ANXIETY** I HAD TO ENDURE BECAUSE I FORGOT I HAD AN **EMOTIONAL SUPPORT PIG**?

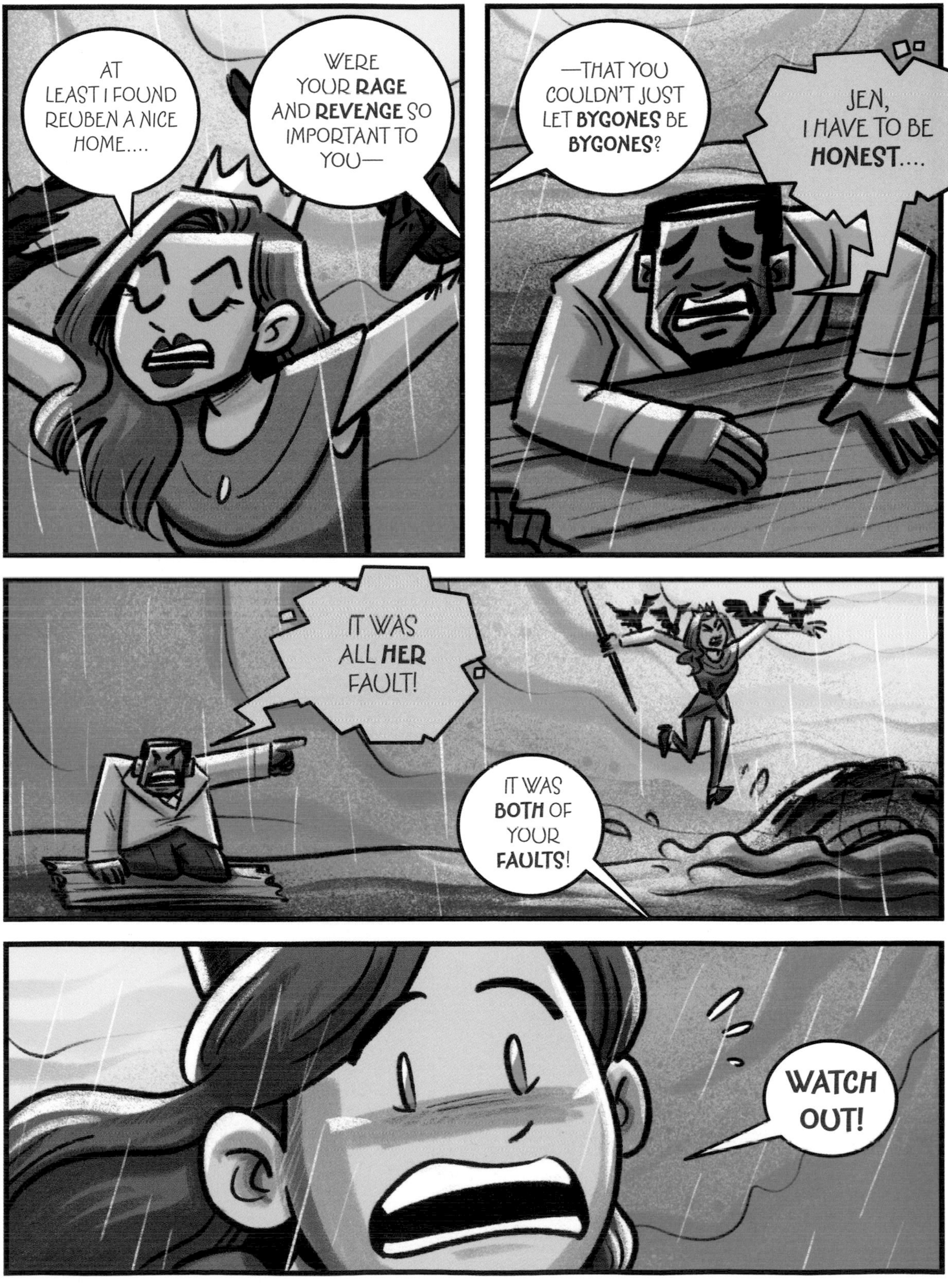
AT LEAST I FOUND REUBEN A NICE HOME....
WERE YOUR **RAGE** AND **REVENGE** SO IMPORTANT TO YOU—
—THAT YOU COULDN'T JUST LET **BYGONES** BE **BYGONES**?
JEN, I HAVE TO BE **HONEST**....
IT WAS ALL **HER** FAULT!
IT WAS **BOTH** OF YOUR **FAULTS**!
WATCH OUT!

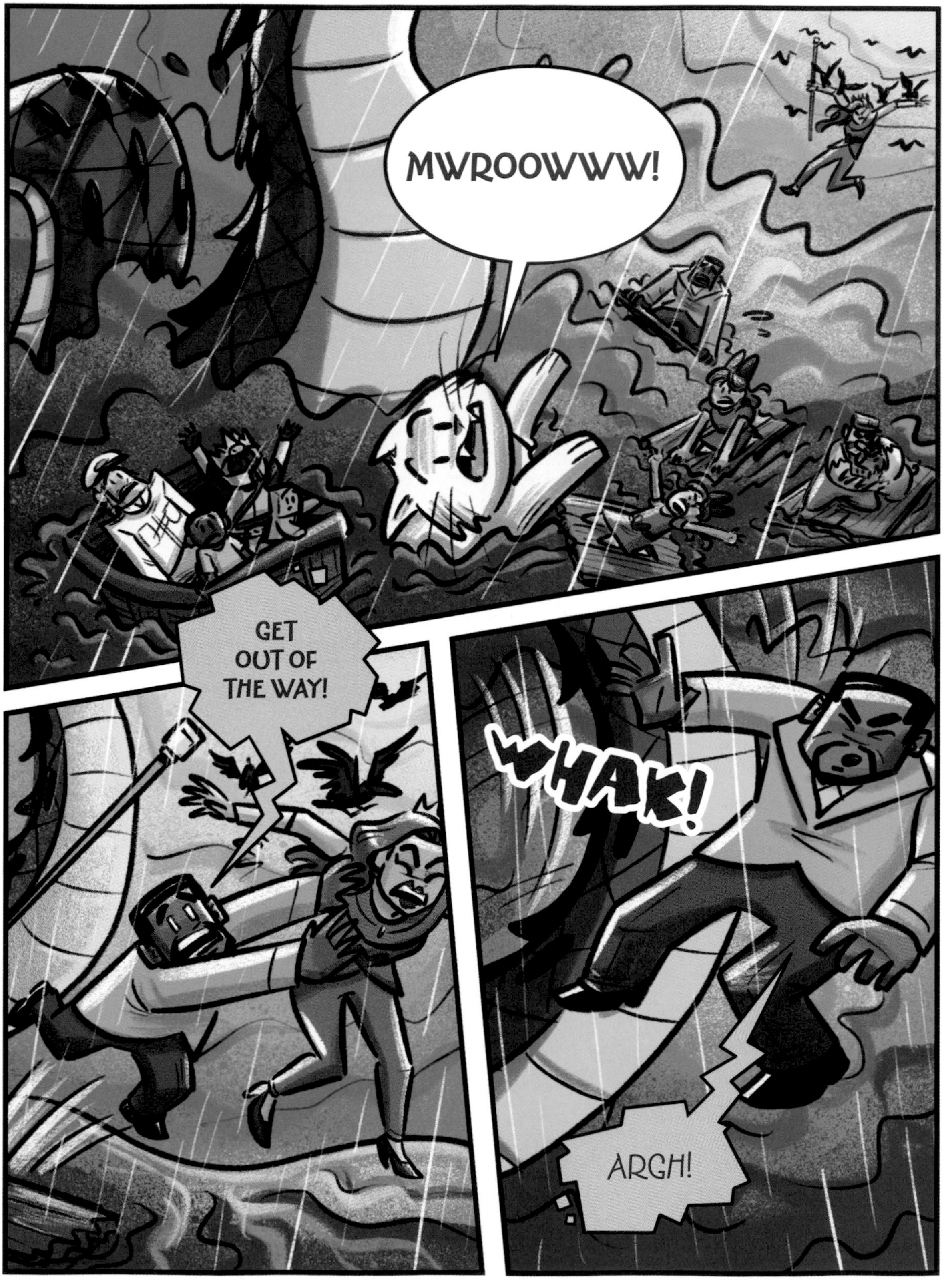
MWROOWWW!
GET OUT OF THE WAY!
WHAK!
ARGH!

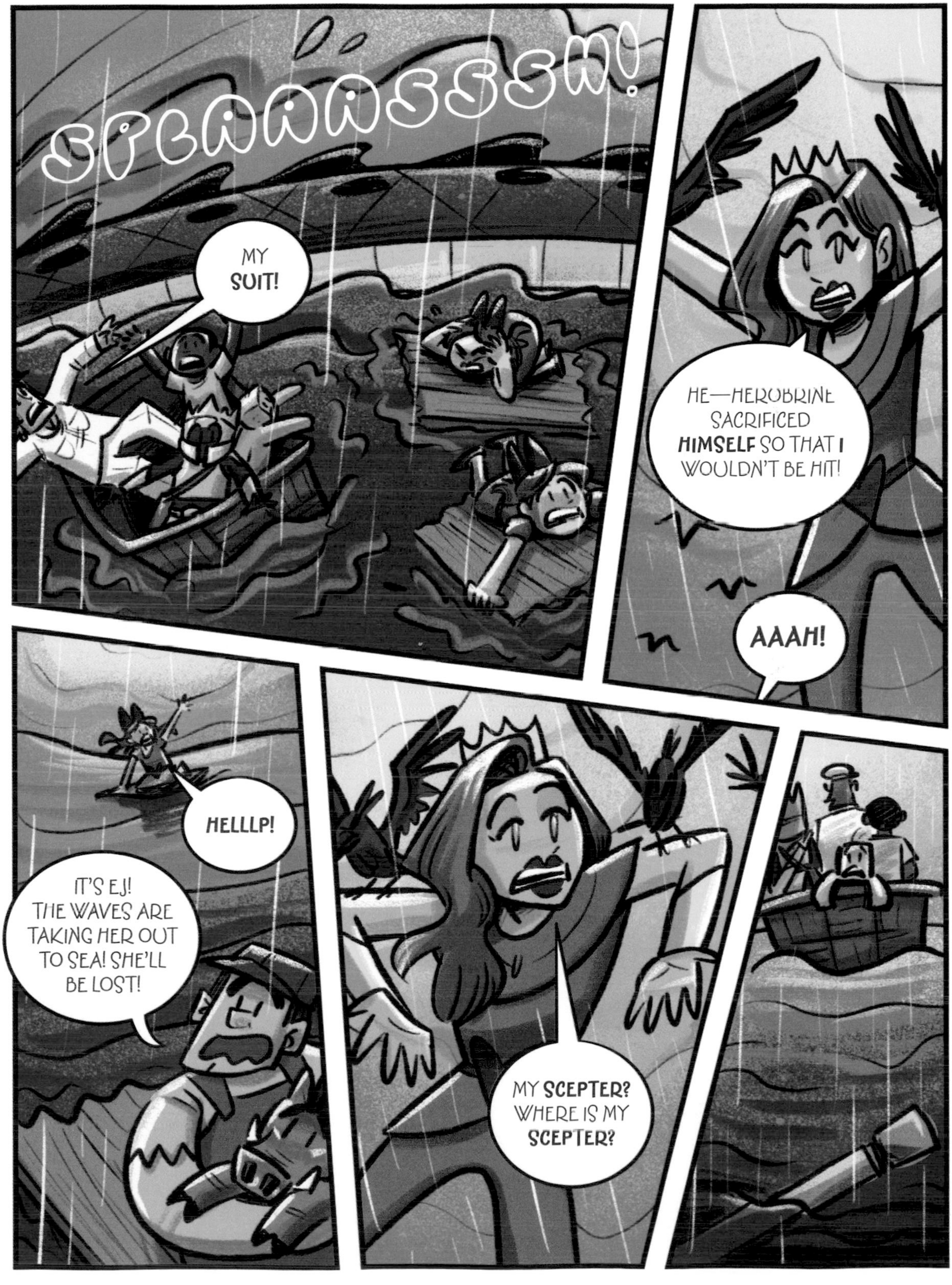
SPLAAASSSSH!
MY SUIT!
HE—HEROBRINE SACRIFICED HIMSELF SO THAT I WOULDN'T BE HIT!
AAAH!
HELLLP!
IT'S EJ! THE WAVES ARE TAKING HER OUT TO SEA! SHE'LL BE LOST!
MY SCEPTER? WHERE IS MY SCEPTER?

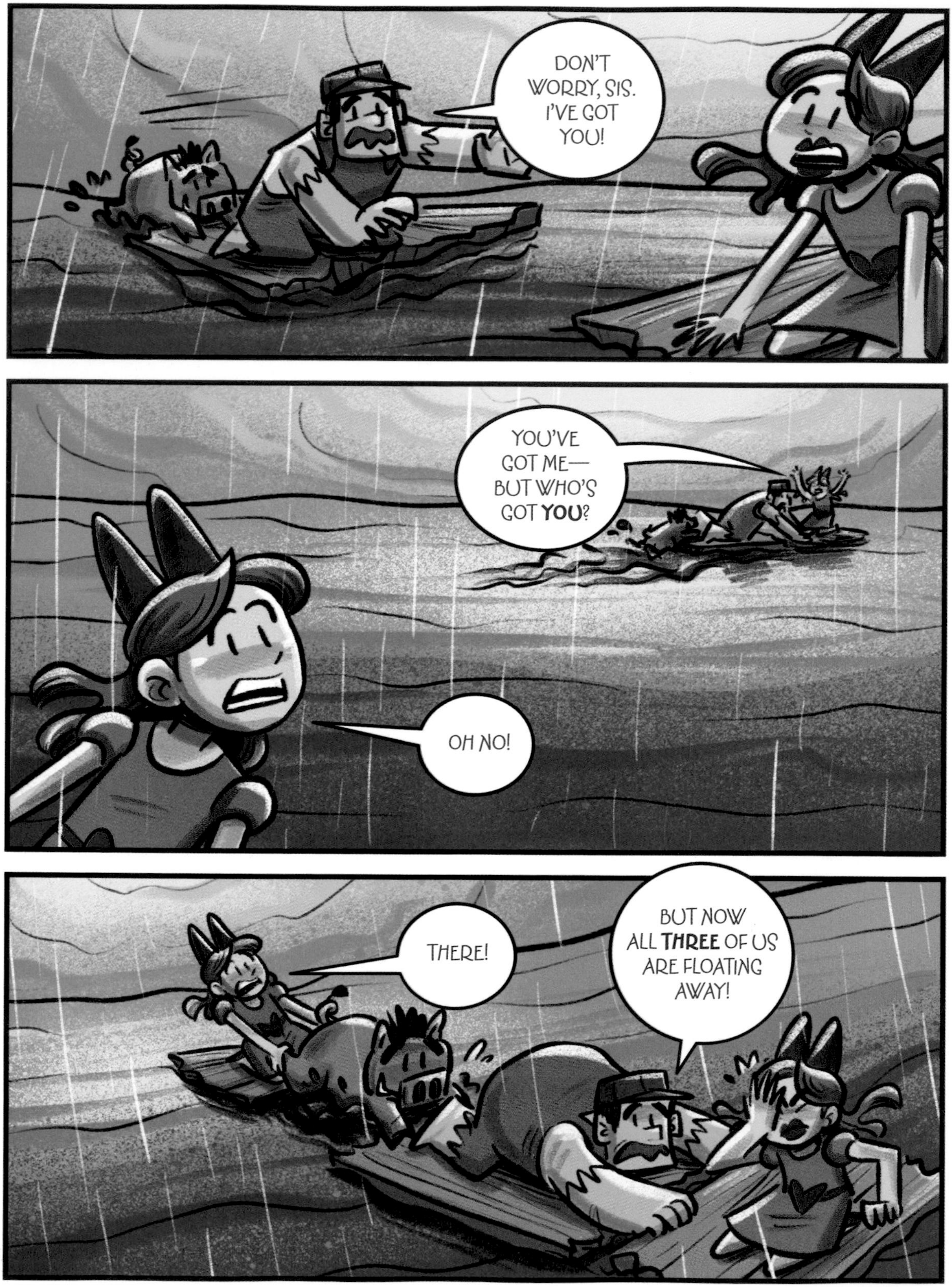
DON'T WORRY, SIS. I'VE GOT YOU!
YOU'VE GOT ME— BUT WHO'S GOT **YOU**?
OH NO!
THERE!
BUT NOW ALL **THREE** OF US ARE FLOATING AWAY!

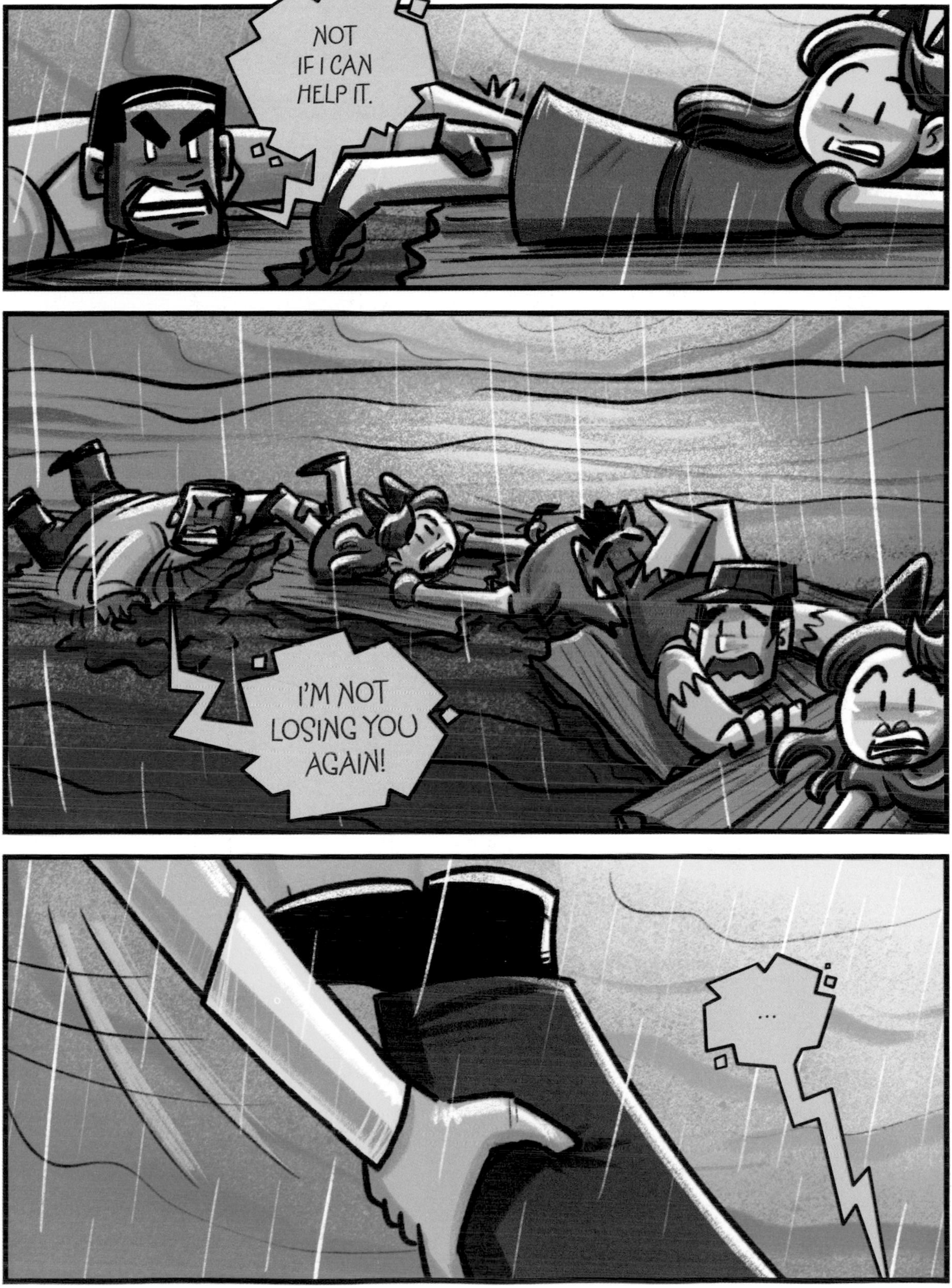
NOT IF I CAN HELP IT.
I'M NOT LOSING YOU AGAIN!
...

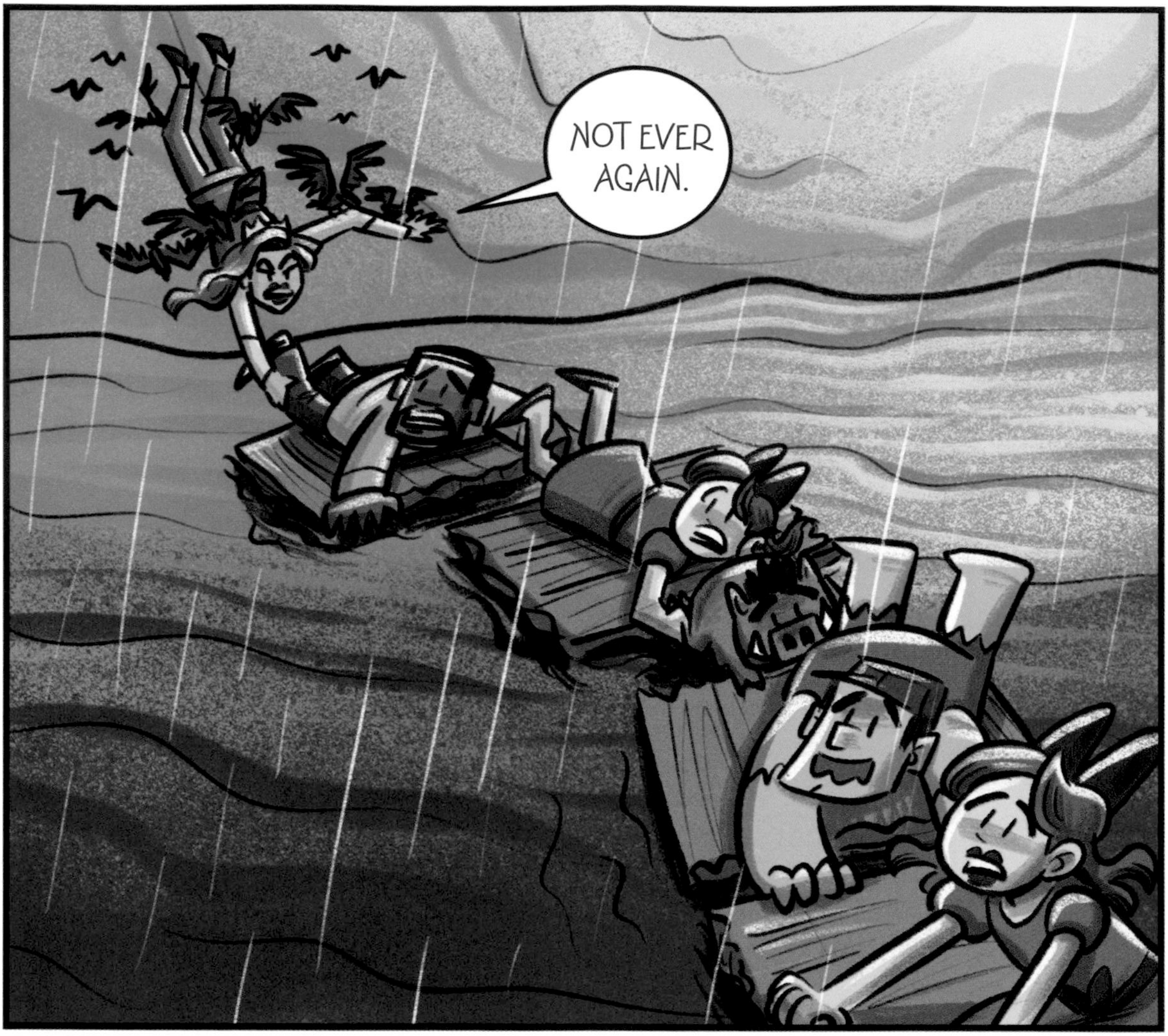
NOT EVER AGAIN.

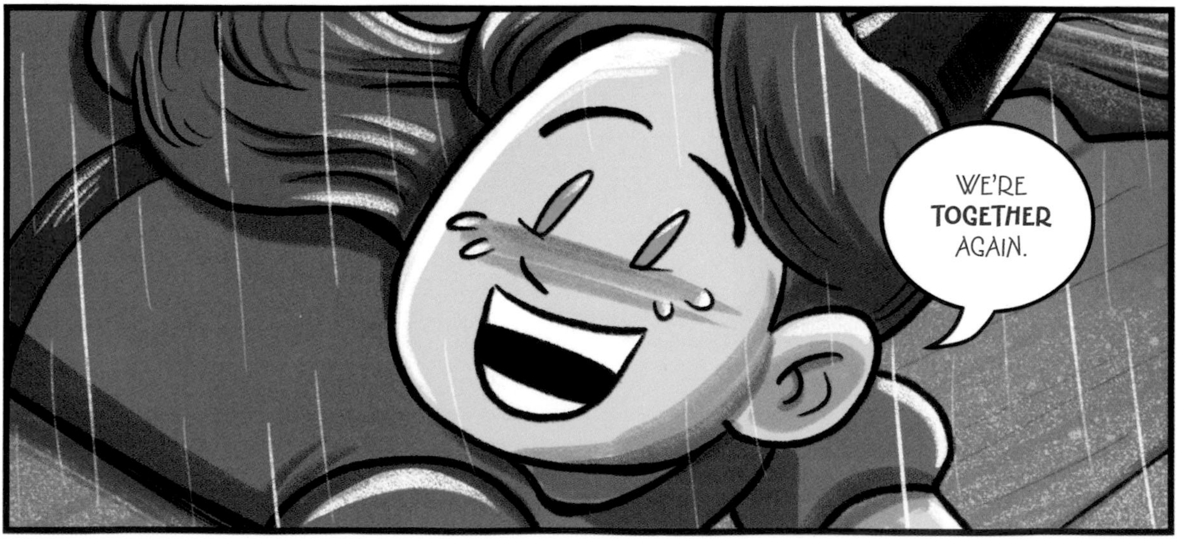
WE'RE **TOGETHER** AGAIN.

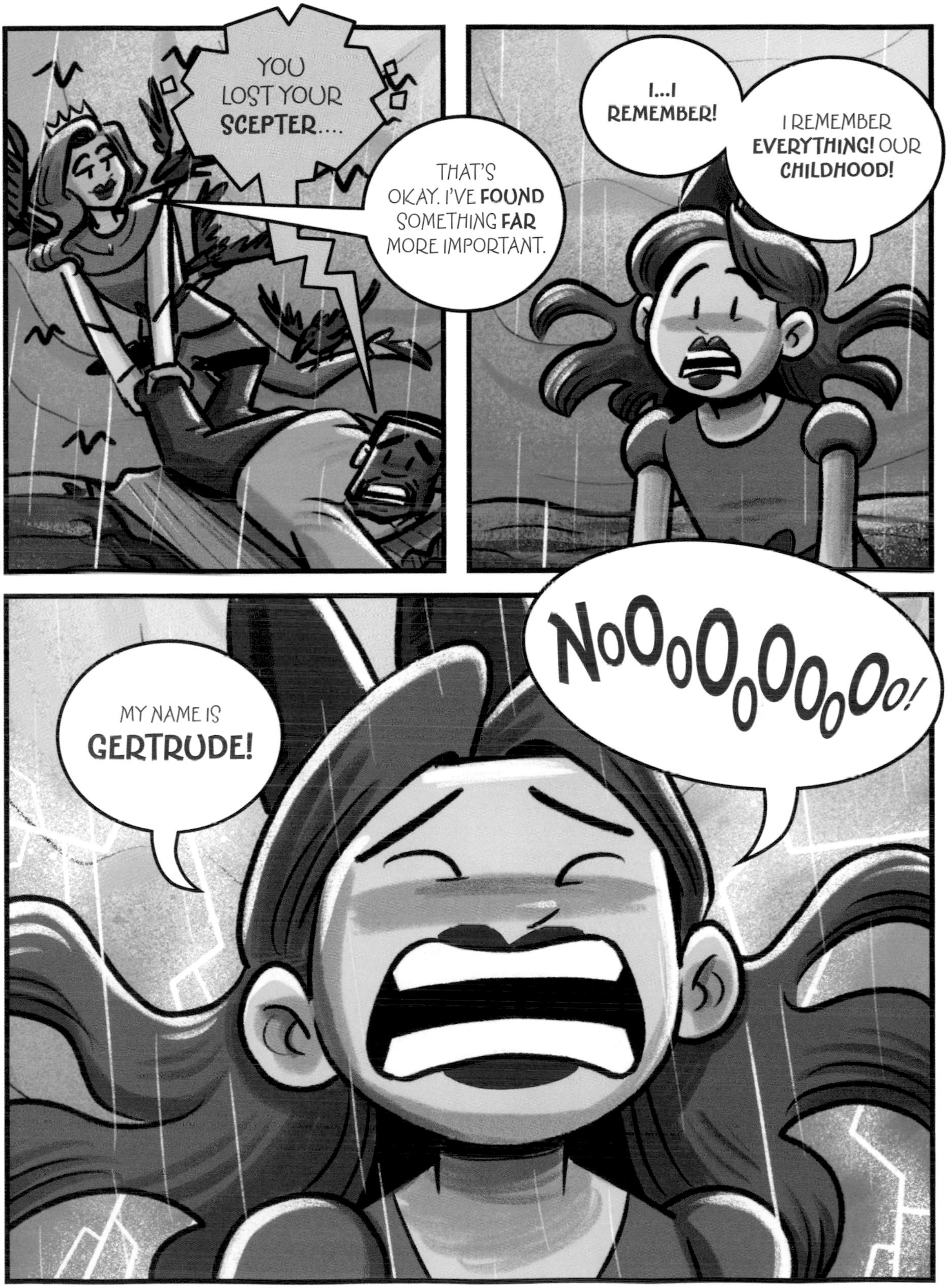
YOU LOST YOUR SCEPTER....
THAT'S OKAY. I'VE FOUND SOMETHING FAR MORE IMPORTANT.
I...I REMEMBER!
I REMEMBER EVERYTHING! OUR CHILDHOOD!
MY NAME IS GERTRUDE!
NOOOOOOOOOO!

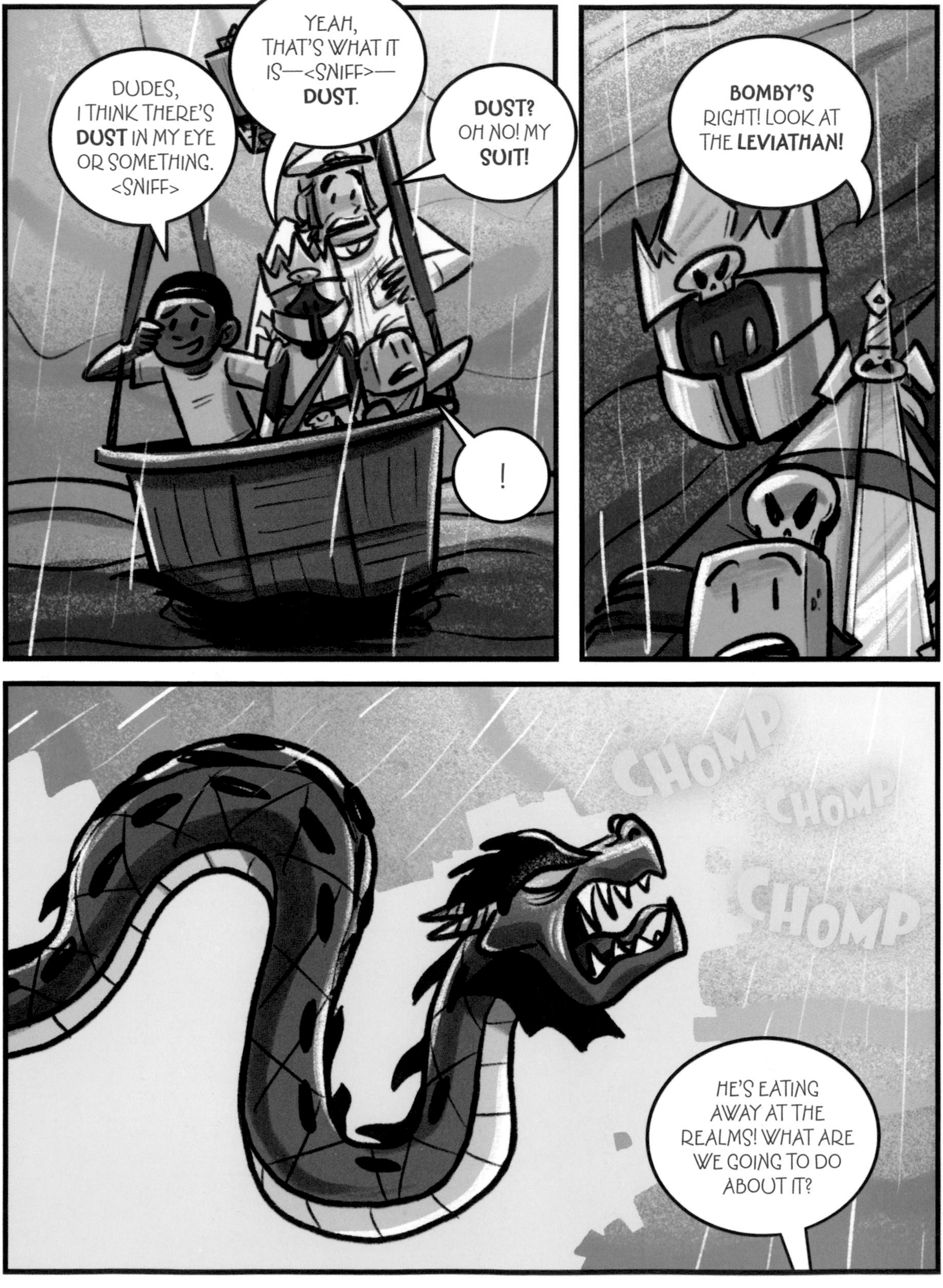
DUDES, I THINK THERE'S **DUST** IN MY EYE OR SOMETHING. <SNIFF>
YEAH, THAT'S WHAT IT IS—<SNIFF>—**DUST**.
DUST? OH NO! MY **SUIT!**
!
BOMBY'S RIGHT! LOOK AT THE **LEVIATHAN!**
CHOMP
CHOMP
CHOMP
HE'S EATING AWAY AT THE REALMS! WHAT ARE WE GOING TO DO ABOUT IT?

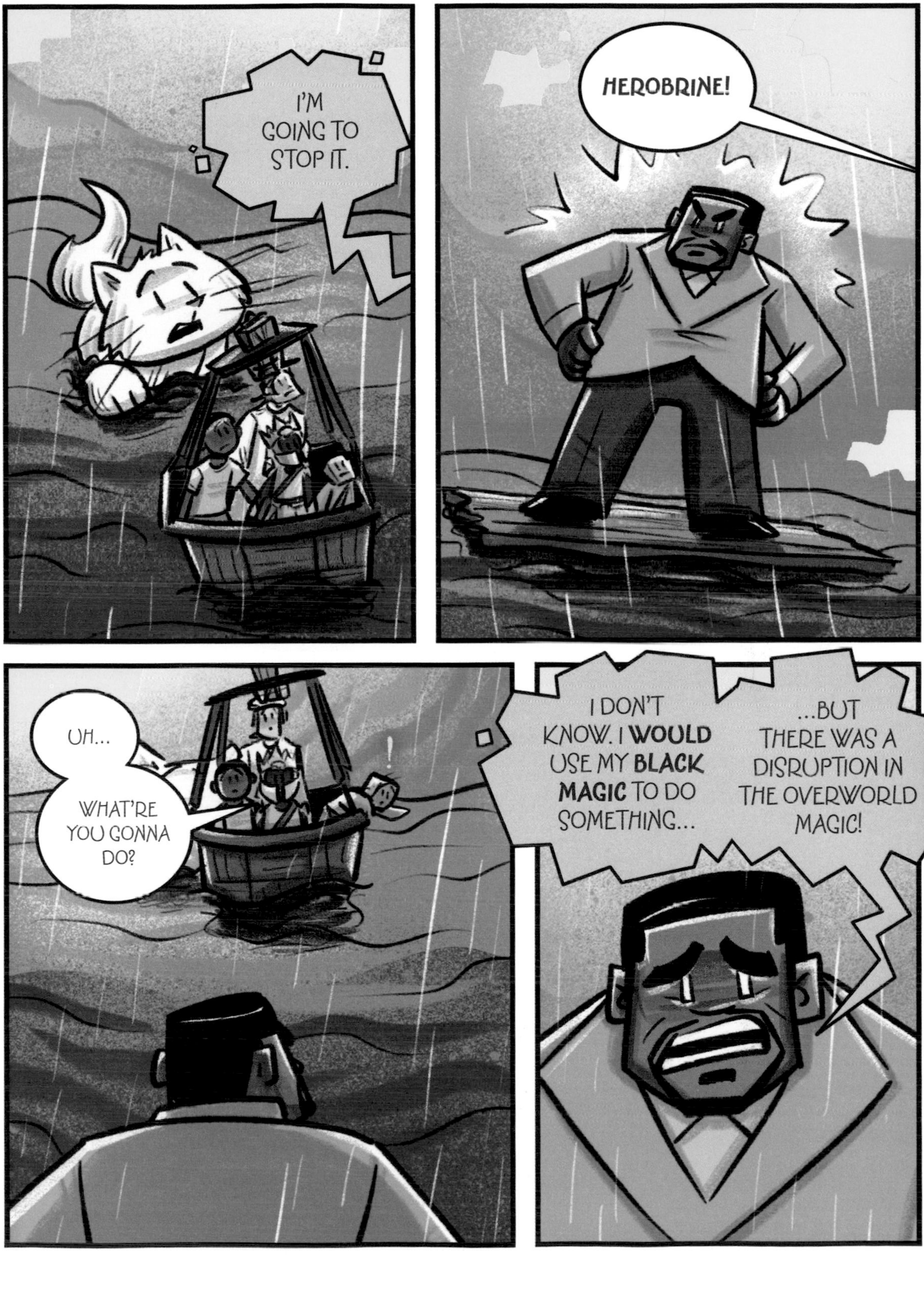
I'M GOING TO STOP IT.
HEROBRINE!
UH...
WHAT'RE YOU GONNA DO?
I DON'T KNOW. I WOULD USE MY BLACK MAGIC TO DO SOMETHING...
...BUT THERE WAS A DISRUPTION IN THE OVERWORLD MAGIC!

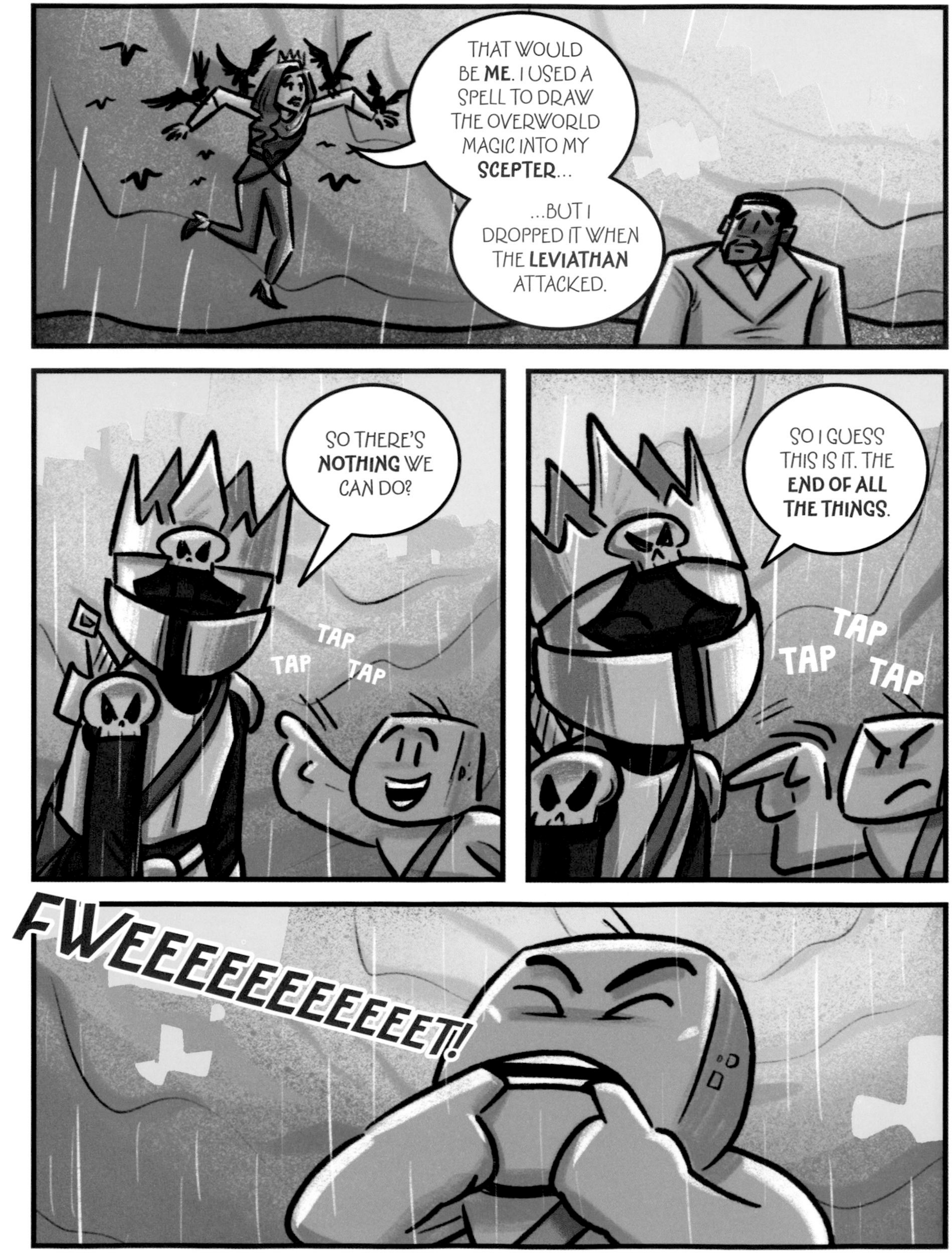
THAT WOULD BE ME. I USED A SPELL TO DRAW THE OVERWORLD MAGIC INTO MY SCEPTER...
...BUT I DROPPED IT WHEN THE LEVIATHAN ATTACKED.
SO THERE'S NOTHING WE CAN DO?
TAP
TAP
TAP
SO I GUESS THIS IS IT. THE END OF ALL THE THINGS.
TAP
TAP
TAP
FWEEEEEEEEEEEET!

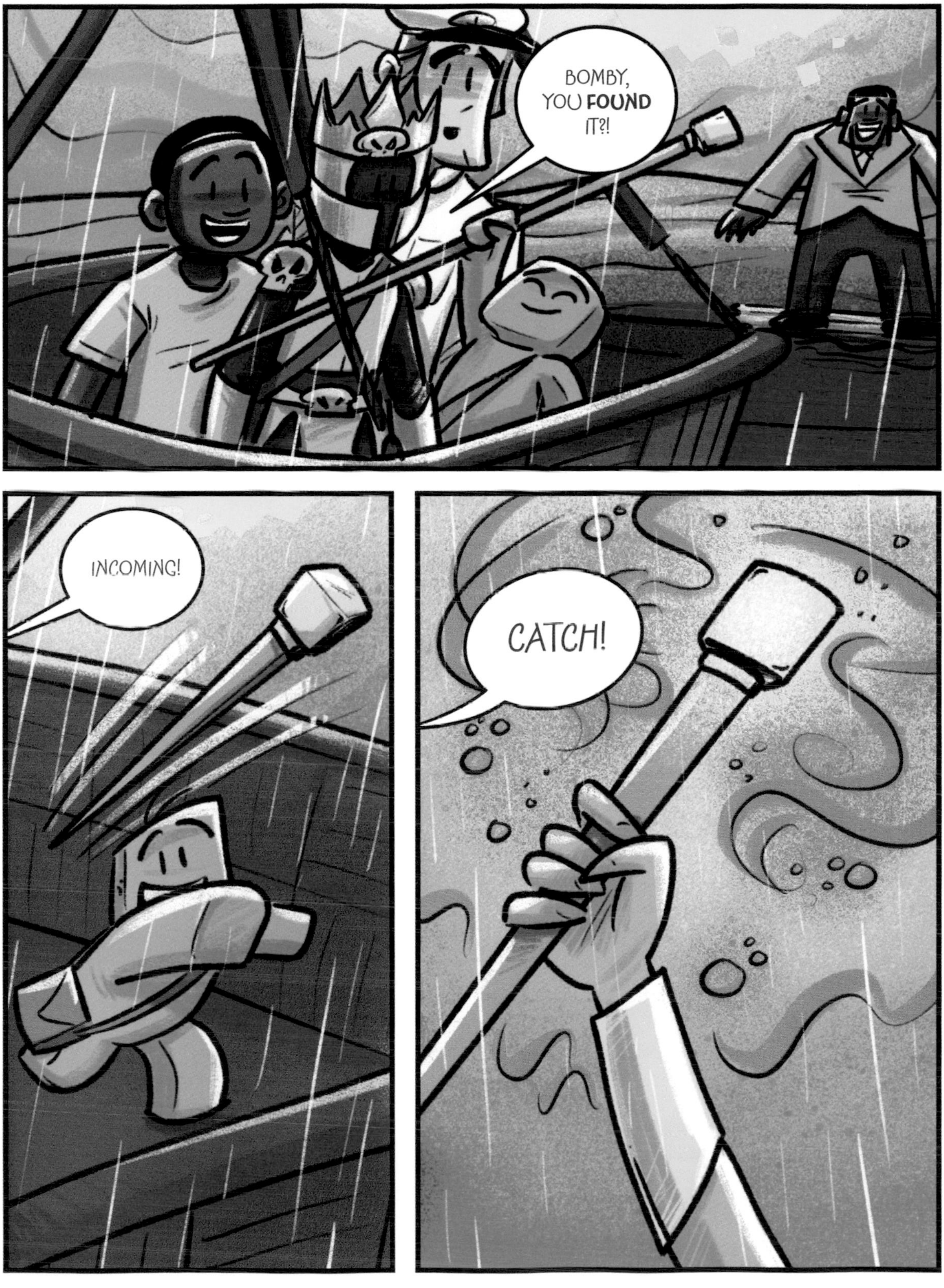
BOMBY, YOU **FOUND** IT?!
INCOMING!
CATCH!

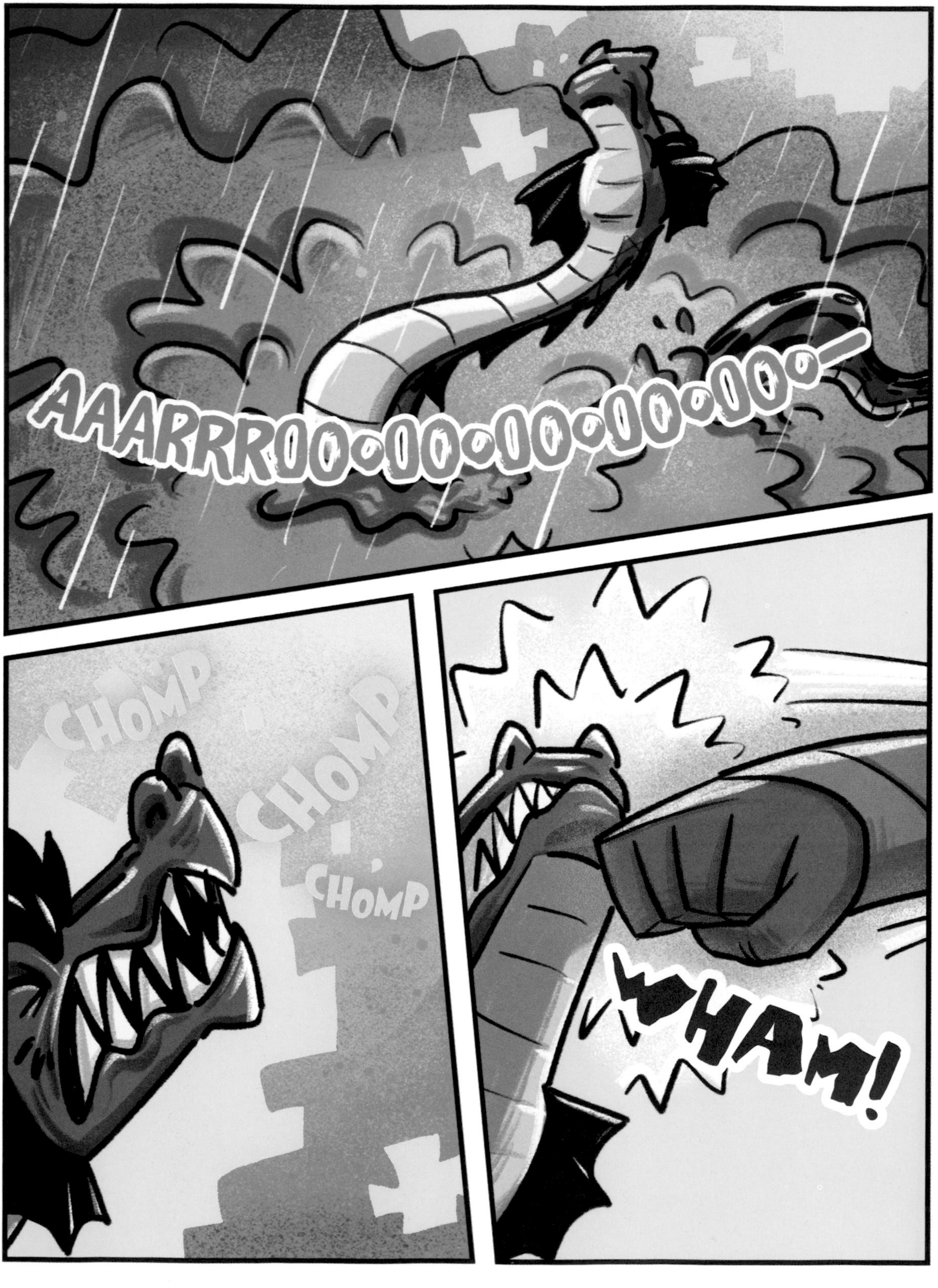
AAARRROO-OO-OO-OO-OO-OO—
CHOMP
CHOMP
CHOMP
WHAM!

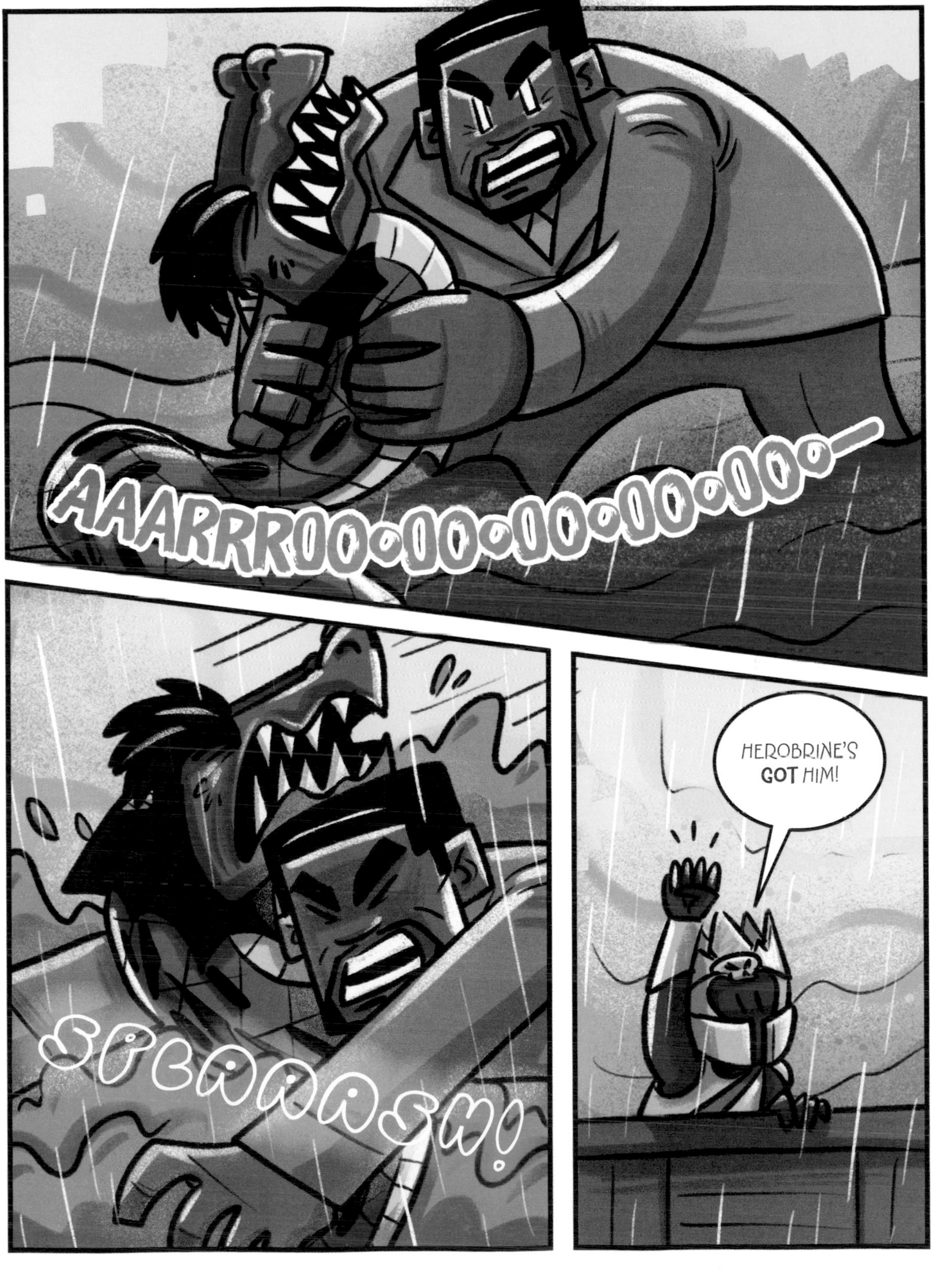
AAARRROO-OO-OO-OO-OO-OO—
SPLAAASH!
HEROBRINE'S GOT HIM!

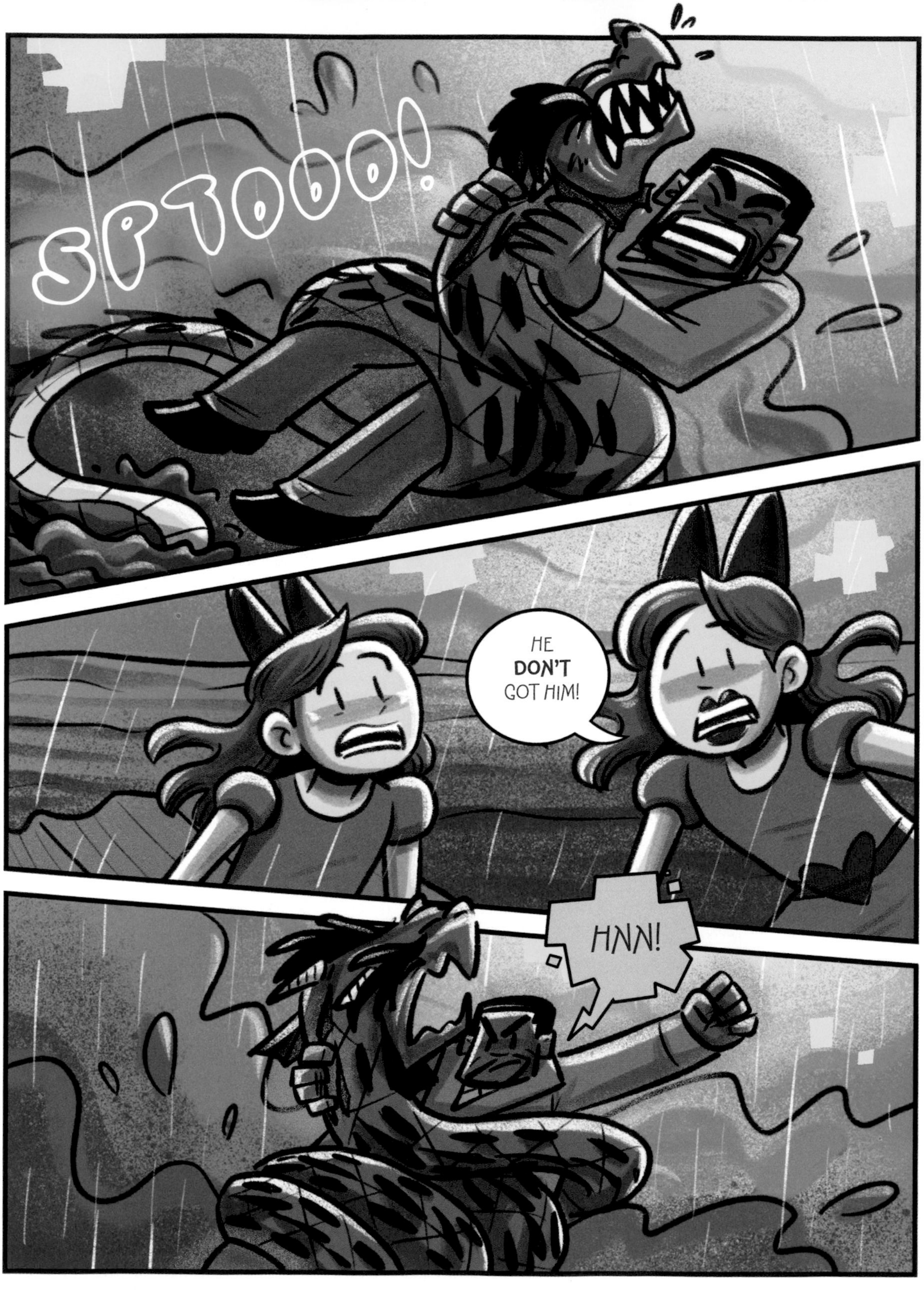
SPTOOO!
HE **DON'T** GOT HIM!
HNN!

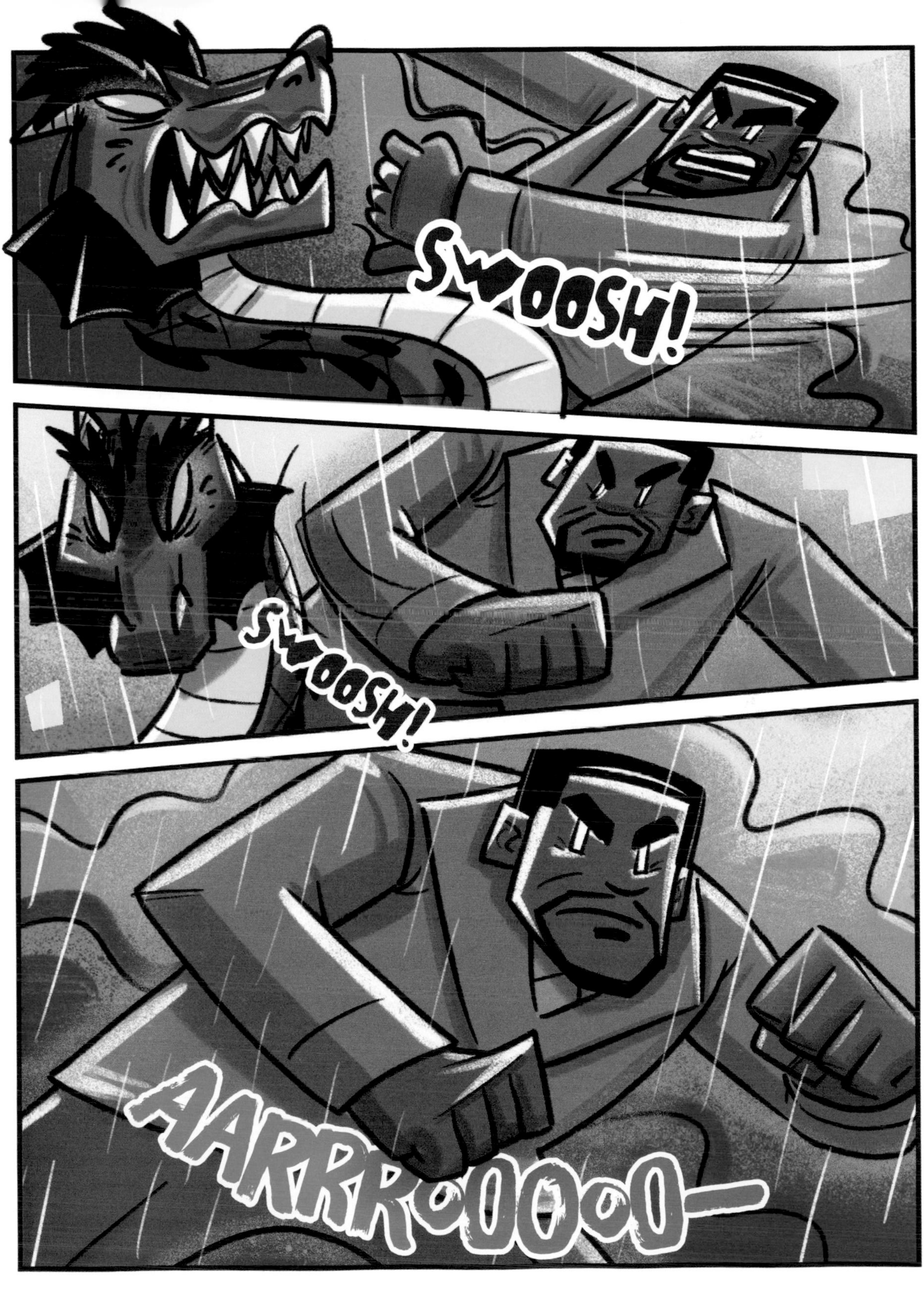
SWOOSH!
SWOOSH!
AARRR-OOOOO-

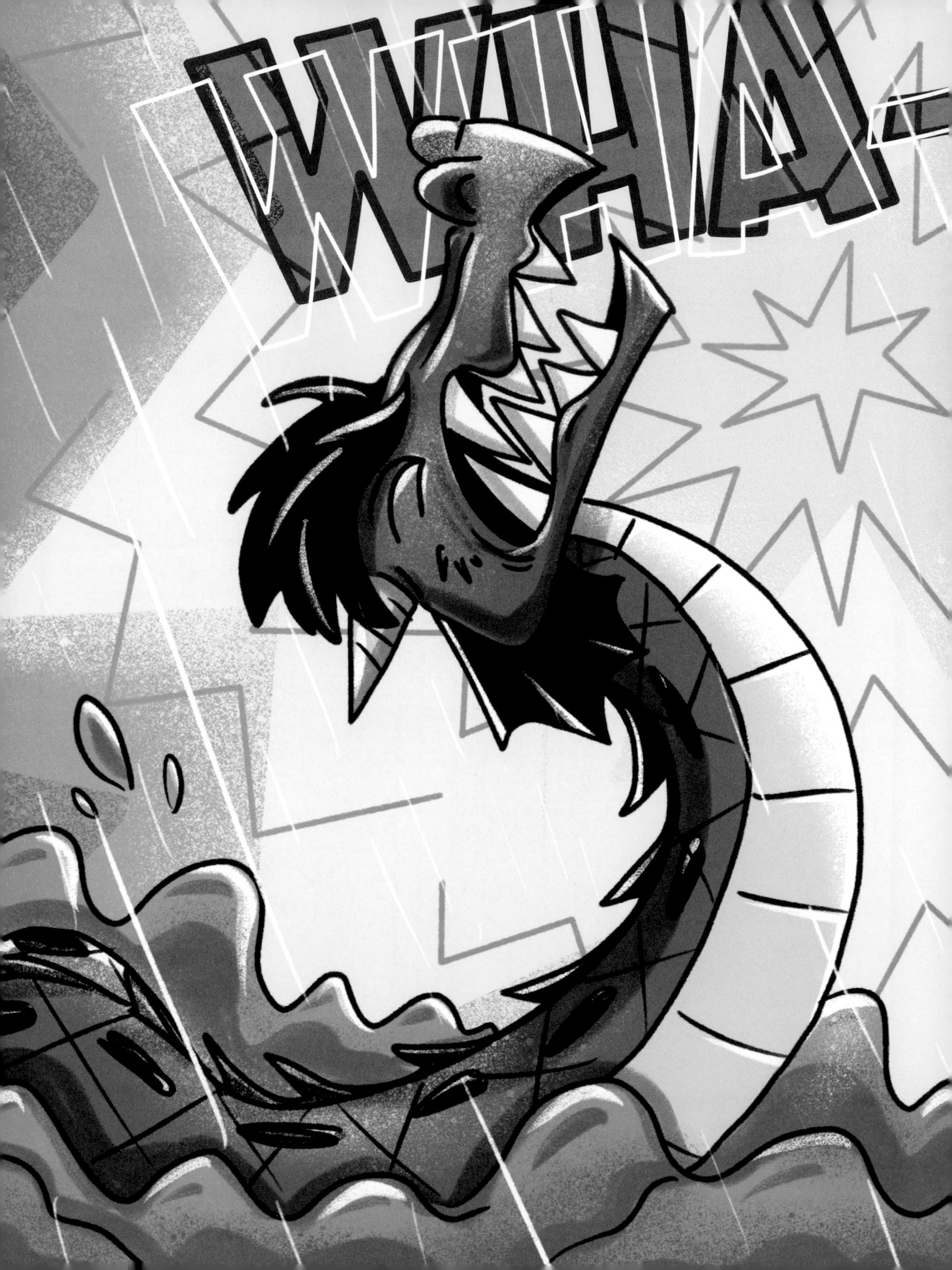
WHA-

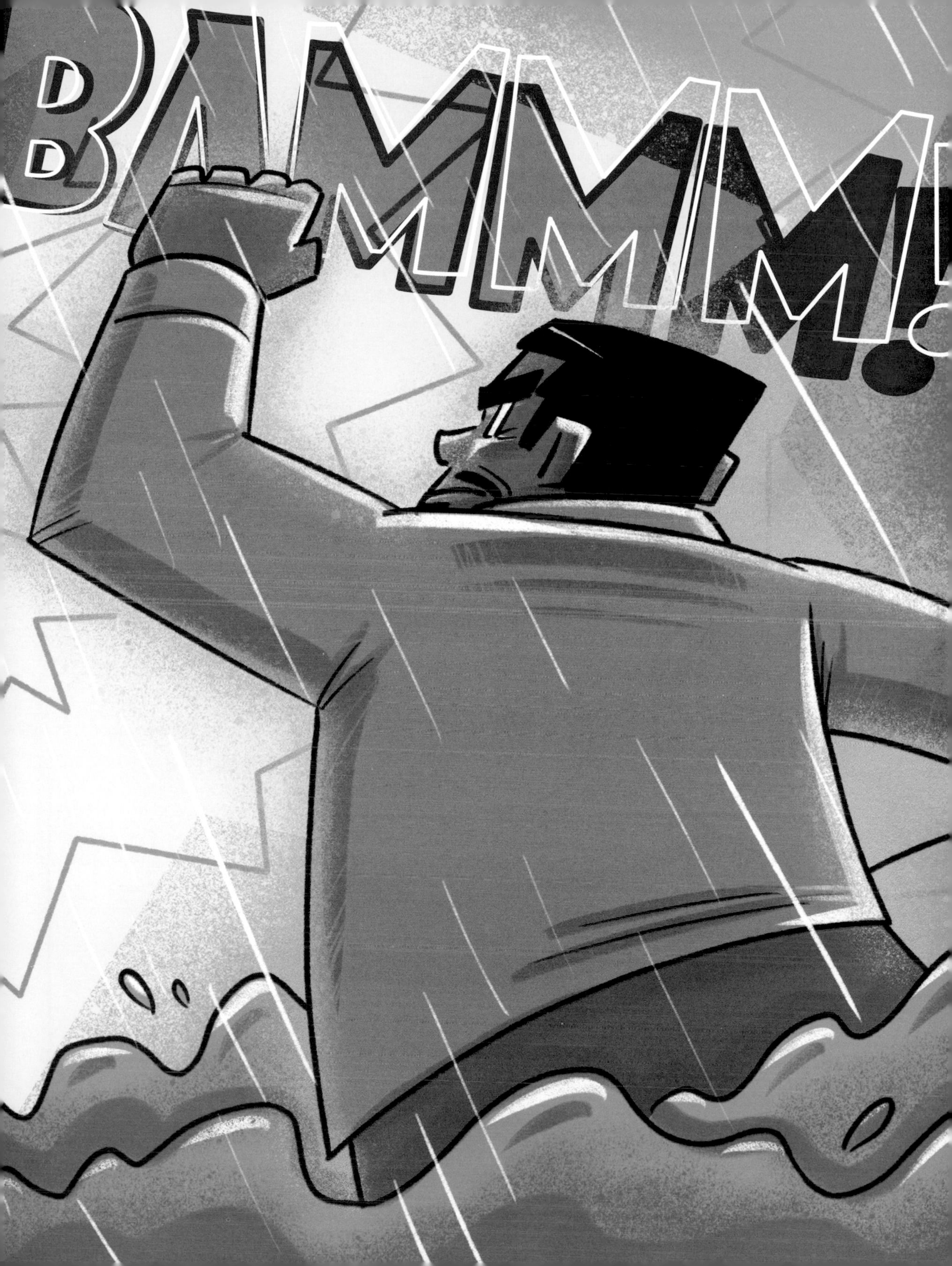
BBAMMMM!

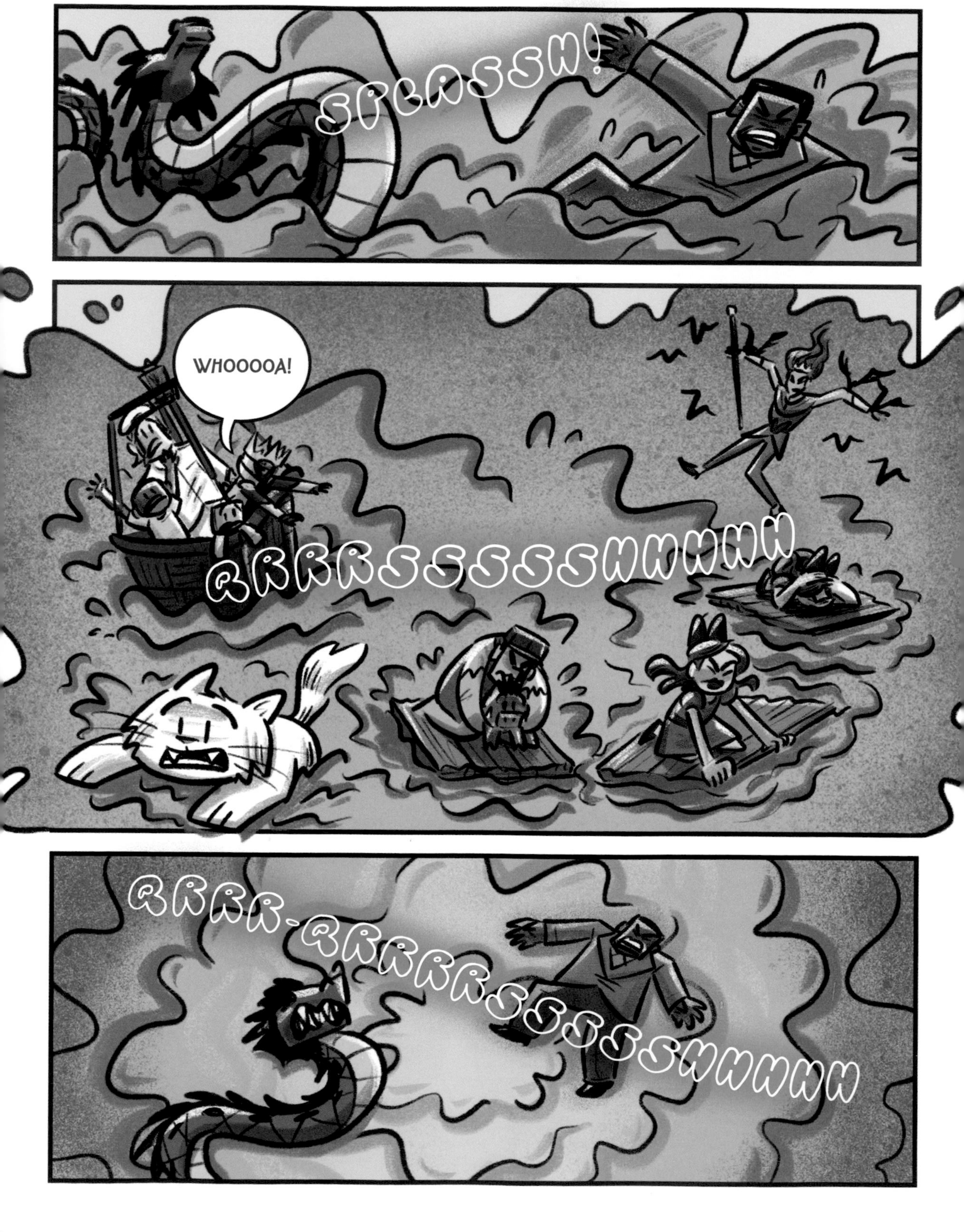
SPLASSH!
WHOOOOA!
RRRRSSSSSSHHHHH
RRRR-RRRRRRSSSSSSHHHHHH

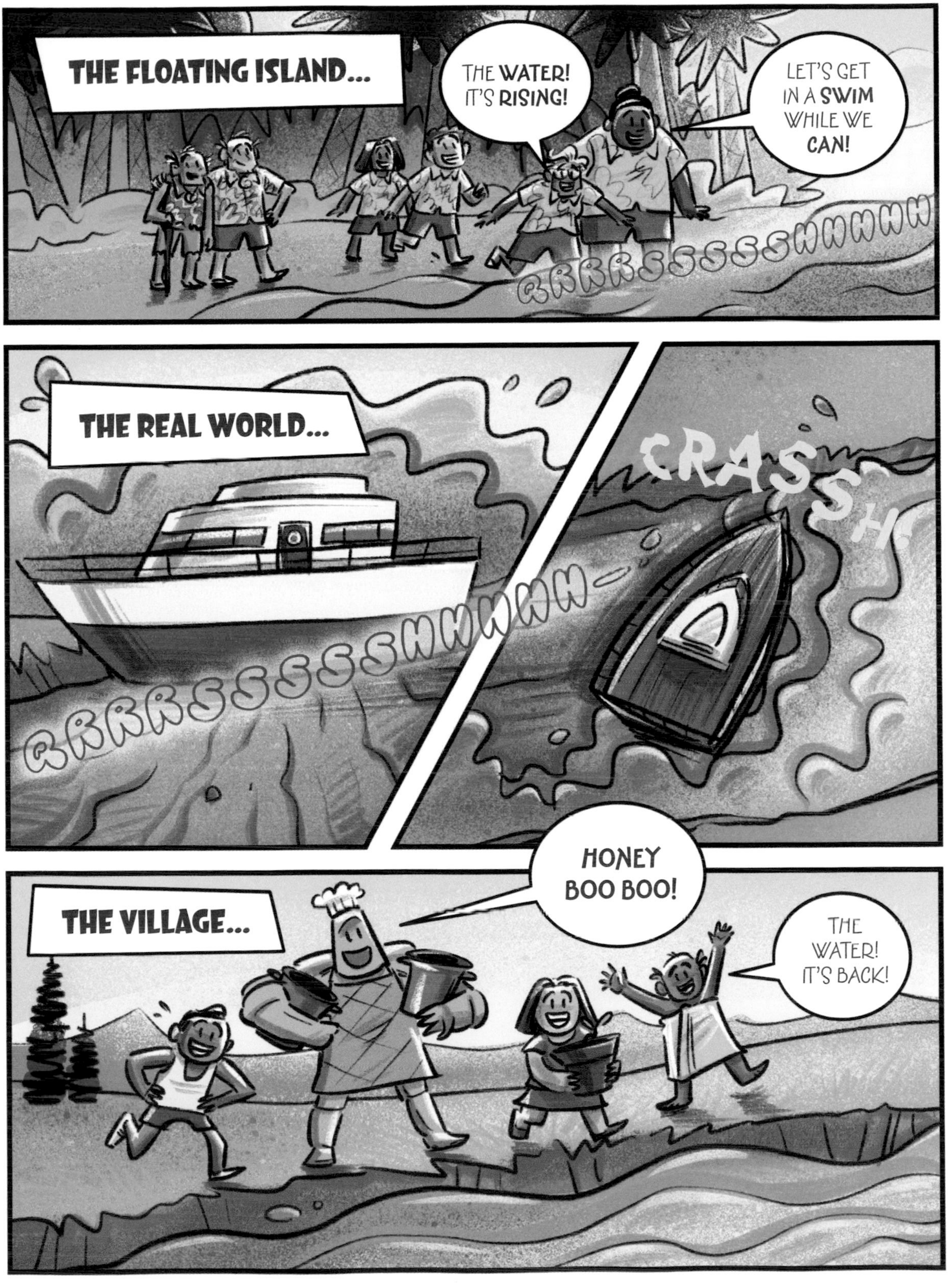
THE FLOATING ISLAND...
THE WATER! IT'S RISING!
LET'S GET IN A SWIM WHILE WE CAN!
BRRRSSSSSSHHHHHH
THE REAL WORLD...
BRRRSSSSSSHHHHHH—
CRASSH!
THE VILLAGE...
HONEY BOO BOO!
THE WATER! IT'S BACK!

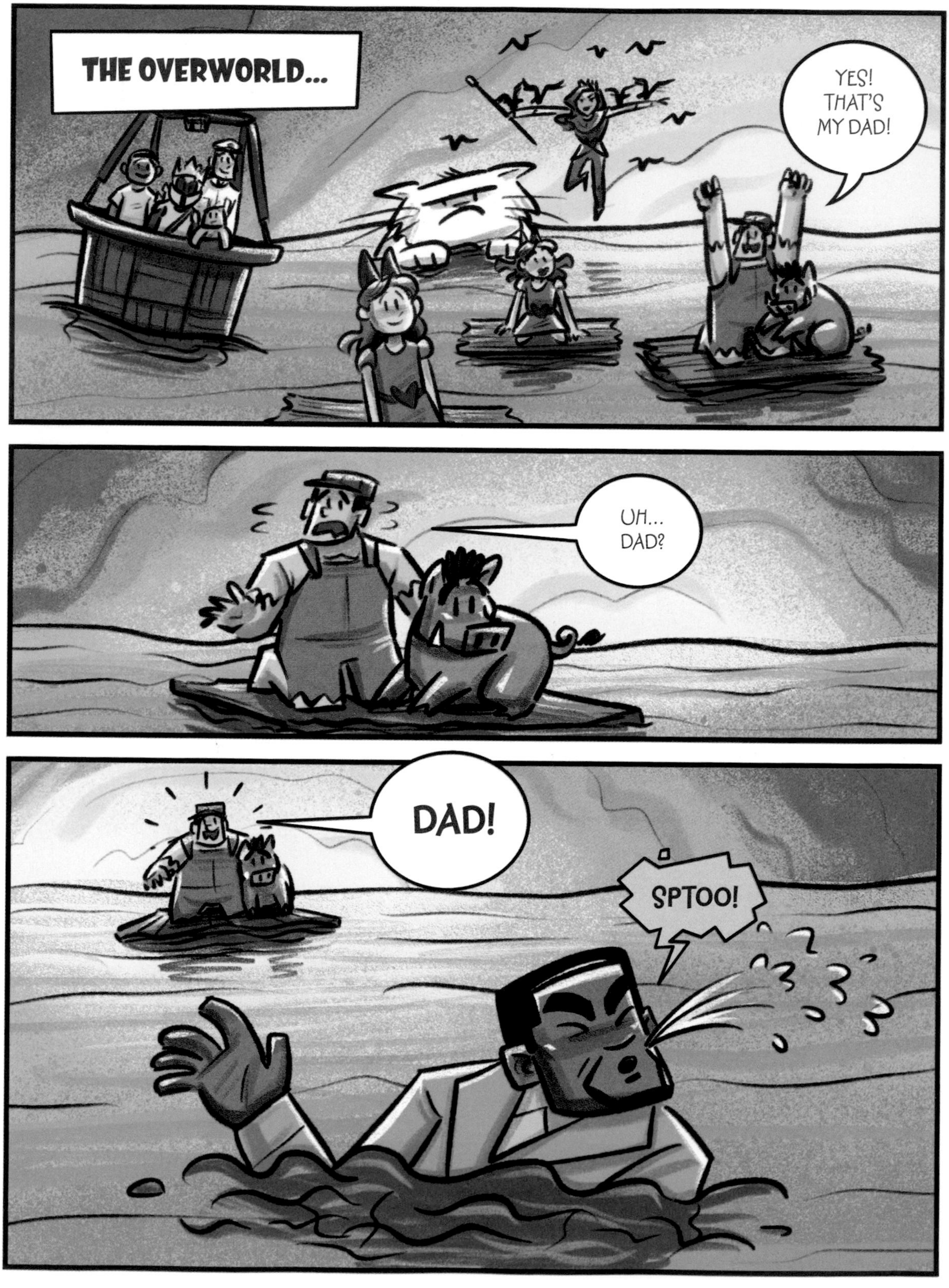
THE OVERWORLD...
YES! THAT'S MY DAD!
UH... DAD?
DAD!
SPTOO!

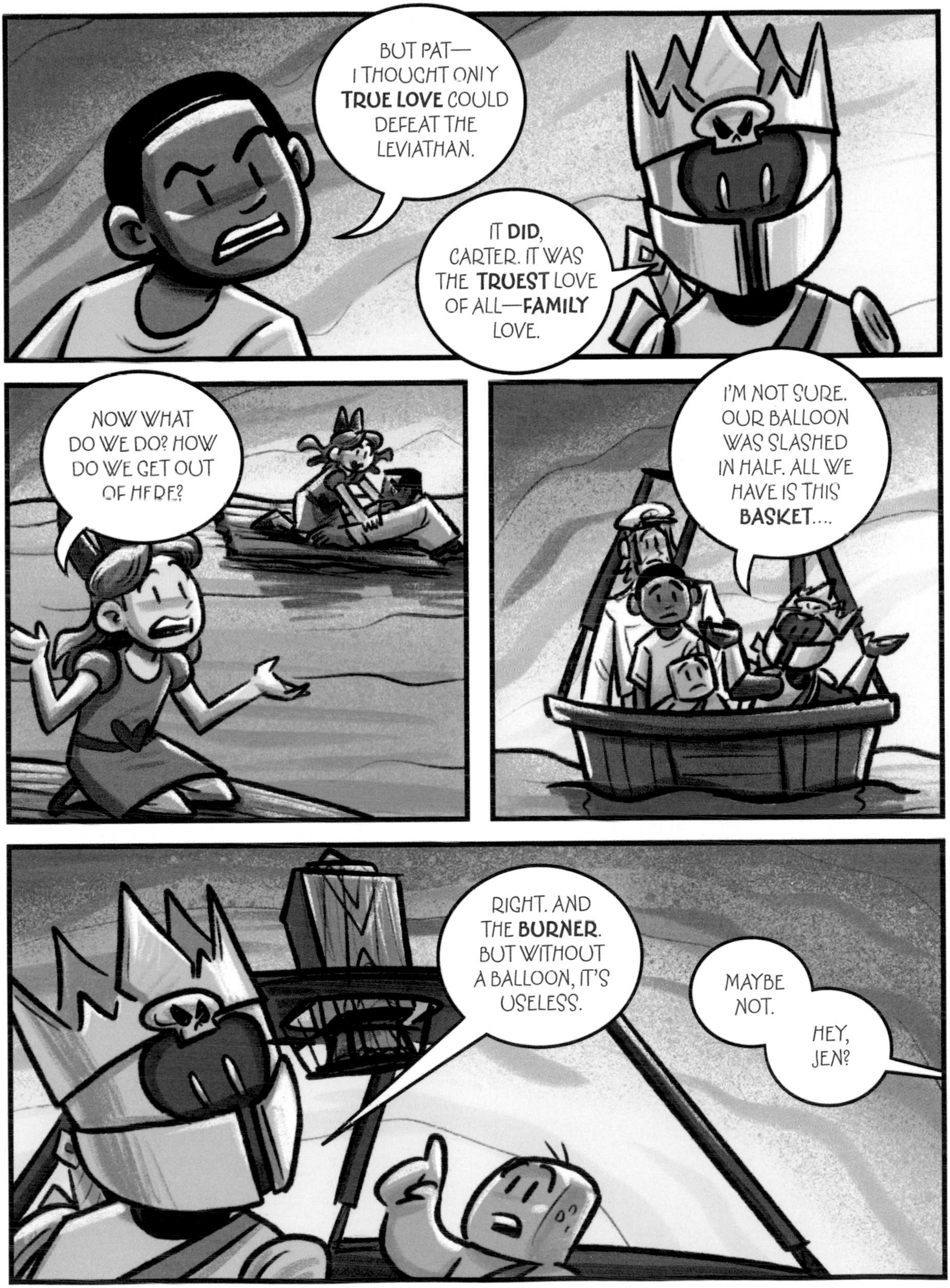
BUT PAT—I THOUGHT ONLY **TRUE LOVE** COULD DEFEAT THE LEVIATHAN.
IT **DID**, CARTER. IT WAS THE **TRUEST** LOVE OF ALL—**FAMILY** LOVE.
NOW WHAT DO WE DO? HOW DO WE GET OUT OF HERE?
I'M NOT SURE. OUR BALLOON WAS SLASHED IN HALF. ALL WE HAVE IS THIS **BASKET**....
RIGHT. AND THE **BURNER**. BUT WITHOUT A BALLOON, IT'S USELESS.
MAYBE NOT.
HEY, JEN?

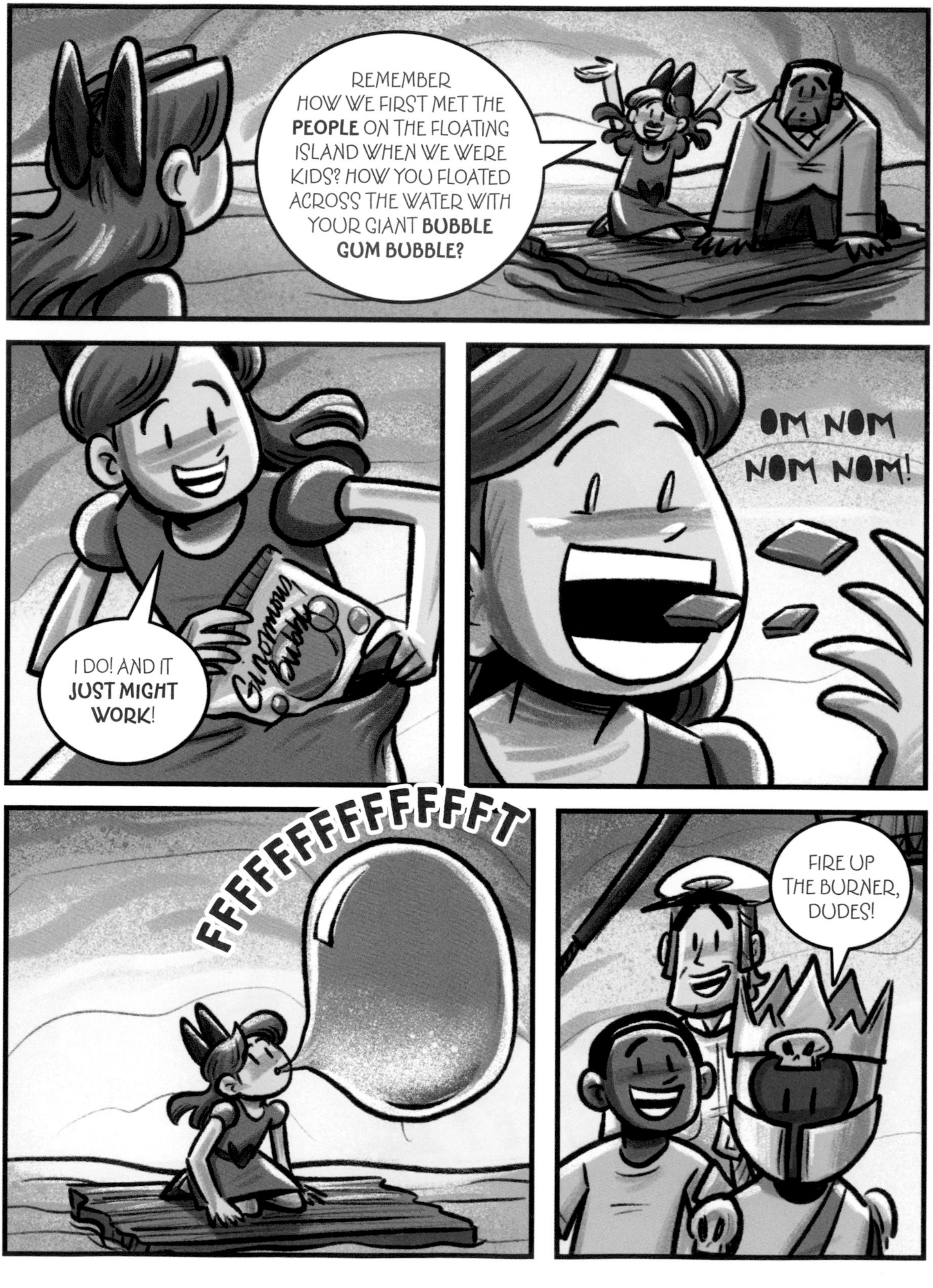
REMEMBER HOW WE FIRST MET THE **PEOPLE** ON THE FLOATING ISLAND WHEN WE WERE KIDS? HOW YOU FLOATED ACROSS THE WATER WITH YOUR GIANT **BUBBLE GUM BUBBLE?**
I DO! AND IT **JUST MIGHT WORK**!
OM NOM NOM NOM!
FFFFFFFFFFFFFFT
FIRE UP THE BURNER, DUDES!

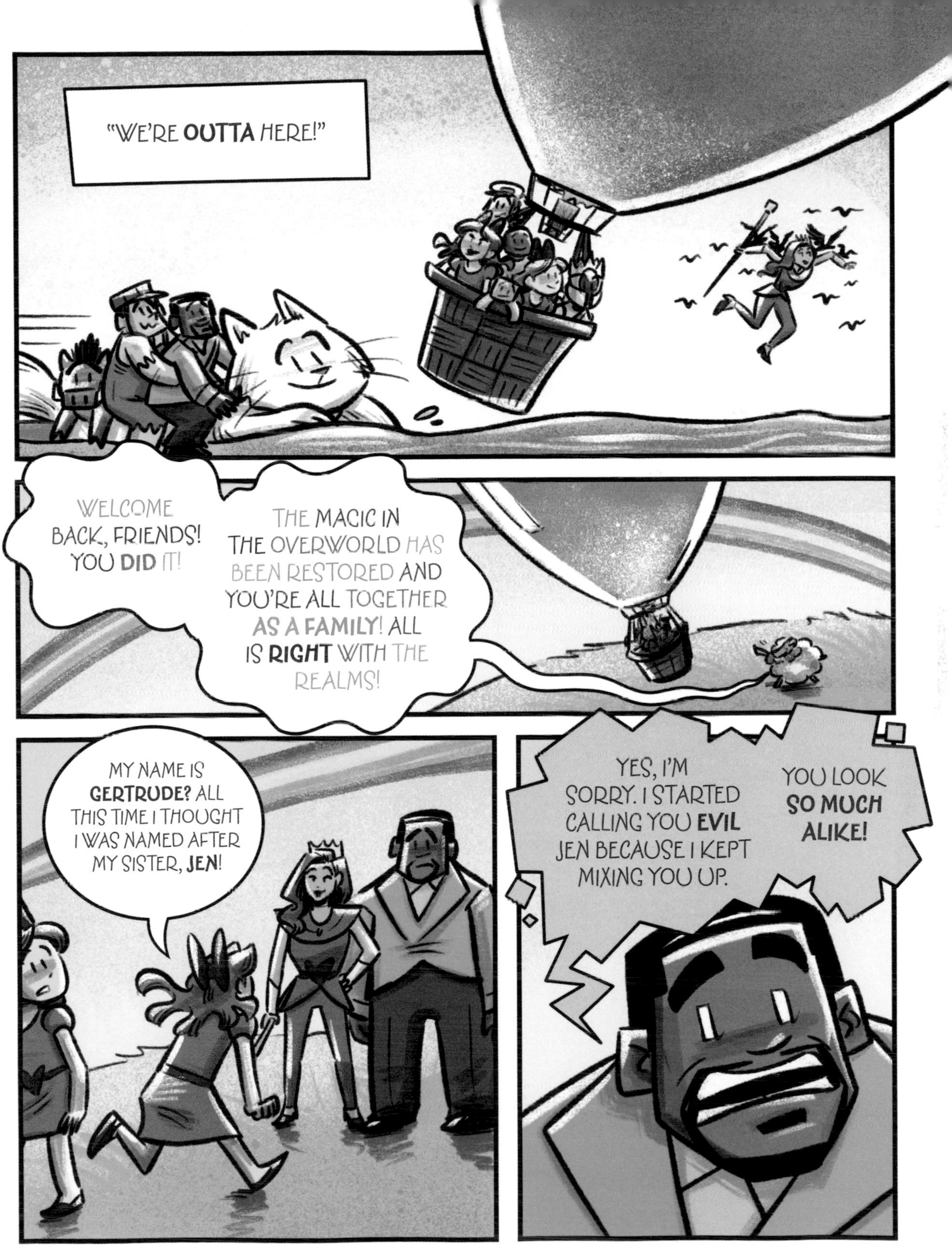
"WE'RE **OUTTA** HERE!"
WELCOME BACK, FRIENDS! YOU **DID** IT!
THE MAGIC IN THE OVERWORLD HAS BEEN RESTORED AND YOU'RE ALL TOGETHER **AS A FAMILY**! ALL IS **RIGHT** WITH THE REALMS!
MY NAME IS **GERTRUDE?** ALL THIS TIME I THOUGHT I WAS NAMED AFTER MY SISTER, **JEN**!
YES, I'M SORRY. I STARTED CALLING YOU **EVIL** JEN BECAUSE I KEPT MIXING YOU UP.
YOU LOOK **SO MUCH** ALIKE!

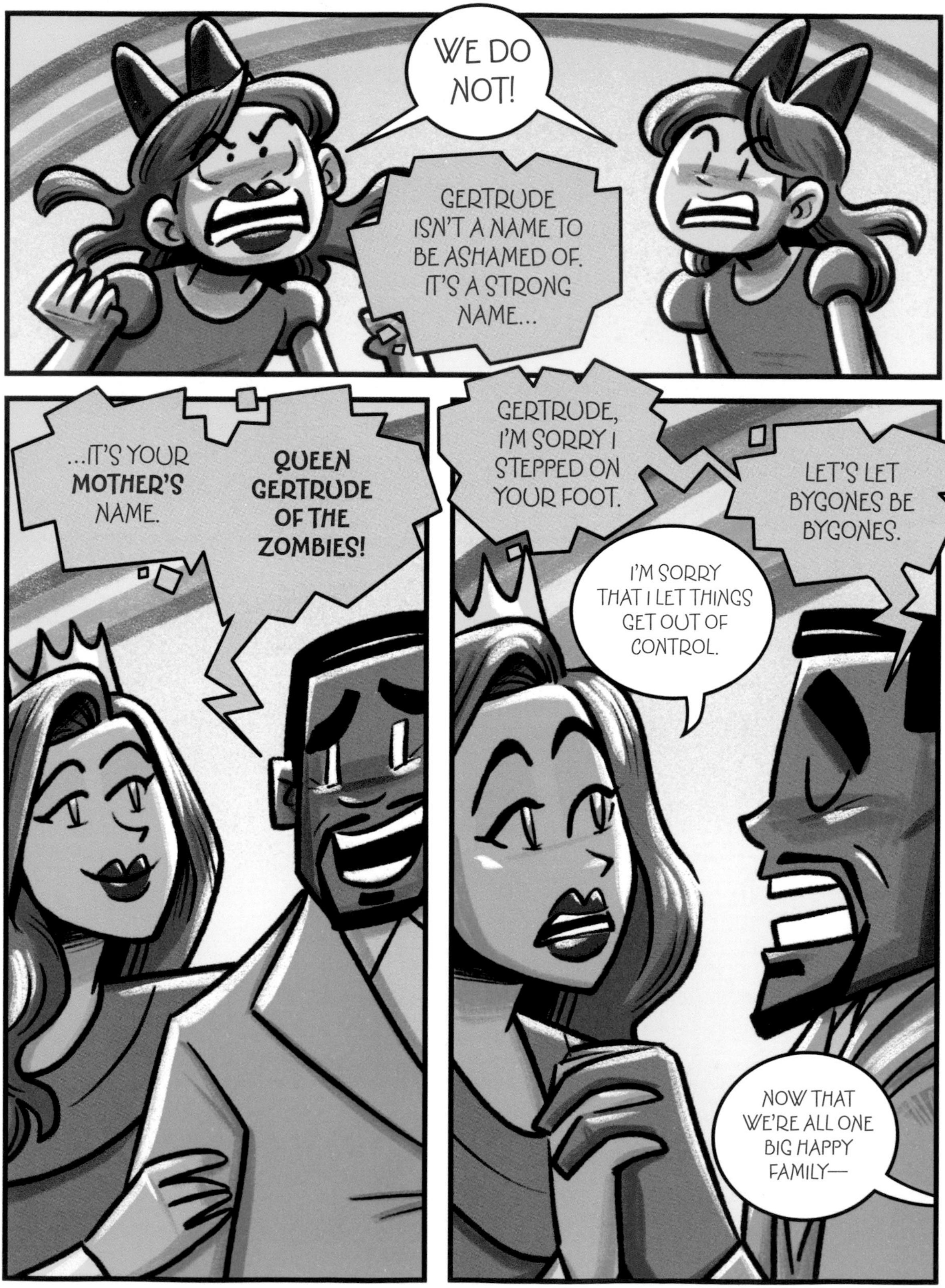

WE DO NOT!
GERTRUDE ISN'T A NAME TO BE ASHAMED OF. IT'S A STRONG NAME...
...IT'S YOUR **MOTHER'S** NAME.
QUEEN GERTRUDE OF THE ZOMBIES!
GERTRUDE, I'M SORRY I STEPPED ON YOUR FOOT.
LET'S LET BYGONES BE BYGONES.
I'M SORRY THAT I LET THINGS GET OUT OF CONTROL.
NOW THAT WE'RE ALL ONE BIG HAPPY FAMILY—

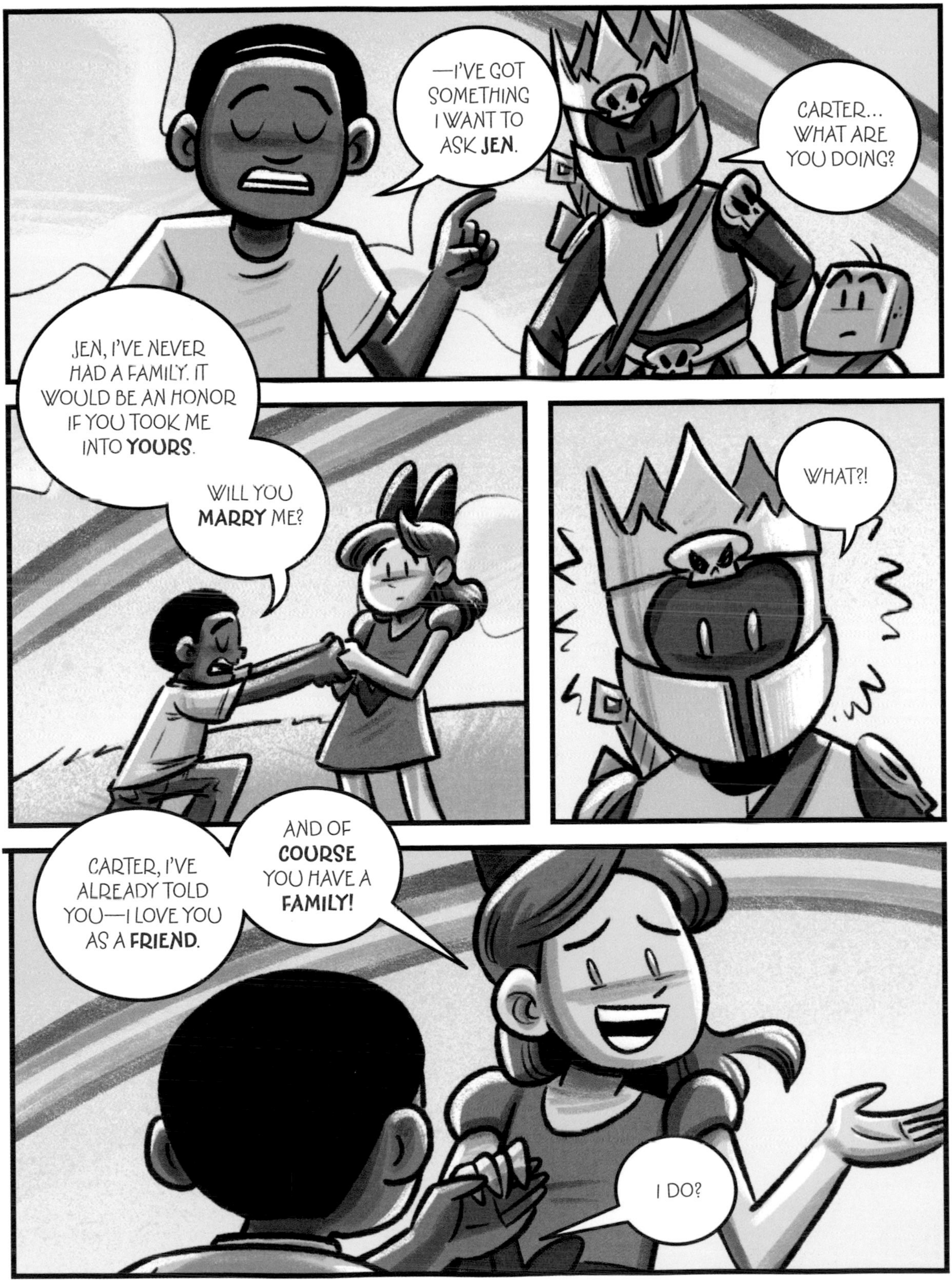
—I'VE GOT SOMETHING I WANT TO ASK **JEN**.
CARTER... WHAT ARE YOU DOING?
JEN, I'VE NEVER HAD A FAMILY. IT WOULD BE AN HONOR IF YOU TOOK ME INTO **YOURS**.
WILL YOU **MARRY** ME?
WHAT?!
CARTER, I'VE ALREADY TOLD YOU—I LOVE YOU AS A **FRIEND**.
AND OF **COURSE** YOU HAVE A **FAMILY!**
I DO?

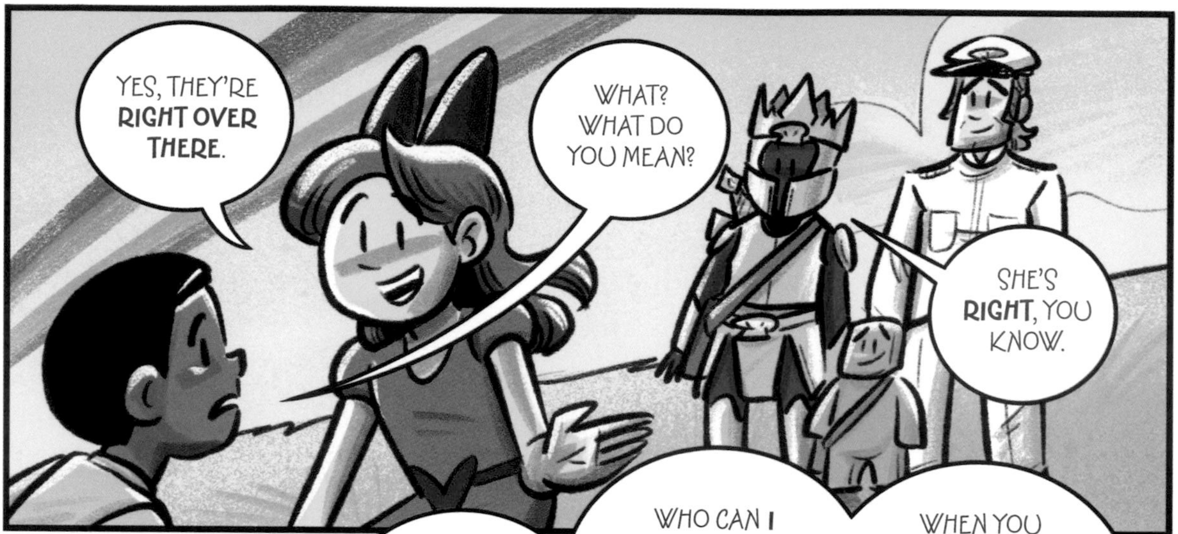
YES, THEY'RE **RIGHT OVER THERE**.
WHAT? WHAT DO YOU MEAN?
SHE'S **RIGHT**, YOU KNOW.

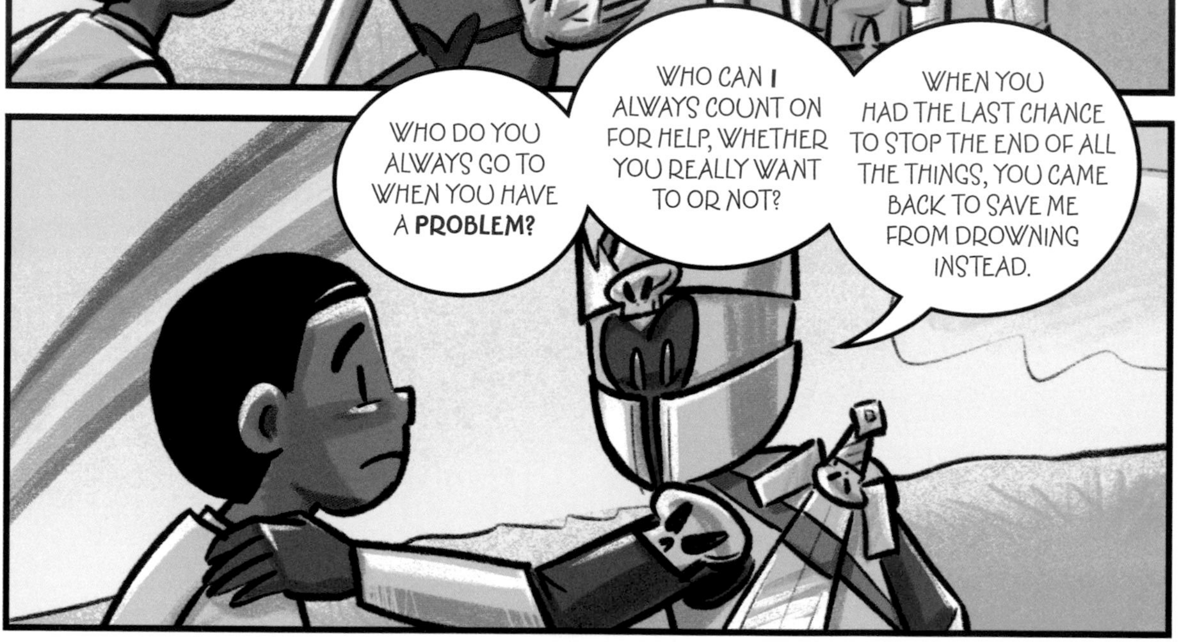
WHO DO YOU ALWAYS GO TO WHEN YOU HAVE A **PROBLEM?**
WHO CAN **I** ALWAYS COUNT ON FOR HELP, WHETHER YOU REALLY WANT TO OR NOT?
WHEN YOU HAD THE LAST CHANCE TO STOP THE END OF ALL THE THINGS, YOU CAME BACK TO SAVE ME FROM DROWNING INSTEAD.

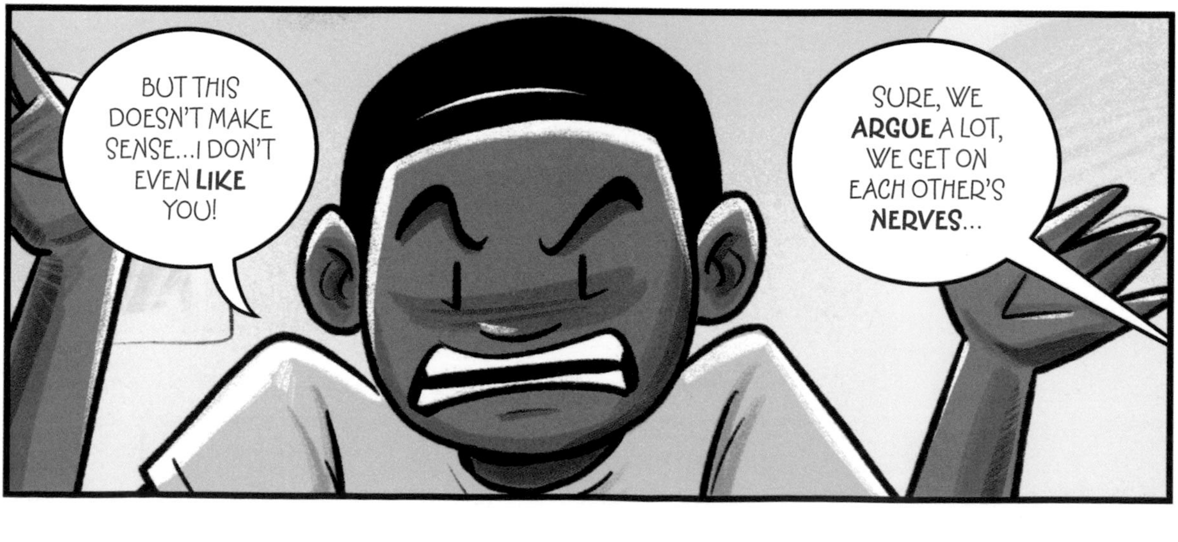
BUT THIS DOESN'T MAKE SENSE...I DON'T EVEN **LIKE** YOU!
SURE, WE **ARGUE** A LOT, WE GET ON EACH OTHER'S **NERVES**...

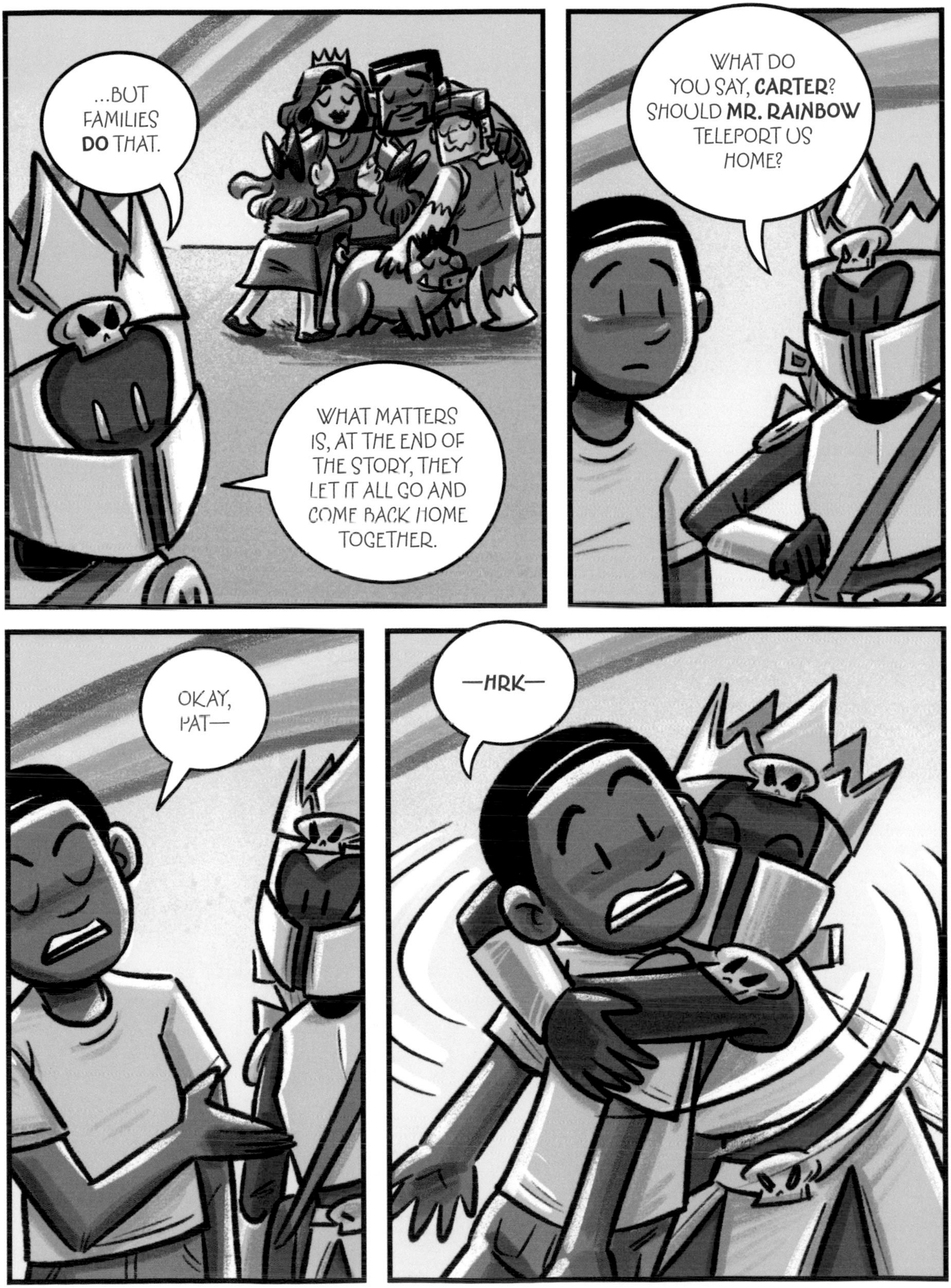
...BUT FAMILIES DO THAT.
WHAT MATTERS IS, AT THE END OF THE STORY, THEY LET IT ALL GO AND COME BACK HOME TOGETHER.
WHAT DO YOU SAY, CARTER? SHOULD MR. RAINBOW TELEPORT US HOME?
OKAY, PAT—
—HRK—

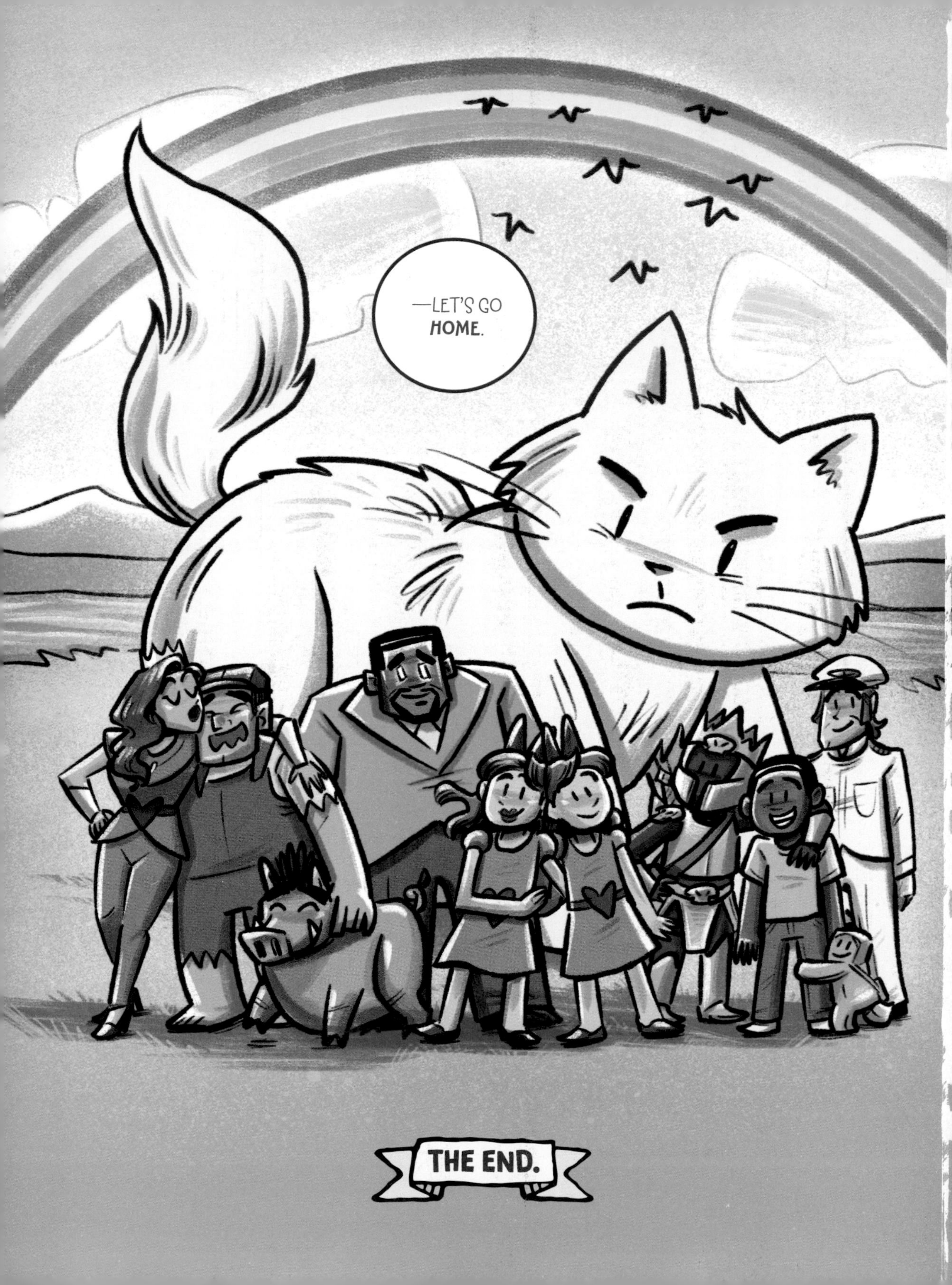

—LET'S GO **HOME**.
THE END.